NURJAHAN

NURJAHAN

JYOTI JAFA

This edition published in 2019

Roli Books Pvt. Ltd.
M-75, Greater Kailash II Market, New Delhi 110 048
Phone: +91 (011) 40682000
E-mail: info@rolibooks.com
Website: www.rolibooks.com
Also at Chennai & Mumbai

ISBN: 978-81-7436-029-8

Typeset in Adobe Garamond Pro by Roli Books Pvt. Ltd
Printed in New Delhi, India

Choosing her words carefully, the Persian Sultana continued, “I’m going to talk very frankly with you, Mehrunnisa. My volatile stepson will one day control the destiny of this vast empire. Many will try to manipulate him for questionable ends, but perhaps you, as his consort, could prevent all that and mould him into a perfect sovereign.”

“What do you mean, Gracious One?” cried Mehrunnisa, while her eyes sparkled with keen interest.

“You are much too intelligent to miss my meaning, Mehrunnisa. Do you think I’m blind to the romantic attachment blossoming between you and Salim?”

Fear and hope jostled wildly in Mehrunnisa’s mind as she followed the Sultana downstairs. A dream took shape, and she imagined herself entering the castle of Agra at the head of a triumphant wedding procession, with Salim riding by her side.

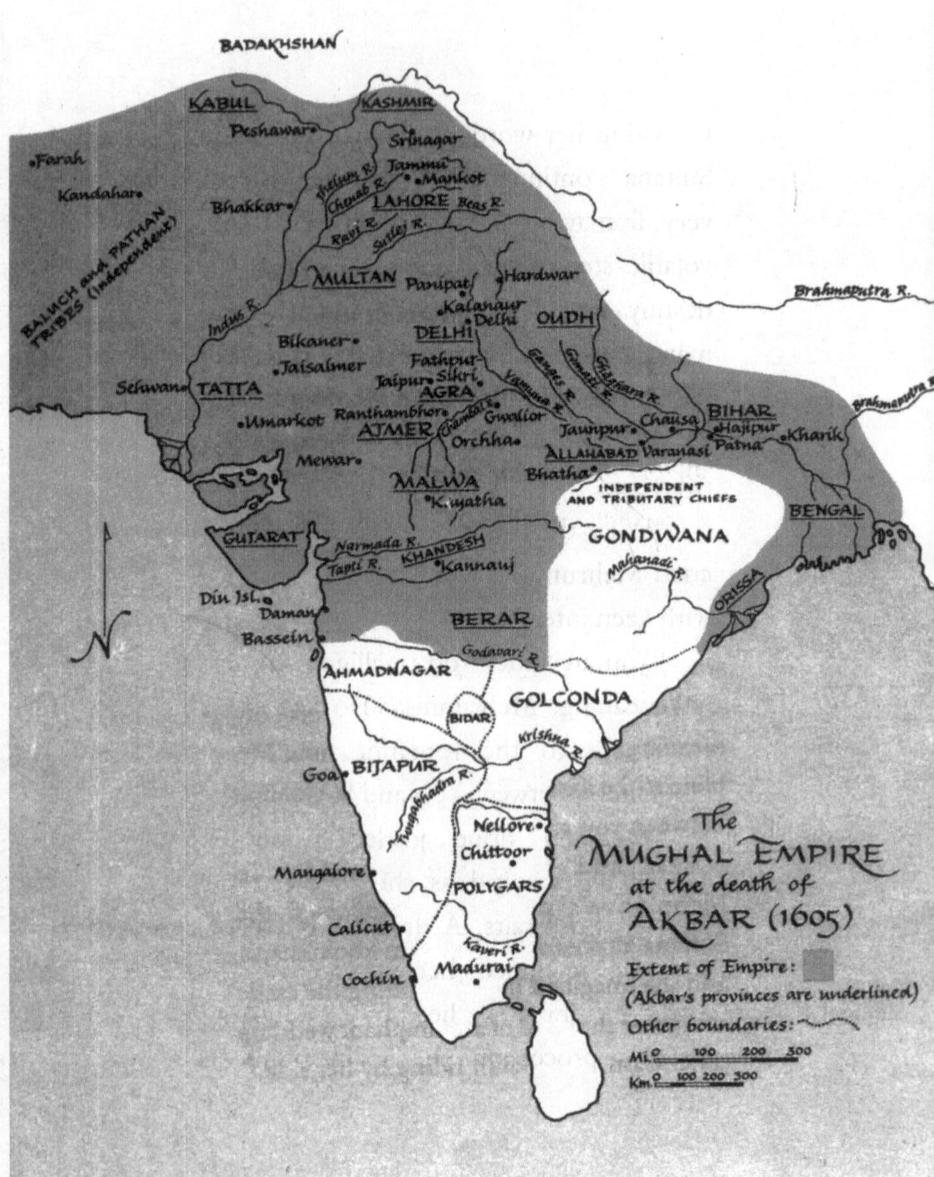
BADAKHSHAN
KABUL
KASHMIR
Peshawar
Srinagar
Farah
Jammu
Mankot
Kandahar
Jhelum R.
Chenab R.
LAHORE
Beas R.
Bhakkar
Ravi R.
Sutlej R.
BALUCH and PATHAN TRIBES (independent)
MULTAN
Panipat
Hardwar
Kalanaur
Delhi
OUDH
Brahmaputra R.
Indus R.
DELHI
Bikaner
Fathpur-Sikri
Jaisalmer
Ganges R.
Gomati R.
Ghaghara R.
Jaipur
AGRA
Sehwan
TATTA
Yamuna R.
Ranthambhor
Gwalior
Chambal R.
Umarkot
AJMER
Jaunpur
Chausa
BIHAR
Hajipur
Brahmaputra R.
Orchha
Varanasi
Patna
Kharik
Mewar
ALLAHABAD
Bhatha
MALWA
INDEPENDENT AND TRIBUTARY CHIEFS
BENGAL
GUJARAT
GONDWANA
Narmada R.
KHANDESH
Tapti R.
Kannauj
Mahanadi R.
Diu Isl.
Daman
ORISSA
BERAR
N
Bassein
Godavari R.
AHMADNAGAR
GOLCONDA
BIDAR
Krishna R.
Goa
BIJAPUR
Tungabhadra R.
Nellore
Chittoor
Mangalore
POLYGARS
Calicut
Kaveri R.
Madurai
Cochin
The MUGHAL EMPIRE at the death of AKBAR (1605)
Extent of Empire:
(Akbar's provinces are underlined)
Other boundaries:
Mi. 0 100 200 300
Km. 0 100 200 300

Contents

Leaning against Jehangir's arm, Nurjahan said, softly, "What shall I ask of you, Sire? You have dowered me with all Hindustan..."

Author's Note

By a strange series of events, a young woman came to control one of history's most fabulous empires, long enough to become a living legend. She was Nurjahan, the Empress of India.

Historically, the name India applied to the whole subcontinent south of the Himalayas, comprising the modern nations of India, Afghanistan, Pakistan, Nepal, Bhutan and Bangladesh. Its vast size, and frequent invasions from its vulnerable mountain passes and unguarded seacoast, led to the development of small kingdoms with their different races, languages, religions and cultures. India's wealth became a fatal burden for its own people and a target for many hardy conquerors.

The Mughals who conquered North India or Hindustan unified the greater part of this immense subcontinent under their rule despite tenacious local resistance. Driven out of his principalities of Samarkand and Fargana, the Timurid Prince, Babur, established the Mughal empire in 1526 by defeating the Sultan of Delhi and then the Rajput confederacy led by Rana Sanga of Mewar. In 1530, Humayun succeeded his brilliant father and experienced many ups and downs, winning and losing his kingdom. Betrayed by his half-brothers who grabbed Kabul and Lahore, and often defeated by Afghan and Rajput armies, Humayun was forced to seek shelter in Persia after the birth of his son and heir, Akbar. There, Humayun acquired a great taste for Persian art and literature at the Safavid court of Shah Tahmasp. The great Afghan soldier and administrator Sher Shah Suri ruled for a brief, but brilliant period. But Humayun was able to win back North India before he stumbled out of life by breaking his neck on his library steps in Delhi as he knelt to answer the evening call to prayer.

The second Mughal conquest of Hindustan in 1556 was due to the efforts of Bairam Khan, whom Humayun had appointed ataliq (tutor and guardian) to his fourteen-year-old successor, Akbar. This courageous, free-spirited boy-king could not endure tutelage, frequently indulging in madcap escapades to show his guardian Bairam Khan – and his protective mother Hamida Begum, his domineering head nurse Maham Anaga, and his demanding Mughal aunts – that they couldn't manipulate him. By eighteen, Akbar had won enough battles to banish his Lord Protector. Bairam Khan was murdered at Surat by some Afghan enemies before he could embark on the pilgrimage to Mecca ordered by his youthful master.

Akbar's dream of an Indian empire became a reality even though the Mughals were foreign immigrants. Descendents of Changhiz (Genghis) Khan and Timur (Tamerlane), the Mughals felt they were Indians despite their Turkish and Mongol blood, Persian acculturation and Arab religion. A practical visionary, Akbar was shrewd enough to see that any stable rule in India must enjoy the support of the Hindus, who were in overwhelming majority. But religious tolerance did not originate with Akbar. It was an ancient Indian tradition honoured even by earlier Islamic warrior kings like Allaudin Khilji, Muhammud Bin Tughlaq and Sher Shah.

The Mughal empire rested on four pillars – the Emperor's personality, the policy of religious tolerance, the Rajput alliance and the balance of power. This last took two forms, external and internal. The external balance was with the Safavids, with whom the Mughals shared control of the Iranian plateau. The symbol of their rivalry was the strategic trade centre, Kandahar, held by the Mughals from 1522 till 1649, then finally captured by the Persians. But neither side wanted to expand and overthrow the other. For the Mughals, the Persians were a safeguard, leaving them free to conquer South India. For the Safavids, the Mughals kept the restless Afghans and Uzbeks in check, giving them comparative security to deal with the expansionist Ottoman Turks to the west.

The internal balance of power was provided by the independent states of South India and the Rajput kings in the north. Akbar, Jehangir, Shahjahan and Aurangzeb fought many wars with the turbulent Rajputs, who constantly threatened the Mughal power centres, Agra and Delhi. The nearest Rajput state, Amber (modern Jaipur), was won over first by a system of mutual accommodation and hard-won concessions. In 1568-69, the two great fortresses of Chittor and Ranthambore were captured. Despite this, Mewar (modern Udaipur) maintained some independence in its remote rocky jungles. But the rest of Rajputana accepted Mughal supremacy.

After that, Akbar's conquests followed steadily. By the time of his death in 1605, Akbar controlled a huge sweep of territory between the Arabian Sea and the Bay of Bengal, including Afghanistan, Balkh and Badakshan up north. In the south, Bijapur, Golconda (modern Hyderabad), Mysore (modern Karnataka), parts of Kerala and the Portuguese colony of Goa remained independent. The Nizam Shahi kingdom of Ahmednagar became a vassal state, revolting frequently till Shah Jahan finally annexed it in 1633.

Akbar took several steps to sustain this empire. He

prohibited the enslavement of Hindu prisoners of war, gave Hindus important government posts, abolished jezia (a hated poll tax on non-Muslims) and the pilgrim tax on everyone. And he married Hindu princesses, encouraging them to practise their religious rites and social customs within the Mughal household. The mothers of his heir Salim and his grandsons Khusro, Khurram (Emperor Shah Jahan) and Shahryar were the Hindu princesses of Amber and Marwar (modern Jodhpur). These matrimonial alliances brought Akbar and his successor Jehangir powerful Rajput brothers-in-law with their armies and administrative skills.

Controversy surrounds these Rajput–Mughal marriages. But there were historical precedents for such matrimonial alliances between Hindu and Muslim royal families. The Raja of Ucch's daughter was Sultan Shahbuddin Ghori's wife. The Bhatti princess Nella, married to Salar Rajab, became the mother of Delhi's canal-building king, Firoz Tughlaq. A Daulatabad princess had married Alauddin Khilji's son. By opting for happy mergers rather than hostile takeovers by the mightier Mughals, the Rajput princes ensured their own survival, protected their subjects from the ravages of prolonged wars and became partners in Akbar's creation of a centralized Indian empire.

The Timurid princes who ruled India were great patrons of learning, art and architecture. Akbar too loved books, specially illustrated ones. But he had a highly disturbed childhood and a very turbulent youth, with little time or inclination for reading. So the myth persists that he was virtually illiterate. Perhaps he was simply dyslexic and had a reading disability. But only a seeker of knowledge could have collected the vast library of nearly 25,000 books which Akbar left his heirs. These included works on history, anthropology, mathematics, medicine, music, veterinary science, engineering, military strategy, natural history, comparative studies on religions, astrology, astronomy, architecture and literature in

Persian, Arabic, Turki, Hindustani and Sanskrit. He also left commissioned translations of the Ramayana, Mahabharata, Bhagvad Gita, Harivamsha Puranas, the *Upanishads* and all the four Vedas to enlighten his Muslim courtiers and foster better understanding of the Hindus.

The Mughals also welcomed men of ability to India. Merchants, soldiers, poets, painters, musicians, architects and jewellers from Turkey, Iran, Arabia, Central Asia, China, Africa and Europe came seeking fortunes at the glittering Mughal court. The Portuguese, the Dutch and the French had representatives in India before William Hawkins and Thomas Roe were sent by James I of England to the Grand Mughal, requesting trading permission for the East India Company. The Europeans brought new scientific, technical and artistic knowledge to Mughal India. They also aroused interest in Christianity and western customs. (But Jehangir's enthusiasm for European novelties did not prevent him from noticing the shoddy workmanship of the silver carriage presented to him by Thomas Roe, and having a far superior copy made by his own craftsmen!)

Even though Akbar was undoubtedly a great monarch, disappointments within his family darkened his last years. His prayers for a son and successor had been answered thrice. But none of these fruit of piety seemed worthy of inheriting what Akbar had created. Salim's younger brothers Murad and Daniyal both died of drink before they were thirty. The fault was no doubt partly Akbar's. For all one's sons to turn into alcoholics smacks of more than mere coincidence.

According to Timurid traditions, a father's territory was divided equally among surviving sons or grandsons. Thus the Mughals had no law of primogeniture and ugly wars of succession became a fact of their lives. Akbar came to the throne without facing strong rivals. But his death, and the death of every other Mughal emperor, was accompanied by upheavals, none more disruptive than the rebellion of Jehangir's eldest son, Khusro.

He was supported by two of the most powerful nobles in the empire – his uncle Raja Maan Singh of Amber and his father-in-law Mirza Aziz Koka, Akbar's eccentric foster brother.

Jehangir was the first Mughal to inherit an empire worthy of the name. Often dismissed as a pleasure-loving dilettante, Jehangir in fact served his nation well. India prospered, and there was peace in the countryside during his twenty-year reign. His essential kindliness made him forgive offenders, including his rebel son Khusro. He insisted on payment of compensation for crops damaged by Mughal troops on the march, abolished or reduced customs dues and tax for policing, established free kitchens for the poor and made sati and female infanticide capital offences. He disregarded the strict prohibitions of Islam while remaining a Sunni Muslim and observed many Hindu festivals and customs. A justice-loving ruler, Jehangir had a gold chain attached to a bell in his bedroom which could be pulled by anyone from below if they wanted to bring grievances to his notice. Jehangir's chief success lay in maintaining the status quo despite shortcomings like indolence and a pronounced taste for opium and wine that would have ruined his health much earlier, without the intervention of his devoted wife, Nurjahan. She was his alter ego; indeed, they were two halves of a perfect whole, bound by their enduring love and trust, rare in royal marriages.

Nurjahan was the de facto ruler of India for sixteen years. Brilliant, beautiful and benevolent, she is admired even now for her creativity. Her poetry is included in anthologies of Islamic literature and she designed one of the loveliest Mughal buildings, her parents' tomb at Agra. But the most intriguing aspect of Nurjahan's life was her ability to dominate the totally male-oriented world of Mughal India from behind the purdah.

The enduring love between a Persian adventurer's daughter, Meherunnisa (Empress Nurjahan), and Prince Salim (Emperor Jehangir) is one of the world's rather few happy romantic sagas.

Prologue

Mirza Ghias Beg's apprehension increased as he peered through a narrow window at a group of Ethiopian horsemen thundering across the square, their helmets glinting in the fast fading twilight. Asmat clutched her husband's arm as the horsemen whooped fearsomely by.

"They'll find us!" she cried. "This is the end!"

"Hush," admonished the Mirza, drawing her close. "Have courage. Look, they are riding away."

An ominous silence filled the empty square as night fell on the turbulent city of Isfahan. Amidst the blurred shadows of the room, the Mirza recalled the harrowing events which had, almost overnight, altered his life. Within days of old Shah Tahmasp's death in the last week of November 1579, his heir Ismail had been found with an assassin's dagger in his throat. The Grand Vezzir had declared himself regent, placed Ismail's young half-brother Shah Abbas on the throne of Persia and proclaimed the decree of exile against Ismail's friends and supporters.

The wailing in the Shah's palace had startled the city and when the tale of treachery and horror was told, the streets were quickly deserted. The bazaars and wine shops, the mosques and public bathhouses called hammamgahs, stood desolate while Shah Ismail's kinsmen began to disappear. And Ghias Beg, who on his cousin Ismail's succession to the throne of Persia had envisaged a splendid diplomatic career for himself, knew that he must abandon his hopes and save himself by flight.

"Do you think the Grand Vezzir will ever allow us to escape? He knows how close you were to Shah Ismail. And if we do, we shall be at the mercy of every bandit on the public highway, and I doubt whether we'll reach Kandahar safely." Gathering her disordered veil close round her swelling body, Asmat moved away from the window.

His wife, reflected Ghias Beg, was understandably distraught. The long journey to the Persian frontier was in any case known to be hazardous. And in her condition, and on horseback, it was bound to be a torture.

"This is not the way I had planned things, Asmat. Do you imagine that I want our next child to be born somewhere in the wilderness? But I have already worked out a plan. We shall try to reach Yezd, and if fortune favours us, join my father's old friend Malik Masud. With his kafila, we shall travel by easy stages to Hindustan. After that, we shall see."

Asmat sighed. "What does the Grand Vezzir have against you? Heaven knows you are a generous, scholarly man. You've never harmed anyone or concerned yourself with Court intrigues or factions. What are we going to do? I've been tortured with doubts and premonitions of disaster ever since that comet appeared in the sky, but I never dreamt that we would become homeless wanderers..."

"Come, Asmat," interposed the Mirza. "Comets have nothing to do with our plight. Who can understand Allah's ways? Perhaps destiny awaits us in Hindustan. All the arrangements are made, and it's time we were on our way. You haven't forgotten your jewels, I hope."

Before she could answer, footsteps sounded on the bare marble floor, and they saw a flickering candle held aloft by their faithful old retainer, Mustapha.

"Hurry, my Lord, hurry!" whispered Mustapha. "The horses are saddled and waiting in the courtyard and I've taken care to provide blankets, food and drink for the way. You must avoid the highway and public caravanserais till you reach Yezd, Master."

Asmat glanced a last time at her home, wondering if the Grand Vezzir's minions would come any moment to batter down the barricaded doors and drag out her treasures: damask coverlets, enamelled goblets, burnished mirrors, fringed and tasselled cushions, precious carpets for which her husband had paid incredible sums.

The nurse stole softly into the hall, leading six-year old Mahamud, sleepy and irritable. Young Asaf followed, asking innumerable questions. Asmat tried to reassure him, and the Mirza warned his sons to make no sound till they were well beyond the city gates. He noticed with satisfaction that they were clad in warm woollen robes, long trousers and astrakhan caps to protect them from the cold night air.

Ghias Beg took up Mahamud behind him and Asmat tied her girdle around Asaf, settling him into the saddle before her. She cast a last lingering look at her home. As long as she lived, the scent of roses would recall to her this ancient courtyard in Isfahan, around which she had expected to raise her family and pass her life. With a quick, low farewell, Ghias Beg urged his mount forward through the small postern-gate.

They rode until they came to an old crumbling archway in the city wall. Eerie noises rose and fell in the darkness around them. The wind whistled through cracks and holes in the wall, and blew dust and dying leaves into their faces. There was not a soul guarding the opening. No horseman was in sight, though they could hear bursts of laughter and snatches of ribald song coming from the soldiers' camp above. The guards had been well-bribed and, if they could get past that archway without being challenged, they might yet escape.

Asmat's heartbeat skipped as she heard a rough oath, and a soldier thrust his lance out of the shadows and barred their way. Her arm crept round her belly instinctively as she tensed in the saddle.

Ghias Beg controlled his startled steed and glanced down contemptuously at the soldier. He drew a bag from his girdle, opened it and scattered gold coins on the ground.

Seizing Ghias Beg's bridle, the soldier said, "What little value you put on your life and freedom! Your wife's jewels, quick, or I'll raise the alarm."

The Mirza's fingers clenched round his dagger hilt. Choking back an oath, he gestured to his wife. The children sat petrified while Asmat fumbled in her loose jhubba, drew out a brocade bundle and held it out wordlessly to the guard. He snatched it from her trembling fingers with a triumphant cry.

Ghias Beg signalled to Asmat and spurring their horses, they galloped away.

Three weeks later, they reached Kandahar.

Strings of fruit-laden donkeys wound their leisurely way towards the city, and a cavalcade of camels, led by muffled riders on Iraqi horses carrying piles of precious merchandise, The Afghan women stood silent as Malik Masud's kafila passed under the city walls and ragged, barefooted children ran along the road to peer curiously at the riders.

They were in the territory of the Grand Mughal at last, after so much weary travel. But he had no cause to complain, reflected Ghias Beg. After his meeting at Yezd with Malik Masud, his immediate problems had been solved and the old merchant had promised to provide a midwife for Asmat in Kandahar.

The northern ramparts of the city thrust themselves above

the high plateau and the minarets of Babur's mosque soared skywards.

Malik Masud gave a signal to his kafila leaders, and the entire caravan turned to camp beside the ancient tanks which marked their traditional halting place. Soon a noisy little settlement grew above the rugged slopes. The Mirza escorted his wife and children into a tent pitched beneath some arar trees.

Asmat looked gaunt and dishevelled and there were dark smudges under her eyes. "It's been a gruelling ordeal for you. But we are safe now, and Malik Masud assures me that as soon as everything is in order he'll send for a skilled Hazara tribeswoman from his cousin's house in the city," said Ghias Beg.

Asmat clenched her teeth against a wave of pain and forced herself to whisper, "Ask for her at once." She sank exhausted on the blankets heaped on the floor.

The kafila's camel drivers were singing hoarsely by their fire when the flap of Asmat's tent opened and a tall dark-eyed woman shuffled in. A scarf covered her head and a shapeless garment hung loose around her spare frame. For a moment, Asmat glimpsed the great roaring fires burning outside, and the smell of wood-smoke filled the tent.

Dil Aram, the Hazara nurse, bent over her where she lay on the rough blankets. To Asmat, the nurse's touch was warm and firm, and a pleasant odour of herbs came from the vessel she held.

Dil Aram spoke gently. "I'm going to raise you up and you must drink this soothing mixture. It will relieve your pain and give you strength to birth the child."

She helped Asmat sit up and drink and went swiftly about her preparations.

Asmat's child was born at daybreak. Dil Aram bustled out of the tent, and placed the swaddled infant girl in Ghias Beg's arms. At that moment the sun rose over the distant mountains and the child opened her eyes. A thrill of pride and tenderness rose in Ghias Beg as he held her close and marvelled at her beauty. He would call her Mehrunnisa, Light of Womanhood, he decided impulsively.

After a lavish repast, Ghias Beg and Malik Masud stretched themselves out comfortably on cushioned carpets in Masud's tent.

Handing the stem of his hookah to the Mirza, Masud observed, "It's always a pleasure doing business with Shahenshah Akbar's customs officials. No harassment; above all, no waste of valuable time in petty quibbling. Everything has been checked, the livestock has been certified healthy and every bundle of merchandise sealed. The customary dues have been paid and now our kafila is free to proceed anywhere in Hindustan."

"I'm glad to hear that, my friend," remarked the Mirza. "You will understand my impatience to reach Lahore. I've an acquaintance there, called Hakim Abul Fath, who is attached to Akbar Shah's Court. He might be willing to use his influence in presenting me to the notice of this strange king, about whom legends are already being told throughout the world."

"Not Lahore," amended Masur. "We are going to Agra, for that's where the Shahenshah is. Persia isn't the only country going through a terrible upheaval. I've had reliable information about trouble brewing in Kabul and Badakshan. It seems that Mirza Shah Rukh has usurped his grandfather's throne, and poor old Mirza Suleiman is on his way to seek aid from Akbar Shah. Maan Singh of Amber has been recalled from Mewar and ordered to proceed…"

"You seem to have forgotten that I am a total stranger here," interrupted Ghias Beg, laughing.

Laying a hand on Ghias Beg's shoulder, Masud said, "Pardon me, Prince. I'll explain things as I go along. Akbar

Shah is Mirza Suleiman's suzerain, so he is bound to help him recover his throne. Maan Singh is the nephew of his Hindu Empress, Jodh Bai. And when I tell you that she is the mother of his heir, Salim, you will understand how powerful Maan Singh is. He could make or mar anyone's career."

Ghias Beg regarded him thoughtfully. "And what makes this king place such trust in infidels? Their ideas should be absolutely different, their meeting points limited."

"Many shared your scepticism, when Akbar Shah banished his Vezzir Bairam Khan nineteen years ago and turned to the traditional foes of his dynasty for alliances. You must understand that there's not a drop of Indian blood in his veins – he descended from Changiz Khan and the great Timur on his father's side. His mother Hamida Banu is Persian. Born in the house of Amarkot's Hindu Rana, taught from childhood by that impossible dreamer Abdul Latif, Akbar Shah believes that his reasoned faith, the Din-i-Ilahi, must prevail, or the lesser patriotism of his followers will disrupt his ambition and his larger conception fail. At his Court all are welcome, regardless of their faith or nationality. I tell you, Isfahan is insipid compared to Agra."

They sat puffing in silence for several minutes. Frowning faintly, the merchant asked, "Didn't one of Shah Tahmasp's daughters marry Akbar Shah? I've been trying to remember her name. Here everyone calls her the Persian Sultana. Her mother was your father's younger sister, and your father made a great fuss over buying her dowry. Ah! I had to send agents to many different trade marts to procure suitable gifts..."

Dismayed, Ghias Beg protested, "I hope you don't mean to present me to her as a long-lost cousin from Persia!"

"Nonsense!" retorted Malik Masud. "She's a close relation of yours. What is Abul Fath's influence compared to that of the Persian Sultana? Has not the Prophet enjoined responsibility on kinsfolk? Allow me to arrange things in Agra."

The thought of Mirza Suleiman made Bilquis Begum rise from the couch where she had been sitting, thinking melancholy thoughts of the life that could never be again.

The news of her father's death followed by her brother's assassination had plunged Bilquis into profound grief. She had been a slight girl of sixteen when she left her father's kingdom for Hindustan, to become Akbar's consort. That had been nine years ago, but she had never got over her nostalgia for Persia, her kindly royal father and the crowd of friendly half-brothers and sisters who had made the Shah's palace at Isfahan a happy place. And now she could never go back.

Seating herself before the toilet table, she called out to her waiting women, "Hurry up, Gulnar, Firoza, otherwise I'll be late for the reception my mother-in-law is holding for Mirza Suleiman's daughter."

Bilquis Begum's maids placed a beautiful jewelled cap on her head and clasped delicate ruby bracelets round her wrists. As they were arranging the veil over her shoulders, she saw Abul Fath's wife standing in the doorway, making low salaams and murmuring compliments.

"Ah, Askadara Bibi. All is well in your household, I hope." Askadara presented a petition. The Sultana unfolded the note, saying ruefully, "Can't it wait till tomorrow? Now I shall be late and the Shahenshah's mother will raise her eyebrows at my tardiness!"

The little lines of worry about Askadara's eyes deepened. The Sultana was in a great hurry and she had not chosen the best moment for presenting Ghias Beg's petition.

But after reading the note, Bilquis looked up and asked, "Mirza Ghias Beg? Isn't he the son of my uncle, the late Vezzir of Khorasan?"

"Yes, Gracious One. And he hopes that out of natural warmth of heart for your own compatriots, you will permit him to enter your service."

"He's a kinsman of mine! We must see what can be done for him," said the Persian Sultana affably. "He must give me all the news from Persia. Bid the Mirza wait on me tomorrow."

Askadara Bibi was all smiles as she helped the Sultana enter her palanquin. "Your command will be obeyed," she said as the curtain was lowered and the bearers prepared to carry the Sultana to Hamida Begum's palace.

Seven years ago, Akbar had begun building the city of Fatehpur. No ancient fortress marked the site that Akbar had chosen for his imperial dwelling; only the modest hut of Sheikh Salim Chisti had stood by the little lake. Fatehpur lay on a plateau commanding the plains of Sikri and Bayana, close to the battlefield of Khanua where his grandfather Babur had defeated the forces of Rana Sanga of Mewar.

Ghias Beg stared critically at the Buland Durwaza which dominated the entire city. It could bear comparison with some of the finest buildings of Iran. He had to crick his head backwards till it hurt his neck, but at last he could read the Arabic inscription over the vast archway.

"Said Jesus (On Whom be Peace), the world is a bridge, pass over it, but build no houses there. He who hopes for an hour has hopes of eternity. The world is but an hour, spend it in devotion, the rest is unseen."

It was a strange inscription, the Mirza thought, for a mighty conqueror and builder. Then he recalled the tales Abul Fath had told of the monarch he was going to meet. Not so strange an inscription after all, for the man who spent his nights in devout philosophic discussions rather than in riotous carousing.

There was great bustle everywhere. A tremendous din rose as the workmen went about their chores under the eyes of watchful supervisors, for the city of Fatehpur was by no means finished yet. Abul Fath was grumbling to his young companion and gesticulating with his hands. A veritable rumble of words fell from his lips on inattentive ears, for Ghias Beg was busy looking about at the white-robed nobles dismounting from their gaily caparisoned horses, at the strange buildings, gardens and courts which lay all around him.

The Hakim was saying, "Oh yes, Raja Birbal, Raja Maan Singh, Todar Mal, Mia Tansen, Prithviraj Rathor, Abul Fazl and his brothers have been given houses around the Palace itself. They walk a short distance and they are ushered into the Shahenshah's presence! At night they retire to their own homes. But we, who work long hours in the public offices, have to ride back and forth between Agra and Fatehpur in all kinds of weather. I tell you, the dust chokes my mouth and the heat saps my strength, yet I am made to rush about at all hours, and the Lord High Steward declares arrogantly that he cannot find suitable lodgings for us."

Abul Fath escorted Ghias Beg across numerous gardens and galleries, pausing a while to point out to his friend the black and white patterned marble courtyard on which the Grand Mughal often played pachisi with live slave girls for pieces. The April kite season had begun, and Ghias Beg saw the Mughal princes Salim, Murad and Daniyal busy flying colourful paper kites with their friends on a sandstone rooftop. Outside the Persian Sultana's apartments armed harem guards demanded their identity.

The Mirza was expected. Hakim Abul Fath was told to wait outside in the corridor.

Discreetly veiled women ushered the Mirza into a chamber facing an open Court, where a tiny fountain tinkled into a basin of jasper. The builder of all this magnificence was seated on a raised marble dais, beneath a sandstone canopy. By his side sat Bilquis Begum, the Persian Sultana, a gossamer veil draped over the jewelled head dress she wore in the fashion of the women of Isfahan and Baghdad, but alien here under these sultry Hindustani skies.

Before Ghias Beg could perform the ceremony of kornish by bowing low and raising his hand thrice to his forehead, Akbar spoke in his deep mellow voice, and the fugitive began to have an inkling of his mesmeric power: "You are welcome at Fatehpur, Mirza, as a kinsman of the Sultana."

Bilquis heard Ghias Beg answer her husband's queries with courteous deference. Tears trembled on her lashes as she listened to the Mirza's tale and mourned her brother's death anew.

Akbar saw Bilquis wince when Ghias Beg spoke of his children and guessed the thought that lay in her mind. Their daughter had lived only seven months, leaving Bilquis inconsolable.

"Begum, why don't you undertake Mehrunnisa's upbringing?" suggested Akbar.

Brightening, she answered, "Nothing would give me greater pleasure. And perhaps Mirza Ghias Beg's sons could become Salim's companions?"

"I too was born on the road between Hindustan and Iran. And my father, Badshah Humayun of blessed memory, was so impoverished by the upheavals in our country that he had nothing except fragments of musk to distribute among his loyal chiefs when they brought him news of my birth," confided Akbar.

Bilquis Begum couldn't help adding: "And the fame of your great deeds and noble generosity has spread to the four corners of our world, my Lord, like that of musk itself. May Mehrunnisa too, be similarly blessed, Inshallah."

As he rose to signify that the audience was over, Akbar said, "We must find some worthwhile employment for you and turn Iran's loss into Hindustan's gain."

Ghias Beg backed out of the chamber and followed the waiting women into the shadowy corridor where Abul Fath sat. The Mirza accompanied him to the stables and they mounted their horses for the long ride back to Agra. As he gathered his reins, Ghias Beg thought of the future that shone brightly again, like the road to Agra which stretched glimmering through tall arching trees in the light of the setting sun.

Mehrunnisa

1

Usually, she enjoyed reading aloud from the beautifully illustrated volumes of fables, history, poetry and love legends kept in the Mughal zenana. Or to sketch, paint and embroider with her friends in some airy riverside chamber while they chatted and played tricks on each other during the hot summer mornings before lunch was served and they could all take well-deserved naps while serving maids fanned them.

Some irresistible urge made her linger in Bilquis Begum's private garden long after her companions had gone into the palace, protesting at her wilfulness.

She sat dreaming now by the edge of a small round lily pool. Tiny striped squirrels, birds in gilt cages and drifting butterflies made this garden on the banks of the Ravi, outside the walled city of Lahore, a place of enchantment.

The spell was broken by the sound of anklet bells and the rustling of women's skirts. Bilquis Begum walked into the garden with her stepson Salim, followed by a bright, bejewelled band of her ladies and maids.

"I assure you, this is the only pair of fantailed white pigeons in Hindustan. They were smuggled out of Basra by that clever merchant, Masud. He knew how I longed for a pair. The Badshah guards them as though they were rare gems," declared the Sultana.

The young girl rose and salaamed low as the Sultana advanced. Salim glanced briefly at her and turned to look at the pigeons with a covetous gleam in his eyes.

His stepmother smiled knowingly. "Ah, Prince, I knew I'd lose my winged treasures once you saw them. No matter; you may add them to your aviary. But promise me the first fledglings hatched from this pair."

Askadara Bibi brought down the cage from its perch on a mango tree, but Salim was not content to gaze at them. With a swift movement he opened the cage and caught the birds with both hands, his rings glinting against their white feathers.

A goblet of sherbat was offered him and he looked around for someone to hold the pigeons while he drank. His glance lit on the face of the young girl standing by the pool, the sunlight playing through her face till he could have sworn her skin was transparent.

Salim beckoned. The wind teased her veil and a lock of hair fell across her brow. She walked towards him, her braids swaying, and he wondered what subtle fragrance she wore. She raised her eyes to his face and he marvelled at their strange colour. Were they black or blue, he wondered, holding out the birds to her. Her long slender fingers trembled as they touched Salim's hand and an involuntary smile flashed on her lips.

"Won't you stay to dine with me, Salim? You came back to Lahore two weeks ago, and you haven't been to see me till now," put in the Sultana cajolingly.

Salim grinned, "I wish I could, but you know that whenever I'm at Court, I dine with grandmother every afternoon. She would casually mention my absence to the Shahenshah, and I'd get a thundering scold for neglecting her. As if anyone could!"

"I hear she's returning soon to the heat of Delhi, though the Shahenshah entreats her to escape summer with him to Kashmir," Bilquis said as they sipped their iced sherbat.

"Don't you know she detests travelling from province to province, and according to her, all these journeys and visits..."

Abruptly he broke off as he heard the flutter of wings. One of his newly acquired pigeons wheeled and circled in the sky, calling to its mate. "Careless girl," fumed Salim, as he turned and asked imperiously, "How did it escape?"

She laughed to see the petulant look on his face and

opening both her hands wide, answered, “So, my Lord!” And away went second bird.

She could see his amber-flecked eyes now, bequeathed by some forgotten ancestor of the Central Asian steppes. And his beautifully moulded mouth was stern in his flushed face.

The stunned women ceased their chatter, fearing one of Salim’s sudden violent rages. Bilquis Begum placed her hand protectively on the girl’s arm. She stopped laughing but continued to gaze at Salim, her face tilted slightly upwards. His handsome fair face, short straight black hair, the drooping moustache over the petulant full mouth, the tapering nervous fingers, the aura of power and arrogance he radiated absorbed her as she stood motionless, waiting.

Was her glance entreating or mocking him, he wondered. Then Salim threw back his head and laughed uproariously at the trick she had played on him. “A fearless maiden, by Allah!”

Taking a step towards her, Salim raised her chin with a finger and after a quick appraisal asked, “Your name?”

A moment passed. Her mouth trembled and a flush spread from her creamy throat to her cheeks and brow. “Mehrunnisa,” she replied in a curiously husky voice.

Nobody spoke. A frightened flutter of foresight skittered in that garden full of Persian women. Something stirred at the back of Bilquis Begum’s mind, some tale Asmat had told of Mehrunnisa lying unharmed under a cobra’s hood.

Deliberately, the Persian Sultana broke the spell that bound her profligate stepson and this closely guarded girl of seventeen.

“She is Mirza Ghias Beg’s daughter and my kinswoman, Prince.” The Sultana spoke with icy hauteur, warning Salim, reminding Mehrunnisa, that she too was a prince’s daughter and no harem slave girl to be casually trifled with.

“Let us go into the palace, the sun is so hot today!”

But she spoke too late. Salim had gazed at Mehrunnisa too long ever to forget her face.

2

Princess of Amber stood on the balcony, watching boats with silken canopies glide past her palace. Her deeply gathered skirt of flame-coloured brocade swirled gently over her hips and its contrasting black border swept the floor as she moved a step closer to the marble fretwork balustrade. A pearl-encrusted veil was drawn negligently over her right shoulder, leaving her jewelled head bare. The brisk spring breeze teased the tassels of her backless bodice as she looked towards the massive bulk of Hari Parbat, crowned with the crenellated towers of the Mughal castle. Kashmir had finally been conquered in 1589 by her father, Raja Bhagwan Das. She wondered if Salim was still closeted with Akbar Shah, discussing the forthcoming campaign against the Afghans, who had broken their treaty and raided the towns beyond the Khyber pass.

The cool spring air was laden with the scent of saffron, and beyond the great forests of pine and deodar rose the snows of the Pir Panchal, glittering through shreds of mist in the sunlight. The entire Court was here in Kashmir on an excursion of pleasure, but this tranquil scene failed to soothe her tumultuous spirit. She was tormented afresh by thoughts of her husband, Salim. Impotent rage engulfed her as she thought of his indifference over the last month. Her life, she felt, had become meaningless, a succession of dismal days spent in idle speculation and nights haunted by fevered dreams and hopeless longings. At Lahore and Agra, she could keep track of him, but here it was impossible to know where he was, or with whom. There were over seventy royal gardens scattered all over the valley of Kashmir and Salim could retire to any one of them with the girl of his choice.

She should have learnt to accept and ignore her husband's amorous intrigues, she told herself sternly for the thousandth time. But the zenana was abuzz with groups of gossiping, whispering women, who seemed to derive vicious delight in seeking her out to drop honeyed words of warning and compassion in her ear while secretly gloating over her fall from favour.

She wondered despairingly how long she would continue to enjoy the title and privileges of Shah Begum. Even her father-in-law Akbar Shah had overlooked the claim of his first wife Ruquiya Begum and elevated Jodh Bai to the rank of Empress. But everyone knew that Salima Sultana, more fortunate than both, was the Grand Mughal's undoubted favourite. Salima Begum and Akbar Shah were first cousins, like Shah Begum and the Crown Prince. And it was well known that Akbar Shah had wasted no time in marrying Salima after her first husband Bairam Khan's murder.

"Princess!"

Shah Begum turned round, an angry sparkle in her eyes. "Quick, Chandra, tell me what you've discovered. Has he been meeting her here?"

The old nurse's thin mouth was drawn in a sharp line of disapproval. With an audible sniff, she answered, "The Prince has been very discreet. But do you know what those Muslim Begums are plotting? Their effrontery is beyond belief! This evening at Bilquis Begum's banquet that little witch is going to sing before the Shahenshah, so that she may charm him into consenting to this unequal match. It is all Salima Sultana's doing, I swear, to rule the Prince through Mehrunnisa!"

Shah Begum gasped in disbelief while Chandra, a distant relation of the Empress Jodh Bai, continued relentlessly: "Don't stand by sighing and praying while your entire future is being wrecked! You must go immediately to the Empress, your aunt, and beg her to intervene before it is too late. If things go on like this, it won't be long before Mehrunnisa is installed in the harem as the Prince's favourite bride."

"You are right. She must intervene. Order my palanquin immediately!" said Shah Begum in her impetuous manner.

Nodding and sighing and grumbling to herself, Chandra hastened off.

Soon, palki-bearers stopped inside the portico of Empress Jodh Bai's palace. Shah Begum waited impatiently for the courtyard to be cleared of all the soldiers, servants, gardeners and loungers before she could alight.

At last the bearers shut the massive outer gate and withdrew, and she flung aside the tasselled brocade curtains to step out of the palki.

The maids at the doorway managed to remain expressionless as they greeted Shah Begum. They were all women of Amber and spoke to her in their own tongue, disdaining the polished Persian phrases of Court. Shah Begum always had a kind word for her mother-in-law's maids, but today she barely managed to murmur the customary words of greeting.

The women exchanged glances and wondered what had brought the Princess at this odd hour to her aunt's palace. They too had heard rumours of Prince Salim's latest amorous involvement, and they could anticipate interesting developments once Shah Begum's grievances began.

Leaving Chandra in the corridor, the Princess passed into the enclosed Court which was a bower of flowers. Under a golden canopy sat Jodh Bai on velvet cushions, chatting affably with Salima Sultana, the mother of Prince Murad. Trays of fruit and sweetmeats and goblets of sherbat were set on a low engraved rosewood table. Two silver-gilt spittoons were already full of apricot and peach stones. Akbar's two consorts were whiling away the pleasant spring morning together, apparently on the best of terms.

As Shah Begum bowed low to them with folded palms,

suspicion flared in her mind. What had they been discussing so animatedly when she had entered?

Salima Sultana was recounting some story of her last visit to Kabul. She was even better travelled than the Emperor's mother Hamida Begum, or his aunt Gulbadan, having seen every noteworthy city in Hindustan, Afghanistan, Badakshan, Persia and Arabia. And strangely enough, she had insisted on leaving her six-year old son Murad in the care of Empress Jodh Bai while she made the holy pilgrimage to Mecca which had lasted seven years.

After exchanging pleasantries with Shah Begum, Salima Sultana rose and took leave of the Empress. She could see that Shah Begum was burning with indignation and plainly waiting to pour a flood of complaints into her aunt's ears.

Jodh Bai gestured with her hands and spoke a word of dismissal to her attendants. She sensed that her daughter-in-law had not come to pay a ceremonial visit and looked with some apprehension at her disturbed face.

Shah Begum was not only the chief wife of her son and the mother of her first grandson, but also the daughter of her brother Bhagwan Das. They had both been born within the high latticed walls of Amber, and in their veins flowed the blood of the Kachwaha clan. The family likeness was evident in their luminous black eyes, matchless pale gold colouring, voluptuous mouths and stately bearing.

"Aunt," whispered the Princess. "My worst fears are coming true. Those Muslim Begums are intriguing and planning to present Mehrunnisa to the Shahenshah tonight! She was invited to accompany Bilquis Begum to Kashmir at his express request, I am told..."

"You should have learnt by now to ignore idle palace gossip, child," rebuked Jodh Bai gently.

"You may judge for yourself this evening whether it's merely idle gossip. A Persian adventurer's daughter trying to insinuate herself into the Crown Prince's life!"

"It's the way of Princes to find diversion and I wouldn't be surprised if Salim made this girl his concubine. My dear child, it's never easy, but your position demands iron self-control and absolute indifference to Salim's intrigues." The Empress was thoroughly annoyed. Her niece was impetuous and emotional; one never knew what she would do in a fit of temper or dejection. But it was exceedingly inconsiderate of Salim to flout convention and ignore his wives. Now there would be a lot of unpleasantness involving everyone.

Shah Begum cried indignantly, "You advised me to ignore all those goings-on when the Prince was dangling after Zain Khan's daughter Saheb Jamal! Nothing would come of it, you said. And yet the Shahenshah had to agree to that match, and now she..."

"Have enough wit and subtlety not to hurl reproaches at my son!" interrupted Jodh Bai. "And I must tell you that Salim cannot bear tears, tantrums and recrimination. You must preserve at least a semblance of affability, no matter what Salim does."

"I thought I could at least rely on *your* understanding and sympathy," protested Shah Begum.

"Does the Amber Princess fear this insignificant girl? You always were a credulous child. Nothing will come of this affair, but just to set your mind at peace, I'll have Mehrunnisa's horoscope cast by our High Priest. After that, we shall know exactly what to do. Compose yourself, my dear."

"Horoscopes!" said Shah Begum angrily. "It is perfectly evident you've not seen this girl."

"If your report is true, we shall spend half the evening watching Bilquis Begum's protege flaunting her accomplishments before the Shahenshah. And I shall know whether to condemn or applaud Salim's taste," rejoined Jodh Bai with a gleam of amusement in her eyes.

Scanning Mehrunnisa appraisingly, Bilquis Begum decided that her elegant embroidered blue kamiz and silvery silk veil were just right with the tight white satin trousers.

"You look very well and I'm glad, for the Prince has a critical eye..."

Mehrunnisa could only blush and stammer incoherently.

Bilquis raised her delicate eyebrows and cast her a quizzical look. "Perhaps you are unaware of Salim's interest in you?"

Her lips parted and then closed again. She dared not repeat what the Crown Prince's favourite sister Arambanu Begum had whispered to her one idle afternoon in the garden. She could hardly confess her own weakness to the Sultana, and Salim's interest might be nothing but a fleeting whim.

Choosing her words carefully, the Persian Sultana continued, "I'm going to talk very frankly with you, Mehrunnisa. My volatile stepson will one day control the destiny of this vast empire. Many will try to manipulate him for questionable ends, but perhaps you, as his consort, could prevent all that and mould him into a perfect sovereign."

"What do you mean, Gracious One?" cried Mehrunnisa, while her eyes sparkled with keen interest.

"You are much too intelligent to miss my meaning, Mehrunnisa. Do you think I'm blind to the romantic attachment blossoming between you and Salim? I have also consulted trusted Sufi peers, Hindu astrologers and crystal-gazing clairvoyants, who all agree that your birth signs, Leo and Capricorn, are in perfect harmony, each providing what the other needs for a happy, balanced life," Bilquis Begum said with deep conviction.

"Allah has endowed you with the intellect and strength of soul required in queens and I believe your Persian education has helped refine both." She paused and took Mehrunnisa's hand affectionately. "It will mean so much to so many and everything to Salim." For a long while she talked earnestly with Mehrunnisa.

Fear and hope jostled wildly in Mehrunnisa's mind as she followed the Sultana downstairs. A dream took shape, and she imagined herself entering the castle of Agra at the head of a triumphant wedding procession, with Salim riding by her side.

Dreams. And here was reality, the hall of Bilquis Begum's apartments, lavish and ornate, decorated with friezes and arabesques. In the corners of the octagonal room stood alabaster and onyx pedestals bearing bowls of incense and ambergris. Little niches cut into the walls held beautiful enamelled vases filled with flowers, bowls of fruit, and sherbat in priceless goblets.

In the centre of the room was a raised marble dais covered with a deep blue carpet patterned in crimson and white, on which were arranged tasselled and fringed brocade cushions, gleaming richly in the light of a thousand candles blazing in huge tinted glass candelabra. The inlaid wooden floor was scattered with rich woollen carpets woven with Persian motifs in Kashmir itself.

Mehrunnisa watched the Mughal *grande dames* in their velvet basques and sequinned veils, their distinctive thumb rings flashing. She saw too the supple, graceful figures of Rajputanis, girdles dangling from their waists and gossamer draperies floating behind, walk with superb self-confidence into this gathering dominated by women of the conquering race.

There stood the haughty niece of the Amber Raja, her black eyes blazing, a dagger stuck in her girdle as usual. Seeing her thus, Mehrunnisa could almost believe the story that with that same dagger, she had threatened Akbar Shah as he sought to trifle with her in an ante-chamber at Agra.

By her side stood Raja Birbal's daughter, a delicate beauty and reputed artist, who had not proved as virtuous, having succumbed to the emperor's wooing to become one of his concubines without legal nikah before the kazi.

Her friends surrounded Mehrunnisa and their gay chatter broke upon her musings.

"Princess Arambanu has just been telling me that besides a fabulous prize, the best singer will receive a month's training in music under Mia Tansen," said Laila, the pretty rose-cheeked daughter of the military commander Mansabdar Jallal Khan Kuraish.

"That could hardly excite you," Mehrunnisa said, smiling,

"You are one of the few girls, besides the Mughal princesses, whom he has condescended to instruct."

"Not because she's gifted, but merely out of friendship for her family," interposed Gulabi with a grimace.

A laugh escaped Mehrunnisa, but she shook her head reprovingly. "Don't pay any attention to her, Laila. I would much rather have that handwritten copy of the Khan-i-Khanan's incomparable poems, which Salima Begum has promised the winner," she declared. "His dohas are so witty yet spiritual."

"Rahim's couplets! Nothing but a collection of heretical songs written in praise of Hindu idols. I'm *positive* he doesn't compose them himself. When would he get the time, pray? One of his pensioners writes them and he gets all the credit."

"Stop repeating malicious gossip, Gulabi. Would the Shahenshah have chosen Bairam Khan's son Abdul Rahim Khan-i-Khanan as his heir's ataliq if he wasn't the most versatile scholar in Hindustan?" exclaimed Mehrunnisa indignantly.

"Oh, everyone knows that he was appointed only due to Salima Begum's influence. Stepson teaching stepson," sneered Gulabi.

Before Mehrunnisa could caution her indiscreet friend, Askadara Bibi entered the chamber with a gold staff in her hand. She tapped the floor with it and announced loudly: "The Shahenshah!"

Everyone rose and bowing low to the floor, touched their right hands to their foreheads thrice in quick succession in kornish. Akbar smiled and returned their salaams, followed by Salim, resplendent in pink brocade and rubies.

Mehrunnisa looked at Akbar, master of a million destinies, absolute ruler of a mighty empire. He shone with power and benevolence. Though his hair had turned grey, his face was still unlined at fifty three and he sat upright against the cushions.

He was robed in a white silk fargal, the flaring coat crossed and tied over the chest with fine cords, and a half-sleeved jacket of pale blue velvet, buttoned with diamonds and embroidered at the edges with gold thread. There was a double strand of large pearls round his neck, and on his turban was a plume of heron feathers secured by an aigrette made of priceless rubies, from which hung the legendary Kohinoor.

She wondered with a quickening heartbeat how she would sing before him. Many declared that Akbar Shah was gifted with the power of divining people's thoughts. What if he guessed hers?

Someone was watching her intently, she felt. Glancing around, she encountered Shah Begum's smouldering, brooding gaze. A strange thought came to her. She could not explain the feeling to herself, yet it seemed to her that Shah Begum, in spite of her secure position as Khusro's mother, was not of the stature required to dominate the Mughal zenana.

At a signal from the Persian Sultana, a slave-girl entered bearing aloft a burning candle and the entertainment began.

Conversation sank to whispers as the candle was placed before Laila. Glancing nervously at Akbar, she salammed and began a sad song. Her style was almost flawless, for Laila had been trained by Mia Tansen, the foremost musical genius in Hindustan. Sounds of acclaim filled the air as the audience cheered her and commented on the various singers who followed her. At last the candle came to Mehrunnisa.

Watching the candlelight flickering over her face, Salim whispered to Bilquis Begum, "Yes, indeed an incomparable beauty! She has eyes like the gems of Khorasan, lips the colour of rubies from Herat!" Oblivious of everyone else, Salim stretched out his hand towards Mehrunnisa in a beckoning gesture. Their glances locked. Mehrunnisa gave him a small secret smile. She marked the ruby studs on his fargal and her quick mind raced. After a little pause she began to sing.

"The ruby button that gleams on your shirt
Is a drop of my blood
That has caught you by the collar!"

The lilting melody soared to fill the hall. Akbar turned to the Persian Sultana. "Ghias Beg's daughter performs delightfully! She is by far the best amateur singer I've heard," Gazing up at Akbar, Bilquis smiled. "Do you think she deserves the prize, Sire?"

Salim touched the ruby button at his throat and laughed softly to himself. He alone could fathom the meaning of her charming verses. A quick-witted beauty, by Allah! What a way she had chosen of telling him of her heart's surrender.

Empress Jodh Bai studied Mehrunnisa thoughtfully and then turned her eyes to her son. The song ended, Salim burst into loud praise, and Jodh Bai cast him a repressive glance, saying, "Restrain your exuberance, Prince."

The applause came to an end and the hum of low voices filled the room, while Akbar conferred with Salima and Bilquis.

Amidst a chorus of comments and congratulations, Mehrunnisa came up to the dais to receive a jade casket full of unstrung pearls from Akbar.

"I've been wondering, was that delightful song you sang one of your own compositions?" he asked affably, as she sank to her knees.

"A poor effort, Sire."

Akbar smiled. "It's evident that you have inherited your father's gift for elegant and original verse."

And graciously, Akbar dismissed her, while Jodh Bai gazed impassively at her smouldering niece.

3

Raja Maan Singh of Amber rose from an ornate lacquered chair as his aunt Jodh Bai entered the apartment, pausing for a moment by a green-and-gold-painted door niche, which resembled an undulating seashell. When greetings had been ritually exchanged, Maan Singh coughed and said significantly, "Your message sounded urgent enough to make me put off several important affairs of state."

"We are perfectly aware that you are immersed at all times in Sultanat affairs. But perhaps in your moments of leisure you could mend matters in your own house?" countered the Empress a trifle ironically as a sudden sharp peal of thunder rang out. Looking her nephew straight in the eye, she continued, "You alone can help me safeguard the future of your sister Shah Begum, which is again under threat."

Amusement flashed in his dark eyes. The pearls in his ears quivered as he laughed and said, "Does my sister still permit herself to be teased by trifles?"

Though he had small regard and no affection whatsoever for Akbar's heir, he had absolutely no intention of becoming involved in another harem intrigue. The feuds of the harem, he was well aware, were merely extensions of the great rivalries in Hindustan. Akbar Shah often declared that he had successfully welded his Hindu, Persian, Afghan, Mongol and Turkish vassals into a harmonious unit. But Maan Singh knew that these ambitious, arrogant men were held together only by the Grand Mughal's ruthless will.

There were factions at Court, factions throughout the country. There were fierce rivalries, family feuds and swift vendettas. And all those warring cliques had their spies, their scandals, their plots. Since they found it impossible to involve

Akbar Shah in their schemes, they invariably wove their webs round his heir, Salim.

Jodh Bai sat silently arranging her cool muslin veil over her bejewelled arms. She directed a penetrating glance at Maan Singh, who was stroking his curling black moustache with an expression of wicked glee.

After the death of her brother Bhagwan Das, Maan Singh had succeeded to the gadi of Amber, and over the years Jodh Bai had come to rely on his calm good sense and unquestioned devotion to herself. Though never an intimate friend of her husband like Abul Fazl, or Raja Birbal, her nephew was undoubtedly the most powerful prince in the country. The epitome of Rajput manhood, endowed with virile good looks and a magnificent physique, he was also a scholar of Sanskrit, an architect and a musician of high repute. Despite his stubborn refusal to join the Emperor's select Din-i-Illahi sect, Akbar Shah had unhesitatingly granted him Bihar in jagir. He also held the rank of Mansabdar of Seven Thousand, and the governorship of Lahore and Kabul. Jodh Bai knew that he possessed in full measure the unique Kachwaha trait of adaptability to the present and foresight for the future. He had succeeded in bringing Amber into the mainstream of Hindustani politics and his ambition for his family knew no bounds.

Reflecting thus, the Empress felt sure that however reluctant Maan Singh would be to interfere with Salim's pleasures, the merest hint of a threat to Khusro's future would waken the latent clannishness in his soul. Salim had belonged from the moment of his birth to the Emperor, to his nurses, his tutors, his Mughal aunts and stepmothers, and to the empire. Khusro belonged to the Kachwahas of Amber.

"You may care nothing for your sister's woes, but you must have learnt by now that your own future will be secure only if Khusro succeeds to the Mughal throne," she said with cool confidence. No one knew better than herself the significance of her marriage to Akbar and of the Rajput alliances that had followed. The Rana of Mewar still disparaged them, without appreciating the advantages bought for the entire Hindu community and their imperilled civilization by these marriage contracts.

"None dare threaten Khusro while I live!" Maan Singh declared, with swiftly blazing eyes. His sword rasped in its scabbard as he swore, "There shall always be a host of Kachwaha clansmen to uphold his claim and protect his life."

The empress silenced him with a gesture. "Yet there are those who are plotting to humiliate us, to undo all our efforts to achieve ascendancy in Hindustan. Those insolent Muslim Begums are confident of success because once more Salim has fallen prey to a pretty face!"

His curiosity overcame his caution and he said, "What can I do about it?"

"Arrange a match for a certain young girl."

His vanity tickled, the Raja cried archly. "What! Must I marry another of your wards, whom your son is beginning to fancy?"

"She wouldn't wed you even if the Kachwahas of Amber would agree to accept a Shia Persian's daughter as their queen!" came the crushing retort. Jodh Bai was in no humour for her nephew's pleasantries. After a long pause, she said, "I want you to find a bridegroom for Mehrunnisa Khanum, eldest daughter of our Lord High Steward, Mirza Ghias Beg."

The Raja reflected a while, glancing silently at his aunt. There was an angry glitter in her eyes, and her face, usually so composed, was flushed today.

"Why? Ghias Beg's daughter doesn't lack suitors, I believe. One hears endless talk about this girl's beauty and accomplishments. And everyone knows that the Persian Sultana has promised her a dowry befitting a Mughal princess."

"Ah, yes!" cried Jodh Bai. "But the Persian Sultana plans

to wed Mehrunnisa to our son Salim." She rose abruptly from the cushioned divan and walked towards an open window, to watch the softly-falling rain.

For a while she stood toying with her bracelets and inhaling the refreshing scent of moist earth and new-washed grass.

Turning towards her nephew, who had strolled over to stand beside her, she said emphatically, "I know what you are thinking. If Salim takes another wife or concubine, it signifies nothing. Shadows do not startle me: but hear this. I've had Mehrunnisa's horoscope studied by the High Priest of Amber, who is the foremost astrologer in this country. He insists that Mehrunnisa shall rule undoubted queen over Hindustan one day; that Khusro's star will wane when she rises to power. Three times, practising the severest austerity, did he cast her horoscope, and every time the answer was the same."

She heard him suppress an oath. Astrology wielded an incalculable influence over Maan Singh. It actually regulated the very tempo of his life, she knew. Deeply superstitious, her nephew would not doubt her reasoning for a moment now, she thought confidently.

"We can't stand by watching idly while the Persians conspire to dominate Salim through this girl. We can't permit Salim to marry her. Mirza Ghias Beg is an intimate friend of yours; you could persuade him to marry her off to someone who could be relied on to take her away from Agra."

All at once he understood her fears and, casting aside indifference, became involved in her plans. Something would have to be done now, he realized. His eyes followed a flight of pigeons winging across the cloudy sky. The rain fell afresh. Choosing his words carefully, he said "It won't be an easy task. If Salim was sent away for a while, perhaps to conduct the campaign in Mewar...?"

The Empress understood. "It shall be arranged," she promised calmly.

4

Just as he finished setting the turban on his head, Mirza Ghias Beg heard Asaf's voice calling to one of the servants in the corridor outside.

A humorous twinkle appeared in the Mirza's eyes when he saw his son. Asaf was resplendent that morning in a pure white silk cabaya, a short-sleeved jacket which fell well below his knees; a jewelled dagger was stuck into his purple brocade cummerbund, his pale lilac turban was adorned with an emerald and pearl aigrette of superb craftsmanship. He wore tight purple satin pyjamas and gold embroidered slippers with enormous curling toes, and brought a whiff of strong attar into the chamber.

"Greetings, father," said Asaf, salaaming low. He straightened up, disclosing an attractive, animated countenance, with wide-set hazel eyes under fine straight brows. With his high-bridged nose, broad forehead and full, sensitive mouth, he bore a marked resemblance to his handsome father, though he lacked the Mirza's height.

"Peace be upon you," murmured Ghias Beg, scanning his son from head to toe. "Tell me, how do you manage to buy such sumptuous raiment and jewels on the modest allowance I make you?"

Asaf grinned, "So the Lord High Steward fails to recognize the Crown Prince's gems!"

With a word of dismissal to his attendant, Ghias Beg moved towards the archway. "I hear the Crown Prince will soon be leaving Agra," he remarked once they were alone on the upper storey of the house.

"But no one in the Prince's suite has heard anything, father!"

There was a slight pause before the Mirza said gravely, "I rely on your discretion not to spread the tale abroad, Asaf!"

As they came to the zenana apartments, Asaf observed with concern, "If your news is correct, my friend Veer Bhatt may arrive from Benaras to find me gone. I had invited him to come and stay with us believing that we would remain here for a few months."

"That's your poet friend, isn't he? The one who is trying to translate the *Rig Veda* from Sanskrit to Persian?" asked the Mirza.

Asaf nodded, and his father said, "In case you leave before he arrives, I shall offer him the hospitality of our house, though I doubt if he'll accept it. Your friend is a high caste Brahmin, while we are despised Toorks!"

"Persians, Father."

The Mirza shrugged, "To the Hindus we are all the same, my son: hated invaders from the northwest. Who can convince them otherwise?"

"Can anyone blame them, Father? We Persians share a two-thousand-year-old Aryan heritage with the Rajputs, but get lumped with our Chagatai Turkish masters because of ugly episodes like the massacre at Chittor after the citadel fell. Even Allaudin Khilji showed more chivalry in 1303 than Akbar Shah in 1568, by sparing the peasants after sacking Chittor."

The Mirza cautioned his son not to repeat such dangerous opinions where tale-bearers might hear them. "The Emperor has human failings like all of us,"

"Failings!" exclaimed Asaf. "He poses as a prophet, a saviour of this divided land. Can anyone justify the frightful slaughter in Malwa – a Muslim kingdom – after Sultan Baz Bahadur's defeat, and the rape of all his wives and concubines by the Emperor's wretched foster brother Adham Khan? Or the unnecessary attacks on the tribal tracts of Gondwana, where its warrior queen Durgavati committed suicide to escape a similar fate?"

Ghias Beg couldn't help agreeing with Asaf. Even though all this had happened before they came to India. Rebels were executed without trial, prisoners tortured and very often strangled in jail. Less fortunate in his councillors than Sultan Allaudin Khilji, Akbar had allowed Sheikh Mubarak and his two sycophantic sons Abul Fazl and Faizi to convince him that he was virtually divine and could do no wrong.

At the threshold of the dining chamber, father and son removed their slippers. Asmat smiled her welcome. She marked the aura of unconscious pride and dignity which surrounded them both; for a fleering instant she wished that Mahamud, her firstborn, had been endowed with their gracious affability. Brushing asidc her thoughts, she busied herself at the dastarkhan.

The Mirza watched his wife's supervision of the morning meal with approval. There was something on the damask-covered board to tempt all her children: tall silver tumblers full of warm milk flavoured with saffron and cardamoms and sweetened with pounded crystal sugar; platters heaped with fried flaky bread, fresh yoghurt, butter, boiled eggs, pickles and kebabs; bowls of figs, grapes and ripe pomegranates from Kandahar. They had come a long way from that impoverished tent in which Mehrunnisa had been born, he thought, and humbly thanked Allah for Asmat's wonderful beauty and intelligence. Asmat had made their home a happy, harmonious place, where no shadows of the past nor furore from the imperial household marred their marriage. Ghias Beg's devotion and contentment often amazed his friends and aquaintances, for no junior wives or concubines dwelt in the Lord High Steward's house. His love for Asmat had grown and deepened with each passing year, and the birth of each new child, till there were six happy brothers and sisters demanding their share of time, love and attention.

He smiled and chatted with the children seated round the dastarkhan on the carpeted floor. As he broke unleavened bread with the words "Bismillah," his eyes rested fondly on his favourite child. He saw so little of her these days; his duties kept him moving about ceaselessly with the Court from province to province.

Mehrunnisa glanced at her father with a warm loving look, then pretended to eat her food. Ghias Beg noticed things about her which he had never noticed before. The transparency of her skin, the dreamy look in her eyes, her softening contours. His daughter's new beauty disturbed him strangely.

Ibrahim, barely a year younger than Mehrunnisa, turned to her with his mouth full and whispered, "There's a fair being held today beyond the Atka Bazaar. My tutor has forbidden it, but I mean to go and enjoy myself. If you want me to buy you some trifles, you must lend me some money."

Mehrunnisa almost laughed at his ingenious way of begging and signalled her assent.

Asaf picked up a silver tumbler and asked, "Another indulgence, Mother?"

Raising her hands aloft, Asmat protested, "Ya Allah! I was practically forced to buy an entire set at the last Meena Bazaar. How can you accuse me of self-indulgence? I don't even care much for the pattern, Asaf."

"Ah, the Mughal Begums are forcing everyone to patronize some new silversmith from the palace atelier," laughed the Mirza.

"We met Ayesha there, brother, but we couldn't give her your message. Her mother wouldn't leave her alone with us!" interposed fourteen-year-old Manija, a lovely, vivacious girl with a restless air about her.

Khadija, a deceptively frail child with a marked resemblance to Mehrunnisa, giggled, "She was so laden with purchases, we couldn't help asking her if she was buying her dowry!"

Grinning, Asaf turned to speak to his mother and ignored his sisters. They enjoyed teasing him about his fiancee, whom he had never seen in his life and whom he would be marrying after Id.

"Mahamud is late as usual. Is he still asleep, or hasn't he returned home yet?" Ghias Beg asked suddenly. An uncomfortable silence fell upon the intimate family group.

Asaf answered at last, with downcast eyes, "He has gone to Delhi with Aziz Koka, Father."

The Mirza sighed. "I wonder, will Mahamud ever learn wisdom? To associate openly with a man who was banished from Court for displeasing the Shahenshah..."

"What has he done *this* time?" asked Mehrunnisa. She enjoyed listening to stories of Aziz Koka's escapades, for he was always involved in endless, intense disagreements with Akbar Shah. Besides, it was pointless discussing Mahamud, who would always go his own way.

"Nothing much, except that while walking in the garden with the Shahenshah a few days ago, Aziz Koka suddenly spread his turban on the ground, fell on his knees and loudly started reciting the evening prayer. The Shahenshah repeatedly ordered him to rise, saying that it was not yet time and gave him a few clouts on the head. But do you think he would budge? He arrogantly gave everyone a lecture on the virtues of prayer. And as a result he has been banished from Court and commanded to proceed to Mecca on Hajj!"

Everyone laughed. "Were you present, Asaf, when Sultan Salim quarrelled with his brother Murad? I heard there was a tremendous uproar at the Palace," asked Asmat. "What was it all about?"

Asaf answered evasively; that was hardly a tale for the ears of his three young sisters, who were listening attentively. But apparently they had heard something, for Mehrunnisa glanced at her brother with cool hauteur, and declared, "Only despicably malicious persons could believe those slanders against Sultan Salim."

"Oh, oh! I wasn't aware that you were such an ardent admirer of our Crown Prince," mocked Asaf softly. "What do you know of him, beyond the tales women whisper in the Mughal zenana?"

Mehrunnisa's colour mounted and her father noticed the way her fingers trembled as she hastily picked up a pomegranate. He was tempted to intervene as Asaf continued to tease his sister. But just then his wife claimed his attention.

"There is something I must discuss with you before you ride to the palace," she said.

At a sign from Asmat, serving maids appeared with basin, ewer and towel at his elbow. Ghias Beg washed his hands, rinsed his mouth and, wiping his fingers, rose from the dastarkhan.

Together they went through a long, shadowy corridor to Asmat's bedchamber. It was a room made cheerful with coloured tiles and hanging lanterns, devoid of furniture except for a large silver-legged bed covered with a chintz-satin palangposh. A long, low, wooden chest carved with scrolls and flowers stood against one wall; niches around the room held mirrors, toilet articles, perfume flagons, books and betel boxes. A small Persian carpet woven with the traditional cypress motif in cream and indigo was spread under the pink sandstone windows which opened on a magnificent view of the river and opposite bank.

Her agitated manner warned the Mirza that Asmat was disturbed about something. He waited, knowing that she would explain things in her own way.

"These were delivered for Mehrunnisa this morning and I thought you had better see them before I confront her." With this cryptic utterance, Asmat walked to the chest where her valuables were stored. Opening the lock with a key she wore dangling from her girdle, she opened the chest and after a moment's search, drew out a small gold casket.

Intrigued, Ghias Beg took it from her and opened the lid. He stared incredulously at the ruby studs which blazed before his eyes.

Suppressing his instinctive fears, he asked: "What mad folly is this? Who has had the audacity to send our daughter these priceless gems?"

"I've been wondering about it myself," she answered. "Do you remember, after the Court returned from Kashmir, Sherrif Khan became a frequent visitor to our house? Early today, my maid Jamila brought me this casket. She swore that Sherrif had bribed her husband to make certain that it reached Mehrunnisa, but she declared she could not carry out his bidding. After all our kindness, she said, she couldn't deceive us, and brought it to me instead."

There was a long pause as her husband studied the gems. "Sherrif Khan indeed! I know perfectly well who sent these rubies to Mehrunnisa. Sultan Salim has a perfect passion for collecting rubies, and these were purchased only a few months ago from a Badakshani merchant. I suddenly begin to understand a lot of things: Mehrunnisa's remarks, Asaf's new affluence, Maan Singh's curiosity."

Ghias Beg's handsome countenance, usually serene, was plainly perturbed. Thoughts which he could not put into words crossed his mind as he paced restlessly up and down. Memories of palace intrigues and their effect on his family's fortunes in Isfahan surfaced in his mind. He was much too wary of imperial connections.

Asmat hesitated a moment, then said, "I'm beginning to suspect, from several hints she has dropped, that the Persian Sultana is determined to make a match between Mehrunnisa and her stepson. What can we do about it? The stories one hears about him are hardly reassuring. He would marry Mehrunnisa today and banish her to some provincial fortress tomorrow to make place in his harem for a new favourite!"

"Has Mehrunnisa ever indicated by word or gesture that she is partial to the Prince?"

"Do you imagine that girls make confidantes of their mothers?" countered Asmat bitterly. "What is to be done now?"

"I shall speedily arrange a suitable match for her so that all this nonsense may be forgotten."

A long sigh escaped Asmat. She glanced at her husband and murmured softly, almost sadly, "Parents make the most elaborate plans for their children… but Mehrunnisa's own kismet will decide her future. Inshallah!"

Suddenly, Mehrunnisa's voice came to them from the garden below. Through the window they watched her sway to and fro on the garden swing, braids and veil flying, feet bare, as she laughed and cried to her sister. "Higher, Manija, higher! Push me up higher still!"

Ghias Beg rode away from his house with the sound of Mehrunnisa's laughter ringing in his ears and a nameless fear in his heart.

5

My Prince, what you ask is impossible! I've never set eyes on your fair charmer, so how can you expect me to paint her portrait? Grant me a glimpse of this houri and I swear to capture her image on ivory for you."

Salim threw back his head and chuckled softly. "Really, Sherrif! Do you think I'll allow anyone to feast his eyes on one whom I've sworn to make my bride?"

They were standing in the Prince's baradari, enjoying the river breeze that blew into the pillared pavilion overlooking the Jamuna.

Sherrif heaved an exaggerated sigh. He was the son of Abdul Hamid Mesowar, the greatest artist of Akbar's Court and also Salim's favourite foster brother. They were both in their twenty-eighth year and had always been inseparable. Outsiders were invariably amazed at the licence and indulgence the Mughals allowed their foster brothers. The institution – born out of a pragmatic physical need to keep alive Mughal princes whose own mothers were unable or unwilling to suckle them – had acquired political overtones, carrying considerable economic gain and social clout. There had been the infamous Atka Khel (foster brother clan) led by Akbar's horrid chief nurse Maham Anaga and her sons, there was the utterly bizzare Mirza Aziz Koka, and then Salim's comparatively moderate foster brothers. Of them, Sherrif, Mahabat and Qutub-ud-din were the three closest to the Crown Prince. But they could seldom agree with each other about anything.

Sherrif bore such a striking resemblance to Salim that many believed Akbar had fathered them both. Qutub-ud-din was a dashing rogue with kohl-rimmed, light blue eyes, voluptuous mouth and very fair skin. Mahabat's slanting hazel eyes, brown hair, high cheekbones and sturdy, perfectly exercised built frame proclaimed his Mongol blood and soldier's qualities.

"Pardon my impudence, Prince. Describe her and I'll draw one of my imaginary portraits, which you may compare to the lady," compromised Sherrif good-naturedly.

Salim's eyes grew tender as he began to speak of Mehrunnisa while Sherrif listened in amazed silence.

"She has a laughing face, a matchless form. Her nose is small, exquisitely shaped, her lips perfect, rose-tinted. Her eyebrows arch like taut bows over her lotus lids. How shall I describe her eyes? Those long large eyes have a strange mesmeric power, though it's impossible to know their real colour. When she moves..."

"Are you raving, Prince?"

"No, you fool! This girl exists."

Sherrif laughed, displaying sparkling white teeth. "My guess is you mean Asaf's sister, to whom I carried those ruby studs. Was there a word of thanks from her? You'd better tread warily. Your great good nature and easy susceptibility to feminine charms are all too well known."

"I know you are cynical, my friend. But this girl is above worldly considerations. I asked her for a self-portrait through my sister Arambanu, and she sent me my own profile. She caps every couplet I toss her, completes every Koranic sourah and knows more riddles then anyone else," murmured Salim.

Somewhere beyond the baradari, one of the clocks brought to Agra by the firangi Khans struck the hour. The quiet of the morning was shattered as a crowd of young men entered Salim's presence. Orange, yellow, pink and white turbans flashed on their proud heads. Barefooted, they stood salaaming while the Prince murmured polite greetings.

The young men launched at once into animated talk, relating all the town gossip and latest scandals to Salim and rallying one another about the forthcoming hunt.

Mahabat, a tall, well-built man with formidable battle skills and rigid principles, said heatedly to Qutub-ud-din, "It's all very well for you to talk of coming home laden with spoils but I refuse to believe that there is any sport in allowing cheetahs to chase and kill deer, while you merely follow on horseback! This is butchery, not sport."

"Don't try to impress me with your airs, Mahabat. If it's all that distasteful, why don't you tell the Prince? I didn't invent this particular form of sport," snapped Qutab-ud-din.

"Don't, Mahabat," advised young Mirza Rustam, already an astute courtier. "Otherwise, you'll be sent packing to some provincial town, or even to Ahmednagar, where the siege is on."

Mahabat cast a contemptuous glance at him. "Don't judge others by your standards. I prefer military duty to playing the sycophant, like..."

Salim joined the group, a pair of gauntlets in his hand. "You two are always quarrelling. I won't allow you to stand arguing here while my father's people kill off all the tigers between Agra and Alwar. And remember, *we* must return with the bigger kill. So stop saying that you hate to hunt with cheetahs, Mahabat, because..." Salim paused, full of glee. "Because I appoint you keeper of my shikar cheetahs from today!"

Loud guffaws greeted this announcement. Wincing visibly, Mahabat protested, "No, really, Prince!"

"You have no choice, my friend. That was an Imperial Command." Salim strode out, his sword slapping against his legs with each stride.

In the corridor, he met Asaf. "I was beginning to think that you were indisposed. What kept you so long? Where is Sher Afghan?"

Mirza Rustam answered, "Gone to hunt with the Shahenshah. Imperial Command!"

There was a fresh outburst of laughter at his sally. Pausing, Salim cried, "What? My champion huntsman purloined by my father!"

He strode into the great sunlit courtyard of the castle, followed by his entourage, and went up to his father who stood amidst his courtiers on the steps of the Diwan-i-Khas.

Placing his hands affectionately on Salim's shoulders, Akbar asked, "Is the light of our life prepared to outshine us today?"

"Who could ever hope to outshine the noonday sun?" rejoined Salim, smiling.

While they stood talking together, Maan Singh came forward. "Everything is ready, Sire, and they only await your command before sounding the kettledrums."

"Warn everyone, Maan Singh, that only the Prince and I will attempt to shoot the tigers. The nobles must content themselves with other sport," commanded Akbar.

The Prince turned away, trying to locate Sher Afghan in that vast crowd.

Sher Afghan saw the Prince beckon to him and, murmuring a word of apology to his comrades, hurried through the crowd to join Salim. He towered over most of the other men. Wiry strength was evident in his massive shoulders, deep chest, long arms and legs. He had to bend down to hear the taunt flung at him by the Prince.

"Traitor!"

A twinkle lurked in Sher's grey eyes while he listened to the Prince's harangue.

"This is a shabby trick!" continued Salim. "If you refrain from exerting yourself in the chase today, I shall reward you handsomely."

"As handsomely as the Shahenshah has promised to reward me if I show uncommon prowess?" inquired Sher, smiling.

"You are an impudent, avaricious man," Salim said.

Just then Qutub-ud-din approached and announced, “Your elephant is ready, my Lord.”

“Do you think I will be perched on that great, clumsy beast while my father’s horse out-distances me?”

“It would be infinitely more comfortable,” murmured Sherrif. “But too conspicuous if you desire to escape unnoticed from the hunt.”

“Comfort be dammed! Am I a zenana houri?” snapped Salim.

“The Prince is in a vile humour, Sher, because of what he calls your duplicity,” said Asaf as they watched Salim mount his superbly trained Iraqi stallion, Dalsingar.

Before Sher Afghan could reply, the resounding thunder of kettledrums and blare of fifes announced to the world the departure of the Grand Mughal from his palace. Beside him rode Salim on his prancing white steed, and in their wake followed hundreds of nobles and huntsmen armed with swords, spears, bows and muskets. The pampered shikar cheetahs came last, sprawled on litters borne by elephants. The hunting dogs and Afghan hounds set up a dreadful commotion, barking and growling as they strained at their leashes, trying to drag their keepers towards the deep woods. A great cloud of dust soon hid the hunting party from the Mughal ladies who were watching the scene from the harem windows.

At a signal from Akbar, the beaters, spread in a vast circle of over twelve miles, began sounding the drums suspended from ropes round their necks. Others held burning flambeaux and together they moved forward, making the circle smaller and smaller while they drove the game relentlessly towards the Imperial party with fire and noise.

There was a great bustle and stir in the forest as boughs snapped, deer sprang from safe hiding places, rabbits scampered towards their warrens, and partridges, quail and pigeons flew frenziedly out of thickets. The cheetahs chased and brought down their prey with marvellous speed and dexterity. The thud of horses' hooves was muffled somewhat by the leaves and grass carpeting the earth.

Signalling to Asaf, Salim cantered away from the main shikar part with Asaf and Mirza Rustam hard on his heels. They rode into a deep thicket. A peculiar stench pervaded the place and the Prince wrinkled his nose distastefully. Asaf was about to suggest that they ride away, when Salim gasped and pointed excitedly towards a small pool. There, amidst a few shrubs and boulders, was a family of tiger cubs basking in the sunlight. Instinctively, Asaf glanced around the clearing, searching for the tigress, but there seemed to be no sign of her.

Temptation stirred in Salim. He had an inordinate fondness for rearing and taming wild beasts and he longed to add those little golden cubs to his menagerie.

Before anyone could guess his intention, he slid off his mount and tossed his reins to Asaf.

Appalled, Asaf protested, "No, my Prince! It would be folly to rob a tigress of her cubs! You may be quite sure she isn't far off."

"Come back, Lord," cried Rustam, shifting nervously in the saddle.

Salim merely signalled to them to be quiet. "Watch well, my friends," he said softly. "I'll be back in a minute with those cubs. And if the tigress approaches, Rustam, you must shoot unerringly."

The little cubs retreated as he advanced but bending down, he swiftly picked up two of the furry creatures and rose again to return to his mount. Suddenly, a mighty roar split the forest air. Through the rippling sun-dappled grass came the tigress, bounding to the rescue of her cubs.

Salim whirled around and froze. Only his heart seemed to thud loudly. Dropping the cubs, he unsheathed his dagger and crouched to meet the infuriated beast. Just one thought filled his numbed brain, born of a hunter's instinct: somehow he would have to plunge his dagger deep into the beast.

For a few horrified seconds Mirza Rustam sat motionless on his mount. Then he heard Asaf shouting, "Shoot, you fool!"

With frantic haste he pulled the trigger and as the musket roared, a tongue of flame leapt from its barrel.

But still the tigress advanced. Asaf glanced around wildly as if looking for some miraculous source of aid. With trembling fingers he drew his sword, wishing desperately he had a javelin instead.

Soundlessly, step by step the tigress advanced towards Salim. He could see her burning yellow eyes now, curiously like his own. And then, as he prepared himself to meet her attack, he heard branches crash wildly.

Through the cleaving foliage a horseman thundered into view. Straight he tore at the snarling tigress, his scimitar glinting in the sunlight. With a single stroke, he chopped the beast's head off. His horse moved away with a shrill, high whinny from the carcass, now spurting blood.

Salim sheathed his dagger and took a deep breath. "Thank heaven you came, Sher!" He wiped the beads of sweat from his brow. "You've saved us all from certain death, my friend."

Holding aloft his blood-drenched scimitar, Sher Afghan dismounted. "What mad folly is this, Prince? Are you a child who needs to be taught to run in the opposite direction when you chance upon tiger cubs?"

The sound of Sher Afghan's laboured breath seemed to fill the forest clearing. The restive horses stamped and snorted and rolled their eyes. Untying his cummerbund, Sher wiped his blade clean and threw away the soiled cloth. Turning on Asaf and Rustam, he began berating them soundly.

Salim interposed, "Nay, Sher! The fault was all mine. I was determined to add these cubs to my menagerie and Asaf couldn't deter me. But you ought to know by now that it's predicted I will die peacefully in my own tent while on a journey!"

"And you believe such a prophecy!" exclaimed Sher Afghan incredulously. "But, then," he said in a lowered voice, "people say you were born under an auspicious spell."

Salim drew off a huge ruby ring engraved with his name and taking Sher Afghan's hand, slid it on his finger. "A token of gratitude for saving my life, Sher. Demand whatever you desire and if humanly possible, it shall be yours!"

Sher Afghan wiped his sweating brow against his sleeve. "Let us not talk about it anymore. If you must thank anyone, thank Allah, who sent me to your aid."

They rode back silently to camp, astir with returned hunters and attendants. A lavish repast was being spread in one of the tents. At a little distance, the game keepers were laying out the day's kill in neat rows: scores of bleeding rabbits and deer; innumerable birds; and the solitary tiger brought down by Akbar's javelin.

Raja Maan Singh was busy supervising everything. Under his pale green turban, his hair was powdered with dust. He saw Salim riding into the clearing and came forward to help the Prince dismount.

Salim grinned easily at his haughty kinsman: "You must have made a fortune betting on the various archers today."

Maan Singh laughed, revealing his square white teeth. He shrugged disdainfully. "These young men bet recklessly. By my reckoning I should gain over six thousand gold mohurs today. But collecting them will be another matter!" Suddenly, he noticed the tiger cubs and stiffened. "How's this, Salim? Whoever carried a tigress' cubs away and lived to tell the tale?"

Before anyone could answer, the Emperor approached. "Did you have good sport, my son?"

"Not mere sport, Sire, but the greatest adventure!"

Everyone stopped talking and clustered round the Prince. Sher Afghan retreated hastily when Salim began lauding his bravery. There were cries of horror and amazement as the assembled nobles expressed their concern and murmured words of thanksgiving to their various deities.

"Salim!" exclaimed Akbar in accents of deep reproach. "No one doubts your courage, but when will you learn discretion?" He turned to Sher Afghan and declared, "We have no words to convey our gratitude, Beg! You have put us under an eternal obligation by saving our son's life. We grant you the jagir of Burdwan in Bengal and raise you to the Mansab of One Thousand Horse. Demand anything you desire and we will not refuse."

"You are generous, Sire. It was nothing, a mere matter of luck." Reflecting a moment, Sher added, "But some day, perhaps, I may approach you for a boon."

"Certainly, Sher," said Akbar, smiling. "I have pledged my word before these Rajput chiefs and you know what *that* means."

"It is high time you gave up these childish pranks, Prince. You can't gratify your whims by endangering your life. After all, you are heir to the throne of Hindustan," rebuked Maan Singh sharply.

Grinning wickedly, Salim rejoined, "You never can resist lecturing me, can you?"

The Emperor interposed, "Raja Maan Singh is right, Salim. It's high time you gave up these thoughtless whims." Turning to Mirza Ghias Beg, who stood close by, Akbar commanded, "See that arrangements are made to feed fifteen thousand destitute for five months from our kitchens, in thanksgiving for Salim's safety."

Before following the Emperor to the dastarkhan, Maan Singh beckoned Sher Afghan and they stood aside talking awhile.

Mirza Ghias Beg noticed an almost jubilant smile on Maan Singh's face when he joined the imperial party at the dastarkhan. "What deep schemes are you hatching, my friend?" he asked casually.

"Our next triumph," came the cryptic reply.

That autumn the people of Agra watched yet another awesome Mughal army preparing to ride forth to conquest: war elephants, horses, camels, cannons drawn by mules, bullock carts heaped with stores and baggage, camp followers behind foot soldiers, the deep reverberation of beating drums, shrill note of war-fifes, clash of cymbals, flutter of pennants and standards bearing Timur's device of a rampant lion eclipsing the sun. And everywhere, the dust from marching feet.

Amidst a shimmer of spears and clinking of chainmail coats, Salim reviewed his troops. Mehrunnisa watched him from the latticed sandstone windows of Bilquis Begum's palace and wondered if he could sense her presence.

Prayers were offered in every temple and mosque and the royal ladies sent sheets of flowers to the shrines of Muslim saints to ensure his safety. On the eve of his departure, the Empress held a grand feast at which ancient Hindu rites were performed and Shah Begum buckled the sword round her husband's waist. Salim's stepmothers, sisters, aunts and wives kept an all-night vigil, praying for his safe and speedy return with the crown of victory on his brow.

Salim longed to meet Mehrunnisa before riding away from Agra; he longed to hold her in his arms and gaze into her eyes and murmur vows of love. And the only person who could arrange this was the Persian Sultana.

Salim walked into his stepmother's apartment and exchanged the usual courtesies with her. When the attendants had withdrawn, he said, "Will you grant me one small favour before I leave Agra, Elder Mother?"

Bilquis smiled and touched Salim's cheek. "Anything you desire, my son."

"Will you send for Mehrunnisa, Gracious One?"

"And draw the wrath of your wife Shah Begum on my head? I've no desire to become embroiled in a dispute with the Amber faction."

But after studying his woeful face, she relented, and reflecting a while, said, "I could take her to Fatehpur Sikri, but that is too far...there must be some valid reason for my trip. No, that won't do, for you've got to leave Agra tomorrow precisely at the time fixed by our astrologers. Ah, I have it! Go to Sikandra early tomorrow morning to offer your devotions at the saint's tomb. The ride shouldn't take you more than half an hour. Mehrunnisa will meet you there."

As Raja Maan Singh was preparing to mount his horse in the Court of Tournaments, the groom holding his stirrup slipped him a note. Maan Singh paused to read it. His mammoth web of spies spread through the entire palace had never failed him yet, he knew. His face grew thoughtful as he tore the note to shreds, casually tossing the pieces away.

He spoke to the groom in his crisp voice, "Find Sher Afghan. Bid him hasten to me in the gallery behind the Naubat Khana!"

He was surprised to encounter Aziz Koka on his way out through the Court of Tournaments. Maintaining his composure, Maan Singh asked, "Back at Court? By all that is logical, Aziz, you should have been on a ship bound for Mecca by now."

With his customary impudence Aziz Koka answered, "Oh, all that is forgotten. Evidently the river of milk that nourished us both is still flowing!"

Maan Singh couldn't contain his laughter. Aziz Koka continued, "I've just had audience with the Shahenshah and I've some amazing information for you."

"What?" demanded the Raja of Amber.

"His Majesty says that he is delighted with Prince Salim. The Prince has actually been making intelligent suggestions in the council chamber. I've been hearing strange stories from my friends. He seems to have lost his indolence and he is suddenly bristling with efficiency. What's all this about his ordering the architects to demolish that old pavilion overlooking the Jamuna near his palace? He is designing new apartments, I hear. Bridals in the air again, eh? Who's the girl this time?"

There was a distinctly annoyed expression on Maan Singh's face. "I'm afraid I haven't your talent for gossip, Aziz," he replied coolly.

Mirza Aziz Koka stroked his beard thoughtfully and studied Maan Singh's face. "Come, come! Nothing goes on in Agra, or Hindustan, for that matter, of which you are unaware. Salim is after something, and knowing him, it is safe to presume he is probably chasing some perfectly ineligible girl. And if his whim is denied, we shall have a rebellious Prince snarling at his fond father."

The Raja of Amber answered with a significant smile, "I'll lay you a wager, my friend. *This* whim of his will not be gratified."

Aziz Koka's sharp slanting eyes glinted maliciously. "One must tread warily when the Amber Raja lays wagers against the Crown Prince!"

6

The shrine of Jamal-ud-din Chisti stood amidst a solitary mango grove, beside a small lake which was deserted save for a few white cranes that stood meditating in the shallow water.

Salim dismounted and hitched his horse to a wooden rail. Removing his shoes, he walked up the steps and through a stone archway leading into an empty sunlit courtyard. At the far end stood the saint's tomb. It was a simple marble slab inscribed with verses from the Koran, covered by a dome of yellow sandstone, enclosed by marble railings to which were tied strips of cloth and garlands of faded flowers. Opposite the entrance was a stone basin, at which Salim washed his hands and feet.

There was a slight commotion outside, the talk of men, then footsteps. And Mehrunnisa stood under the arch, draped from head to toe in a dark shawl, carrying a fragrant sheet made entirely of flowers sewn over transparent silk.

Salim helped her spread the sheet of flowers over the tomb, then knelt beside her. They both lifted their hands in supplication and began praying silently.

When they rose, he saw misery in her deep amethyst eyes. "When shall I see you again, Prince?" she asked.

"Very soon. As soon as I can contrive to return from Mewar," answered Salim. "Several veterans have assured me that those rebels are incapable of resisting a determined assault."

"I wish you could take me with you. I have the most unreasonable, dreadful premonition. Something tells me this is going to be an intolerably long separation. I've never been so afraid, my Prince. This morning, all the omens were inauspicious, and I wonder, I really do..."

Salim drew her to him. "Mehrunnisa, Mehrunnisa! Be courageous, my loved one!" For a long moment they clung together.

'I must leave now, but when I return from Mewar, Elder Mother will arrange our betrothal. But you must not linger here. Have you an escort to see you safely home?" said Salim at last.

"Bilquis Begum sent me with an offering to this shrine in her own palanquin. My nurse accompanies me and all the palki-bearers are trusted slaves," she answered, touched.

The Prince kissed her forehead and said farewell. "I never realized that this would be so difficult, Mehrunnisa!"

Tears trembled on her lashes as she whispered, "Allah's peace abide with you!"

Then he was gone. The sound of his horse's hooves grew fainter rill she could hear them no more.

The shrine attendant came to collect the Prince's offering, but seeing the young woman's tear-stained face, withdrew silently.

She remembered an old saying and tore a strip from her rose silk veil. Murmuring an ancient Persian charm, she tied the piece of cloth to the railing of the tomb, praying for her lover's safety and swift return.

The road between Agra and Sikandra was deserted, except for a couple of rustic youths driving cattle to pasture. The palki-bearers chanted in low tones as they moved along briskly.

Dil Aram refrained from questioning Mehrunnisa, though she longed to know what the Prince had said. She lifted the curtain a little, and peered out at the sun-drenched countryside. They were being carried through a forest of enormous banyan trees. Several chattering monkeys swung from their aerial roots, and she could see crows, mynahs and green parrots on the branches.

The palki-bearers came to a halt all of a sudden,

confronted by a group of masked men crashing through the undergrowth.

"Robbers," Mehrunnisa whispered, "What shall we do now?"

"Sit absolutely still," commanded the chief bearer. "We'll fight off those cowardly knaves!" He ordered the others to set down the litter and draw their swords. Hearts pounding, Mehrunnisa and Dil Aram sat with clasped hands and tried to pray. They could hear the rough oaths and sounds of strife as blows were exchanged and swords clashed.

Suddenly, above the tumult and confusion, Mehrunnisa heard the pounding of hooves and a horse clattered up the road.

The horseman reined in his mount so violently that it almost sank on its haunches. Quickly grasping the situation, he drew his sword and rode straight at the masked bandits. They scattered before his fierce onslaught and disappeared through the trees.

Mehrunnisa raised the curtain and sat staring at their rescuer. The flushed face beneath the turban was unfamiliar to her.

The man's grey eyes feasted on the vision of beauty seated in the palanquin. Her voice fell sweet on his ears as she thanked him. And his heart was lost.

"Allah be praised for sending you to rescue us," murmured Mehrunnisa. "That was nothing," he said with an effort, still staring. "I'm amazed at the audacity of those rogues. The police officials must hear of this outrage. People should be safe to travel, at least in the vicinity of Agra."

"Please," interrupted Dil Aram. "You must not mention this to anyone. We are just returning from the saint's shrine at Sikandra and never imagined that such a thing would happen so close to the capital. Since all is well, you need not mention this affair to anyone, my Lord."

He kept staring intently at Mehrunnisa until she veiled her face to escape those relentless eyes. Dil Aram pulled down the curtains, the bearers lifted the litter and with repeated thanks to their rescuer, moved on.

"Who could she be?" he wondered aloud. From the palanquin he assumed that she was the daughter of some great house, perhaps even a Mughal princess.

Thoroughly intrigued, he determined to follow the girl. Only when he had ridden half-way to Agra did he remember the purse which Raja Maan Singh had entrusted to him for the old attendant of Sheikh Jamal-ud-din's shrine. That would have to wait. First, he would discover that girl's identity.

At a discreet distance he followed the palanquin, till it passed through the gateway of Mirza Ghias Beg's large mansion.

Without hesitation, he rode in on the pretext of meeting Asaf. The gatekeeper informed him that Asaf was out. Tossing him a coin, the horseman asked, "Who was in that palanquin, my friend?"

"Mirza Ghias Beg's daughter, returning from an errand on behalf of the Persian Sultana," said the gatekeeper boastfully.

"Her name?"

"Mehrunnisa Khanum."

7

At first Sher Afghan hesitated, but his burning impatience compelled him to seek Raja Maan Singh's advice.

He had dressed with great care in dark blue cotton pyjamas and a cool pink-striped cabaya edged at the neck and hem with a narrow gold border. His pink muslin turban was encircled by a strand of pearls to which he had pinned a plume of heron feathers. His lavishly embroidered shoes had enormous curling toes and exactly matched the crimson velvet scabbard of his sword.

He managed his capering steed skilfully through the crowded streets. All around him was the bustle and stench of Agra. Even though sweepers swept out every street and cleaned the drains twice daily with long bamboo brooms, garbage accumulated in the bazaars. A woman with a naked baby astride her hip turned to stare after him as a group of ragged boys scattered before his horse. Sher Afghan rode past water carriers sprinkling the dusty road, lumbering oxcarts, barbers squatting on their heels while they shaved their early morning customers, dhobis driving small over-burdened donkeys and boys spinning wooden tops.

In the noisy Atka Bazaar sat rows of dealers, carefully measuring out grain and cloth. On blue and red rugs spread out on the pavement was a great display of shining objects – pots and pans, images of brass and marble, slippers embroidered with silver, stuffs splashed with sunlight – silks, velvets, Benaras brocades and Dacca muslins, all spread out to tempt the passing crowd.

He rode past sweetmeat shops around which children and grown men coifed in red and white turbans stood greedily eating savoury halwas and syrupy sweets.

From a narrow side lane came a funeral train, with a Hindu corpse wrapped in white gauze. He reined in his horse to let the cortege pass. The bearers went by, men followed with clashing cymbals, some holding lighted flambeaux, all chanting the sacred syllable, "Ram! Ram!"

He came at last to the lofty gate of Raja Maan Singh's palace, into which a train of camels was disappearing. Falcons whirled and screamed before the red image of the elephant god Ganesh, set in a niche over the portico. The massive whitewashed walls were tattooed with designs in many colours: elephants, tigers, goddesses, trees, soldiers with shields and swords.

On three sides of the square courtyard were buildings of red sandstone crowned with turrets and projecting balconies supported by square stone pillars. Beyond the five-storied facade of Maan Singh's palace lived his mysterious household. No one knew the exact number of his wives or offspring, but they were rumoured to be numerous.

Maan Singh was standing in his armoury, talking seriously to his chief armourer. Sher Afghan was ushered into the vaulted chamber. The walls were hung with swords, shields, spears, axes and spiked iron clubs, sufficient to arm a small force. Some muskets of Portuguese make were stacked in a corner against the wall. A strong smell of leather, wood and oil hung in the air. Maan Singh dismissed his armourer and turned to greet his guest.

There was a knowing smile on his arrogant face. "Ah, Sher Afghan! Welcome. Is it urgent business or idle pleasure which brings you here?"

"I've come to seek your advice."

The Raja led him by the elbow through a cool verandah into a small comfortable room filled with books in wall shelves and gilt- framed paintings of bygone rulers of Amber. Some low lacquered chairs stood around the carpeted room.

Maan Singh bid his guest seat himself. He studied Sher Afghan's lean, grey-eyed face, which showed good blood and the instinct of command. While they talked, attendants came in with sweetmeats on jewelled platters and rose sherbat in tall silver tumblers.

The dusty ride through crowded streets had made him thirsty. Sher sipped the iced sherbat and commended its flavour.

"This is a very special sherbat made from the roses of Amber. And the ice makes it very refreshing on a warm day," agreed Maan Singh. Fresh blocks of ice were brought down by boat from the Himalayas every day for all the Mughals, their relations and ministers.

Although he could guess what had brought Sher Afghan to his house, he sipped slowly, appreciatively, with half-shut eyes, while Sher Afghan mustered his thoughts.

"I've always been curious about you, Sher," said Maan Singh finally. "They tell me you are of Persian descent, though it is generally believed that you're an Afghan."

"That is one of life's ironies. The Afghans destroyed my family, but I shall be called Sher Afghan for the rest of my life. They slaughtered all the Persian Begs when they reconquered Herat, and I was the only one of my house to escape alive. Somehow, I made my way through Kabul to Lahore, where a fortunate incident brought me to the notice of Mirza Abdur Rahim, and he introduced me to Sultan Salim. I was hoping that the Prince would give me an independent command during this Mewar campaign..."

"Don't permit yourself to be disheartened. Have you considered taking charge of your fief in Burdwan instead of chasing glory on battlefields?" said the Raja of Amber. "Anyway, if you are determined to follow a soldier's career, I'll request Aziz Koka to include you amongst his officers when he takes reinforcements to Ahmednagar..."

Sher set down his glass on the tray. "It is not that which brings me here; those things could be arranged later. I came to ask if you could speak to Mirza Ghias Beg on my behalf."

An amused smile played about Maan Singh's lips. "What about, my friend?"

"Mehrunnisa Khanum. His daughter. I wish to wed her, and only you can broach the subject to Mirza Ghias Beg, since I have neither kith nor kin to undertake this delicate matter."

"Hmm. It is no ordinary girl you aspire to wed. The Persian Sultana has already destined her for another." He raised a hand, silencing Sher Afghan's query. "You wouldn't understand even if I told you."

"What am I to do? This is unbearable!"

"Don't despair, my friend. Remember the boon you had from Akbar Shah when you saved Prince Salim from the tigress? You may still attain your heart's desire if you move swiftly."

Sher nodded, his eyes sparkling in swift comprehension. He wrung the Raja's hand. "You can't imagine how deeply indebted I am to you! I met this girl when I agreed to carry your offering to the Chisti shrine, and I haven't been the same man since then! Believe me, if things work out, I will pledge you my sword, my very life, my Lord."

The Raja of Amber laughed and said something about youth.

Mehrunnisa was standing at a window when Raja Maan Singh and Sher Afghan rode into the outer courtyard of her house. They were followed by a train of turbanned retainers carrying trays covered with brocade cloth.

She recognized him immediately. How he had stared at her that day when he had rescued her! As though sensing her presence, Sher Afghan looked up from his horse, straight at the window behind which she stood hidden.

Her sisters and several maids came to look at the cavalcade. They giggled and commented on the size and style of the Amber Raja's retinue, and tried to guess the identity of several young noblemen who stood about in the courtyard.

Soon the men went indoors, and after a while, Dil Aram came to call her, saying, "The Begum wants you." Mehrunnisa found her parents in the reception room. They looked amused about something. Perhaps the visitors, who seemed to have just departed, had brought interesting news.

"What, another son for the Raja? Does he bring us sweets to celebrate the event?" she asked with a laugh.

Asmat placed her hands on her daughter's shoulders. "The Raja of Amber brings you betrothal gifts on behalf of Sher Afghan, who should rightfully be called Ali Quli Beg Istajlu of Herat, of noble Persian blood like us."

Already the maids were carrying trays full of jewellery, embroidered cloth, perfume flagons, nuts, sweetmeats and fruit.

For a moment, Mehrunnisa stood staring incredulously at the procession. Suddenly she understood her mother's meaning and her laughter died. There must be some mistake, she thought wildly. Her parents could never compromise her like this.

In a trembling voice, she protested, "I can't understand this! You can't accept these gifts without first knowing my wishes."

"You will do as the Shahenshah commands," Mirza Ghias Beg interposed firmly. "The Raja of Amber came to negotiate marriage terms, and I can't tell him to wait while my daughter makes up her mind!"

"Surely you will give me time to consider this proposal, Father?" she countered, whereat Asmat began berating her.

When all her mother's arguments failed, the Mirza spoke again with concern, "Try to understand, Mehrunnisa. We cannot flout Akbar Shah's command. He has already *promised* you to Sher Afghan, and if we defy him, he will send us away. We will be fugitives again, daughter."

"It's true!" thought Mehrunnisa. The Mughals, like the Rajputs, had a kink in their minds about honouring promises, no matter what the cost. She recalled stories of Badshah Humayun actually seating the water carrier who had saved his life on the throne for one day, and Babur smashing all his jewelled wine cups and flagons after the battle which made him master of Hindustan. Akbar Shah would show no mercy. Everyone stood silent. An unacceptable marriage or another family upheaval? I'm only a girl, she thought bitterly as she bowed her head, pretending not to notice Asmat's sudden sharp breath of relief. Only a girl. Ya Allah, teach me patience. Give me strength…

Nurmahal

1

Hamida Begum stared thoughtfully at the sparrows fighting in her courtyard. Over the years confused and contradictory reports about Salim had continued to sadden the Mughal zenana. The rift between Akbar and Salim had widened perceptibly after Empress Jodh Bai had died, broken-hearted, in the summer of 1603. And ever since the Raja of Amber had brought Prince Khusro back to Agra, people speculated openly about the Mughal succession.

Intrigues grew more involved and at last the Dowager Empress Hamida Begum decided to interfere in her son's affairs, something she had carefully avoided doing since Akbar had banished Bairam Khan.

Oddly enough, in spite of all his voluptuous frivolities and indifference to convention, Hamida Begum still loved her eldest grandson dearly. His defiance of Akbar pained her more than she cared to admit to anyone. Having flouted his father on every occasion and having shirked all his duties as Crown Prince, Salim was travelling on a dangerous road. Something must be done, thought the old Begum, before Salim plunged himself, and all Hindustan too, into the dark abyss of civil war. She made up her mind to intervene and bring about a reconciliation between her son and grandson.

That evening, Hamida Begum invited her daughters-in-law to dine with her. Salima and Ruquiya were both Mughal princesses. And Hamida Begum had always had a special affection for the Persian princess Bilquis, whose father Shah Tahmasp had rendered her beloved husband Badshah Humayun such valuable aid when they were driven out of Hindustan by that Afghan usurper, Sher Shah Suri. The Begums sat on the marble terrace overlooking the garden, chatting affably and chewing paan. The air was laden with the lingering sweetness of grapefruit trees in lower; fountains splashed soothingly and a refreshing breeze flew through the trees in the lamplit garden.

Somehow, the talk always came back to Salim. The Begums tried to cajole their mother-in-law out of her sombre mood. Hamida Begum's bearing was dignified in spite of recurring illness and great old age. She was held in affection and esteem by all who knew her, for with her wise, tranquil ways, she maintained harmony in the Grand Mughal's zenana.

Salima Sultana vehemently denied some of the stories about Salim, her favourite. But the Dowager Empress countered, "Are you blind to the intrigues going on here, Salima? Everyone is encouraging my son to bestow the jagirs and privileges of Crown Prince on young Khusro. And Salim is making absolutely no effort to appease his father!"

Very different emotions made the three ladies think of Salim. The Prince had failed to fulfil their earlier expectations, and over the years Bilquis had grown indifferent and Ruquiya Begum contemptuous. Only Salima continued to defend him, but then, there had always been a perfect understanding between them. It was commonly believed that her affection for Salim had increased after the premature death of her own son Murad. She always declared that Salim reminded her greatly of her grandfather. But indolence had never been one of their grandfather Babur Shah's vices, thought Ruquiya, her green eyes snapping.

"These intrigues and conspiracies will always surround princes. You should ignore idle gossip, Gracious One. You know the peculiar ways of sycophants and self-seeking amirs," interposed Salima.

The Dowager Empress sighed, "I've never understood the sudden change in Salim. Do you remember the years of prayer and penance before his birth? And everyone rejoicing when Sheikh Salim Chisti's prophecy was fulfilled, and Salim was born… the love and care lavished on him by us all… what could have turned my happy grandson into an opium addict?"

Bilquis glanced up at her, and said, "I think he never recovered from the loss of Mehrunnisa. He has always believed that the Shahenshah deliberately humiliated him by forcing her to marry Sher Afghan."

"Nonsense!" exclaimed Ruquiya. "That trifling affair couldn't have meant anything to Salim. He was never famous for constancy."

Bilquis Begum sighed, "Whatever the reason, we know that Salim has embarked on a disastrous course. His brutal butchery of that pious, harmless man, Abul Fazl, his…"

"That pious man," interrupted Salima angrily, "did his best to cause mischief between father and son! He paid for his rashness with his life."

"We are wandering from the point," murmured Hamida Begum. "It's Salim's future, not Abul Fazl's death, which concerns us now. I wouldn't be so apprehensive if my grandsons Murad and Daniyal were alive today." Pensively, she added, "Daniyal always called his musket the Bier of Death, and indeed the wine smuggled to him in its muzzle was his undoing. Who can understand Fate's tortuous ways? The tongue shouldn't utter rash words, my daughter," She sank back against the cushions with a tearful sigh.

"What exactly is Khusro after, I wonder," murmured Bilquis.

A faint smile flickered on Salima's lips. "Isn't that obvious? Khusro is like wax in the hands of his uncle Maan Singh and we all know what the Amber faction wants. And now that unpredictable man, Aziz Koka, has joined Khusro's clique. Was it wise, I wonder, to marry Khusro to his daughter? I foresee trouble, nothing but trouble ahead…"

"My grandfather Babur's empire shall not become the plaything of unscrupulous amirs!" declared Ruquiya with a vehement toss on her haughty Mughal head.

"Let us be more optimistic, Ruquiya. May Allah grant my son a very long reign! However, I've called you here today to discuss a scheme for reconciling Akbar and Salim."

Thoroughly aroused by her cousin's remark, Salima retorted, "And I'm equally convinced that Salim is no rebel. People are determined to estrange father and son, and they report all his words and actions to the Shahenshah with a thousand distortions."

"Haven't you read his insolent letters?" demanded Ruquiya. "What reason has Salim, his father's pampered darling, to behave like this?"

"For years Salim's ideas were scorned and disregarded, he was literally forced to oppose his father's policies."

"Didn't he realize that this would lead to an open breach? A son's first duty is to obey."

"Have you ever tried to understand how everyone was trying to belittle Salim? Are you not aware that the Raja of Amber, Abul Fazl and Aziz Koka were encouraging the Shahenshah's hostile attitude, so that Salim was forced to escape to Allahabad? You know they were planning to try him for treason, Ruquiya."

"You may find excuses for him, Salima, but we all know that Salim was always prone to passion and error. He has always been capricious and implacable and I believe his haughty, turbulent spirit scorns a position he finds inadequate to his ambition. Evidently your foolish stepson, Rahim, failed to instil obedience and filial love in his charge."

"What chance had poor Rahim when Salim's own mother and aunts never missed a single opportunity for pointing out his faults and shortcomings to his father?" said Salima Begum scathingly.

The Dowager Empress commanded sharply, "That's enough, you two. I'm determined to frustrate all these attempts to estrange my son and grandson. I've decided to send you to Allahabad, Salima. I'm sure you could persuade Salim to end his fractious disputes with his father."

With her clear-sighted intelligence, Salima realized that Khusro's return to Agra could take an ominous turn. Some people considered Hamida Begum meddlesome, but she felt that her mother-in-law often contrived to find solutions to tricky problems.

Hamida Begum ordered her women to prepare the dastarkhan. Dinner was served and the Begums sat in a circle round a low octagonal stool, talking as they ate.

Nibbling a sweetmeat, Salima Begum asked, "What do you suggest I tell Salim, Ruquiya Bibi?"

"It's no use asking me. You must use your own judgement." She signalled and serving maids brought her basin, ewer, and towel. She washed her hands and picked cardamoms from a box presented to her.

After a while she said, "You must permit me to depart, Venerable One. Khurram is still running a high fever and I can't trust my women to look after him."

Hamida Begum smiled indulgently. Akbar's childless first wife had been entrusted with the upbringing of Salim's third son, Khurram, and she had become engrossed in the boy. Khurram's trifling ailments agitated her beyond belief and she spoiled him shamelessly, but it was touching to see her devotion.

"Go, by all means, and send Khurram to visit me when he recovers."

Before leaving, Ruquiya turned and remarked, "An idea has just occurred to me, Salima. Why don't you consult Haji Yusuf, the caretaker of Sheikh Salim Chisti's shrine, before going to Allahabad? His predictions are invariably fulfilled. I've often consulted him about Khurram. The other day he made an amazing prophecy after studying Khurram's horoscope. Haji Yusuf swears that he shall reign undisputed king over Hindustan one day. Who knows…"

Deeply disturbed, Hamida Begum warned, "Don't repeat this preposterous prophecy to Khurram. It could cause untold harm. It might even warp his soul and turn him into another recalcitrant prince, Ruquiya."

The Begum salaamed, and withdrew with a cryptic smile. Bilquis laughed, and said something about Ruquiya's predilection for astrology. Hamida Begum continued to discuss the Allahabad trip with Salima. Like her son, Hamida trusted and favoured Salima Bibi most of all the Mughal princesses. Hamida Begum couldn't help recalling how her husband Badshah Humayun with blessed memory had loved complicated astrological studies, and how accurate his chart of Akbar's horoscope had proved. She must remember to pass on to Salim the unique zodiac circle carpet and tent commissioned by his grandfather, in which family members and intimate friends were made to sit according to their birth signs on special occasions connected with the lunar calender. Did she have this special understanding and tolerance for Salim because he was so similar to his grandfather, with his love of learning, elegance, ease, opium and wine?

Four days later, Salima Sultana left by barge for Allahabad with Akbar's consent. But before she could fulfil her mission, news of the Dowager Empress' death reached her.

Thinking that the time of bereavement would be ideal for reconciliation, Salim set out immediately for Agra with his stepmother.

He was thrilled at the sight of the domes and minarets of Agra rising across the great tawny plains. The rugged red walls and massive bastions of his father's fortress rose to dominate the city.

Followed by his vast retinue, the Prince rode into the fort of Agra. There were resounding cries of welcome from the ministers and mansabdars lining the gateway. From the Naubat Khana rose the thunder of drums and clamour of fifes, announcing his return to the city.

Through a succession of great courtyards the horses pranced till Salim came at last to the steps of the Diwan-i-Khas, where the Grand Mughal stood, surrounded by his grandsons, Khusro, Perveiz and Khurram. They were resplendent in brocade robes with jade-hilted daggers stuck in their cummerbunds, their plumed turbans aglow with jewels in the sunlight. Khusro's eyes were wary, but his half-brothers rushed to welcome their father with radiant faces. Salim smiled at his sons, and tossed a greeting to Khusro, but his face was inscrutable as he rendered homage to the Emperor.

Everyone watched, amazed, as Salim's marvellously trained elephants sank to their knees when he threw himself at his father's feet. They trumpeted and raised their trunks in salute when Akbar raised his son and clasped him in a close embrace.

Later, when Salim had retired to the zenana to visit the ladies, people gathered in little groups. Most of them believed he would be restored to favour, but a few said that the Emperor had made a gesture of forgiveness to silence the Begums and to reassure his subjects, the rayaya.

Aziz drew Maan Singh away from his kinsmen into a secluded garden. "Did you hear the first words Sultan Salim spoke to the Shahenshah after the reception? That he had missed the scent of the fragile roses of Agra all these years!" His voice held a note of indignation.

The Amber Raja smiled. "That's a Mughal trait, Aziz. Now I for one would feel relieved if Salim continued to spend his time planning gardens, painting pictures, writing poetry and flying pigeons. Harmless pastimes."

Aziz Koka grinned sardonically. "There's little that's

harmless about any of the Mughals. A queer turbulent family it has always been from the time of Timur, tortured by internal hatreds that often lead to fratricidal wars." And after a little pause, he added, "What's going to happen to Khusro now?"

Maan Singh silenced the Khan-i-Azam. "You talk rashly, my friend. You seem to have made it a hobby! Treat Salim with deference and curb your tongue or you'll bring disaster on us all."

Aziz paid no heed to this but answered with a shrug, "You may say what you choose, but I'm convinced that despite this splendid public reception, the differences between those two will never be resolved."

Maan Singh frowned. "It's a tricky situation. There's hope for Khusro yet. Don't let anyone have an inkling about our ultimate aim, Aziz," he warned.

Aziz Koka only laughed, and urged his friend to stop agitating his mind over trifles. They parted amicably enough.

2

From the Court of Tournaments, Salim looked towards the royal balcony where Akbar sat with his grandsons. In the gallery behind stood gorgeously arrayed nobles, while eager spectators thronged the terrace below to watch the elephant fight. Along the walls of the courtyard stood mounted soldiers, holding spears and swords which glinted in the sunlight.

Khusro's masterly horsemanship drew cries of admiration from the courtiers. The youthful handsome prince, magnificent in a gold-striped crimson robe and jewelled turban, returned the salutes of the courtiers with exaggerated courtesy before cantering up to his father.

From the music gallery came a tremendous outburst of drums. Akbar leaned forward from his cushioned throne, and his fanbearers paused an instant to watch the elephants come into the arena.

At a signal from the Emperor, the mahavats urged their elephants forward. Giranbar, the pride of Salim's herd of fighting elephants, raised his trunk and trumpeted loudly. Prince Khusro's black beast, Abrup, stood flapping its ears, evidently excited by the repeated prodding of his mahavat; Akbar's elephant, Ranthaman, stood near the arched gateway leading towards the other gate of the fort.

Salim gave last-minute instructions to his mahavat, Khusro cheered Abrup, and all the assembled courtiers exchanged bets. People jostled each other for a better view.

Nodding knowledgeably, the Emperor said to Khurram, "Can you smell the offensive discharge from Giranbar's eyes? That elephant is in musth; he will undoubtedly win today. Khusro should have chosen another opponent for his elephant."

He looked up in time to see them charge each other with tremendous fury. The earth seemed to tremble, and their trumpeting cries filled the spectators with awe. The elephants moved with marvellous swiftness, their tusks menacing. Their trunks twined and twisted, their huge legs lashed out. And soon their gleaming hides were covered with blood and dust.

Giranbar poised his great right foreleg and gave Abrup a tremendous kick. With a loud cry, Abrup broke through the wooden barricade and retreated towards the gateway, causing several spectators to stampede in panic. In the confusion, a soldier tripped over his lance and floundered under the advancing beast's legs.

The mahavat, who had somehow managed to cling on, could not stop him trampling the prostrate soldier. He died, shrieking horribly. And at that moment, Giranbar charged up and knocked Abrup sideways with his massive forehead.

Khusro watched his father's elephant repulsing Abrup's counter attack with growing annoyance. Khurram cheered loudly from the royal balcony. Akbar gave a nod, and the elephant-keepers brought up Ranthaman to aid the weaker beast.

At this, Khusro's attendants cheered, but Salim's men shouted loudly, "No, no! Take Ranthaman away!" The noise and confusion increased.

Khusro rode up to his father, and cried impetuously, "How dare your men interfere! It's the custom, and Ranthaman shall come to my elephant's help!"

"Your elephant's cowardly behavior seems to have turned your head. You should learn to accept reversals with dignity."

"That's a lie!" shouted Khusro with rising passion. "Abrup was trained by my Amber uncle. He's unmatched for valour. I could swear that someone has drugged my elephant just to humiliate me!"

Several curious people crowded around to overhear their

exchange. Frowning heavily, Salim said, "Take care, Khusro, before you try my patience too far." Khusro swore furiously and rode away.

Suddenly, Salim saw his attendants running down the terrace steps and vaulting over the balustrades. They were yelling and cursing, and hurling stones at Ranthaman to chase him out of arena. Akbar watched enraged. The elephants ran blindly round the Court and soon the entire place swarmed with fighting, grappling men, whom the guards could not control.

"Unfair, Sire!" shouted Khusro, charging up to the balcony, but the tremendous uproar drowned his words.

The Emperor sharply commanded Khurram, "Go down immediately and tell your father to stop this shameful exhibition!"

Khurram found his father trying to restore order amongst the brawling men. He raised his voice above the hubbub, and repeated the Emperor's words.

"Assure my father that the miscreants shall suffer. I will stop this contest immediately."

Glancing around, Salim caught sight of Mirza Ghias Beg, who was trying to put a stop to the riot. Beckoning him, Salim commanded, "Tell your men to set off some fireworks. That alone can shock those elephants into obedience."

The sudden explosion of crackers and rockets startled everyone. Salim's anxiety increased when instead of halting, the elephants began running amuck and trampled several spectators to death. Horses reared and neighed, dust rose in clouds, and men shouted incoherently, trying desperately to escape from the path of the maddened beasts.

The elephant-keepers made several attempts to calm them down and lead them out of the Court. But suddenly Giranbar and Ranthaman charged and crashed through the great arched gateway opening on the river with a tremendous sound. Into the Jamuna they thundered headlong, the mahavats completely powerless to hold them back.

Realizing that the disgraceful behavior of his attendants had resulted in this stampede, Salim dismounted and went swiftly to the Imperial balcony. For weeks, the Emperor had been ailing and Salim knew that any form of excitement could make him feverish again. Moreover, Khusro would have to be pacified and this disgraceful affair handled with tact.

"Sire, I don't know how to apologize for this unseemly uproar. I'm sorry to see Khusro deprived of satisfaction, and will gladly bestow two of my best elephants on him."

By now the courtiers had opened their ranks to admit the enraged prince. "Do you deny that your cowardly attendants behaved so shockingly without your orders?" he cried.

"Restrain yourself, Prince!" retorted Salim. "I admit the fault of my attendants, and I will recompense you for your loss, but I won't listen to impertinent language."

"No!" declared Khusro. "My men shall not suffer because my father's men behaved so rashly." He cast a venomous look at Salim.

"Either you obey us, Khusro, or retire immediately," stormed Akbar, his face flushed with mounting anger.

"Can't you see, Grandfather, that's just what he wants! He wants me disgraced and banished so that he and his murderous followers may hold undisputed sway over Hindustan!"

Salim stared with anger and shocked disbelief at his son.

"How dare you say such things?" shouted Akbar. His eyes were bloodshot, and the mole on his nose grew pronounced. People watched him apprehensively, and his physicians grew alarmed.

Maan Singh and Aziz begged the Emperor to retire before he had another attack of fever.

"Out of my sight, both of you! This is insufferable!"

Maan Singh tried to offer an apology for Khusro's

behavior, but Akbar silenced him with a few angry words and retired.

And everywhere people wondered... was Khusro in disgrace?

It was an October night and the air was laden with the scent of champak flowers. From the garden of his palace came a cool breeze, accompanied by strains of music from a pavilion beyond the fountains. Salim leaned against a marble column, indolently enjoying the night scene. As he sipped his iced wine, he became aware of the romantic possibilities of the soft, dark night.

From behind, a disapproving voice spoke. "While your enemies are plotting in the fort, my Lord, you are lost in contemplation more suited to a poet than to a prince whose patrimony is in danger!"

Salim answered languidly with half-shut eyes, "My days belong to cares and dreams of empire; my nights are my own. While the Grand Mughal lives, I may indulge my poetic humours, Mahabat."

"There is news from the palace that he has had a relapse and I don't trust Prince Khusro's adherents," declared Mahabat emphatically. "Aziz Koka and the Raja of Amber, what plots are they hatching? I wonder. Surely you will pay a courtesy visit to the Emperor?"

"I've had enough of the Imperial Palace for one day," rejoined the Prince. "Tomorrow I shall go as usual..."

The sentence was never completed, for an usher approached in a distracted manner, bearing his golden staff of office awkwardly. By the light of the candles Salim could see the man hesitate before he spoke.

"Pardon, my Prince! Your orders were not to admit anyone to your presence, but there's one who demands immediate audience," he said.

Trying to keep annoyance out of his voice, Salim asked, "Who is it?"

"Ghias Beg!" exclaimed a voice, and the bearded Mirza, visibly agitated, pushed past the guards into the pavilion.

"Couldn't your business wait till tomorrow, Mirza?" asked the Prince, in a vexed tone.

Striding right up to the Prince, Ghias Beg retorted, "Nothing less serious than the future of the Mughal empire could have brought me out of the fort of Agra at such an hour!"

He drew a dagger from his girdle. Its hilt was set with a single large yellow diamond, surrounded by rubies that sparkled in the dim light.

'The Shahenshah's dagger!" exclaimed Salim. He could see that Ghias Beg was exhausted by his long ride. "Sherbat for the Mirza!" he said, and the usher vanished.

A vague fear lurked in Salim's heart. He turned the dagger over in his hand, wondering how it had left his father's possession. Waking or sleeping, the Emperor always kept this dagger, gifted by the Sultan of Golconda, by his side for he believed that the yellow diamond was a talisman.

"The Shahenshah is sick, perhaps fatally sick. He has commanded me to summon you to his bedside. As a token of good faith, he has sent his own dagger, that you may be convinced it's no trick," said Ghias Beg, guessing the Prince's thoughts.

"Mahabat, rouse the escort! I can't understand this. What has been happening at the palace? When I left his august presence, my father was not indisposed."

"The Shahenshah retired immediately after the elephant fight – a sad affair, my Prince – to the zenana, where the Begums coaxed him to eat his usual meal. When he sent away every dish untasted, the Sultanas offered him slices of musk-melon, newly arrived from Kabul. After returning to his apartments, the Shahenshah complained of a violent pain in the abdomen, and Hakim Ali of Gilan and other physicians were summoned. Meanwhile, seeing that his condition was rapidly deteriorating, Mirza Aziz Koka approached him and asked what his orders were regarding Prince Khusro. The Shahenshah waved him away, and asked whether you had been informed. Raja Maan Singh then answered that a message would be sent in the morning. But my master beckoned to me, and giving me this dagger bid me hasten to summon you to his bedside," explained Ghias Beg.

Salim's tawny eyes grew thoughtful; he tugged at his drooping moustache as he listened, and became aware of his changing status.

"Hurry, my Lord!" urged Mahabat, entering the pavilion. "The ahadis are mounted. Asaf has just ridden in with the news that Raja Maan Singh's soldiers have fortified the palace!"

Salim's blood thrilled with keen exhilaration as he saw the domes and battlements of the Mughal castle rise against the night sky. He was entering the great gateway unannounced, and tomorrow, ah, tomorrow, he might be master of this castle and all Hindustan!

By the light of numerous flambeaux, Salim could see the feverish activity going on in the palace. Mansabdars and ahadis stopped dead to see him at this late hour, wondering about him even as he wondered about their loyalty.

Mirza Ghias Beg conducted him to the Emperor's sickchamber. The first person he noticed as he walked in was his son, Khusro. At the foot of Akbar's bed stood the grandees of Hindustan. Salim couldn't see their faces clearly and the dim lamplight hid their expressions from his prying eyes.

3

The impetuous cry of the muezzin calling the faithful to prayer from the minarets of the castle mosque woke Mirza Ghias Beg from fitful slumber.

"Allah ho Akbar!" rose the fervent cry.

Ghias Beg performed his ablutions hastily, spread his small prayer rug on the floor, knelt with his face towards Mecca, and began the ritual morning prayer.

A faint rosy flush tinted the pearl grey sky; and the first twittering of birds could be heard in the deserted garden court as Ghias Beg stepped out on his way to resume his duties.

It had been a frantic, anxious night, and Ghias Beg had toiled relentlessly to perform his office of Lord High Steward. Apart from his night ride to fetch the Prince, and all the alarms and anxieties of that tumultuous day, he had had to find accommodation for Sultan Salim and his attendants, and the numerous nobles who had taken turns to keep vigil in the Emperor's antechamber. He tried to ignore his headache and began to tackle the day's work: accounts to check, meals to supervise and orders for the day to be given to the heads of various departments. And he hoped that since the Emperor would not be visiting the zenana, the Begums' incessant demands from the Imperial storehouses would cease for a few days.

Walking across the gardens to the pillared portico running along Khusro's palace, the Mirza saw two figures striding up and down, talking together in low tones.

Throughout the night, men had gathered in little groups, discussing the Emperor's illness and the succession. Mirza Ghias Beg had not allowed himself to be drawn into these speculations, for he had no desire to embroil himself in any intrigue.

In the faint light he could make out their profiles as they turned away, too engrossed in their deliberations to hear his footsteps on the marble flagstones. He coughed to announce his presence to Raja Maan Singh and Aziz Koka, but they did not seem to hear. Instead, a flood of alarming words smote Ghias Beg's ears.

"Salim, Emperor?" spoke Aziz Koka. "Have you forgotten his behaviour at Allahabad? I, for one, would not serve such a ruler!"

Maan Singh's deep voice came to Ghias Beg. "I agree. Khusro's young. We can teach him to carry on with Akbar Shah's excellent work... abolition of jazia, freedom of worship for all men, confirmation of our jagirs, mansabs and tides, justice for all. Above all, no whimsical behaviour, no military expeditions beyond the Hindu Kush..."

They walked away and their words came faintly: "Will the Shahenshah settle the succession on Khusro? If only he would commit himself and put an end to all speculation! I foresee trouble ahead for us, Aziz, for Salim is not without adherents."

Aziz Koka answered briskly, "If Sultan Salim will compromise, the kingdom of Kabul for him... if not, he shall drink the poppy juice. He is always talking about regaining Timur's ancestral kingdom, and we can encourage him to lead a campaign against Samarkand. There are infinite possibilities and we'll rid ourselves of him, I'm sure. And once the treasury is ours..."

Ghias Beg suppressed an involuntary shudder. He wondered if Salim would be forced to wade through blood and corpses to his father's throne. He returned immediately to his private apartment and sent an attendant for Ram Das Kachwaha, one of the few men whose integrity was unquestionable.

Ram Das Kachwaha found Ghias Beg standing on the massive ramparts behind the Hall of Private Audience, lost in deep reflection. After a long pause Ram Das said, "Surely you didn't summon me here to admire the sunrise over the Agra plains?"

Ghias Beg glanced around quickly and regarded him with a queer little smile. "Be serious, my friend. This is scarcely the time for your little ironies. I've got a feeling that the Amber Raja will soon control everything here. And you know what that means..."

"You are right," responded Ram Das with a thoughtful expression on his lean, lined face. "There's an appalling atmosphere in the palace, and everyone knows that a struggle between the Mughal princes is inevitable. I've already been subjected to a lot of pressure from Maan Singh to withdraw with my men from the guard house, but I told him I'd retire from my post only at Akbar Shah's command. I believe the hakims have given up all hope of recovery..."

"He's unconscious most of the time, and nothing seems to revive him," confided the Mirza. "I had resolved not to become embroiled in this affair, but I can't stand by and let Aziz and the Raja of Amber seize the Imperial treasure and all the secret records. Somehow we've got to prevent this."

The Kachwaha chief, renowned for his valour and selfless devotion to Akbar, declared emphatically, "I'll do it! My kinsmen and I will guard the Imperial treasure house, and I swear the seals shall remain inviolate." After a thoughtful pause, he continued, "Who could have imagined that Akbar Shah's illness would spark off such terrifying rivalries?"

"Yes, indeed," sighed Ghias Beg. "You had better collect your men, and I must confer with the Sayyids of Barah and the young Prince of Marwar. Proceed cautiously, I beg of you."

"Don't worry, I'll take care of everything." And with this assurance, the Kachwaha chief hurried away.

Salim stood in his father's chamber, surrounded by arguing physicians.

"And I say that the potion prescribed by Hakim Ali has helped to aggravate His Majesty's suffering," declared Hakim Muzuffer. "He deserves to be trodden by elephants for erring in his diagnosis!"

Hakim Ali's parchment-like face seemed piteous to Salim. "It is merely human to err, Hakim Muzuffer. Continue to seek some remedy for my venerable father, Hakim Ali. No punishment shall be inflicted on you at anyone's malicious suggestion," he said soothingly.

Akbar stirred, opened his eyes and gazed directly at his son. Salim promptly bent over his father, trying to catch his murmured words, but Akbar's eyes had already shut and his voice faded away in sleep.

Looking down at the old monarch, Salim tried to analyse his own feelings. He had felt awe, resentment, love and admiration in turn for this man. For fifty years, his father had dominated everyone, sweeping the entire land on the tide of his will, introducing strange precepts of justice and tolerance into his despotic rule. His father was something more than a great ruler, perhaps the greatest emperor the world had known: a mystic, a dreamer, a sage whose dreams had transcended earthly glory and power.

Staring at the weary, white-haired man, Salim made a sudden resolve: come what may, he would not darken the last days of his father with a struggle for the crown involving Khusro and all the nobles of Hindustan. The time for reckoning would come later. He left quietly for his own lodgings outside the palace.

Next morning he received a sealed note from his stepmother Salima Begum warning him to stay away from the castle, as there was a conspiracy afoot to kidnap and imprison him.

Salim reclined on a divan, smoking his hookah and discussing the situation with his friends.

"I'm hardly ignorant of the intrigues and secret councils

going on around my father's bed. Should I go or stay, Mahabat?"

Mahabat threw up his hands and exclaimed, "The throne will be lost if you don't visit your father, Prince! And that's just what the Amber Raja wants."

"I really don't think that would be wise. Begum Salima Sultana has lived through three reigns, and knows the implications of palace coups and noblemen's intrigues. I've learnt to trust her judgement. There's something afoot in the palace, something sinister and dangerous," said the Prince contemplatively.

"But the Shahenshah will never overlook your absence. He may recover to reign for many, many years," argued Asaf.

For a moment, Salim was silent; then, knitting his brows, he removed the stem of his hookah from his mouth. The sickly sweet smell of opium filled the air.

"If Allah wills it, the throne of Hindustan shall be mine without struggle some day," murmured Salim.

"What prevents Maan Singh from poisoning the Shahenshah while you sit here?" Mirza Rustam asked.

"Ah, Rustam, you wrong the worthy Raja. Leave poison to lesser men. He'll fight and scheme for his precious nephew, but he won't stoop to poisoning my father."

The curtain was suddenly raised and Mirza Ghias Beg, barefooted and sombrely-clad, entered.

Salim sat up, all indolence gone from his face. "What news, Mirza?"

Ghias Beg salaamed and said, "Raja Maan Singh has sworn the Hindus on Ganga water, and the Muslims on salt, to uphold Prince Khusro's claim to the throne."

Angry shouts from Salim's companions filled the pavilion. Above the din of excited voices, Salim's command rang out, "Let the Prince of Marwar be summoned from his camp outside Fatehpur. He has sworn to support me. And call your brother Ibrahim, Asaf. Let a messenger depart immediately to Bikaner with my firman requesting Rai Singh's immediate presence at Agra."

Asaf and Mirza Rustam bustled out to fulfill these commands, and Salim turned to Mirza Ghias Beg.

"What news of my father?"

In an anguished voice, the Mirza said, "My Lord, this morning the Shahenshah declared that his life will end when the eternal flame in the Hall of Worship goes out. Your presence is essential by his bedside."

He saw a strange look pass over Salim's face.

The Prince rose resolutely. "Come, Mahabat, let us go."

Accompanied by a thousand mounted Imperial guards, the ahadis, Salim arrived before the great gateway of the Mughal castle. He swore furiously when he found the gates shut.

"What does this mean? Have those perfidious amirs shut the gates against me? Look towards the ramparts, Asaf. Can you see the gunners loading the cannon? I'm beginning to realize that Salima Begum was right after all!"

Mahabat declared impetuously, "Let us ride forward, Prince. They dare not keep the castle gates shut when you demand entrance."

Frowning, Salim wondered aloud, "Could they have shut the gates on my father's orders?"

"That's impossible!" Asaf burst out vehemently. "He is almost in a coma, he knows nothing; he orders nothing these days. Aziz Koka and Maan Singh are responsible for this."

"Shall we storm the castle?" asked Mahabat.

"Yes, Prince!" shouted the ahadis, holding their javelins menacingly.

"No!" commanded Salim in a sharp, incisive voice. "You fools, don't you see that's just what Maan Singh wants. An excuse to blow us all to pieces! While Akbar Shah lives, my troops shall not besiege his castle."

Khusro observed this tumult from a watchtower. The dust and noise, the neighing of horses and the thud of hooves, the menacing clink of armour and flash of steel, the shouted oaths and curses disturbed him strangely. He had a sudden impulse to cry out and to order Mirza Azia Koka to throw open the gates. The moment passed; he saw his father wheel around and thunder away with his force.

Khusro sighed with relief. As he came down the steps, his father's arrogant face rose up before him, and the old feelings of hatred and revulsion overpowered rational thought. A scowl marred his face as he walked swiftly towards the Emperor's palace. He wondered what the outcome of this open confrontation with his father would be.

Khusro found his grandfather lying on the great ornate bed, busy with his prayer beads. Outside a strong wind howled.

"Is that you, Khusro?" asked Akbar, his eyes still shut.

Startled, Khusro asked haltingly, "How did you know, Grandfather? Is it true, what some people say, that you are gifted with second sight?"

For a moment, the young man was really frightened. What if the Emperor could read his terrible thoughts? Khusro found the perfumed chamber stifling despite the ceaseless swishing of fans.

"We know your footstep, child," murmured Akbar with a wan smile, "What was that commotion outside?"

Khusro had a hideous feeling that his grandfather was watching and knew everything, that he would yet recover. Maan Singh threw his nephew a warning glance.

"Does the noise and heat disturb you, Grandfather? Would you prefer to retire for a few days to Babur Shah's garden across the Jamuna?"

Akbar tried to raise himself up, but he fell back exhausted. His attendants hurried forward and made him comfortable against the bolsters. So deep was his feeling of tragic foreboding that he made a superhuman effort to rally his powers.

"Answer my question, Khusro."

Khusro stood silent. The amirs and mansabdars ceased their whispering.

At last, Maan Singh spoke, "Sultan Salim's troops are besieging the castle, Sire. We can deal effectively with the rebels if Your Majesty consents to leave the castle."

At last Akbar understood. It was far, far worse than anything he had imagined. With a shock he realized that he had inadvertently allowed Khusro to loose inside his palace an awesome conspiracy that could result in the destruction of his entire life's work. The spectre of fratricidal war, more terrible than death itself, rose before Akbar's weary eyes.

"Who has presumed to shut the castle gates in Salim's face? Hasten to Salim, and bid him come to receive our sword of state. Let everyone understand that Salim is undoubted heir to the throne of Hindustan." Akbar's word was still a command.

Khusro found the nobles and attendants avoiding his eyes as the news spread through the palace. He turned away from them contemptuously. Soon they would be grovelling and scraping before his father, he knew.

The windows of Akbar's room overlooking the river Jamuna had been flung wide open at his command and a cool breeze ruffled the hangings.

With immense compassion, Akbar said, "My son, reconcile yourself. Death is Allah's decree, of Him alone are life and sovereignty. The world cannot contain me anymore. Take up your burden and discharge your duties manfully."

Before the assembled vassals, Salim bowed at his father's feet and solemnly walked three times round his deathbed. Then he took his father's sword and girt it round his waist. Slowly he raised his father's turban and set it on his own head.

The Chief Kazi of the realm fell on his knees beside Akbar's bed, and began reciting the Kelamah Shihodet, the Sourah Neish and the Adeilah prayers from the Koran.

Salim heard his father gasp, "Ya Allah, Allah!" and the body he supported grew suddenly limp in his arms.

From the courtyard below came an agonized cry, loud and lamenting: "The Flame! The Eternal Flame is out!"

In a mournful voice, the Chief Kazi intoned, "The Grand Mughal is dead! That tall cypress tree, the glory of this worldly garden, is laid on the bed of desolation! From the snares of Death there is no escape!"

For a few moments, his pronouncement hung in the air. Then all the assembled princes and nobles turned their gaze from the dead Emperor to his son, and the terrifying realization came to them all at once that Salim was now master of all Hindustan, master of their destinies.

But Salim's eyes were fixed on his son, who seemed frightened and horrified. In that death-hushed chamber, he perceived the almost imperceptible nudge Maan Singh gave Khusro.

With apparent meekness, Khusro came forward to render homage to Salim.

4

The Khutba proclaiming Salim Emperor was read from every mosque in Hindustan.

The coronation durbar brought a dazzling array of people to Agra: provincial governors, generals, amirs, rajas, and mansabdars came from far-flung Mughal outposts; ruling chieftains from Sindh and Afghanistan, Badakshan, Kashmir, Ivishtwar and Khorasan rode in with their retinues.

Never before had the people of Agra seen such magnificence, such splendid extravagance.

For forty days and forty nights, the rayaya enjoyed entertainments, banquets and fireworks at the new Emperor's expense.

Embassies came from neighbouring kingdoms, from the Deccan Sultanats and from the Sheikhdoms of Arabia. The Portuguese, the Dutch and the English sent envoys to obtain firmans bestowing trade privileges. These firangis, though widely travelled and attuned to oriental sumptuousness, were dazzled and impressed by Agra despite their doughy faces. Their gifts paled into insignificance besides the countless treasures in the Grand Mughal's perfumed palace.

At the coronation, a hush fell on the assembled princes and nobles as Salim entered the Diwan-i-Am and stood before the throne. An outburst of music and the thunderous chorus of cheers from the assembly almost drowned his loudly acclaimed tides. "By the grace of Allah the Magnificient! Render homage to Nur-ud-din Muhammud Salim, henceforth titled Badshah Jehangir, the world-subduing King!"

Flanked by fanbearers and mansabdars carrying the insignia of the House of Timur, surrounded by his sons and watched by the Mughal Begums, Jehangir sat enthroned, receiving the homage of his nobles.

Mirza Ghias Beg saw the glow of pearls, the sparkle of rubies and diamonds set in the Mughal crown. Sunlight filtered in through the arched windows of the Diwan-i-Am and an aura of light surrounded the Emperor. Inshallah! Let it be a light-filled reign, he prayed. He had been appointed Dewan of the realm, with the tide of Itmad-ud-Dowlah, and he felt confident of the future.

Asaf caught a glimpse of shimmering veils and flashing gems from his place opposite the fretwork gallery in which the Mughal Begums and princesses were assembled. He could hear the murmur of voices and the tinkling of women's ornaments as they sank to their cushioned seats. For a moment memories of his sister Mehrunnisa flashed through his mind. If the old Emperor hadn't interfered, she would have been seated with them now, probably laughing with the others at the awkward progress of the fat Raja of Marwar towards the throne.

With the practised eye of an artist, Sherrif absorbed the impressions of the Durbar: all crimson and gold, splashed with orange and blue, and the numerous turbanned heads plumed with white. And everywhere, a profusion of gems.

From his place close to the throne, he glanced at the gold-embroidered hangings, the glowing colours of the Persian carpets, the curling incense smoke rising from jewelled censers, the filigree lamps and tinted crystal lustres.

He studied the silent rows of men, covered from head to foot in jewellery, standing behind gold and silver railings according to their rank. How many of them, wondered Sherrif, really meant to uphold their oath of allegiance?

The gods be praised, young Khusro had heeded his advice and changed his recalcitrant attitude, thought Maan Singh. The Prince had uttered dark threats, declaring that he would not be thwarted of Akbar's promise to the throne of Hindustan, and he had spent hours reasoning with his nephew. But Salim was crowned now, and they would have to wait and watch.

The memory of that bygone day, when his aunt had ridden to a moment of destiny at Sambhar, came to Maan Singh. Jodh Bai had brought beauty and ancient Aryan blood into the Mughal line. He wondered if his aunt's spirit watched Salim from the high jharokhas today. His sister, he knew, was jubilant at her husband's coronation. Undoubtedly, she was empress now, with the high-sounding ride of Badshah Begum.

There was a sudden tumult in the courtyard below. Aziz Koka, restored to favour through the intervention of Salima Sultana, frowned at the clatter of hooves and the shouted commands. He grew perturbed and wondered if Khusro's men were causing some disturbance outside. He glanced out, and saw the gold-staffed ushers escorting his brother-in-law Abdur Rahim into the Diwan-i-Am.

Salaaming at every step, the Khan-i-Khanan approached the Mughal throne. It moved him strangely to see Salim, the young prince he had tutored so lovingly, seated in regal splendour upon Akbar's throne. Then Mirza Abdur Rahim's eyes fell on two pedestals flanking the throne: one held a pair of golden scales, on the other stood a silver cow and a gold lion, drinking out of the same vessel. Understanding this symbolic representation of justice and tolerance, he smiled his approval at Jehangir and presented his gift, an uncut emerald of astounding size.

Rahim realized that the empire, his one-time ward, Jehangir had inherited rivalled those of China, Turkey, Persia and Rus. He recalled how hard Akbar Shah had striven from a very young age to achieve this. It had involved coping with the harem ladies, leading armies against neighbouring kings, a treacherous half-brother and recalcitrant chiefs, reorganizing Mughal administration on patterns set by Sultan Alauddin Khilji and Sher Shah Suri, and negotiating alliances with the Rajput Rajas and Deccan Sultans. He himself had just made it in time for the coronation ceremony, travelling fast from

Burhanpur in the Deccan, to which he knew the new Emperor would force him to return.

The Emperor's face lit up with a charming smile as he thanked his old ataliq. It never ceased to amaze Jehangir that this avowed Sufi mystic was also the best Mughal general bar none.

Mahabat Khan watched Khusro clutching the double strand of enormous pearls he wore about his neck. This restless prince, he realized, would seize the first opportunity to create trouble. Khusro's movements would have to be watched carefully; Mahabat knew that his partisans had not yet accepted reality.

Behind the harem screen, Begum Salima Sultana prayed silently for her stepson. For a moment she seemed to sense the presence of bygone Mughal Emperors around Jehangir; her husband and her grandfather Babur. Was it true, she wondered, that at certain moments in one's life, one's ancestors came from beyond the celestial veil to render aid? She would discuss this later with her other stepson, Rahim.

When at last the ceremony was over she rose to go. Then her eyes fell on Badshah Begum, Empress of Hindustan and Princess of Amber, who was rising amidst a rustling of skirts and a flurry of veils. She stood aside, and waited for the Empress to pass into the pillared portico leading to the harem. Her enormous brown eyes filled with tears as she realized afresh that she was only Akbar's widowed queen now.

Jehangir's nerves, never calm, were being frayed by the trouble in Afghanistan. He wondered if his appointment of Sheikh Abdur Rahman, son of his old enemy Abul Fazl, as Diwan of Punjab, was a wise one. He was notoriously headstrong, whimsical and indifferent to the interests of the public.

The Sisodias of Mewar continued to plunder convoys bringing revenue from the ports of Gujarat or carrying pay and supplies to the Mughal armies in the Deccan. Reports came from Bengal of growing Afghan insolence; from Punjab came rumours of the rise of a new militant Hindu sect, followers of a man called Nanak. The Mirzas of Kandahar were quiet, but Jehangir knew of the secret gifts and embassies sent them by the Shah of Persia. The governor of Gujarat complained that foreign merchants were carrying away precious merchandise from Hindustan without paying adequate duties.

The wives and concubines of his dead brothers Murad and Daniyal had to be allotted jagirs or disposed of creditably in marriage, the education of his orphaned nephews supervised, suitable matrimonial alliances made for his nieces.

There were endless problems everywhere. Jehangir was aware of a restless search within his soul for deeper fulfilment. Increasingly he found himself seeking out Mirza Ghias Beg and his younger sons, knowing that they were totally devoted to him.

The Mirza had a marvellous mind. His conversation ranged from statecraft, revenue administration and army organization to poetry and mathematics, calligraphy and painting, the principles of horticulture and hydraulics, aesthetic arrangement of gardens, fountains, pavilions and apartments; to the subtle effects of precious stones on the wearer, the appropriate perfumes and wines and fabrics for different seasons. For Jehangir, Ghias Beg's unfeigned interest and sympathy were balm for his unsteady nerves.

Asaf was subtle and profound, an adroit leader of men and a lover of learning. He knew more about Sanskrit poetry and Hindu philosophy than any other Muslim nobleman, with the exception of Abdur Rahim Khan-i-Khanan. He had a fund of amusing stories gleaned from Persian and Hindu classics, and anecdotes culled from various sources. Yet he was a superb horseman and marksman, and his stable of fine horses was much envied. Jehangir had always found in him an excellent companion, an athlete, a robust pleasure-seeker, a man who could match him cup for cup without succumbing to intoxication.

And Ghias Beg's youngest son, Ibrahim Khan Fatehjung, already a seasoned warrior at twenty five, bore a marked resemblance to his sister Mehrunnisa, with her irrepressible sense of fun. Jehangir came to love him with an abiding affection and gave his own niece Naseem to Ibrahim in marriage.

But he couldn't overcome a deep-rooted distrust of Ghias Beg's fantastically handsome, swaggering eldest son. Tales of his amorous intrigues ran through the city of Lahore, where Mahamud preferred to live. His reputation for profligacy matched only that of Mirza Ghazi Beg Tarkhan, ruler of Sindh and Multan. Every courtesan in Lahore and Agra claimed friendship with this son of the Dewan of Hindustan.

Jehangir had admonished Mahamud several times for rowing past the Imperial castle on an illuminated barge with singers and dancers, which was a privilege reserved for the Mughal princes and those of Timurid lineage alone.

Mahamud's first wife was Aziz Koka's niece and he was attached to Khusro's suite. And Jehangir knew that he deliberately encouraged Khusro's hostile attitude. If Mahamud didn't mend his ways, he would be forced to banish him from Court, despite his affection for Ghias Beg, thought Jehangir.

Months later, when he received the homage of Sher Afghan, Chief of Burdwan, the hauntingly beautiful face of Mehrunnisa, his lost love, rose with standing clarity before his eyes. And at last he began to understand the obscure longing which tormented him day and night.

They dined together that evening, and in the course of conversation, Sher Afghan told the Emperor that they had a six-year old daughter now, called Ladli.

"What, only one child to show for all these years?" Jehangir said lightly, though pain ripped through his breast. Sher Afghan smiled and shrugged.

Feigning indifference, Jehangir asked, "And your lady? Has she accompanied you to Agra?"

Sher Afghan shook his head, his clear grey eyes serene. "Well, Sire, she preferred to stay at Burdwan to manage the estate during my absence." He had not been surprised at her refusal. And he had been too wise to insist that she came to Agra with him.

Jehangir stared at the ruby ring on Sher Afghan's left hand. "You still wear my ring, Sher?"

Looking straight into Jehangir's eyes, Sher Afghan answered, "It is my talisman, Sire. I'm never without it. I owe my life to it, I believe, and my family's well-being."

Jehangir understood. He picked up his gleaming goblet in which floated ice and slices of peaches.

His mind became engrossed with plans. There must be some way of reclaiming Mehrunnisa. He would set Meer Sudder Jahan to examine the various Hadits pertaining to divorce law according to Islamic Shariat, he decided.

5

As the months passed, Jehangir became increasingly aware of the rivalry between the men who had been appointed to high office.

Sherrif had remained unchanged despite his great good fortune. No trace of hauteur had crept into his bearing; his light brown eyes were full of candour, his mouth broke readily into smiles. He had a calm, determined air about him which won the affectionate respect of most men, though there were many who envied his rise and disliked his appointment as Grand Vezzir. But they masked their feelings behind words of fawning praise.

Only one man baited Sherrif mercilessly and that was Aziz Koka, the former Grand Vezzir.

One day, summoning Aziz, Jehangir said, "I don't tolerate any feuds or vendettas at my Court! I want you to extend the hand of friendship to Sherrif." Jehangir paused to sniff delicately at the rose he held. Glancing away from Aziz, he continued, "He has shown me unquestioned loyalty and gratitude, unlike certain persons I could name."

Aziz heaved an exaggerated sigh. "What do you advise? I am all obedience, Sire!" And all the while his impertinent slanting eyes gleamed with mischief.

"Invite my foster brother to your house, and break the bread of friendship with him. The aged and elderly should be kind and discreet in their dealings with younger men."

With a low obeisance, Aziz Koka said, "To hear is to obey!"

A few days later, on a particularly cold winter night, Sherrif, Asaf, Mahabat and young Ibrahim gathered at Mirza Aziz Koka's palace.

Torch light flickered on the pink sandstone walls, throwing

weird shadows on the faces of the alighting guests. The Khan-i-Azam stood at the threshold in the pillared portico, clad in a quilted satin robe, fur-lined slippers and cap. Over his shoulders was draped a dark Kashmir shawl, incredibly light and warm. He greeted his guests with a jest and welcomed them to his humble abode.

They entered a gilded and painted banqueting hall. Heavy brocade curtains had been rolled down over the windows to keep out the cold night air. The floor was spread with brilliant-hued Bokhara rugs. Charcoal glowed in silver braziers and gleaming gilt lamps swung from peacock-shaped marble brackets while divans spread with tapestried Chinese silk stood against the walls. Enamelled gold aftabas and goblets stood on low sandalwood stools.

Sherrif declared ruefully, "If this is a humble abode, Mirza Aziz, then surely Paradise must resemble it! But where are your houris?"

At a signal from Aziz, slave girls with enticing faces entered and poured wine for the guests. Ibrahim sipped and gasped; the wine was liquid fire roaring down his throat.

Aziz Koka began to chat animatedly with Asaf, relating an amusing tale involving Deccan pundits, temple dancers and himself. There were hookahs prepared with opium, and Aziz Koka held forth on the rival merits of opium from Patna, Malwa and Mewar. There was nothing to compare with the white poppy of the Afghan highlands, asserted Asaf, while Sherrif praised the more potent Persian variety that was specially imported for discriminating buyers.

Mahabat was uncomfortable and wished the entertainment was over. He was not used to these devious old men, who mocked with their eyes and cajoled with their tongues.

Surprisingly, Sherrif found nothing offensive in Aziz Koka's house. Here was exuberant luxury, an interior as unrestrained and colourful as the Mirza's own personality. Peacocks and lotus flowers seemed to obsess Aziz, for even the cushions were covered in a silk interwoven with these two motifs.

Aziz Koka could seldom resist exhibiting his intimate knowledge and understanding of Akbar Shah. On the pretext of displaying an album of paintings to Sherrif, Aziz explained, "This picture of my royal foster brother riding an elephant across that bridge of boats is also from real life. He often indulged in such escapades when we were young to show his guardian Bairam Khan, his mother Hamida Begum, and his stern Mughal aunts that they couldn't manipulate him."

In Sherrif's view, the characterization of people and animals had gained greater depth and complexity under the new emperor's patronage. Preferring quality to quantity, Jehangir had reduced the staff of the royal studios soon after his accession. He encouraged his favoured masters to paint with increased subtlety, softer colours, less turbulent rhythms and more harmonious designs. Indeed, elegance was the keynote to his royal foster brother's personality, Sherrif couldn't help reflecting.

Ibrahim whispered to Sherrif as they reclined side by side on the divan. "Do you think our amiable host has some entertainment provided for tonight? Or does he intend talking only about himself? Where are all his sons?"

Overhearing the last remark, Aziz Koka said, "I must apologize for the absence of my sons, Ibrahim. Young men have so many engagements, you know."

"I hear you will soon be wedding Rao Amar Singh's daughter, Mahabat," remarked Aziz after a little silence.

Mahabat smiled and nodded assent. His mother had arranged the match and the Emperor had given his gracious consent.

"You are wise," continued Aziz, smiling. "A man must have four wives, not because the Prophet advocates it, but because he needs a Persian to talk to, a Turkish dame to manage his household, a Hindu to nurse his children, and a Khorasani to whip as a warning to the other three."

An outburst of laughter greeted this sally, though Sherrif wondered if the Mirza was trying to provoke him, since his own mother was a native of Khorasan.

A steward came and whispered in Aziz Koka's ear. He nodded and soon some of the famous courtesans of Agra were ushered in, followed by Aziz Koka's musicians. They salaamed and seated themselves on one of the rugs, and began singing a brisk melodious song, its words double-edged.

When his guests grew merry and flushed with wine Aziz signalled to his attendants. Serving maids attired in festive robes entered, carrying platters heaped with aromatic dishes. With hospitable words and gestures, Aziz Koka gathered his guests round the dastarkhan. The brocade cloth was spread with round silver salvers and bowls piled with steaming hot delicacies. Well-trained servants came to help them wash and dry their hands.

Aziz Koka broke flat unleavened bread into five pieces to start the meal. Soon Mahabat was biting with obvious relish into chicken fried in a rich curd gravy, crushing the bones with his strong white teeth. Mirza Aziz tasted a little pullao, nibbled a sweetmeat and kept up a steady flow of words. Ibrahim selected venison kebab and turned to compliment his host.

"Delicious. You have a Kashmiri cook?" added Sherrif.

"Yes," answered the Mirza. "A Kashmiri for meats, a Bengali for sweetmeats, a Mathura Choubey for halwas, a man from Marwar for papads, another from Jaipur for pickles, a Banaras Brahmin for vegetables, a Pathan for baking naan, a Persian for pullao, a Shirazi for kebabs, a Mongol for cheese, a Konkanese for fish, and innumerable men to help them. And I also have..."

"I'm quite convinced that your kitchens, worthy Mirza, are presided over by geniuses second only to the Badshah's cooks!" broke in Sherrif, laughing, and the Mirza threw up his hands in mock humility.

Sherrif then ate a pickled meat cooked in oil and vinegar, flavoured with garlic and tangy spices. "I have never tasted anything quite so succulent before." Glancing up at his host, he exclaimed, "What new recipe is this, Mirza Aziz?"

"Ah, you wouldn't allow me to tell you, my dear Sherrif. That is pickled wild boar, shot and cooked by one of my Rajput retainers."

Sherrif recoiled instinctively. He pushed away the platter and cried angrily, "Unclean! You have deliberately tried to defile us, Mirza Aziz!"

"Nonsense, Sherrif. Did you know that the wild boar is herbivorous? I suppose wild herbs give its flesh such flavour. And boars are cleaner than fowls, which peck in abominable places." Aziz laughed and slapped his thigh, delighted at the infuriated expression on Sherrif's face. Suppressing an oath, Sherrif rose angrily from the dastarkhan.

"Come, Sherrif," chaffed the Mirza. "Surely you feast often enough with your Rajput friends. They also eat pork and I'm sure you don't sulk away from their feasts in anger."

"The Rajputs have the decency to respect our prejudices. Beware lest some retribution overtake you for your levity, Mirza Aziz!"

Asaf, Mahabat and Ibrahim also stood up. The situation was rapidly becoming extremely unpleasant, realized Asaf.

"Spare me your lectures, dear Sherrif," murmured Aziz with his impassive face. "Even Akbar Shah used to say that beef and pork, their eating or not eating, has nothing to do with religion."

"Did you call us here to humiliate us?" demanded Sherrif, his chest heaving with suppressed fury.

"Come, come, you are no true friend of mine, Nawab, to accuse me thus. Yet your father was my dearest friend.

He painted the walls of this very chamber in which I have endeavoured to break the bread of friendship with you. Tchak! Tchak! Never would I cause sorrow to the son of that celebrated artist, whom even Akbar Shah honoured."

Sherrif stepped forward, his face grim. "You'll pay for this effrontery."

And without a word of thanks or leave-taking, he turned on his heels, followed by his friends.

He brushed away Asaf's hand from his shoulder when Asaf tried to calm him. "We all know his waspish, unconventional ways. Mirza Aziz can't control his tongue, and he delights in annoying people. Don't quarrel with him, Sherrif."

"I'm determined to avenge this insult, Asaf. There are documents in the secret state archives which could annihilate him, and the old fool knows nothing about them. But I do."

"He's mad, Sherrif," said Asaf soothingly. "Anyone else would have tried to placate you, but I'm beginning to believe he's mentally deranged. Forget this affair."

6

Divorce?" gasped Sherrif.

What in the world had revived memories of that long forgotten affair in the Emperor's mind, he wondered. There would be endless trouble if Jehangir tried to espouse every pretty female he had dallied with as Crown Prince. Princes were expected to be much more serious. Careful, he warned himself.

Pulling at the pearl in his ear, he protested, "I wouldn't wager this pearl against my life after uttering this word to Sher Afghan! He came meekly enough to render homage after your coronation, but have you ever wondered why he refused all appointments and begged leave to retire to his estates in Bengal? Or why he has professed to be satisfied with his fief of Burdwan, instead of exchanging it for one in Punjab, as you suggested to him?"

"It was impossible for me to force Sher. I can't begin my reign by repudiating my father's firmans. Then too, Sher is the undoubted hero of a group of Afghan chiefs whom I can't possibly alienate. After Khusro's revolt and the open support given to him by most of the Rajputs and many of the highest amirs in the realm, an Afghan uprising in Bengal would be disastrous for the Sultanat."

Sherrif was utterly exhausted after the long journey from Agra, undertaken in the debilitating August heat in obedience to a peremptory command from the Emperor. He had been only one night in Allahabad, and he began to fear that Jehangir was about to send him on an imprudent mission to distant Bengal.

As though reading his thoughts, Jehangir said, "That's why I am sending you as my envoy to Bengal. Cultivate Sher

Afghan and at the appropriate moment suggest the divorce on the ground that Mehrunnisa has not borne him any male heir. You can offer Sher the choice of espousing a number of lovely young noblewomen, whom I shall endorse generously. But I want no scandal or ill-will resulting from this. You will be discreet and tactful, as you value my honour and friendship, Sherrif."

Jehangir gazed at the tranquil splendour of the river flowing down below. At the hour of sunrise a great multitude came to bathe in the holy river, and scantily clad women thronged the ghats and plunged into the water with offerings of flowers and coconuts. The sight of those female forms draped in drenched, transparent saris always amused him, for Hindu women were notable prudes otherwise. But today only the thought of Mehrunnisa absorbed him, and the scene below failed to divert.

He turned to his friend and said wistfully, "I've never understood, Sherrif, why the one woman I desired so desperately was snatched away from me."

Thousands of pigeons flew overhead; peacocks raised raucous cries from the gardens. Inwardly deploring Jehangir's seriousness, Sherrif tried to speak of other things.

Pointing to the bathers at the ghats, he said, "Do you realize, Sire, that all those men and women are chanting sacred verses, imploring the holy river to remove from them the stains of their sins. I remember that your father would only drink water brought from the river Ganga. Did he also believe in its mystic powers?"

"Mystic powers!" scoffed Jehangir. "I and all the Mughals drink Ganga water for one simple reason. We know that it has medicinal properties. It contains certain minerals essential for good health. So many mysterious phenomena can be rationalized, Sherrif, if people take the trouble to investigate myths."

Sherrif smiled, thinking that he had succeeded in diverting

his foster brother's mind. He turned gratefully towards the cool morning breeze blowing up from the river.

The Emperor said sharply, "There's nothing you can teach me about the manners and customs of the Hindus. My father took good care to acquaint us with every religion under the sun. We had learned mullahs, kazis, pundits, and even Jesuits to educate us, and you know it."

"Of course, Akbar Shah transcended the limitations of race and religion. I've always wondered, Sire, how your noble father could have been simultaneously a great practical statesman and a transcendental mystic..."

Casting a stern glance at Sherrif, Jehangir interrupted, "I haven't summoned you all the way from Agra to rehash all the religious discourses and speculations we both heard as young boys in the Ibadat Khana at Fatehpur Sikri. Let us speak of Bengal and Sher Afghan. Do you know that I have recalled Maan Singh from Bengal? Qutub-ud-din Koka is the new governor, and you may rely on his help, but don't disclose the actual purpose of your visit to anyone."

"Sher Afghan is not one to meekly yield what you covet," warned Sherrif. "It is not going to be a simple question of talks and arguments and negotiations. We'll have to intimidate him somehow."

The Emperor couldn't help wondering again why all the omens and predictions about Meherunnisa becoming his wife had proved false. For deep within his soul he believed what the Sufi, Hindu, Buddhist, Jain and Hebrew mystics said about each human soul inexorably fulfilling its Karmic destiny before achieving release or nirvana from the cycle of rebirth and reincarnation. Until he merged with his soul's beloved, Mehrunnisa, what hope had he of the magnificent final merger with their Universal Creator?

They continued strolling along the ramparts of the Allahabad Fort. From the ancient caves beyond the palace came sounds of stone-cutting, of scaffolding being erected, shouts of overseers and the monotonous chorus of masons.

Repairs to these monuments depicting scenes from Hindu mythology had been an annual feature since Akbar Shah's time, and he had decreed their preservation. This reminded Jehangir of Shah Begum's tomb, which was already under construction beyond the city of Allahabad, where he planned to ride in the evening to supervise the planting of fruit trees. The Amber Princess had loved fresh fruits.

Jehangir sighed as he thought of his dead wife. Always tempestuous and unpredictable, she had swallowed a fatal dose of opium when news of her son's revolt had reached her. Ah, well, that was over and done with. It was the future which concerned him now, thought Jehangir.

Flinging an arm around Sherrif, he said, "You who have slept by my bedside since infancy, can't you guess how lonely I am? Is there one among my queens or concubines who can be a true companion? Of my children, the first-born son shows his filial love through revolt! He is eager for the sword and diadem of empire. In time, my other sons will also turn ambitious. Daughters, they are wrapped up in their own little pleasures and petulances, scandals and jealousies."

With a deep sigh, he continued, "Wherever my eyes turn, I see the work of Akbar Shah, my father. Is there nothing I can create? Will I leave behind no lasting record of conquest and triumph? But Mehrunnisa has the strength of soul my consorts lack. You can't imagine what torments I suffered when my father snatched her away from me and gifted her to Sher Afghan!" Jehangir's voice was tremulous with passion.

Since they were children together at Fatehpur, they had bared their souls to each other. The milk that had nourished them both bound them closer than ties of blood or kinship.

"You should send Asaf to tackle Sher Afghan. He is good at that sort of thing."

Jehangir frowned. "That is out of the question. I don't want Asaf to have even an inkling about this affair."

"That is impossible," objected Sherrif in his forthright manner. "Asaf is no fool. There is bound to be a great deal of speculation if you send me all the way to Bengal."

"Everyone will believe that I am sending you to represent me at Qutab-ud-din's daughter's wedding. After all, you are a close relation of his wife. It's an excellent opportunity for meeting Sher without giving rise to undue talk, Sherrif. He is bound to attend the wedding."

"There is a faster and less devious way of achieving your desire, my Lord. Bir Singh of Orchha is your man," suggested Sherrif softly, hoping to give a new turn to the scheme.

"Undoubtedly. But, friend of short memory, am I to order the murder of a man who once saved me from a hideous death? Such is not the way of the Mughals!"

"Then send him to Mewar against the Rana," Sherrif urged. He wanted no part in this affair, he profoundly detested this whole coil of intrigue.

Jehangir glanced disdainfully at his foster brother. "And have the entire world saying that Badshah Jehangir sent Sher Afghan to war and certain death to wed his widow? No, Sherrif. These stratagems won't do. But divorce is allowed under Islamic law, and a divorced lady is free to wed anyone."

Sherrif knew that from his youth Jehangir had been obsessed with law, legality and justice. He stood rubbing his chin, assailed by many doubts.

At last he spoke. "I'll go on your errand, even at peril to my life."

Jehangir smiled charmingly. "You are the only man I trust in all Hindustan, Sherrif. May Allah guide you on the road to Bengal!"

7

After a week, Sherrif set out on the hot, long road to Dacca with a small entourage.

They splashed across countless streams and crossed huge forest tracts where tigers, thugs and herds of wild elephants roamed. Sherrif was amazed at the excellence of the Great Road built by Sher Shah Suri more than seventy years ago, now kept in wonderful repair by a succession of Mughal governors.

In Dacca the new Governor had built a magnificent palace. Thousands of men, women and children had been rounded up to complete the buildings in record time, in spite of an edict prohibiting forced labour. Gardens, pavilions, fountains and canals had been rapidly laid out, turning the provincial capital into a flourishing luxurious place.

Bengal's exotic vegetation of varied palms, towering teak and sal trees, fruit-laden bananas and papayas, and wild flowers caught his artist's eye. So many shades of green shimmered in the rice fields stretching between the Ganga and the Himalayan foothills. Even the birds here were different. Sherrif, despite the urgency of his mission, couldn't help stopping now and then to sketch the great hornbills, multicoloured pheasants, herons, pelicans, cranes, snow-white storks and black darters lining streams and jheels, which he would paint later as gifts for his foster brother Jehangir's collection.

Tents had been pitched under coconut and betelnut palms to lodge the numerous wedding guests. Many of Qutub-ud-din's relatives had journeyed to Dacca all the way from Agra and Lahore, and almost all the mansabdars of Bengal.

The town bustled with activity. Open air markets sprang up round the encampments. Hawkers came with fish and fowl, a vast variety of vegetables, fruit, condiments and spices. They demanded exorbitant prices for their goods, knowing that the Governor's stewards, preparing to feed thousands of guests, would gladly pay anything to get enough supplies.

In the zenana apartments of Qutub-ud-din's palace, Benazzir, the bride-to-be, sat beside her mother, Sakina Begum, choosing and rejecting from a pile of clothes and jewels, while around them festive ladies reclined on cushioned divans, eating sweetmeats and drinking refreshing iced sherbat, gossiping and chewing paan. In the canopied courtyard sat a group of women singing traditional wedding songs to the accompaniment of drums, while the younger girls pirouetted, their braids flying in the air, colourful skirts flaring.

Several dusky-eyed ladies were having palms decorated by slave girls proficient in the art of applying henna, while they chattered excitedly of the singing and dancing, the banquets with brilliant fireworks to be held every night.

The pillared corridors were festooned with garlands of heady, perfumed flowers. And outside the zenana, it seemed all Dacca was astir with gaiety. Tomorrow the daughter of Qutub-ud-din, Governor of Bengal and foster brother of the Grand Mughal Jehangir, would be married to Darab Khan, son of Mirza Abdur Rahim Khan-i-Khanan and grandson of Bairam Khan, Akbar's one-time guardian.

Sakina, the Governor's elegant lady, sat attended by Mehrunnisa, Ratna, the young bride of Prince Madho Singh of Amber and her cousin.

In answer to Sakina's query, Mehrunnisa spoke of her daughter Ladli's fluency in Persian, Arabic, Turkish and Urdu.

"Has your cousin Sherrif brought any letter or messages from Laila?" inquired Mehrunnisa.

"No, he hasn't. Through I must say that Laila would have definitely written to you if she had known that her husband was coming all the way to Dacca. We were delightfully surprised when he arrived without any warning from Allahabad."

"My husband says that Sherrif Khan is the most powerful amir in all Hindustan today. He even succeeded in having Aziz Koka imprisoned," declared Ratna in an awed voice.

Her cousin spoke up languidly: "Really? But he is only the son of a painter, I hear."

Sakina exclaimed sharply, "Only the son of a painter? Let me tell you that my aunt married his father, who was the foremost artist of Akbar Shah's Court, and what is more, he is the grandson of Nizam-ul-Mulk, who was the chief Vezzir of Shah Shuja of Shiraz. And Sherrif is descended through his grandmother from the Prophet himself!"

"Really," mocked the sceptical Rajputani. "Every Mughal amir claims descent from Hazrat Mohammed! He must have had innumerable offspring..."

"Not half as numerous, I assure you, as the progeny of your Sun God!" came a swift retort from Mehrunnisa.

Some of Sakina's friends smothered their laughter, but many smiled outright. They knew that no one bested Mehrunnisa in verbal badinage.

Putting down her tumbler on a stool, Mehrunnisa rose, "There's your sister beckoning me, Sakina. I had promised to help her decorate the bridal chamber, and I suppose I shall have to leave you for a while."

Regarding Mehrunnisa's retreating figure with a fascinated eye, Ratna asked curiously, "Sakina Begum, is it true that Sher Afghan's wife was the Badshah's sweetheart before her marriage? They say she was the most beautiful girl at the Mughal Court, and I must admit she is incredibly lovely even today."

Sakina looked away, picked a nut from a salver and thoughtfully began chewing it. "It all happened so long ago. I've forgotten the details, Ratna. Of course, there were many stories..."

A serving maid approached, breathless with excitement, "Mistress, the baraat is approaching the palace."

This news created a flurry of anticipation among the assembly of matrons and young maidens. From a distance came the sound of beating drums, music, laughter, the jingle of harness and clipclop of hoofs and the slow tinkling of elephant bells.

The women ran up to the rooftops, chatting and giggling and gently shoving one another, all decorum thrown to the winds in their eagerness to watch the bridegroom's arrival.

Dust rose in billows to mingle with the coloured powder, candy sugar, flower petals, coins and rosewater showered on Darab Khan and his entourage. Paupers scuffled with children for the largesse scattered so lavishly.

The Khan-i-Khanan and his son were greeted and embraced by Qutub-ud-din and his kinsmen and escorted into the palace.

Next morning, her aunts led Benazzir to a low platform in a shaded part of her mother's courtyard for the henna ceremony. Carpets had been spread around it for those who wished to watch, and in a corridor sat singers. The tray of henna, prepared according to custom by the bride's mother-in-law, was brought.

Sakina touched Mehrunnisa's shoulder and said coaxingly, "Your designs for henna are justly reputed to be the loveliest in all Hindustan. Won't you decorate my daughter's palms today?"

Mehrunnisa laughed. "What a shameless flatterer you are, Sakina. But I will gladly do anything to make your lovely daughter lovelier."

She sat across from Benazzir and mixing the henna paste to the correct consistency, began tracing a delicate design of miniature flowers on Benazzir's palms with an ivory stick.

The singers began their song and the guests clapped in time to the drum beat. Slave girls carried tray after tray of bridal gifts into the courtyard. Everyone turned eagerly to examine the costumes, jewels, perfume flagons and toilet articles, loudly acclaiming Darab Khan's taste.

Intent on her task, Mehrunnisa did not hear one of the maids calling, "Purdah! The Master is coming!"

The other women drew their veils across their faces, and peeped between their fingers at the Governor. Qutub-ud-din walked into that feminine assembly with smiling lips and animated eyes. An expectant thrill ran through the women, for his amorous adventures were the talk of Dacca. Not content with his wives and concubines and his numerous delectable slave girls, Qutub-ud-din stalked and courted married women assiduously.

Benazzir, draped from head to foot in brilliant scarlet, glanced at her father and smiled shyly. As he smiled back, Mehrunnisa's profile caught his attention. Completely unaware of his gaze, she continued her task.

Beckoning his wife, Qutub-ud-din drew her apart into an inner chamber for a private discussion about the numerous wedding ceremonies.

Before returning to the male quarters, he asked casually, "Who is that lady decorating Benazzir's palms?"

Sakina frowned. "Why do you ask? That is Mehrunnisa, wife of Sher Afghan and daughter of Mirza Ghias Beg."

"Out of sheer idle curiosity, my dear."

After the wedding, only Sherrif and Sher Afghan remained as guests. On some pretext or another, the Governor urged Sher to prolong his stay, and Sherrif declared that he was in no hurry to begin the tiresome journey back to Agra.

Sherrif regaled them with Court gossip, Qutub-ud-din arranged hunts and entertainments and the days passed pleasantly.

No one could have guessed from Sherrif's demeanour that he was longing to return to Agra. His cautious queries had drawn an outraged oath from Sher, and Sherrif had realized that no inducement would make him consider divorce. The problem seemed insoluble. Sherrif spent an entire morning composing a letter entreating the Emperor to forget the whole affair.

That night Sherrif found Qutub-ud-din in high spirits. "My huntsmen have sighted a rhinoceros in the swamp across the river, and I propose to take you both hunting tomorrow. This is a wonderful opportunity, Sherrif. They don't usually drift so close to Dacca, you know."

Sherrif rejoined ruefully, "The prospect of being trampled, gored, or ripped open by a rhinoceros doesn't delight me!"

Qutub-ud-din grinned, showing sharp white teeth. "You've been listening to Sher's harrowing hunting yarns, I'll wager. He likes everyone to believe that hunting rhinoceros is extremely hazardous, while he quietly makes a fortune out of their horns."

Sher Afghan smiled, but refrained from comment. Qutub-ud-din continued, "Don't let him daunt you. I guarantee your safety, and promise you the horn as a trophy to display to envious friends in Agra."

"Is this going to be a long trip?" inquired Sher. "I'm anxious to return home before Friday, you know. There are several matters requiring urgent attention at Burdwan."

"We'll be back the same evening," Qutub-ud-din assured him. "It's barely a few hours' ride. I wonder if your lady is as anxious to return home as you are, Sher. They say that this is the first time she has stirred beyond Burdwan in nine years."

He poured wine for his guests and said, "Such amazing devotion! Now my own wives are always clamouring to visit their relations; they preferred living in Agra where they were always attached to some Mughal Begum or Princess..."

A slight frown creased Sher Afghan's brow. He tried to remember something Mehrunnisa had said about the Governor, but it eluded him. Soon he was involved in Qutub-ud-din's plans, and the matter slipped his mind.

Before sunrise next day, Qutub-ud-din and his guests, escorted by several huntsmen, crossed the river over a bridge of boats and rode towards the swamp.

The rhinoceros, wallowing peacefully in the mud, seemed apparently indifferent to all the din and clamour created by the huntsmen to draw him out of the water. But when they began beating gongs and pelting him with stones, he grew infuriated. Clambering clumsily from the mudhole, he bellowed loudly and charged towards the group of horsemen.

Qutub-ud-din and Sherrif moved their horses to safety behind a clump of trees, but Sher Afghan halted his mount and asked for a javelin.

The rhinoceros charged towards Sher with incredible speed. Sherrif watched, amazed. He had never imagined that such a large, clumsy beast could move so fast.

Sher Afghan whirled his horse expertly out of the charging animal's path, aware that the rhinoceros could not change direction. Holding aloft his spear, he wheeled the horse around, ready for another onslaught. The rhinoceros dug up tufts of grass with its horn and snorted viciously.

An exhilarating feeling came over Sher, his body and mind became vibrantly alert. He had done this thing so often before that he knew instinctively the exact spot through which he could pierce that tough hide.

With perfect timing, he galloped towards the charging beast. One moment his spear was embedded in its flesh, and in another, the shaft snapped with a twang that could be heard over the thud of hoofs and the excited cries of the men.

He choked back an angry oath as the momentum of the action threw him off his horse. As he fell heavily to the swampy ground, a confused vision of hoofs and horn and heavy armoured hide thundered past him, but he forced himself to rise.

Sherrif realized in that instant that none of the others, though experienced hunters, had made a single move to stop the rhinoceros which was preparing to attack and maul Sher Afghan. Raising his musket, he took careful aim and fired, refusing to believe that he might not get that difficult head shot. Sherrif's bullet pierced the rhinoceros' left eye. It cried, stumbled, and sank to its knees.

Sher Afghan watched the animal die with horrible suspicion in his mind. His mouth was grim, and his breath came loud and furious. He strode up and wrenched Qutub-ud-din down from his horse.

Towering over him, Sher demanded, "What treachery is this?"

Pushing away his hands, Qutub-ud-din said coldly, That was just bad luck. It could have happened to anyone. Watch your tongue, Sher Afghan. There are other tempers and swords besides your own!"

"Ya Allah, Qutub-ud-din! That spear should not have snapped. It was your personal weapon," cried Sher furiously.

"So what?" sneered Qutub-ud-din with an insolent glint in his eyes.

The forest seemed to press oppressively around Sher. It became at once an evil, dark place, though the trees were behind him, and before him stretched the open grassy swamp. He became aware of Qutub-ud-din's men standing silent and menacing in the background. All at once he realized how cunningly the trap had been set for him.

Qutub-ud-din laughed. In an instant, Sher Afghan's sword flashed out.

"I'm beginning to understand everything now. And you, Sherrif. Was it on this errand, was it to procure my death that you came to Bengal?"

Sherrif protested instantly, "Would I have shot down that rhinoceros if I had desired your death? Put down your swords, you fools."

"Do you think I will swallow his insults?" cried Qutub-ud-din, raising his sword. "One of us will die before this is settled."

Ruthlessly they fought, filling the forest with the sound of clashing steel and laboured breath. While they were locked in bitter battle, Sherrif stood by gazing helplessly. Sher Afghan attacked Qutub-ud-din with stunning force. The Governor parried the blows as best he could, and Sherrif could see the glint in his murderous eyes.

Once Qutub-ud-din slipped on the slushy ground and lost his footing. Sher Afghan waited for him to recover his balance. He received a cut on his left shoulder, and a dark stain spread over his fargal. Panting, he parried the next thrust, and with a swift motion of his wrist, wounded Qutub-ud-din, drawing blood from his breast.

Running up to the combatants, Sherrif shouted, "In the name of Allah! Stop this senseless fight."

"Get back, Sherrif," warned Sher Afghan, and rushed to attack his opponent.

Long and hard they fought, steel against steel, each parrying stroke with stroke. Both were excellent swordsmen, but Sher Afghan had the mightier arm. Qutub-ud-din had grown soft with luxurious living while Sher had kept himself in fighting form.

Qutub-ud-din's lifeblood was ebbing from the wounds inflicted on his chest and arms. His breath came in gasps and the trees swayed before his eyes. He reeled, unable to avoid Sher's deadly thrust. The sword entered his stomach and clutching his wound, he fell to the ground.

Seeing their master fall, the Governor's men rushed on Sher Afghan. Sherrif watched them surround him, repelled yet fascinated by the gruesome scene before him.

Though he fought valiantly, Sher Afghan had no chance against that pack of retainers howling for his blood. Nor could Sherrif prevent them from hacking his old comrade to death.

When at last he fell, a ring of dead men surrounded him and Sher Afghan's body was a mass of wounds.

Sherrif stared with dazed disbelief at the dead men sprawled at his feet. He thought of his cousin Sakina, and of Mehrunnisa, but above all of Jehangir. This was going to have disastrous repercussions in Agra, he knew.

8

That night, Sherrif took charge of Qutub-ud-din's palace. He had already sent messengers galloping to notify the Emperor, though how Jehangir would react to the news from Bengal was open to conjecture.

Apart from concern for Qutub-ud-din's wives and dependents, Sherrif was troubled by thoughts of Mehrunnisa.

Her situation in Qutub-ud-din's house was insufferable. She had heard him speak of her husband's death with stunned disbelief; and when the bodies had been carried in, her self-discipline had been superb.

It was Sakina who had turned hysterical and hurled invectives at Mehrunnisa. Everyone had stood aghast till Sher Afghan's little daughter had pushed her way through the crowd of staring, speculating women to tug at her mother's arm. And it was only then that Sherrif had heard Mehrunnisa making soft, mournful sounds.

He had found it impossible to take his eyes from her face as she bent over her husband's body and at long last he understood his foster-brother's inability to forget her.

According to ancient custom, he should have summoned her father or one of her brothers to take charge of her. But keeping his original mission in mind, Sherrif had decided to notify only the Emperor.

Mehrunnisa's first feeling when she heard Sherrif's pronouncement had been one of anguished shock. Her second thoughts had been of concern for Ladli's future. But for the next few days, she was busy settling her husband's affairs at Burdwan, where Prince Madho Singh of Amber had insisted on escorting her in his usual impulsive, chivalrous manner.

Though her eyes were swollen, she had no more tears left. After grief came resignation and relief; she waited for the summons from Agra which she knew would come.

By the time a month of deep mourning had passed, Sherrif had come with an Imperial escort to convey her to Agra. There was never any question of her refusing to go. She knew as well as Sherrif that the Emperor's commands had to be obeyed.

Her father had written to inform her that her brother Ibrahim would meet her at Patna. Anyway, there was nothing to keep her in Bengal now. Akbar had made it impossible for Mughal noblemen to pass on power and wealth by introducing the law of escheat to India. At death, everything a mansabdar owned reverted to the Crown. Inheriting anything from a father's estate depended entirely on the Emperor's approval. Since Sher Afghan had killed not only his viceroy in Bengal, but also one of his foster brothers, all her husband's estates, jewels and effects had passed to the Emperor. She knew that henceforth she and her daughter would be totally dependent on their sovereign's whim.

For nine long years, she had trained herself not to speak or think of him, but now her cruel inexorable destiny would bring them face to face again, brooded Mehrunnisa.

After months of weary travel, they reached Agra at last. The sounds and smells of Agra smote Mehrunnisa, arousing a thousand memories. She peered through the curtains of her high-domed bullock chariot at the sandstone walls of the Mughal castle visible in the distance, and her thoughts were all of Jehangir.

Her daughter exclaimed suddenly, "Why have they stopped? Have we reached my grandfather's house, Mother?"

Mehrunnisa frowned. The cavalcade had indeed halted. She supposed that now her brother must be taking leave of Sherrif and preparing to escort her with his own retinue to her father's palace. But a moment later, she saw Ibrahim cantering up to her chariot. She wondered at the grim expression on his handsome, youthful face.

"What is the matter, Ibrahim?" she asked as he reined in beside her.

He answered, frowning heavily, "I don't know if my father is aware of this change. It seems that Sherrif has just received a written command from the Badshah to convey you to the Mughal castle with your child and nurse. I can't understand it. This is most irregular. But we dare not question his commands."

Ibrahim heard her gasp and refrained from adding that he feared this would give rise to a lot of unpleasant talk. That old affair of hers, of which he had never heard the details, would be raked up again, and her position, already pathetic, would become insupportable.

Mehrunnisa cried in a distressed voice, "There must be some mistake, Ibrahim! The Badshah cannot wish to deprive me of my family's company at such a time. Let me speak to Sherrif."

Sighing, Ibrahim answered, "It would be useless, my dear sister. The instructions are quite explicit. You are to be conveyed to Begum Salima Sultana's palace, where our mother is waiting to receive you."

"Are you going to see the Badshah?" asked Ladli in an awed whisper.

Mehrunnisa did not answer. The driver flicked his whip over the bullocks and the chariot lurched forward.

They entered the portals of the Mughal castle and Mehrunnisa heard the gates clang shut behind them.

She had expected the impetuous lover of her maiden days to receive her immediately, but the days passed, and her hope for a private audience remained unfulfilled. She contented herself with glimpses of Jehangir at crowded zenana functions.

Days turned into weeks, weeks into months, and yet he did not send for her. Then news came from Bengal that the Afghans of the Sur and Lodi tribes had joined hands to rise in revolt against the Mughal throne. Jehangir had marched up to Patna with his troops to suppress the revolt, she heard.

But he had been back now for days, and soon it would be a year since she and Ladli had arrived at Court. Did preoccupation with Sultanat affairs leave him no time for her, she wondered, piqued at his neglect.

She didn't know how sternly he held himself in rein or how often his eyes sought her from the latticed windows as she walked in the zenana gardens. He wondered what she thought and felt, and wished that he could end her suffering.

In the zenana, Mehrunnisa had her own apartment, where she was allowed to receive her immediate family, had attendants to wait on her, and every possible comfort she could desire. She was not permitted to step out of the palace, but her old friends began visiting her when they realized that she was not in disgrace.

The monotony of her existence was broken only when Moharrum, Ramzan, and the night of Shab-i-Raat came, or when one of the Hindu festivals was celebrated at Court. She mourned on Moharrum, kept the forty-day Ramzan fast, offered prayers and ritual gifts for her dead husband's soul on Shab-i-Raat. But for her the joyous festival of Id had become meaningless.

Salima Begum ignored her pleas for removal to her father's house, and Mehrunnisa repeatedly wished that the more amenable Persian Sultana was still alive.

Her most frequent visitors at the Mughal zenana were her sister Manija and Sherrif's wife Laila. It was from them that Mehrunnisa heard the details of her eldest brother Mahamud's miserable death at Lahore after Khusro's disastrous revolt.

Her father's fears for Mahamud had been justified. His

plot to assassinate the Emperor after Khusro's capture had failed, and with several others he was tried for treason. All her father's efforts to placate the Emperor's wrath had proved futile and her brother had been beheaded.

Manija spoke bitterly of Mahabat's zeal in implicating Mahamud, and of the ensuing trouble between Asaf and Mahabat. "Mother was amazed when the Badshah continued showing favour to our family. Indeed, everyone speculated about his strange behaviour."

After Manija's departure, Laila said tartly, "If your sister wasn't so scatterbrained, she would know precisely why he indulges your entire family."

"Hush," whispered Mehrunnisa. "Be careful how you speak of him. We are surrounded by spies."

"Pooh!" said Laila airily, and plunged into clever but slightly malicious verbal sketches of all the Emperor's relations.

Mehrunnisa couldn't help laughing, but she said resolutely, "I wish you wouldn't talk nonsense all the time, Laila. It was bad enough when we were young girls together in Bilquis Begum's charge, but now your husband is the Grand Vezzir, and your behaviour could endanger him."

Abruptly, Laila asked, "Do you know why my husband went to Bengal last year?"

"To honour Qutub-ud-din," answered Mehrunnisa scathingly. Laila peered into a mirror and fussed with her veil. She turned and tapped Mehrunnisa's cheek playfully. "That's what everyone thinks, my innocent, but you should know better."

A sudden suspicion flared in Mehrunnisa's mind. She turned pale and gasped. Her eyes grew wide with disbelief. "No, it couldn't be! No, no!"

"He told me the whole story himself, my dear," answered Laila with a maddeningly superior smile on her pretty, plump face. "Of course, he has always known his foster brother's secrets."

Seeing the stunned expression on Mehrunnisa's face, Laila continued, "I've always been honest with you, and I suppose you're wondering why he didn't act sooner. But you'll have to agree that he could have hardly done anything so long as Akbar Shah lived."

"Stop, Laila!" cried Mehrunnisa.

"What is worrying you? It's not as though you loved Sher Afghan."

"Allah, aid me," whispered Mehrunnisa, staring distraught at her friend.

When Dil Aram found her mistress pacing under the cypress trees in the garden, clad only in flimsy muslin, she realized at once that something was wrong. She guessed that Mehrunnisa was thinking again of Sher Afghan's atrocious death. At times Dil Aram felt that she deliberately recalled every gory detail to punish herself.

'This will never do," said Dil Aram, casting a shawl around her shoulders. "You will catch a chill, and be miserable for weeks, my child. Remember, you are quite unused to the severe Agra winter after all those years spent in humid Bengal."

Mehrunnisa thanked her nurse, but kept her head averted, as if to hide some uncontrollable emotion.

Never had she endured so long, so miserable a night as this. Towards morning her distracted thoughts began to lose all coherency; she fell into a confused and feverish sleep.

Next day, she was totally unprepared for Arambanu Begum's visit. They sat on a marble bench in the sun-drenched court, and discussed her problems.

"I have spoken to my brother about you, Mehrunnisa, but he says that as your liege lord, it is his duty to look after you and your child."

"He could grant me a widow's pension, if he fears that I will be a charge on my ageing father, though he could hardly be considered impoverished."

"Why complain, Mehrunnisa," said the Mughal Princess, complacently eating almonds from a bowl. "Here you have every comfort and luxury that a woman's heart could desire."

"I wish he would understand that I desire none of these things. My father's home would be a more suitable place for us than the Grand Mughal's zenana."

The Princess smiled knowingly. "Come, Mehrunnisa! Don't be so dense. Surely you understand that my brother has no intention of ever letting you depart from his palace? He had once planned to make you his bride. If you have forgotten it, he at least has not!"

Mehrunnisa rose. She plucked a rose from a nearby bush, crushed its petals, and said, "Ten years is a long time. Sher Afghan's widow is no match for the Badshah of Hindustan."

Arambanu laughed and said archly, "Do you know what my brother said yesterday? He declared that if I was so concerned with your welfare, I could take you hawking sometimes. He is sure that you miss your daily rides and has placed a beautifully trained Arab mare at your disposal."

For a moment, annoyance at his audacity made her silent. Then she said with suppressed vehemence, "Surely the Badshah overrates the normal human capability to adjust to new circumstances? Widows don't hawk all over the countryside, and he knows it!"

Princess Arambanu said sharply, "I wish you would stop hurling that word 'widow' at me. All Agra knows you won't remain one very long."

"You know, I'm, really worried about my brother," she confided when Mehrunnisa did not respond. "Not only has his health deteriorated, but his restlessness is also increasing. And you know that makes him ill-tempered. His passion for hunting has grown to an unnatural extent, and again he is drinking to excess."

"Does it surprise you?" Mehrunnisa asked. "He has fallen

a victim to the obvious failings which accompany unlimited opportunities for self-indulgence."

"Is that what you think? Actually, I believe that boredom and loneliness are driving him to excess. Salim feels that there is no one to share his ideas, no one he can confide in, no one who understands him."

For a long while they sat silent. Rising, Arambanu said with a teasing smile, "Think of my poor brother suffering the pangs of unrequited love. Is it unrequited, Mehrunnisa?"

9

Salima Sultana invited Mehrunnisa to visit her almost daily. Everyone knew that the Dowager Sultana took a particular interest in the young widow, and Mehrunnisa could not help being flattered, though she kept wondering if the Begum would help her escape from this gilded captivity.

As she alighted from the palanquin in Salima Begum's portico, she heard someone whisper, "Whose palanquin is that?"

"Mehrunnisa's!" answered a spiteful voice. "The woman whom the Badshah keeps hidden away. They say..."

The rest was lost as the voices sank low.

The Sultana received Mehrunnisa affectionately. At sixty-three, Salima Begum still retained traces of the fragile beauty which had captivated the old emperor, and her gracious affability had never ceased to amaze Mehrunnisa.

At a signal from the Sultana, serving maids carried in trays of sweetmeats and sherbat. "You must taste these coconut cakes. Raja Maan Singh sent them this morning in honour of the birth of his first great-grandson."

After sipping her sherbat, the Sultana carefully selected paan from a gilt casket and offered them to Mehrunnisa. She settled comfortably against the velvet bolsters, and picked up a leather bound volume lying beside her.

Opening it, she said, "Have you read this charming new version of Fizuli's *Laila.* Isn't the calligraphy remarkable? And what do you think of the illustrations with their minute details? They were painted at my son's command by Abul Hasan. There are only three copies of this work in Agra. One belongs to your father, the other to my stepson Abdur Rahim, and this one is for you."

Mehrunnisa thanked her, and glanced through the slim volume. "The illustrations are indeed unusual. But Fizuli's poem is a mere imitation of Nizami's earlier, and, if I may add, far superior work. Nizami created a poem of supreme artistic dignity which has been imitated by poets everywhere!"

"I grant your partiality for Persian poets, but let us be objective, Mehrunnisa. The story originated in Arabia, you must admit, and it was the Persians who borrowed it. Salim insists that there never could have been such besotted lovers. It was originally meant to be a mystic poem, like Kabir's impassioned hymns which have often been misunderstood."

"Well, Gracious One, anecdotes about Majnu were circulating in mystic circles long before Nizami's time. As the sages say, the beauty of every human being is a reflection of divine beauty. Majnu saw Allah in his beloved, and people cried sacrilege when he stood before the Kaba and said 'Ya Laila!'"

The Sultana smiled tenderly at Mehrunnisa. Her tired old eyes brightened, and she said, "Ah, yes, I know what you mean. In the words of Gulsheir, 'What use to me is a mortal Laila? I shall break with Laila and then only the Lord remains!' Love, madness, poetry..."

Something in Mehrunnisa's face made her pause. She had become increasingly aware of Mehrunnisa's strange unhappiness. She wondered what made this young woman so depressed. Suddenly, memories of her first widowhood came to her, and she realized with a slight shock that today was Bairam Khan's death anniversary. Later, she would perform fatiha and dispatch her eunuchs with alms to the various mosques and shrines.

"My memory is not what it used to be. I had almost forgotten that my first husband, the Lord Protector, was killed on this very day forty-seven years ago."

Mehrunnisa said nothing. The Begum sighed and

continued in a reminiscent tone, "We were on our way to Mecca at the Shahenshah's command. I was only sixteen then, and my stepson Rahim was a child of six. I thought I would never recover from that tragedy, and today I can't even recall his features clearly. Fortunately for me, my aunt Hamida Begum had me brought to Court, and my cousin married me when the prescribed period of mourning was over."

She studied Mehrunnisa intently. She saw the colour drain from her face, and marked how she sucked in her breath.

This girl was far too intelligent to pretend that she did not understand her. Sher Afghan had been dead two years now, and Mehrunnisa still wasted her youth keeping up the pretence of mourning for a husband she had never loved. Even if she was eleven years younger than Salim, she would soon be too old for anyone.

Salima Begum decided that she would summon Asmat tomorrow, and make it clear to her that this nonsense had gone on long enough.

"You know, till I became Sultana, the running of the harem and other important jobs like the arrangement of banquets, celebration of birthdays and festivals, granting of pensions and purses were in the hands of the Shahenshah's aunt Gulbadan Begum. It has always been so among us Mughals. But perhaps because I was myself a Mughal princess, the Shahenshah began entrusting me with all these tasks. And when Salim came to the throne, he continued to rely on me for the management of all zenana affairs."

"It must be trying at times," murmured Mehrunnisa politely.

"I'm much too old for all this now. But there is no one to whom I can delegate responsibility. Even if Shah Begum had lived, her haughty ways would have brought her into intense conflict with Salim's other queens and concubines. And will you believe it, Khurram's mother, the Marwar Princess, has refused, actually refused, to involve herself in what she call worthless worldly affairs!"

This made Mehrunnisa laugh. The Begum went on, "I don't think it is funny. She reserves all her strength for metaphysical disputes and attempts to explore the fifth dimension. She meditates for hours and believes that she has learnt the secret of astral travel. She even goes to the extreme of pretending that she is in direct communion with her God!"

"All her family are extremely devout, I believe," murmured Mehrunnisa.

"That is what my husband used to say. He wouldn't permit anyone to upset her, and he always maintained that she was almost as devout a mystic as her great-aunt Meera Bai. Have you ever heard the story of Akbar Shah's visit to the shrine of Eklingji in the heart of the Rana's territory to meet Meera? Yes? Ah well, he was young and headstrong then..." Salima Begum sat lost in old memories. "His guardian, Bairam Khan, often deplored his recklessness..."

Afterwards, Mehrunnisa realized that she should have kept silent and allowed the old lady to run on. But something made her exclaim, "And when the Lord Protector Bairam Khan was murdered in Gujarat, many blamed the highest person in the land!"

Salima Begum stared at the young woman in stunned disbelief. With superb self-control, she answered quietly, "They were utterly misguided, or jealous, or both."

10

Jehangir waited and hoped, and another year passed.

Tales of Mehrunnisa's virtue and piety spread throughout Hindustan, and in many languages bards sang of the strange-eyed woman kept captive by the Emperor in his castle at Agra. It made a wondrous tale, of a woman who refused a crown and repudiated a throne.

Mehrunnisa busied herself with Ladli's education and tried to drown her sorrow and suspicion in constant work. Indifferent to her parents' pleading, she drove herself to frenzied activity: embroidery, painting, writing. Soon the wives and daughters of Jehangir's courtiers were buying her delicately embroidered veils, her finely painted portraits and note sheets, her illuminated copies of fashionable poetry.

Incredulous, amazed, and outraged in turn, Jehangir found her behaviour exasperating. He wondered what mad folly compelled her to defy him and decided that he had humoured her long enough.

And then, suddenly, after four long years, Mehrunnisa found herself travelling beyond the outskirts of Agra in Salima Sultana's train. They were bound for Lahore. The Emperor planned to visit Kabul, and despite his urging, Salima Sultana had decided not to accompany him. With the Emperor in Kabul, Mehrunnisa thought she would be spared those distressing glimpses of him in the zenana at least for a few months.

The Imperial party returned to Lahore at the beginning of winter. Jehangir's new apartments were not yet ready for occupation, and Mehrunnisa heard that he was camped with his entourage in the Dilkusha gardens across the Ravi.

On the very evening of his return he determined to visit her. Asaf had warned him that it was pointless to pursue her;

his stepmother had spoken of her strong will and urged him to forget Mehrunnisa. But Jehangir had already resolved on his return journey from Kabul to confront her finally.

This time he would demand an answer directly from her. Even before he strode into the zenana eunuchs had alerted the women, and they gathered in groups on the balconies, waiting for the Emperor's appearance. With one swift word, he dismissed them and sought the apartment where Mehrunnisa was lodged.

Mehrunnisa came slowly across the courtyard. Her snowy veil swept the floor behind her; her hair, unbound, hung to her knees in black ripples. To Jehangir, her downcast eyes were brilliant gems in her pale face.

Without a word she salaamed. A tremor shook her as he stepped forward and clasped her hands. Her vision was blurred by the flash of his crimson fargal, but his ruthless amber eyes drew her gaze against her will.

"Dismiss your maids," Jehangir said. She made a sign, and instantly they were alone.

"Come." He took her hand and led the way to a small pavilion enclosed by arches, where a carpet and cushions were spread.

"Will you offer me no refreshment, daughter of Ghias Beg?" asked Jehangir, looking deep into her eyes.

"Sher Afghan's widow has nothing to offer the Badshah of Hindustan."

"Well, Mehrunnisa?" demanded Jehangir, ignoring her remark. "Didn't you understand what I told Salima Sultana, Arambanu and Asaf to convey to you? I have lost all patience with your excuses, and have come to demand an answer. You have mourned Sher Afghan long enough."

Impatience made Jehangir's voice harsh. This was the first woman to refuse him, the only woman he had always desired, and he was beginning to fear that he would lose her.

Then she heard him say in a softer tone, "I have sought you day and night, my soul's beloved. Everyone wonders at your wilfulness, and I, who am called Lord of the World, beseech you, only to be spurned with harsh words!"

Turning away, Mehrunnisa said in a trembling tone, "Sire, I beg you to cease this relentless persecution. I am a helpless, defenceless woman, imprisoned in your vast palace. I appeal to your sense of honour and justice – permit me to depart quietly to my father's house with my child."

"Why do you repudiate me? I have asked you repeatedly to marry me, to assume the veil and diadem of Empress of all Hindustan! I have not insulted you by forcing you to become my concubine. What has made you so remorseless, you who once swore eternal love?"

Mehrunnisa could hardly contain her tears. With a sudden, fretful gesture, Jehangir asked, "Is it because of your brother Mahamud's execution? That had nothing to do with us, nothing at all! Let us forget your brother. Though I grieved for your parents, who are so loyal, I could not pardon him. Do you realize that he had sworn to assassinate me?"

Mehrunnisa did not answer. Jehangir continued, holding her hand firmly in his grasp. "You were destined to be mine; you belong to me. Why then have you become a guarded citadel? Do you wish to be besieged and captured by assault? No, Mehrunnisa! You were born to rule, to receive homage, to have the treasures of this earth laid at your feet. In all fairness, at least give me a reason for your refusal."

Mehrunnisa swayed, she grew faint and would have fallen but for Jehangir's steadying arm. The mosaic floor of the pavilion blurred under her eyes as she gasped, "Sher Afghan, my husband, whom you had murdered in Bengal!"

A sob escaped her. She saw only her husband's corpse, heard anew the wailing in Dacca.

Jehangir's eyes grew furious, his ardent face grew cold.

So this was what she has believed all these years, he thought. "What makes you think so?" he demanded with careful control.

Mehrunnisa's first instinct was flight. But she knew that she could not retreat now. And he had not even bothered to deny her accusation.

"Sherrif Khan's presence when my husband was butchered by your minions. Was Sherrif Khan impelled by ambition or avarice?" she flung at him.

Anger flared again in Jehangir. "How dare you?" he shouted, turning to Mehrunnisa as though to strike her. His eyes snapped dangerously. "How dare you fling these filthy lies at me? I magnanimously forebore with Sher Afghan when he wheedled my father and married you! And why? Do you imagine it was out of concern for you? No! You were a spineless girl, afraid of my father's given word. I was helpless only because Sher Afghan had once saved my life!"

He drew a familiar ruby ring from his finger and thrust it at her. "When they brought me this, I cursed Qutub-ud-din."

"Yet the men who treacherously killed that valiant warrior went free," she said with a weary sigh.

"By the Prophet, not one of them lives!" swore Jehangir.

She was filled with nothing but vast disbelief. She leaned against a pillar and sobbed convulsively. The people called him just, and yet she knew that he was liable to passion and error, capricious in his favours and implacable in resentment. She thought of Abul Fazl, her brother, and all the others who had aroused his wrath and lost their lives.

Jehangir argued with her, stormed at her, and finally pleaded with her. She wept uncontrollably, fighting her doubts. Her mind was in turmoil, she didn't know what to think.

She looked deep into his tawny eyes, and slowly, very slowly, her fears began to recede. I believe him, she thought, amazed.

"Mehrunnisa, will you always deny me happiness?" His eyes were now sad and questioning. His fingers brushed her face. "Must I lose you forever, my love?"

Suddenly, the overwhelming realization came to her that she loved this man, and always would, no matter what he did or what the world said of him.

She knew that if she refused him now, she would never see him again. Hope and fear and wild desire surged through her as he turned to go.

"Wait, Sire!" she called in a tremulous whisper.

Jehangir turned around, read the answer in her eyes. And gently, very gently, he touched her face and began to kiss her.

Mehrunnisa awoke on her bridal day to find the world full of fragrance and light. Dozens of vases filled with her favourite roses had been placed around the room. Through the balcony of Salima Begum's private palace on the lake she looked at the soaring majesty of Hari Parbat, and smiled to herself, delighted that Jehangir had insisted on being married in Kashmir.

The day sped swiftly in various ceremonies. After the ritual bath, Mehrunnisa was escorted to a gold dais placed before a large mirror and there her sisters and sisters-in-law began to dress her in her bridal finery.

She had refused to wear the traditional crimson robes offered by Salima Begum. Instead, she had chosen a glowing yellow brocade, the colour of spring, woven with tiny pomegranates outlined in gold. Her gossamer veil, also yellow, was embroidered with pomegranate flowers. She was jewelled with rubies, aglow with them. Her high-necked robe was buttoned with ruby studs at which the women marvelled.

"Another gift from the Badshah!" exclaimed her sister Manija.

Mehrunnisa caught her mother's eye and smiled. She was tempted to tell Manija that these rubies were his first gift, had lain in their mother's jewel chest for years, and she had known nothing about them till that morning.

That morning, Mehrunnisa had also received from Salima Begum a magnificent necklace of black pearls, an heirloom of the Timurid House, always presented to the favourite wife of the reigning Mughal.

"Those pearls were first bestowed by my ancestor Timur on my great-great-grandmother and are said to possess some strange mesmeric quality. Ah! You smile, but some day you will agree with me, Mehrunnisa," the old Sultana had told her.

At Mehrunnisa's request, the Emperor had restrained himself, and agreed to a quiet ceremony at which only her immediate family and his sisters Arambanu and Khanum Sultana would be present. Salima Begum had insisted that the wedding itself be held at her palace, and only the wedding banquet in Mirza Ghias Beg's garden on the Jhelum.

But no one had been able to restrain Jehangir's wedding gifts to Mehrunnisa, which included eighty lakh asharfis in gold, five hundred sumptuous costumes, necklaces of priceless pearls, chokers set with diamonds, rubies and emeralds, countless other ornaments and perfume flagons, bags of musk and ambergris, massive bracelets and anklets encrusted with precious stones, glowing shahtush shawls, slippers embroidered with seed pearls, stacks of khinkhab and atlas silk, muslin and cloth-of-gold.

Mehrunnisa smiled when Sherrif handed her firmans bestowing on her Rampur, Kanauj, and Kandahar, her birthplace, in jagir.

Jehangir had also sent her elephants and horses and palanquins with enamelled gold handles. And she became the first woman ever to hold the command of thirty thousand troops.

At the auspicious hour appointed by the Court astrologers, Jehangir arrived with his friends and waited with growing impatience for his bride to appear in the flower-decked balcony.

Garlands of jasmines, roses, and pearls hid Mehrunnisa from his piercing gaze. The music ceased and the ceremony began.

When he heard her low response to the kazi's question, Jehangir's elation soared. For him this was an end and a beginning. An unknown peace filled his heart, and he looked forward with keen anticipation to renewing his interrupted love.

The dance would go on for a long time. The garden with its multicoloured lanterns, soaring fireworks and splashing fountains was like Jannat itself, murmured the guests. A spectacular banquet was in progress, conducted with infinite dignity and taste by Mirza Ghias Beg to celebrate his daughter's nuptials.

Beyond all sound of revelry stood a marble pavilion on the edge of the river Jhelum. To this the Emperor's sisters led Mehrunnisa. With laughter and arch remarks, they brought her into the fragrant flower-filled bridal chamber, and left her alone.

While she watched the flickering flames of the perfumed candles, Jehangir came in and for a long time stood silently gazing at her. She trembled, and shut her eyes for a moment before meeting his amber gaze steadily.

She woke next morning, to watch from his arms, the sun rise over snowcapped mountains. Jehangir gazed ardently at her and buried his face in her hair.

"Mehrunnisa."

"My Lord?"

"The sun seems pale compared to your bewitching radiance. I shall call you Nurmahal, Light of the Palace."

Her long reign had begun...

impatience for his bride to appear on the flower-decked balcony.

Garlands of jasmines, roses, and pearls hid Mehrunnisa from his piercing gaze. The mullah arrived and the ceremony began.

When he heard her low response to the kazi's question, Jehangir's elation soared. For him this was an end and a beginning. An unknown peace filled his heart and he looked forward with keen anticipation to renewing his interrupted love.

The dance would go on for a long time. The garden with its multicoloured lanterns, soaring fireworks and splashing fountains was like Jannat itself, murmured the guests. A spectacular banquet was in progress, conducted with infinite dignity and taste by Mirza Ghias Beg to celebrate his daughter's nuptials.

Beyond all sound of revelry stood a marble pavilion on the edge of the river Jhelum. To this the entourage escorted Mehrunnisa. With laughter and arch remarks they brought her into the fragrant flower-filled bridal chamber and left her alone.

While she watched the flickering flames of the perfumed candles, Jehangir came in and for a long time stood silently gazing at her. She trembled and shut her eyes for a moment before meeting his ardent gaze steadily.

She woke next morning, to watch from his arms, the sun rise over snow-capped mountains. Jehangir gazed ardently at her and buried his face in her hair.

"Mehrunnisa."

"My Lord?"

"The sun seems pale compared to your new shining radiance. I shall call you Nurjahan, Light of the Palace."

Her long reign had begun.

Nurjahan

1

Ladli sat talking to Prince Khurram beneath the spreading branches of a mango tree.

Bright-plumaged birds twittered through the garden, peacocks strutted across the lawns, trailing pure white feathers along the green grass. Little slave girls ran about, shooing them away from flower beds.

Ladli's young mind had lately become obsessed by thoughts of her father and the manner of his death. She had overheard whispered conversations between zenana women, and doubts about her mother's version of the horrific story were beginning to assail her. Khurram was in an affable mood today. Perhaps he would answer her forthright questions without turning pale or walking away.

"Tell me, Prince, how did my father die in Bengal?" she asked, sullen suspicion on her wistful, heartshaped face.

Surprised at her abrupt manner, Khurram paused. "Surely your mother the Empress has told you something?"

Ladli nodded. What her mother had actually said was that she must forget all that and learn to behave like a Mughal princess now.

"My father... was he brave?"

"Yes, he was. The tallest and most fearless man in Hindustan, Raja Maan Singh always says."

"Do you remember him?" she asked eagerly.

"As if I had this moment seen him striding across the courtyard at Agra, ready to mount his horse and ride away to war. He once killed a tiger with a single sword stroke, thus saving my father's life. That was when my grandfather Akbar Shah gave him the jagir of Burdwan."

Her long grey eyes brightened for a moment, but again

she grew pensive. Ladli's mind went quickly over the entire course of happenings; how her father had been murdered, how her mother had been brought to Agra and how she had held the Emperor off for four long years while yet living within the Mughal zenana, till at last the Emperor had made her widowed mother his Empress, calling her first Nurmahal and then, inevitably, Nurjahan – Light of the World. Would she ever learn the truth about her father, she wondered.

She was about to say something but the words died unspoken. Ladli saw the Emperor approaching with her mother by his side. Rising, she salaamed and stood with bowed head and folded hands before him. He raised her chin with his forefinger, and playfully pinched her cheek. She blushed and tried to move away.

Nurjahan talked affably with Khurram while Ladli tried to compose herself.

Flinging an arm affectionately round his son, Jehangir asked, "And what were you discussing so seriously with Ladli?"

"This girl," said Khurram with a twinkle in his enormous black Rathor eyes, "asks the most impossible questions." Ladli threw him an outraged glance.

They chatted for a while, then the Emperor passed on to another group of girls, his daughters and nieces, while Nurjahan sat on the edge of a marble pool, and called to her women to bring puffed rice for the gold fish.

Khurram drew his stepsister down on the bench and resumed their conversation. Ladli and Khurram were great friends. She remembered the day when she had slipped and fallen on the marble steps at some zenana function. Her mother had been in disgrace then; she used to earn a living by selling her embroidery to wealthy noblewomen. Khurram had helped her up while others had laughed, and she could never forget his kindness on that and several other occasions.

And now she was the Emperor's adopted daughter. He

had given his solemn word to her mother that Ladli would one day marry his heir. But at fourteen she was already beginning to love Khurram, her stepfather's devastatingly attractive and interesting third son, and cared nothing about the imprisoned Crown Prince, Khusro.

"What a strange little creature you are, Ladli," remarked Khurram, studying her face intently. "So pensive and timid and scared. What do you fear in the Grand Mughal's palace?"

"Only you," she whispered.

Khurram's eyes widened with astonishment. "I would never hurt you, little sister," he said in a low indulgent tone.

Khurram knew that Ladli's position in the Mughal zenana was not enviable. Being Nurjahan's daughter, she enjoyed the privileges of a Mughal princess, but his own sisters and cousins detested her. They dared not slight or insult Nurjahan, who controlled everything in the zenana, but on Ladli they wreaked subtle vengeance.

Once they had invited her to a garden party and failed to turn up themselves. They were constantly saying unkind things about her appearance or manners in the hearing of their waiting women; they ignored her at Court functions and often forbade their companions from speaking to the lonely young girl. So Khurram indulged her and laughed at her whims.

After a while, an eunuch came to summon the Prince, and Ladli went indoors.

From a window, upstairs she watched the constant activity in the forecourt of the castle of Lahore. People were arriving and departing; there was the clatter of horses and tinkling of bells as the nobles descended from caparisoned elephants. She saw farashes scurrying up and down the corridors, and great amirs and rajas waiting patiently at the portal of the Emperor's apartment for an audience. There was a commotion when her grandfather Mirza Ghias Beg arrived, accompanied by his sons. And she could feel the eternal sense of urgency as messengers rode in from the four corners of the empire with news.

There was never a moment of peace here, mused Ladli. The afternoon would be enlivened by military reviews, combats between elephants, and sport with dogs, cheetahs or bears. At night there would be a banquet with music, dancing and fireworks.

Ladli realized that over everyone and everything lay the spell of her mother's magic smile and gracious ways. Sometimes she wondered at her seemingly fragile mother's boundless energy. She spent her mornings interviewing the Imperial stewards and granting audience to the ministers and generals who thronged the Court, talking to one about the sad state of the irrigation canals between Firozpur and Agra, rebuking another for the shocking condition of some provincial palace she had just visited; listening patiently as a list of promotions in the army was read to her; advising on some case of justice brought before the Emperor's Court. Jewellers and artists and craftsmen incessantly sought her patronage; poets and writers would submit their works to her for her verdict.

In the forenoon, a majlis would be held in the zenana at which the women could approach her for favours or recount all the news. Supplicants never went away empty-handed from her palace; no widow or orphan left without a pension or promise of help.

Ladli could not help admiring the efficiency and tact with which her mother had undertaken the education of indigent noblemen's daughters. The reputation of her private academy had spread throughout Hindustan, and very soon haughty Rajput and Mughal princes were petitioning her to accept their own children as her wards.

She had watched, fascinated, as her mother renovated palace after palace, adding exquisite light touches to the heavy, ornate apartments favoured by the old emperor, Akbar

Shah. She had watched her mother design the enamelled tile panelling which covered the walls of Lahore fort with lively scenes of elephant-fights interspersed with mosaic floral panels. And the majestic Badshahi Mosque in the bazaar with its red sandstone and white marble inlay work, which had launched a new trend. Ladli knew just as well as the Emperor that Begum Nurjahan had designed the zodiac series of gold coins commemorating the seventh year of Badshah Jehangir's reign. There were elaborate plans afoot for redecorating the forts of Agra and Kabul; workmen laboured frenziedly to complete her mother's private pavilion at Agra before they returned in October.

That summer in Kashmir, her mother had launched a fresh revival of Persian fashions. One evening she had appeared at a banquet with a small velvet cap encrusted with jewels and decorated with heron plumes. The very next day the Emperor's other wives had ordered similar caps. As soon as a thing became fashionable, the Empress would discard it, only to bring something new into vogue. It was she who, with her perfect figure and flawless creamy skin, first robed herself entirely in embroidered white muslin, which made her seem almost ethereal, and launched a rage.

But her mother's influence, Ladli reflected, did not end with fashion and patronage. Her name was stamped on all the new coins; no firman was issued without her seal and signature. Ladli had once heard her stepfather say jovially to her uncle Asaf, "I have sold the crown of Hindustan to Nurjahan for a cup of wine and a piece of kebab; she may do as she likes with it!"

There were many who whispered about her mother's strange, mesmeric hold over the Emperor. Ladli recalled a poem she had read recently, one of Meera Bai's devotional songs:

"Kanha have I bought.
The price he asked I gave.
Some cry, 'tis great, and others jeer 'tis small.
I gave in full, weighed to the utmost grain
My love, my life, myself, my soul, my all!"

Kanha, Ladli knew, was the shepherd-god worshipped by the Hindus. And she believed that her mother's love for her stepfather had traits of a similar idolatry.

She felt insecure, lonely, and bereft. Her wonderful father was dead, and she had lost her mother to the Emperor.

That year Nurjahan decided to hold the Meena Bazaar in her own private garden at Lahore. This was laid out amidst sparkling canals and splashing fountains, enclosed by towering trees and intricately carved pavilions with elaborate balconies and marble terraces. Peacocks preened on sun-warmed domes and kiosks, and the flower beds swelled with glorious roses, and rare purple iris, even tulips, which Nurjahan had procured through the Persian Ambassador.

Merchants from many lands had gathered with magnificent wares to tempt the ladies of the Mughal Court. The secluded harem women would indulge in an orgy of buying and spending, and eagerly anticipate the Emperor's visit to the Bazaar.

The garden was full of laughing, gossiping women on that pleasant March morning; they seemed to form an intrinsic part of the lovely landscape. Brilliant-hued veils draped proud heads, skirts swirled amidst the rich warm colours of the flowers and sunlight sparkled on gold and jewels.

When Begum Nurjahan arrived, surrounded by her retinue, everyone turned to greet her. The women became increasingly aware of her incomparable charm as she passed from group to group and spoke graciously to everyone. She halted where patterned silks, velvets and brocades were flung enticingly.

Her niece Arjumand, Asaf's daughter, was hesitating between a sky-blue velvet and a richly striped crimson atlas silk from Samarkand.

"Buy the crimson atlas," advised Nurjahan. "It goes better with your hazel eyes and lovely rich colouring. Wait! I'll make you a gift of it, with that little matching brocade basque and gold-fringed veil. You must wear them when I see you next."

Arjumand smiled gratefully, a dimple emphasizing her right cheek. Nurjahan passed on, happy in the knowledge that she had given her favourite niece pleasure. There came the sound of male voices and laughter, and she looked towards the arched gateway, through which Jehangir entered the garden. He was surrounded by his sons and nephews and followed by the young eunuchs who carried aloft his gem-encrusted umbrella, with the inevitable cheetahs at his heels.

As they performed the ceremony of greeting, the women grew more animated. The presence of so many men in the garden added romantic insinuations to the frolic of the Meena Bazaar, as Nurjahan well knew.

Women flitted from shop to shop, finding a welcome relief from the tedium of household affairs and young girls coaxed money out of indulgent mothers. The exhilarating scents of the garden mingled with the perfumes they wore, and made them all slightly giddy.

Under gaily striped awnings and patterned canopies were spread rugs piled with a profuse variety of goods. A ceaseless babble of voices rose as the white-bearded merchants sought to attract the noble ladies with tales of distant places from where their merchandise had come. Year after year these old men brought their wares to the Meena Bazaar. They had their regular customers amongst the women, and they knew that a well-told tale could charm them into buying almost anything.

Each stall was unique. There were colourful birds in gilded cages, strings of bangles and gold lace strung up to catch the sunlight. Velvets and muslins, silks and brocades, and gossamer Benaras tissue veils; fringes and tassels to brighten costumes or cushions. Odoriferous drugs, unguents, powdered henna, incense sticks, perfumes and scented oils. Herbs and spices, pendants and amulets concealing magic scrolls from holy shrines. Dangling girdles to encircle dainty waists, tinkling anklets and toe rings for the feet of zenana houris. A profusion of jewels and pearls; glittering silver-ware and gold goblets. Enamelled candlesticks, mirrors, combs and curio boxes; inkstands, feathered quills, fans made of ostrich and peacock feathers. Figurines of sandalwood, ivory and jade; vases made of precious metals, toys and dolls and musical boxes; glass, crystal and porcelain. Slippers of every size and shape, made of velvet or brocade. An astonishing variety of fruit, dates, figs and nuts. A sweetmeat stall and a paan shop, another selling bottled sherbats and essences; all of them hung with flower garlands and silk bunting, all crowded with fashionably dressed women bargaining zestfully.

Twenty-year old Khurram was enjoying himself immensely. He was beginning to acquire a reputation with women, and many were the glances cast at him by unattached girls. He caught within the veils the glow of dark eyes, and within the eyes, mysterious promises with which he was already too familiar.

The Mughal princes were mingling with the horde of lovely young girls, vying with each other in cajoling some of them into romantic attachments which might lead to secret correspondence, exchanges of gifts and trysts in private places. Nurjahan meanwhile had joined her husband, and was conducting him around the stalls.

"Isn't she lovely?" whispered Gulabi, who had recently returned from Gujarat, where her husband Zaffar had been serving as Governor. "Did you ever imagine that our delightfully capricious childhood friend Mehrunnisa would become that rare, formidable creature, a perfect queen? But tell me, why are we still at Lahore? Has she told you when she intends returning to Agra?"

"Oh well," shrugged Laila, critically appraising Gulabi's toilet and deciding complacently that her own sapphire satin costume was in infinitely better taste. "I don't know how long we'll stay here. This has always been her favourite city. She says that Agra belongs to Akbar Shah; he's all over the place!" Laila laughed meaningfully.

"Just look at her!" exclaimed Gulabi, "I can swear she has never seen those two provincial women before. They travelled up with us from Gujarat, and have never been at Court. Yet Begum Nurjahan is talking to them as though she knows their family, their province and their husbands perfectly well."

"That's how she has acquired a vast following. She invites the wives and daughters of all the vassals to her receptions and treats everyone with courteous affability. They return home laden with gifts and goodwill, and my husband often says jokingly that this country is being run on women's gossip..."

"I hear she has not yet despaired of being with child by him," interrupted Gulabi in a confident undertone.

After a thoughtful pause, Laila said, "People don't realize it, but Begum Nurjahan's greatest quality is to recognize and accept reality. She knows that she will never bear children again. All she cares about is him."

Gulabi wasn't really paying attention to Laila. Her eyes were fixed on Aasf's eldest daughter Arjumand. "That girl is much too lovely to remain unnoticed by these insatiable Mughals," she remarked. After a while she gasped, nudged Laila, and whispered, "Oh, no! Do you see what I see?"

Arjumand was standing before a shop where many rare objects were displayed. She picked up a crystal ball inside which a kaleidoscope of forms and colour whirled. Discarding it, she bought a pair of peacocks made of enamelled gold and lapis lazuli, with cunningly concealed springs to make them dance. Then her eyes fell on a wine cup of purest white jade, its edges fluted, and the handle shaped like a ram's head.

"How much?" she asked the dealer, thinking that it would make an excellent gift for her grandfather, whom she adored.

"Seventy-five gold mohurs."

Calculating swiftly, she realized that was all the money she had left. Arjumand tossed him her purse and stretched out her hand for the cup. Just then someone else grasped it firmly. Both hands drew back and Arjumand looked up into the face of Jehangir's third son.

"Forgive my discourtesy. It seems that we both desire the same thing. No matter, please keep it." Khurram spoke with delightful haughtiness.

Though her pulse raced, Arjumand answered with perfect composure, "You may have it, Prince. I only wanted it as a gift for my grandfather."

Khurram discovered that the girl standing before him had a beauty all her own, not vivid or vivacious but full of gentle grace. A luminous serenity seemed to enwrap her, giving her a tranquil dignity far beyond her years. Her veil had blown off her head and she wore a plain gold nose ring from which dangled a single flawless pearl, and he noticed that her bare feet were not painted with henna. "An unwed maid, by Allah!" thought Khurram.

"And who is your grandfather, fair one?"

But Arjumand had already turned and fled, leaving the cup and forgetting her purse in her haste.

"Princess!" cried the merchant. "Your purchase."

"Here, give it to me," commended Khurram, flinging him a gold coin. "I'll see she gets it."

The Prince saw her talking to Ladli at the bookstall, but as he approached them, she slipped away, losing herself in a crowd of women.

Ladli showed him an illuminated folio of poems. "Malik Mohammed Jaisi's *Padmavat*," she exclaimed with animated eyes. "I've been wanting it for such a long time."

"Let me buy it for you." Then he asked as casually as he could, "That girl in the violet costume you were talking to. Who is she?"

Ladli raised her eyebrows in amazement. "You mean you don't know? Why, that's Arjumand, my uncle Asaf's eldest daughter!"

"My thanks!" he cried, and hastened away.

Khurram finally caught up with Arjumand on the terrace. "This is yours, I think," said the Prince with a look that she could neither ignore nor mistake.

Her pulse quickened as she took the cup from him. For a long while they stood motionless, their glances interlocked.

At that moment, Jehangir saw them from a pavilion where he sat sipping wine. "Nurjahan, the men of my family seem to have a pronounced weakness for the girls of your house!"

She glanced towards her niece and stepson, smiled, and wondered if anything could be gained from Khurram's obvious interest in her bewitchingly beautiful niece, Arjumand. Nurjahan reminded herself that the prince was already married to Mirza Abdur Rahim Khan-in-Khanan's granddaughter Kandahari, who was also related to half the Mughal grandees, including Aziz Koka. But she would see what her father the Grand Vezzir thought of another Mughal alliance, decided Nurjahan.

Jehangir smiled knowingly at her. Very often they could read each other's thoughts, and though it was thrilling to communicate so perfectly, it could also be disconcerting at times, felt Nurjahan. But already her mind was busy with plans.

Ladli followed Khurram with her eyes. She had seen him accosting Arjumand, seen them standing on the terrace. With an expression of frozen melancholy on her face, she thought, Khurram would remain just another stepbrother.

2

Stepping into her hammamgah, Nurjahan closed her eyes, and with a sigh of deep contentment inhaled the aroma of roses filling the small chamber. Every day, huge baskets of freshly gathered roses were sent to her palace to scent her bath water, and their heady fragrance never ceased to thrill her.

She kicked off her slippers, and a maid stepped forward to disrobe her. Nurjahan surrendered her body to the expert waiting women. While she sat before a mirror, draped in a soft towel, they massaged her head with scented almond oil to keep her hair glossy and black. Then the women conducted her to an alabaster bench beside the sunken bath. She allowed her old nurse, Dil Aram, to massage her whole body with an unguent of almonds ground in milk and liberally scented with saffron. Dil Aram rubbed the pale orange paste slowly over her whole body. Nurjahan relaxed and allowed herself to become limp under the experienced hands of her nurse.

Daylight had no access to this cool marble chamber. In the centre were great basins of jasper into which running water fell from a fountain built into the wall. Thousands of tiny mirrors gleamed on the ceiling like diamonds in the darkness, reflecting the light of numerous tiny lamps burning in niches. All the lights and mirrors cast a pearly sheen upon Nurjahan's translucent skin.

Unlike the other Mughal queens, she refused to conduct interviews or listen to petitions while at her bath. "Bathing is much too private. I use that time for refreshing my body and mind," she had told her ladies, indifferent to protests.

The women poured water on her and washed the almond paste away. Then they shampooed her hair with a special mixture prepared from pounded amlas and soap-berries. They helped Nurjahan into her rose-filled pool, and she floated pleasurably in the warm scented water, sensuously rubbing the rose-petals over her face and bosom.

She had craved luxuries from those early days, when she first glimpsed the splendour of Bilquis Begum's apartment, but on her terms. Now she surrounded herself with a degree of splendour and opulence unequalled by any other Mughal queen. All the resources of a vast empire were at her command, and she had the flair to use them to the greatest advantage. She guarded her beauty like a precious jewel, spending hours lavishing fastidious care on herself before facing the world.

As she stepped out of her bath, permitting her women to dry and robe her, Sherrif's wife Laila entered and informed her that the widows and orphans were assembled in the courtyard to receive alms.

Nurjahan glanced with approval at her friend's elaborate costume. "That shade of pink becomes you, Laila. Why don't you wear it more often? I shall come down as soon as I'm dressed."

Laila helped her to the bench and threw a thick shawl over her shoulders. Dil Aram rubbed Nurjahan's hair and held it over a brazier burning incense, until her hair was completely dry and lay in shimmering waves down her back.

She stood still as Laila tied the tassels of her backless bodice and slipped a delicately embroidered salmon satin kamiz over her head.

Adjusting the long tight sleeves, Nurjahan said, "Remind me to speak to Khurram about finding a place in his entourage for your eldest son, Laila. He cannot spend his entire life playing chess with the Badshah."

"Nothing would give me greater happiness than to see my sons creditably employed," said Laila, arranging the veil over Nurjahan's shoulders.

Just then Gulabi bustled into the chamber and said,

"Gracious One, the betrothal gifts are arranged in the antechamber."

"My thanks," smiled Nurjahan. "I shall see them before proceeding to my father's house for the ceremony. I hope you haven't forgotten that amethyst and diamond choker which Arjumand admired so much."

"Nothing has been forgotten, and everything arranged in a way calculated to please the most critical eye," Gulabi assured her with a quick gesture.

Nurjahan laughed and countered, "Well, you could scarcely call my father or brothers critical, but if you are hinting at my fussy sister-in-law, you are quite right!"

Dil Aram frowned her disapproval, but relented when she remembered that her mistress, Laila, Gulabi and Ayesha had all been girls together in Bilquis Begum's palace long before her mistress became Empress and Ayesha had married Asaf.

Guessing her nurse's thoughts, Nurjahan turned to her affectionately. "You must put on your festive robes, dearest nurse, for you shall accompany me this afternoon to watch Arjumand's betrothal ceremony." And gathering the folds of her veil around her, she walked out. A smaller chamber adjoining her bedroom contained the arched mihrab facing Mecca, with beautiful emerald and lapis lazuli calligraphy extolling the ninety nine names of Allah. Her treasured hand-illuminated Koran lay wrapt in blue velvet on an ornate ebony and mother-of-pearl book stand. Tucking the prayer veil correctly over her forehead and arms, she lit the precious agar and the scented candles. Sinking to her knees in all humility, Nurjahan did sajdah to her Creator, prayed earnestly with upraised palms, took up her specially blessed amber prayer beads and silently chanted the secret incantation taught to her by a famous dervesh.

After performing her devotions and distributing alms, Nurjahan sat down at her dressing table. A strong fragrance of attar of roses permeated the air. One of her ladies combed and plaited her long black hair and set a delicately designed jewelled head-ornament aslant over her head so that the teardrop pearls fell over her right brow. Another screwed diamond-studded gold anklets round her feet. Gulabi stood ready with the shimmering shawl she would throw over her costume.

She had dressed with extra care today. There was to be a grand banquet at her father's house for Khurram's reception. He had just returned from Khandesh, and Arjumand's betrothal ceremony was also to be held that day.

She wanted them all to see that though Arjumand was young enough to be her daughter, it was she, the older woman, who looked more beautiful and could charm without effort. She had invited some of the reputed beauties of Agra to share with her the delightful duty of entertaining the Emperor and his sons. She was no longer afraid of losing him, no longer unsure of her own allure.

Two years of marriage had been enough to make her realize that the demanding lover she had married was too indolent a man to bother much about his patrimony. If the country was going to be ruled, it would be ruled either by Khurram or Perveiz, with the aid of the scheming, unscrupulous men who thronged the Court.

Very early during their marriage, she had decided that she would not allow her stepsons to grasp all the power. She had begun making decisions when he was too drunk or indisposed to concentrate on affairs of state, and very soon he had escaped from the tedium of day-to-day administration by entrusting more and more responsibility to her.

All those who expected promotion or patronage had begun turning to her, and her father and brothers had begun to enjoy more prestige and influence than the Mughal princes themselves. The haughty nobles found themselves deferring in all matters to the imperious Begum, and throughout the country, her will was law.

She was troubled only by fears for his health when he refused to give up opium. Only yesterday when she had tried cajoling her husband with his welfare uppermost in her mind, Jehangir had retorted: "Nurjahan, I flavour my existence with opium just as you flavour yours with power. Opium eases pain, soothes fatigue, provides instant energy, enhances potency... and induces blessed sleep!"

When Nurjahan murmured involuntary protest at this lecture, he continued, twinkling, "Its use is sanctified in Hindustan by the very gods! Its medicinal and therapeutic value has been proved over the centuries by Ayurvedic and Irani doctors. The opium poppy is a universal healer. It should be worshipped as a magical plant!"

"You forgot the Unanis – the Greco-Roman doctors. They commend it too," she riposted, abandoning the struggle with a sigh – for the moment.

The preparations for Khurram's betrothal turned her thoughts to the only person in Hindustan who would not bow to her will. She had often hinted and cajoled, but the Emperor's eldest son had not agreed to wed her daughter Ladli.

It had been reported to her that on hearing of her plan, Khusro had jeered, "What! Marry Begum Nurjahan's daughter, and turn myself into another of her puppets? I have some hope of escaping from this prison; but that woman would imprison my mind and soul."

Well, he needed to learn that she was not to be denied her least whim; whoever did so would find life uncomfortable. Some day, Khusro would have to change his mind. And Ladli was still so young, reflected Nurjahan, there was time enough to settle her betrothal. Meanwhile, she was thankful that there was no opposition to the match between her stepson and her niece. Even Khurram's mother, that haughty indifferent princess, had been charmed by Arjumand's shy grace. Besides, it suited her plans so well to bind Khurram to her own family by this alliance.

As her palanquin was set down in the portico of her father's palace, she thought once more that her happiness would have been complete if only she could have simultaneously announced Ladli's betrothal to the Crown Prince.

3

When the annual rains made the Aravalli hills green, and filled the lakes of the Rana's land to overflowing, Prince Khurram pitched his camp under the shadow of Chittor, intent on the subjugation of Mewar.

The Emperor's orders had been explicit: the people had to be won over somehow into accepting the sovereignty of the Mughals. Khurram felt that the Rana and his followers were behaving in a foolhardy manner, and wondered how the ruler of a small principality expected to win an armed conflict with Mughal might.

In this age and time it was not possible for any prince to keep aloof from the mainstream of Hindustani politics. Yet many at Court took secret pride in the chivalry of Mewar and applauded the decision of a race to maintain its independence, no matter how high the cost.

The Prince conceded to Arjumand that Rana Amar Singh and his followers were gallant foes, but in the interest of national solidarity, they could not be allowed to remain outside the hegemony of the Mughals. Mewar was rich and fertile, though the long-drawn-out struggle with Akbar Shah had weakened her resources. Yet here, Khurram felt, was material for great generals and statesmen. Once Mewar surrendered, the undoubted talent of her rulers could be put to creative use.

He was amused to find his wife openly championing the Rana's cause. "They have been sovereign princes for centuries, haven't they?" she argued with quiet authority. "What right have we to force them into a treaty unwillingly?"

Khurram had never guessed that his young bride possessed such keen political perception. But after all, she was the daughter of one of the most gifted ministers of the realm, and the grand-daughter of Ghias Beg, that sagacious and liberal statesman.

For the duration of this campaign, Khurram's household was lodged in the hill fortress of Kumbhalgarh. Built by Rana Kumbha in the heyday of Mewar's glory, it was one of the most strategically important and historically famous castles in Hindustan.

From the lofty towers of this really rather shabby and cramped fortress, Arjumand gazed down upon the far more interesting valley strewn with lakes, ancient monuments, and thick jungles full of tiger, panther, leopard, bear and antelope. Eagles flew over the wooded hills fading into a smoky sky.

Across the slate grey hillocks lay the famous marble shrine of Ranakpur, with its lovely statues and carved pillars said to rival those of the Jain temples at Abu and Dilwara. She would enjoy exploring all these new places, but the continuing hostilities between the Mughals and Mewar made such trips dangerous.

She was sick of being cooped up in the palace set apart for her use, tired of walking daily in the same small garden, mediocre beyond belief, though doubtless once the pride of some long-dead Rajput queen. She missed the artistically designed pavilions, terraces, fountains, paved walks and formal flower beds which she had known since childhood. Arjumand pined for her own family, for the space and luxury of the Mughal gardens at Agra and Lahore, for the endless round of Court pleasures.

A plan occurred to her, and she sent one of her maids to summon Satiunnisa Khanum, her inseparable companion and confidante, to whom her aunt Begum Nurjahan had entrusted the charge of the entire household.

"What is it, Princess?" asked Satiunnisa. "I've been busy unpacking your bridal chests which have arrived from Agra at last. Just in time, too. The rain and damp might have damaged everything. Though now I am beginning to wonder if it was worthwhile, having all those things brought to Mewar. Who except your own waiting-women will appreciate your wardrobe in this castle, where nothing ever happens, and no fetes are held? I wish we had gone to Kabul and Kandahar with Begum Nurjahan. The Mughal princesses themselves would have envied you your dowry!"

Arjumand laughed at her voluble friend. "I've got a delightful surprise for you. We are going to spend the whole day diverting ourselves in the little grove by that lake down in the valley. I find Kumbhalgarh particularly depressing today, and nothing amuses me."

Satiunnisa's intelligent, good-humoured face softened. "That's scarcely surprising since the Prince is away. You haven't yet learnt to reconcile yourself to a warrior's ways. The lure of battle, cravings for the crown of victory, which woman can compete with these?"

Arjumand smiled and dispatched Satiunnisa off to supervise the packing of food. As Satiunnisa stood directing the kitchen maids, she felt a vague misgiving in her mind. Would the Prince have permitted his bride to venture so far from the castle? But if he were here, he would be devoting his days to diverting Arjumand and they would doubtless be out hunting, hawking, bathing, or simply exploring the countryside.

Arjumand's words had sent a flutter of excitement through her suite, which was composed mostly of young matrons or unmarried girls of her own age. They were all delighted at the prospect of an outing.

Arjumand sat on a boulder beside the lake, dangling her shapely fair feet in the water, humming to herself while engrossed in thoughts of her husband. Scented oleanders, huge tamarinds, banyan, neem, intoxicating mahuwa, wild fig and clusters of yellow flowering shrubs covered the banks of the lake. Peacocks and ringdoves welcomed the clouds with their cries. Down the narrow defile of the gorge leading out of the valley came a herd of spotted deer to drink at the lake.

Suddenly, a shadow startled her and she looked around to see two swarthy soldiers standing behind her with drawn swords.

Instinctively she covered her face, a swift anger rising in her at the audacity of her bodyguards to come upon her thus. She was about to order them off, when she noticed their saffron turbans and dark, arrogant eyes. A sudden suspicion flared in her mind, and she glanced around and saw that her escort was nowhere in sight. Her women appeared stunned and frightened, and some stood weeping hysterically.

Her dazed disbelief gave way to fright. The realization came to her all at once that she was helpless in the power of this hostile band. No one would ride to her aid because no one in the castle of Kumabhalgarh would imagine that the Rana's warriors had dared appear so close to Prince Khurram's camp.

She determined to brave it out, ignoring their spears and daggers.

"Since when have Rajputs made war on women?" The taunt had its effect, for she could see their leader wince.

He hastened to protest, "We mean you no harm! But I'm taking you captive to the Rana, my master. He will fix your ransom with the Prince."

"Do you imagine the Prince would care if you kidnapped me?" Arjumand asked, playing for time while her mind raced and she wondered how she could extricate herself and her women from this predicament.

The warrior smiled wryly. "He will not refuse. Surely Prince Khurram will give up anything rather than bear separation from his bride, the beloved niece of Nurjahan Begum."

So he knew her identity, and had waited in ambush for

her to walk into his trap, followed Arjumand. This meant there were spies in her own household, or at least in the castle of Kumbhalgadh, who kept the enemy informed of her movements. She would deal with them later. The immediate problem was to evade capture. She was on the verge of argument when she read the relentless purpose in his eyes: he wouldn't listen to her. But as long as she did their bidding, she and her companions would be safe. If only she could summon her escort...

"Your escort is powerless to protect you, Princess. They have already been dealt with as they deserve," said her captor, as though guessing her thoughts.

He ordered Satiunnisa to blindfold her mistress and forced them to enter a palanquin. "We will let the other women go free after we have been gone an hour. No one will be able to find our trail even if they give the alarm at the castle."

Arjumand could hear her women shrieking and moaning hysterically while her palanquin was carried away.

"That's what comes of self-indulgence!" wept Satiunnisa. "And what are they going to do to us, Princess?"

"Nothing," answered Arjumand and tried to pacify her friend. "Don't be afraid. Think of it as an adventure you can narrate once we are back safely in Agra."

"Don't joke, Princess. Aren't you afraid?"

"I was at first. But then I grew angry and now my anger has turned to admiration. You must agree that these are desperately courageous men. How my aunt will laugh at this tale!"

Sadunnisa sighed. "Let us pray that we return alive to Agra. Do you realize that we may never see the Empress again?"

They endured slow, jolting travel before the palki-bearers stopped and a voice, which she presumed belonged to the man who had organized the kidnapping, commanded, "Open to Himmat Singh Hara!"

The great spiked gates of the small fortress flew open, and the party of sixteen mounted men escorting the palanquin passed into the secret retreat of Rana Amar Singh.

Immediately, Arjumand and her companion were ushered into the Rana's presence. When the Rana heard Himmat Singh's tale he swore with indignation. "You fool! Have you forgotten that for untold centuries, we have consigned our women to the flames rather than let them fall prey to the enemy, and honoured the wives and daughters of every other race? How did you dare capture Prince Khurram's bride? Himmat Singh, this infamous deed of yours will put the mark of shame on my forehead!"

Unabashed, Himmat Singh firmly declared, "I did what I thought was my duty, Sire. I meant no harm or insult to the Begum. I was thinking only of you. For thirty years your family and mine have shed their blood for the freedom of Mewar! Now I have brought you the key to Chittor. The Badshah himself will agree to exchange her for Chittor."

"Himmat Singh, you are a good warrior, but a poor strategist. I will deal with you later. Now summon Karan Singh," commanded the Rana.

Himmat Singh went out shamefaced, and a little later the Rana's short, stocky heir strode into the hall, "Your commands, Father?"

He stopped in mid-stride and breathed in sharply. Before him stood the loveliest woman, Hindu or Muslim, that he had ever seen in all his life. Her gossamer veil could not dim the brilliance of her eyes or the sheen of her fair skin. Who was this gorgeously arrayed beauty? Obviously a Muslim of noble lineage. What was she doing in his father's council hall, wondered Karan Singh.

He was amazed at her serene bearing and dignified reserve. After the Rana had spoken, she uttered no threats or recriminations, but requested him in firm accents to arrange for her immediate return to Kumbhalgarh.

Karan Singh exclaimed impetuously, “Princess, forgive the folly and discourtesy of our men. It is late and the jungle path treacherous. Rest under our humble roof tonight. Tomorrow, I will escort you back to your husband.”

Next morning, with beating drums and flying banners, Prince Karan Singh of Mewar escorted Arjumand back to Kumbhalgarh. He was received outside by Khurram, who had just returned from Chittor.

What they said to each other, no one knew. But after that first meeting, each was convinced that he had found his soul’s brother. And so began the incredible friendship between the Rana’s heir and Jehangir’s son.

4

On his return to Ajmer, Khurram found that his stepmother had commenced building pavilions and gardens on the bank of Anna Sagar, and had run into difficulties over the question of canals.

A few days later, she took him on a tour of inspection, and Khurram praised everything he saw. Already, many fruit trees had been planted, paths paved, flower beds made ready to receive the winter seed. The high embankment she had commissioned was dominated by a broad terrace and a colonnaded arcade, which connected two marble pavilions roofed with glazed Persian tiles. It was embellished inside by inlay work in pietra dura. Khurram knew she was partial to this stylized Persian decorative form.

A brisk cold breeze set the lake water lapping against the stone steps where the royal barges for the Begums were moored. While she conducted him through the garden, Khurram exclaimed, "That grouping of cypress trees around the raised dais canopied with red sandstone is superb. And I see that some of your roses are already flowering. That's an unusual yellow creeper."

"Yes, it's quite perfect, or would be if that unimaginative imbecile who calls himself the royal plumber could lay the underground pipes as I desire. Come, Khurram, advise me. You've always had excellent taste and I must admit that your knowledge of building and hydraulics surpasses mine."

Smiling good-humouredly, Khurram followed her to the arcade. Nurjahan pointed to the shallow scalloped onyx basin in its centre, from which a single jet of water spurted upwards.

"The water should flow underground and then cascade over the sloping, scalloped wall on the garden side. And there, where it straightens abruptly, I want it to fall into that marble pool, thus creating an artificial waterfall," she explained, gesturing with her hands.

"I've understood the problem. By tomorrow you will have your waterfall," he promised. Nurjahan smiled her thanks and led him indoors, where refreshments had been laid out.

"How is Arjumand? I haven't seen her this morning. She's still resting after her journey, I suppose. Let me warn you, Khurram, that Arjumand is more delicate than you would believe, and you mustn't demand too much from her," said Nurjahan, pouring sherbat for her stepson.

Khurram laughingly rejoined, "I wish you could have heard Karan Singh's opinion of Arjumand. She defied them all, and made those valiant warriors feel like little erring boys! She'll survive. Can you imagine what my grandfather's reaction would have been if he knew that your pampered niece had succeeded in achieving something he had longed and schemed for all his life?"

"She's remarkable," agreed Nurjahan with a pleasant smile. "And I think you did a wonderful thing when you received the Rana's heir with friendship. I'm also glad that the Rana of Mewar accepted the amnesty which you had the prudence to offer and the generosity to observe in spite of one or two unfortunate incidents."

"I'll never forget the sight of Karan Singh's face when he rode into Kumbhalgarh and found the Mughal troops mounted for war! From his talk I gathered that Raja Maan Singh was responsible for the original misunderstanding between our grandfathers. Is that so?"

Shrugging her shoulders, Nurjahan said, "There are so may stories about Maan Singh that one doesn't know what to believe. The chiefs of Amber once owed fealty to the Ranas of Mewar, and there was a lot of unpleasantness when your grandmother married the Shahenshah. But I distinctly remember that Rana Pratap once wrote to Akbar Shah asking for a treaty. But he changed his mind after hearing from that Rathor hothead, Raja Prithviraj, his nephew by marriage. And immediately afterwards, Prithviraj died."

"Ah, yes, I remember now. That was a year of deaths, and I've often heard my grandfather say that the charm of the majlis was lost with Prithviraj, music fled with Tansen, and with Birbal all mirth. Towards the end, only Aziz Koka and Maan Singh remained," he said with a thoughtful frown.

"And now the Amber Raja is dead too..." mused Nurjahan.

"Perhaps it's just as well. Had he lived, he would have convinced my father that the terms of our treaty are far too generous. Do you know what Mirza Ghias Beg said to me last night when we discussed Mewar? He believes that Akbar Shah and Rana Pratap, each in his own way, epitomized an ideal, and had they ever met, they could have settled all their differences."

"He's probably right."

"Karan Singh made some amazing revelations to me. All he wants is the withdrawal of Mughal garrisons from Mewar, a pledge that we will honour the sanctity of the shrine of Eklingji, and recognize the Rana as a sovereign prince within the borders of Mewar. They are prepared to pay homage to my father if Chittor and their family heirlooms are returned to them, and a pledge taken that no girl from the Rana's family will ever be demanded in marriage by any Mughal. They are utterly disinterested in personal gain, while we are ruthlessly determined to wield absolute power."

He sipped his sherbat and added thoughtfully, "There's something remarkable about a people who have suffered intolerably and yet retained their faith and culture."

"That's just what my father says," Nurjahan agreed. "Can you believe it, he and Maan Singh were always the closest of friends..."

"Ah, but then Mirza Ghias Beg is justly famous for his conciliating ways," interrupted Khurram.

"It's strange, but none of us are in the least like him. Only Arjumand, perhaps, to some extent. I take violent likes and dislikes, my brother Asaf can't abide fools, and Ibrahim was always a hothead. Manija's satire has a biting edge, and Khadija has a streak of frivolousness in her that makes one wary of confiding anything to her," Nurjahan said. She picked up a bowl of grapes, and offered them to Khurram.

"I think the Badshah will agree to everything except Chittor," she went on. "We cannot allow the Rana to fortify it, or even to reoccupy it." She glanced significantly at him, and said in a softly ruthless voice, "After all, this is not going to be a treaty between equals, Prince...they must always look to the Mughal throne with reverence."

Khurram nodded in agreement, but refrained from comment.

"Tell me, have you discussed this with your father?"

"No. I imagine that won't be necessary. We can easily arrange everything without troubling him," said Khurram with an inscrutable expression in his large eyes.

"Surely you realize that the Badshah alone has the authority to make treaties." There was a hint of hauteur in her voice.

Nurjahan knew that her stepson had a genius for military affairs, an unerring tactical sense, the resolution and tenacity of purpose essential to a great prince. But she couldn't allow him to make treaties and set up a pernicious precedent all under the guise of sparing his father trouble and boredom.

"Ah, you know what I mean, Gracious One. My father dislikes dull administrative details, and this treaty must not be delayed. Think of the prospects and possibilities it will open up for us in the Deccan and the far South: our communications secure, our territories enjoying peace, our armies free to take the shorter route through Mewar to the coast. I don't have to convince my father of the futility of the Mewar wars."

"I understand all that but you must consult your father. He promised to come here after granting audience to the English Ambassador. This man, Thomas Roe, speaks Turkish, I believe, and you can imagine the Badshah's delight. He must be questioning him eagerly about his sea voyage, but I expect him here before noon."

Khurram realized that she, and she alone, would decide the ultimate terms of the treaty. She managed to mould the Emperor anyway she chose, while insisting all the while that nothing could be done without his approval or consent. Khurram couldn't help wondering yet again what unfathomed strength lay behind her infectious gaiety and gracious ways. He had already learnt that there was much more to his beautiful, scintillating stepmother than anyone guessed.

Those who witnessed the entry of Prince Karan Singh of Mewar into the city of Ajmer would never forget the sight. Seated on a matchless charger, Pratap's grandson came to render homage to the Grand Mughal. In his train rode the seventeen great vassals of Mewar... the Chiefs of Salumbar, Deogadh, Shivrati, Sadri, Gogunda, Delwara... the Rathors of Ghanerao and Badnor, the proud Chauhans of Bedla, the Jhalas and the Haras... all those who had shed their blood and lost their fortunes in the Rana's wars.

Prince Karan was received outside the city gates by Khurram, attended by the Grand Vezzir Itmad-ud-Dowlah Ghias Beg, the Amir-ul-Umra Sherrif, the Khan-i-Azam Mirza Aziz Koka, the Khan-i-Khanan Mirza Abdur Rahim, Jehangir's brother-in-law Mirza Shah Rukh of Badakshan, and the Rajas of Amber, Marwar, Bikaner, Lucknow, Orchha and Datia.

Ghias Beg glanced at Sherrif, and with unspoken consent, they dismounted. Their example was immediately followed by all the others. Thus leading their mounts, and themselves on foot, the proudest collection of rajas and amirs in Hindustan formed a guard of honour for Pratap's descendants.

The men of Mewar rode through the streets of Ajmer with jaunty self-assurance, almost arrogantly, as though in a triumphal procession. The kettledrums boomed and the city went mad with joy.

Shouting blessings, women and young girls strewed the streets with flowers and the wealthy Jain merchants of the town showered gold coins over the Mewar Prince. Khurram wondered if these people realized that they were participating in a great historical event.

When they entered the ancient citadel of Ajmer, built hundreds of years ago by the last Hindu emperor of Delhi, a tremendous outburst of drums and blare of fifes announced the event to the world.

Seated in the curtained alcove to the right of the throne, Nurjahan felt deeply stirred by the scene being enacted in the great audience chamber before a thousand incredulous eyes.

For days, everyone had surmised and speculated on Jehangir's reception of the Mewar prince. Now, almost instinctively, as though it were the only fitting thing to do, the Emperor stepped down from his gem-encrusted throne and crossed the carpeted hall to the threshold where Prince Karan stood flanked by Khurram and Mirza Ghias Beg.

Jehangir greeted the Prince amidst awe-filled silence, and escorted him to the seat of honour prepared for him to the right of the throne.

This was not the reception of a defeated foe who had come to render homage; this was the unprecedented welcome accorded to a hero on his return from an arduous, glorious campaign, thought the Empress, amazed.

Turning to Khurram's mother Queen Jagat Gossain seated on her right, Nurjahan quipped, "Let's hope this makes the Rajputs realize that chivalry and nobility are not the prerogatives of any single race, Highness."

"To me it's only another example of the Badshah's Rajput blood rising to the occasion," came the smiling rejoinder. Karan Singh seemed to accept the Emperor's behaviour with perfect equanimity, as though he had always known that this was the only reception befitting a grandson of Rana Pratap. But Nurjahan knew that the Rana's heir had come on a desperate quest, and with one single great-hearted gesture her husband had restored his self-esteem and acclaimed the valour of the House of Mewar.

Jehangir and Karan Singh exchanged gifts after signing the treaty, and the celebrations began.

There was a mellow sense of good fellowship amongst the Mughals and Rajputs, a sense of rest after struggle, ease after effort, as the tired warriors of Mewar recovered from countless campaigns.

Later Nurjahan held a select reception, to which she invited Karan Singh and his son Jagat.

She was robed in saffron silk in his honour, and Prince Karan reflected that he had never seen such beauty and grace, or so many jewels on one person before. Begum Nurjahan was decked from head to toe with emeralds, and the huge solitaire ring she wore on her right hand flashed green fire as she returned his greeting with a graceful gesture.

"I believe Ajmer is somewhat similar to Udaipur, Prince," remarked Nurjahan affably, conducting him to a divan.

She was amazed to hear him answer in chaste Persian, "Udaipur is like no other place, Gracious One."

The Emperor laughed and said, "Wait till you visit the valley of Kashmir. I have often declared that Paradise could only resemble, but not surpass Kashmir."

He glanced at Nurjahan, and she said with nostalgic longing, "I'm beginning to wish that it was already spring and we could carry the Mewar princes in our train to Kashmir. There they would see sights to gladden the soul, mountains from whose summits the snows never melt, peaceful lakes, tumultuous streams, the most varied vegetation, and all the flowers of Persia which refuse to thrive in the hot, arid plains of Hindustan: glades carpeted with tulips, hyacinths and nargis! But tell us, Prince, how did you acquire such fluency in the Persian tongue, for I believe none of your house has ever journeyed beyond the frontiers of Mewar?"

Karan Singh answered with a deprecating smile, "Though we were always thundering from battlefield to battlefield, our grandfather Rana Pratap insisted on educating us and our small retinue always included a tutor or two. Once our troops were fortunate enough to capture a renowned scholar from Akbar Shah's camp. Perhaps you remember Sheikh Habibullah. He taught us to speak, read and write Persian, Arabic and Urdu. A saintly man, he wandered with us from place to place, and became very attached to us. But last year he expressed a desire to make the pilgrimage to Holy Mecca before old age overcame him. So my father sent him with an escort to Surat, and they saw him safely embarked on a pilgrim ship."

The Mewar Prince expressed a desire to visit the shrine of the miracle-working Sufi saint Khwaja Moinuddin Chisti, who had come to this ancient Rajput stronghold from Persia in 1191. He had received the land on which his world famous Dargah stood from the legendary last Hindu ruler of Delhi, Prithviraj Chauhan.

Nurjahan couldn't resist teasing the Rathor princess Jagat Gossain, "Despite his liberal religious policy and valour, you must admit that Prithviraj Chauhan's celebrated elopement with the Rathor princess Sanyogita of Kanauj cost him the overlordship of North India."

Karan Singh felt that the Empress was right. The combined armies of all the Hindu Princes led by his heroic ancestors and

Maharaja Prithviraj had been routed in 1193 by the Afghan freebooter, Muhammad Ghori, and Muslim rule firmly established in Punjab and Delhi.

Arjumand led Karan Singh to a group of her friends and soon Khurram had to rescue him from a bevy of pert princesses, who were teasing and questioning him mercilessly from behind their veils.

After pouring wine for the Emperor, Nurjahan turned to young Jagat Singh, a shy ten-year-old boy, and asked, "Are you enjoying your visit, Prince?"

Jagat Singh stammered incoherently. The Emperor intervened, saying, "I have a delightful surprise for you. Tomorrow you must accompany me to the stables and choose two pure-bred Iraqi horses for yourself. I believe you prefer animals to books and toys. Or is there something else you'd rather have to remember your visit?"

The young prince cast an inquiring look at Khurram, and found him smiling encouragement. Taking a deep breath, he blurted, "I'd rather have Chittor!"

Everyone gasped in amazement, but Jehangir roared with evident approval. Nurjahan smiled at her husband and all eagerly awaited the Emperor's reply.

Slapping the young prince on the back, Jehangir cried, "This child has the courage to demand what no one else dared mention!" With a courteous gesture, he continued, "Chittor is yours, Jagat Singh."

The prince thanked him, and the banquet began.

Prince Jagat had never feasted in such opulence before. He suffered agonies of apprehension lest he make a social blunder. He watched Begum Nurjahan's dainty ways and realized that he could scarcely go wrong if he imitated this fastidious lady. He copied her manners, valiantly resisting the urge to raise the curry bowls to his lips and lick his fingers after wading through a mound of pullao.

Throughout the meal, Jehangir related sparkling anecdotes, and the Mewar Princes were amazed to find no word of Sultanat Nurjahan affairs on his lips. Prince Karan noticed that the Emperor seemed very partial to fish, for he urged them repeatedly to taste the bewildering variety of fish dishes set before them.

After the banquet, Nurjahan announced, "My dancing girls and musicians will entertain us for a while and then we can adjourn to the open balconies to watch the fireworks."

The musicians struck up a gay dance tune and after a moment two slender, sinuous girls came twirling into the hall. They were clad in diaphanous skirts and veils, and as they postured and pivoted to the rhythm of drums and anklet bells, they tossed back their veils. Everyone gasped.

"What's this?" cried the Emperor.

Prince Karan blinked his eyes in rapid amazement, and Jagat Singh cried, "It's a trick!"

"No, no, Prince. They are masked to look alike," said Khurram, laughing. "Or cleverly made up," interposed Arjumand.

Nurjahan smiled and said lightly, "Wrong, Arjumand. They are identical twins."

"These delightful ideas occur to you alone, Nurjahan!"

And all at once, Prince Karan began understanding a lot of things that had baffled him ever since his arrival at the Mughal Court.

5

Once Mewar was quiet, Nurjahan urged the Emperor to expand Mughal commerce, to launch ships and wrench the mastery of the eastern trade routes from the foreigners. There was so much she longed to achieve, but balking all her plans stood the Abyssinian minister of Ahmednagar.

Despite all her efforts and the diplomatic missions of the Khan-i-Khanan Mirza Abdur Rahim, the Ahmednagar Sultan was vacillating. And it was to cajole him into a treaty that they were here at Mandu within two years of the Rana's surrender.

How different everything was from that time in Ajmer, mused Nurjahan, returning to her apartments after a long session in the council chamber with her father, Asaf and Mirza Abdur Rahim.

Her numerous nieces welcomed her back animatedly, and teased her to play a game of polo with them in the park before sunset. Thinking that the exercise would refresh her, the Empress agreed, and the girls went off to dress. A message was sent to the stables, Dil Aram bustled about her mistress and Laila helped her change into a cool muslin costume.

But just as she rose from her toilet table, Queen Jagat Gossain, Khurram's mother, was announced. The Rajput princess wore a colourful bell-shaped silk lehenga, deep-necked backless choli and a gauzy green tie-and-dye odhni so typical of her homeland, Marwar. Her bare legs and midriff kept her much cooler than the harem pyjamas, veils, and long-sleeved tunics considered proper by the Mughal Begums. Nurjahan begged the Queen to seat herself and called for refreshment.

When sherbat was poured and the maids withdrew, the Rajput Queen asked, "How long are we remaining here, Nurjahan?"

"The Badshah is enjoying his visit; he finds plenty of sport in Malwa's incomparable forests. He can settle the affairs of Gujarat from Mandu and yet remain in close touch with Agra. And of course, the presence of all his sons here delights him as nothing else could."

"The Badshah's departure from Agra seems to be a signal for the young amirs left behind to cast off all decorum and restraint! These abductions must cease, Nurjahan, or they will lead to family feuds and much bloodshed, besides..."

"Ya Allah! What on earth are you talking about?" interrupted Nurjahan, puzzled.

With a stern glance, Jagat Gossain continued, "I am speaking of your precious nephew, Abu Sayeed, who abducted Ratan Singh's granddaughter from her own house!"

"Whose house should he have abducted her from?" asked Nurjahan. She added mischievously after a pause, "And abducting brides is a time-honoured Rajput practice."

Queen Jagat Gossain launched into a tirade against Asaf's son.

"Just a moment," interposed Nurjahan with a militant sparkle in her eyes. "Do you think it was well done of your brother, Raja Gaj Singh, to involve himself in an affair with Gulabi when her husband was away at Kabul, quelling an insurrection among the Afghans?"

"The morals of your precious friend are no concern of mine," countered the Queen in tones of unbelievable pomposity. "But you ought to have some control over members of your own family..."

"Speaking of abductions, is there any truth in the legend of Rupmati and Baz Bahadur?" asked Nurjahan, restraining her laughter and trying to change the subject.

After careful consideration, Jagat Gossain said, "It all happened before I was born. She was the daughter of a Hindu king, a beauty with the voice of a goddess, they say. Hearing her sing while he rode beneath her castle, Baz Bahadur, Sultan of Malwa, fell in love with her and carried her off to his kingdom, and made her his favourite wife. This palace, and the Jahaz Mahal, were built for her by Baz Bahadur. Here Rupmati died, waiting in vain for her lover to rescue her from the Mughal governor, Adham Khan. They say her spirit wanders here; she still sings upon the tower overlooking the river Narmada, calling to Baz Bahadur at the twilight hour."

Knowing that Jagat Gossain had a natural predilection for probing the depths of everything irrational, Nurjahan said, "Has anyone ever seen her ghost?"

The Rajput Queen answered in a tremulous whisper, "Some say she rides in the forests around Mandu with a hawk on her wrist to lure Mughal hunters to their doom; others say they have seen her bathing in the lake around the Jahaz Mahal, but I must say that though I've kept long vigils, I haven't seen her yet."

The Empress laughed. "What a superstitious story! Surely, my dear sister, you are not credulous enough to believe these tales. Let us come back to reality. I'm going to play a round of polo in the park with my nieces. Do join us; the exercise will refresh you."

"A Persian game!" scoffed Khurram's mother, aware of her unsuitable clothes.

"Ah, but I'm Persian too. The Badshah insists that the Rathors are superb horsemen, the best in all Hindustan. But I say no. The Persians were famous riders long before the Rathor dynasty rose to fame."

"Is that what you think? Send one of your maids to fetch my riding costume and we shall see," came the swift retort.

"There's no need," said Nurjahan with a winsome smile. "You must have the new pink muslin habit, with its matching striped turban, which my seamstresses completed only this morning. Laila Bibi shall help you disrobe."

From a balcony above the park, the other Mughal ladies watched the Empress playing polo with Queen Jagat Gossain.

"Miracles will never cease!" whispered Arjumand to her cousin Ladli. She was amazed afresh at the incredible friendship that existed between her aunt and her mother-in-law. She herself, fiercely jealous, couldn't abide the sight of her husband's other wife, Kandahari Begum, who, Allah be praised, had been left behind in Agra.

What Arjumand did not realize was that the Persian Sultana had trained her ward for the very role she was now performing. There was an atmosphere of mesmeric fascination about her aunt which always affected the people around her. She invariably treated the Emperor's other two wives with charming deference. And Jagat Gossain, with her Rajput traditions, her privileged and unassailable position as the mother of two sons, her arrogant indifference to people's opinions, could hardly descend to jealousy.

Next morning at sunrise, Jehangir and Nurjahan went hunting in the Malwa forest. Khurram and his brother Shahryar accompanied them on horseback, and on two elephants came Arjumand, Ladli and some of Jehangir's daughters, followed by a select band of noblemen.

Nurjahan gazed around appreciatively. The plains of Malwa threaded by the distant Narmada lay on one side; on the other towered the cliffs of Mandu. Here the people were cheerful because of good crops and flourishing commerce with the port cities of Gujarat, she thought. She had not been prepared for the beauty of Mandu, whose charm was enhanced by the tragic legend of its lovely queen. From her elephant she saw pink and white lotus flowers afloat on the placid waters of Rupmati's lake.

Gradually, the huge fortified city was left behind and they entered a forest full of tall towering trees and hidden forest pools. The elephants plunged through tracts lying in deep shade pierced only by amber sunlight. Sometimes Nurjahan caught sight of spotted deer darting through thorn thickets and monkeys swinging from tree to tree.

The royal party halted in a clearing where a variety of animals were being held captive in a vast enclosure. The growl of panthers and angry snarl of tigers filled the forest, but this was not how Nurjahan wanted her shikar.

"Is this fair, Sire?" demanded Nurjahan.

"Forget your scruples, Begum. You desired to shoot tigers, and here they are. Don't imagine that I'll permit you to hunt them in the open forest."

Nurjahan bit her underlip and refrained from comment. He carefully loaded and primed a gun and handed it to her. She rested her cheek on the butt and steadied the weapon against her shoulder.

"Take your time and aim carefully. The English Ambassdor is watching and I want him to see what a splendid shot you are," the Emperor whispered.

"Is this one of the latest gifts?" He nodded assent, and she said, "You may point out any tiger and I guarantee to kill it with a single shot,"

Everyone watched the Empress. Sherrif, ever ready, laid a bet with Mahabat. Thomas Roe, the Inglis Khan, watched the proceedings with skeptical eyes. There was a deafening report, and he was amazed to see a tiger lying dead. There were comments and cries of admiration from the courtiers.

"Well done!" smiled Jehangir, reloading her gun. "Now try for that panther."

Nurjahan laughed. "That's easy." She took careful aim, held her breath and pressed the trigger. The huntsmen exclaimed when she got a difficult head shot.

"You may ask for anything you desire if you can shoot two more animals with single shots," said Jehangir with a delighted smile.

Within minutes, Nurjahan shot down two more tigers. "I've won the boon!" She gave him the musket and said, "But I shall always prefer bows and arrows."

"Incredible!" cried Khurram, riding up to his stepmother's elephant. "I wouldn't have believed that you were such a marvellous shot!"

"What is so incredible, Prince? After all, the Empress was taught to shoot by that incomparable hunter, Sher Afghan!" exclaimed Aziz Koka in his usual acrimonious manner.

He was prevented from further remarks by Asaf, who perceived the look of angry chagrin on the Emperor's face.

"Ya Allah!" he said in an undertone. "Do you wish to be interned at Gwalior again?"

The evening was mild, and a slight breeze ruffled Nurjahan's veil as she stood in Rupmati's high pavilion at the edge of Mandu's cliff. Half-hidden in the forest below lay sandstone and marble structures built long ago by a forgotten dynasty of Pathan kings. Nurjahan murmured a verse from Hafiz and sighed.

She heard Jehangir exclaim, "What are you doing here all alone?"

"It's wonderfully cool up here," she answered and turned to smile at him.

Jehangir drew her into his arms. He noticed that her dense black hair was plaited with thousands of little pearls and clusters of gems hung from her ears. She looked amazingly fresh and cool, while the morning's hunt had left him exhausted.

For a long while they stood gazing down the gorge towards Dhar. Noticing her air of abstraction, Jehangir asked in halting accents, "Did Aziz Koka's remark awaken memories of your life with Sher Afghan?"

She was startled by the undertone of despair in his voice and forced herself to answer lightly, "As if I ever pay any attention to that atrocious amir!"

'It would be insufferable if you grieved secretly, Nurjahan!" declared Jehangir passionately, gripping her shoulders.

"How can I reassure you?" Nurjahan asked quietly. "If I regret anything, it's those years spent away from you."

He stood silent, thinking thoughts he could not utter. After a while, he sighed and said, "There are times, Nurjahan, when mad doubts possess me and drive me to despair."

Nurjahan knew that the agonizing business of dispelling his doubts was futile, anyway. We all have our private terrors, our shadows and secret fears, she thought. This was something that would recur every time Sher Afghan's name was spoken aloud. Deliberately changing the subject, she asked, "Have you discussed Malik Amber's forthcoming embassy with my father, Sire? There are several points on which he seeks clarification, and nothing can be done without your command."

"I haven't had a moment to spare today, Nurjahan. There was the hunt this morning, and afterwards the Inglis Khan presented the gifts from his king. There's an amazing horse-drawn chariot you will enjoy driving about in. And there was the usual afternoon Durbar. Then I took a short rest and made some notes in my journal. Which reminds me of my promise. You may demand anything of me for this morning's superb display of shooting skill."

Leaning against his encircling arm as they strolled up and down, Nurjahan said softly, "What shall I ask of you, Sire? You have dowered me with all Hindustan, fulfilled every whim, every desire…"

Reflecting a moment, she exclaimed, "The sea, my Lord! I've never seen the sea. You must take me to the shores of Gujarat and show me the sea."

Jehangir laughed and bent to kiss her. "You are amazing! All right, if that's what you want. We shall go to Surat immediately after Malik Amber's visit. But it will have to be a short visit, because I'm determined to be in Kashmir before

May. I have always found the Agra summer intolerable."

"North of the ocean and south of the Himalayas lies the land of Hind," Nurjahan murmured in imperfect Sanskrit.

"You've spent the afternoon closeted with my ataliq Mirza Abdur Rahim!" exclaimed the Emperor.

"How did you guess?" she demanded.

'There were times in my childhood when I wondered if Sanskrit literature consisted only of this verse from Shankaracharya. The Khan-i-Khanan never missed a single opportunity for quoting it. Were you discussing this Ahmednagar affair?"

"We went through the same frustrating arguments. There were our proposals, Malik Amber's counter-proposals, a barrage of information about Ahmednagar from the Khan-i-Khanan, Aziz Koka's violent contradictions, and my father's attempts to achieve some understanding. And of course, Khurram and Perveiz have their own ideas about what is politically advantageous and in keeping with Mughal dignity. At this rate, Malik Amber will arrive at Mandu before anything is settled. He's to come immediately after the Navroz festival..."

"I'm positive it's Aziz Koka who encourages all the intrigue and indecision," interposed Jehangir with a slight frown. "You should read his secret correspondence with Raja Ali Khan of Khandesh, intercepted by my father's spies. Malik Amber is hardly the person to cherish any illusions, but Aziz Koka encourages him to pretend that he's on an equal footing with us Mughals."

Nurjahan gave a gurgle of mirth. "What a lot of our time we waste discussing Mirza Aziz! Anyone else, knowing himself to be under a cloud, would have tried to placate his sovereign. But not Aziz! He goes from folly to folly, and I'm beginning to believe he is totally mad."

Arjumand had come to visit her aunt. She looked refreshingly lovely in white, woven with tiny gold motifs, set off by the triple strand of enormous emeralds and pearls clasped round her neck. Flowering motifs were the latest rage for decorating everything from woven silks and muslins to jewellery and pietra dura inlay work on marble walls.

She found Begum Nurjahan's apartments strangely quiet. No one was in sight, only Ladli sat alone on the terrace, strumming her sitar.

"My mother isn't here," she said, looking up with a little smile.

"Have you heard the news?" asked Arjumand, seating herself beside her cousin.

Ladli shook her head. "About what? There always seems to be so much going on."

Moving closer, Arjumand spoke with a shudder. "A messenger just arrived to say that a few days back the Kangra Prince Arjun Deo fell fighting in Bengal, and that his young wife Nandini, one of my dearest friends, committed sati. I've come to request my aunt to send someone to fetch her infant son. He shall be my ward, and perhaps become companion to my son Dara. It's horrid, Ladli, absolutely horrid! How can my father venerate a religion which sanctifies burning women alive?"

Ladli sighed. "It's terrible, I agree. But then, even Akbar Shah couldn't keep these Rajputs from following their cherished customs. Don't you remember when Raja Maan Singh died, six queens and fourteen concubines climbed his funeral pyre? They believe that the wife who burns herself with her husband's corpse dwells with him forever in the mansions of heaven." She touched Arjumand on the arm. "Don't grieve, dear. Some things are beyond human understanding."

After a little pause, Arjumand said, "Since you are all alone, Ladli, come along to my apartment. Your brother has promised to come, and perhaps young Shahryar will join us.

We can play cards or chaupar, or chat, or listen to music, whatever you wish."

"Indeed, I'd love to come, but my head aches dreadfully. It must have been the peculiar miasma of the forest and the monotonous motion of the elephant. But my mother insists that I must learn to hunt, though I don't see what sport there is in shooting down animals held captive in an enclosure. I saw a little fawn, all bleeding and trembling, a pathetic sight..." Ladli said in that strange, disconnected way she had of speaking.

Arjumand gave her a meaningful glance and laughed. "You don't like being with the Badshah, is it?" Ladli strove to deliberately change the subject, for she had not the least desire to discuss her stepfather with Arjumand. "Hear this riddle!"

"At evening came the rogue, and with my tresses toyed
With sweet audacity and with never a please.
Snatched a rude kiss, then wooed me with caresses."

"Who was it, dear?"

"Your lover!" cried Arjumand.

"Oh, no, the breeze!" said Ladli playfully and they both laughed.

"Did you make that up yourself?" asked Arjumand.

"No, it's one of Bihari's riddles. His works are delightful," Ladli answered.

"Oh, a Hindu poet!" Arjumand exclaimed with a deprecating gesture. "I prefer the poetry of Persia and Arabia, but my father is devoted to Hindustani scholars and always has some staying in our house at Agra. But you know all that. Come along, now, before Dil Aram stops us for a sermon."

In Arjumand's rooms, Ladli found herself listening to Khurram narrating some anecdote about his meeting with Malik Amber. The old pain stirred in her heart again, and she realized that she had been foolish to come here with Arjumand only to watch her flirting outrageously with her own husband.

"I don't know when we shall return to Agra," said Khurram in answer to a question from Arjumand. "There's so much to be done before we receive Malik Amber. The local governor has planned entertainments for my father; Aziz Koka is here with all the Deccan officials, and the details of our treaty with Portugal have to be arranged. Jahandar's expeditionary force has to be equipped for Bengal. Oh, well, I suppose Ladli for one is perfectly happy to be away from Agra."

Studying her fingernails, Ladli said, "It's ridiculous, but I never know how to get on at Agra. My mother is always telling me to be gracious to the young Rani of Amber and to remember to treat the Queen of Marwar with deference. I'm supposed to know that Mah Begum repeats everything to her brother, Mirza Aziz; and above all I have to be careful of what I say to Princess Bahar, for she always twists one's words to make them sound absolutely outrageous. One has to be constantly on guard, constantly evasive. Arjumand does it superbly without seeming the least bit artificial, but I stiffen up."

Arjumand coloured and said, "It's just a question of never saying anything controversial or hurting anyone's feelings."

While they were talking, Arjumand's maids spread refreshments on a low octagonal stool. They all sipped sherbat and ate cardamom-flavoured sweets from silvergilt salvers.

At a remark from Ladli, Arjumand began triumphantly cataloguing the virtues of her first child, Jahanara, and praising the clear intelligence of her infant son Dara. Ladli had to sit and listen to these maternal effusions and sympathize with Shuja's teething troubles. Arjumand's three children, born in shockingly rapid succession, seemed to absorb her entirely.

Khurram agreed with everything his wife said. Only Shahryar sat with a bored, petulant expression on his beautiful face. He seized the first opportunity to plunge into an account of his recent ride in his father's new English coach.

A sense of defeat and disillusionment came over Ladli. She must get away, away from Khurram's sharp eyes and Arjumand's coaxing remarks, from Shahryar's stupid chatter. She wanted to shout at him to shut up, she wanted to throw something at this pink-faced boy who ought to have been a woman.

"Why so silent, Ladli?" asked Khurram, studying her brooding face and clenched fists.

"I think I'll go and see the children before they sleep, Arjumand." Without waiting for an answer she fled, escaping into the corridor.

"Ladli is growing into an astonishingly attractive girl," Khurram remarked. "But tell me, Arjumand, why does she behave so strangely? Is she beginning to fancy herself in love?"

"Oh, no. She never talks of anyone, she never grows agitated, she never blushes at the mention of any young man's name. And we are such good friends that I'm sure she would have confided in me. Perhaps it's better for her to be fancy-free, for my aunt is determined to marry her to the Crown Prince, Khusro."

"Ambitions!" sneered Shahryar, not quite eighteen yet, the youngest of Jehangir's sons, and consequently allowed much liberty by everyone, except his mother, Queen Jagat Gossain.

"You'd better show some ambition yourself," retorted Khurram. "Do you know what the old noblemen call you? Good-for-nothing! It's high time you devoted your energies to more worthwhile things than pigeon-flying and singing."

"But you have a beautiful voice," Arjumand assured Shahryar, trying to soften her husband's words.

Shahryar shook with a sudden wild spurt of laughter. "As long as Begum Nurjahan is satisfied with me I don't have to work or study or do anything I don't wish to! So who cares for your opinions, Brother!"

6

That morning, Nurjahan had risen much earlier than dawn, so that she could luxuriate in her bath and perform her morning devotions peacefully. By sunrise she was arrayed in a magnificent jade silk costume, ready to receive the homage and good wishes of her ladies and waiting-women.

It was the Emperor's fiftieth birthday, and she had organized a great many ceremonies and fetes in honour of the occasion.

The women were dressed as though for a wedding. A hundred different things had to be done before the Emperor came to the zenana for the ritual weighing. She smiled as her sister Manija and Princess Arambanu entered the courtyard.

They exchanged greetings and gossip, and Arambanu said, "I have a message from my elder mother Ruquiya Begum. She is indisposed, and will be unable to attend tonight's banquet. But you are to make sure that my brother visits her before midday to receive her blessings."

"Certainly. And now that you are here, dear Princess, will you take charge of the endless gifts and nazars pouring in from the nobles and rayaya for your brother? Get one of the young girls to make a list, for tomorrow we'll have to return them in some form of inam. Manija, please see that the trays of attar and paan at my portico are kept replenished. Do you know, several nobles sit there gossiping for hours, chewing paan after paan! Last year we ran out of paan and Queen Jagat Gossain's women went round repeating the story to everyone!"

Arambanu exclaimed with an amused smile, "Everyone says that the things you serve are the most delicious, Nurjahan, and cannot be bought elsewhere. And last year, when you ran out of paan, my brother laughed at the joke, and gave you

Swat in jagir to meet the expenses of your paandan."

While the Begums were indoors drinking fresh pomegranate juice, the Emperor was announced. Immediately, they all went out to welcome him, and presented their gifts.

Ladli's hands trembled as she bowed before her stepfather, offering him twenty-one gold asharfis. He thanked her profusely and said, "What would you like to have, Ladli? You know that on this day all the children ask for whatever they desire. But you never demand anything, my child." Jehangir studied his timid stepdaughter and thought it was a pity she was so unlike her mother. She still felt alien in the Mughal palace, though he had done his best to make her feel wanted.

Ladli was about to murmur that she had no request to make, when she saw her grandmother Asmat entering the courtyard. Impulsively, ignoring her mother's frown. She said, "Will you please grant me permission to stay for a few weeks at my grandfather's house?" Anything to escape from the Mughal palace now that Khurram was back from Burhanpur, thought Ladli, and was relieved when Jehangir nodded kindly.

Then Jehangir went round the courtyard, touching pile after pile of rice, cloth and coins which would be distributed to the poor and needy on his behalf. Prayers were chanted and another knot was tied to the silken cord, by means of which the Mughals traditionally kept count of their birthdays.

Nurjahan handed over her husband's horoscope to the chief astrologer, who would study it and make a forecast for the coming year. The Emperor's fortune, she knew, affected the whole country. If it was a good year for him, the people would prosper, but if the omens were inauspicious, his subjects would suffer from drought, disease and disaster.

Massive golden scales for weighing the Emperor had been placed in the centre of the courtyard. The sun shone down on the resplendent figure of Jehangir being weighed against gold and silver, jewels, myrrh and frankincense, spices, grain, and bales of brocade. This solemn ceremony had been introduced by Akbar, and all these articles would be distributed among the poor later. Hindu priests chanted ancient Vedic mantras, while on a balcony above, the singing girls sang laudatory verses specially composed for the occasion.

Nurjahan was busy distributing money to buy fodder for cattle and grain for birds, which her stewards would later scatter through the city streets. She touched the customary offerings which would go to the shrine of Sheikh Salim Chisti at Fatehpur, her husband's patron saint.

Cauldrons of piping hot halwa for the rayaya were carried out from her private kitchen. She received all the courtesans and dancing girls of Agra, assembled there to receive their customary annual gifts. And she sent purses to all the poets, musicians, painters, architects, craftsmen, and all the palace servants.

By midday, Princess Arambanu looked exhausted and Manija was ready to drop from fatigue. But Nurjahan appeared perfectly fresh and composed as she entered her palanquin to go to the banquet at Salima Sultana's palace.

This birthday feast had become a tradition of the Mughal house, and the ageing Sultana took pains to ensure its success. There was a relaxed, informal atmosphere in her palace, for only members of the immediate royal family were present. After greetings and courtesies were exchanged, they settled down on the cushioned carpets spread round the dastarkhan, where a sumptuous repast was laid out.

"Perveiz has been talking to the Inglis Khan, Begum," remarked Jehangir. "But I've told him he must consult you, since Surat is part of your jagir."

Everyone stopped talking and glanced at the Empress. Nurjahan said affably, "We can discuss the matter tomorrow, Prince, or whenever you find it convenient." She had her own ideas about the English and Surat, and she was not going to spoil this banquet by entering into an argument with Perveiz.

Turning to her stepdaughter Bahar, she asked, "When do you expect your husband back from Kabul?"

"How should I know?" snapped the Princess with a venomous look. "Who should be better informed about all the comings and goings than you?"

Salima Sultana intervened deftly. "How did you find Ruquiya Bibi today, my son? Does she still plan to visit the shrine of Sheikh Salim Chisti during the Urs fair?"

"Yes," said Jehangir, ignoring his daughter's highly disrespectful remark. "She's determined to go. I couldn't dissuade her. Bahar, you must accompany her and see that everything is made as comfortable as possible for your grandmother at Fatehpur," he commanded, knowing that she detested Fatehpur.

Ignoring her protests, he added, "Somehow I can never make even a hunting expedition to my father's old capital. It lies so empty and desolate, although my sister Khanum Sultana does her best to keep the palaces and gardens exactly as they were in my father's time. I wonder if any future Mughal will care to make Fatehpur his capital again?"

Salima Begum sighed. Would one of these young princes ever have the courage or audacity to repopulate Akbar Shah's dream city? Doubtful. She decided that future generations would merely come to gaze and wonder what manner of man had created those magnificent palaces and marvellous gardens. She remembered so vividly Shah Mansur's arguments with her husband about the impossibility of creating an efficient water supply at Fatehpur. He had been young then, and had refused to be deterred from his purpose. And it was lack of water which had ultimately driven him away from Fatehpur, she mused.

She studied her stepson, who was fifty years old today. He hasn't changed, thought Salima, or matured. He's still a charming prince, but Akbar Shah's premonitions have been amply justified. All his life, Salim has evaded responsibility and seldom exerted himself on anyone's behalf. It is Nurjahan who rules while he escapes from reality, and diverts himself in his private world of gardens and paintings and opium and wine.

But Nurjahan had her good points. Dressed in her favourite green and silver, and wearing the exquisite emerald and pearl necklace presented by the feudatory amir of Swat, Nurjahan looked utterly regal. Besides her breathtaking beauty, gaiety and wit, she possessed iron self-control and calm good sense. She had curbed Salim's drinking and discouraged his swift, cruel reprisals against recalcitrant vassals. She cared for him with utter devotion and a tender solicitude. What more could any one expect? But sometimes she wondered where her stepson's irresponsibility would ultimately lead the Mughals.

Jehangir's second son Perveiz looked at his stepmother and scowled. So now she has been given Surat in jagir, he thought. And anyone who wished to discuss import trade affairs would have to deal with her. She had unbounded influence over the Emperor, and people said that she used it in favour of the poor and downtrodden. But not once had anyone heard her pleading for Khusro, who was lying in prison while everyone gathered here to feast and gossip. He would soon give her something to think about, if she imagined that she could have everything exactly as she liked.

Perveiz did not need Mahabat Khan to tell him that year by year Khurram's influence in the realm was increasing. Because he spoke little, and demanded nothing, preferring not to become a supplicant for his stepmother's favour, the courtiers thought him strange, and her faction ignored him. But his father trusted him, and held him in esteem. The moment had come when he must stake all, and approach his father...

Khurram wondered what made his elder brother look so grim. Was it something the Emperor had said, or had the news from Bengal, where young Jahandar, their fourth brother, was repelling an invasion by the King of Arakan, perturbed him? Or was he piqued about Surat?

Nurjahan saw Perveiz set down his wine goblet with a determined air. She watched him rise from the cushioned carpet. Something was about to happen, she felt.

Perveiz would have been handsome, but he had broken his nose in childhood. This gave him a certain fascination which drew ardent glances and audible sighs from the young girls. He was the darkest of her stepsons, a golden brown man with full lips and candid brown eyes, his resolute chin disguised by the closely trimmed beard he affected.

Like his mother Saheb Jamal, he had a passion for pearls and his father indulged him. Only that morning, in return for his birthday gifts, the Emperor had given Perveiz a chaplet of sixty pearls, each one of which had cost Akbar Shah ten thousand gold mohurs.

Everyone gasped as Perveiz cast himself at the Emperor's feet, and his voice, pleading and poignant, filled the banquet hall.

His behaviour puzzled Jehangir. "What is the cause of this, Perveiz? What have you to complain about?"

Still kneeling, Perveiz cried, "I can't endure this! I and my three brothers pass our lives in hunting, banqueting and in every kind of indulgence and luxury, while one brother, the eldest of us all, has been condemned now for *fifteen years* to drag out a wretched existence in his solitary prison at Gwalior!"

Jehangir winced. He glanced at Nurjahan, and wondered what made Perveiz plead for his stepbrother. Such a thing had never happened before, and he didn't know what to say. Perveiz had certainly chosen his time well, though. On his birthday, he was expected to grant all requests. The gold-leaf-covered paan prepared exactly the way he liked by Nurjahan tasted strangely bitter, and he spat it out into the jewelled spittoon near his feet.

Bahar and her sisters were thrilled. They were all ardent supporters of Khusro, and now they besieged the Emperor and began clamouring for mercy. Nurjahan sat motionless, her beautiful face impassive.

"Perveiz, have you forgotten that your brother Khusro has repeatedly plotted against my life?"

Perveiz protested, "Ah, Sire, my brother was misguided, deceived into treacherous behaviour by those ambitious, scheming amirs!"

"No, Perveiz," said the Emperor resolutely. "When Khusro planned my assassination, Raja Maan Singh was in Bengal and Aziz Koka imprisoned at Gwalior. His misguided companions were punished with death, but after every plot, I pardoned Khusro, not wishing to stain my hands with the blood of my first-born son, though that son wished for nothing less than my death!"

Prostrating himself on the floor, Perveiz implored, "Though my brother has not been entirely blameless, he has suffered long enough. You have always said that clemency is the particular and most becoming attribute of kings. Pardon Prince Khusro, Sire, and restore him back to favour."

Perveiz's mother Saheb Jamal and Queen Jagat Gossain added their entreaties, while Jehangir's daughters set up a dreadful commotion. Nurjahan watched Jehangir sitting perplexed and bedevilled amidst these ladies.

Jehangir found it impossible to parry their urgent supplications. "Can you swear that your brother will never again behave in the same disloyal and refractory manner?" demanded Jehangir.

Perveiz called for paper, pen and ink. Salima Sultana made a sign to her waiting-women and the writing material was produced. Perveiz put his seal and signature on a blank paper saying impetuously, "My noble father and sovereign Lord! Fill in the conditions, and I will give my only son as hostage for my brother."

A black scowl darkened Khurram's brow. With Khusro's release his own position would change drastically. Khusro and Perveiz, with the backing of a vast majority of nobles and rayaya, would slowly begin to wield great power. And if Jahandar returned from Bengal at the head of a victorious Uzbeg army, his own plans for the future would need adroit handling. He became impatient for the feast to end, so that he could go and discuss this affair with his father-in-law, Asaf Khan.

Answering the Emperor's entreating glance with a radiant smile, Nurjahan said, "Perveiz pleads for his brother and he asks nothing for himself."

"Perveiz, you amaze me," sighed Jehangir. "Khusro brought sorrow to my father Akbar Shah, he brought grief and death to his own mother. I gave him everything a prince could desire. Even though he fortified the castle of Agra against me, I forgave him, but within months of my coronation, he chose to attack me at the head of a rebel force. But now, since you are all determined that Khusro should be released, I will send Perveiz to bring him from Gwalior. Let everything be done with befitting dignity and splendour."

The Mughal Begums broke into incoherent praise, and Perveiz went away to carry out his father's commands, a sudden happiness vivid in his eyes.

There were immense, jubilant crowds to greet Prince Khusro as he rode in procession through the city streets, as the rayaya welcomed their beloved prince after almost fifteen years. A shower of flowers and rice fell from all the windows and balconies, increasing to a veritable storm as Khusro's elephant passed below.

Asaf was not amongst those who rejoiced at Khusro's

release and reinstation as Crown Prince. He had smiled and murmured appropriate words of welcome to Khusro but behind the smiles he hid a deep resentment. All his plans for his son-in-law's future ascendancy would now be nullified. He was amazed at his sister for allowing such a thing to happen. Now Khusro would be free to roam from province to province, disputing her authority and jeopardizing the future of their entire family.

Asaf was beginning to regret the impulse that had led him to confide in Mahabat the other day: "What madness possessed Prince Perveiz that he pleaded with the Badshah and effected Khusro's release? Hasn't Khusro caused enough trouble already? With Khusro behind prison walls, Perveiz might well have become his father's heir!"

"True," Mahabat had answered, with a searching look in his eyes. "But I know Perveiz from infancy: I have been his ataliq. There has always been a deep friendship between Khusro and Perveiz, an understanding that goes beyond the ties of blood. Perveiz is intensely loyal by nature, and he's convinced that the throne belongs after his father to Khusro, or to Khusro's son."

Nurjahan, aware that the Mughal family was surprised at her behaviour, aware of the wondering courtiers, was standing on the roof under a domed kiosk, watching her stepson's entrance into the castle of Agra.

She saw her stepsons, clad in splendid robes and riding on gorgeous elephants, followed by courtiers on prancing horses and attendants holding aloft yak tails, peacock feather fans and gilt maces, mail-clad horsemen and camel-mounted musketeers. Sounds of music and enthusiastic greetings drifted upwards.

"It's a great day for the Mughal house," declared Saheb Jamal, pleasure radiating from her face. "How happy Shah Begum would have been today if she had lived to see her son restored to favour! But I haven't told you, Nurjahan, how delighted I was when my son Perveiz had the courage to approach the Badshah. And you, with your persuasive words, urged him to consent!"

Nurjahan looked at the frail, tender-hearted Begum smiling so charmingly at her. "I hope you will grace my banquet tonight, dear sister. I have ordered a delightful entertainment; you will enjoy it immensely."

Perveiz's mother rejoined pleasantly, "Of course, my dear. You always think of such pleasant things; no wonder the Badshah prefers your society to that of poor creatures like us!" Then, looking towards the river thoughtfully, she continued, "But tell me, where is Khurram's mother today? Is she indisposed, or has she decided not to watch Khusro's triumphant return?"

"No, no!" laughed Nurjahan. "It's not Queen Jagat Gossain who is indisposed. It's my niece Arjumand who has chosen this day of all days to give birth to her fifth child! And you know Khurram's mother would not allow her to go to my father's house for her confinement."

Nurjahan was affable and talkative today, almost excessively so, thought Saheb Jamal. "Your niece Arjumand is an admirable lady. She's beautiful, courageous, modest, pious, and fertile. Khurram is fortunate to have such a wife."

For a moment Saheb Jamal thought about her daughters-in-law. Of Perveiz's four wives, only the first had given birth to a sickly son. Then her thoughts turned to Khusro's wife, Rozana, who had shared his long captivity with such fortitude. Aziz Koka's daughter, amazingly enough, had always been docile and devout. She would have to send some tokens of affection to her stepdaughter-in-law.

Leaning her elbow on the stone parapet, she asked, "What gifts aid you send Khusro's wife?"

Nurjahan shrugged and said, "What could I give at such

short notice? I've sent her one hundred brocade costumes, a bag full of jewels for her serving maids, and the ruby and diamond set which belonged to her mother-in-law."

With an incredulous gasp, Saheb Jamal exclaimed, "What! Shah Begum's jewels that Ruquiya Begum gave her? They are probably the finest gems in the family, Nurjahan."

"They belong by tradition to the eldest daughter-in-law of the Mughal house. And somehow, I can never wear any of the jewellery worn by Khusro's mother."

Saheb Jamal stood quietly on the terrace. The remark did not call for an answer, but even so she felt uncomfortable.

"Shall we go down, Nurjahan? The sun is much too warm."

They parted, and the Empress walked through a corridor into which light streamed through marble slabs cut in delicate fretwork. She reached her own apartments, which overlooked the river. Here over the years the loveliest silk carpets, jade carvings, Chinese statuettes and eggshell-thin hand-enameled porcelains, gem-studded flasks, goblets and spoons, crystal candelabras and glass lamps, embossed gold and silver-legged divans and stools, brocade canopies adorned with birds of paradise, embroidered velvet bolsters and silk cushions, interesting books and albums of paintings, and specially crafted musical instruments had been collected by the discerning Empress.

A cool half-light floated over all the gem-encrusted arabesques on the roof and walls. It was warm in spite of the ceaseless swishing of khas-khas, made of vetiver fans dipped in water, and she was thirsty. She called for water, and Dil Aram presented a frosted silver tumbler to her mistress from which Nurjahan drank thirstily.

"Where is Ladli?"

"On the terrace with the other princesses, watching the procession. Shall I summon her?"

Nurjahan put down the tumbler on an onyx stand. "No, let her be. But I want you to make sure she looks her best this evening. And ask someone to summon my brother Ibrahim to the audience chamber. There's an urgent matter I wish to discuss with him."

She could hear her ladies and serving women bustling in the corridor outside. Dismissing them, she sat in her alcove, reflecting on what she would say to Ibrahim. If the Crown Prince agreed to her offer, without mentioning a word to anyone, she would help him begin his career afresh. She would move heaven and earth to marry her only child to the Mughal heir, and if Khusro was wise, he would accept her terms. If not, then he would find out how disastrous it was to oppose her.

That evening Nurjahan received her guests in a crimson costume encrusted with pearls. Rubies flashed and sparkled on her forehead, her throat, her arms.

Her stepsons swaggered into the pavilion, a laughing, apparently friendly group of young men. They were tall and arrogant, and they spoke to her with great dignity, their festive robes and jewels blazing under the perfumed lamps. The heady fragrance of jasmine, rose, and incense burning in amethyst bowls enveloped the pavilion. Beyond the fountains, Khusro saw fireworks soar and scatter. His stepmothers, sisters and aunts crowded around to greet him with tender words.

The Emperor entered the pavilion to the strains of music. At once, everyone rose to greet him and a fresh flurry of talk and laughter filled the air as he sank upon the cushioned throne.

He smiled at Nurjahan, whose beauty and exuberant spirits never ceased to thrill him. There was not another woman in the gathering, either among the Begums or young princesses, who could rival her, he thought, glancing around. He whispered something, and Nurjahan's incomparable laughter pealed out.

She made a gesture of homage to the emperor, spoke a word of welcome to Khusro, asked a question of Khurram, smiled at Perveiz, and laughed indulgently at Shahryar.

She offered Jehangir wine in a gem-encrusted goblet. He drank and passed the goblet to his son Khusro, who occupied the seat of honour on his right hand. Nurjahan watched her stepsons circulating the goblet amongst themselves, and noticed her husband's obvious delight at this scene of harmony and reconciliation.

Khusro's thoughts were grim as he sipped the wine. He looked at his stepmother, and remembered Ibrahim Khan Fatehjung's words. Would she remain so amiable when his answer was conveyed to her tomorrow? Or would he be deprived of his new freedom and honours at her whim? His wife had urged him to accept Begum Nurjahan's proposal. But he, amazingly enough in a polygamous society, had been faithful to his only wife for seventeen years, through good fortune and adversity, and he found the very idea of espousing Ladli, or any other woman for that matter, repugnant.

One thing was certain. Begum Nurjahan's family formed one vast conspiratorial ring around his father, and they would not permit him to fold his hands and languish peacefully at his father's Court. He was bewildered by everyone's friendliness, but he knew that he must tread warily. The future lay uncertain and menacing for him.

At a signal from Nurjahan, serving women carried in tray after tray piled high with smoking hot, aromatic delicacies. More wine was poured, and the Emperor drank joyously in the company of his sons. Talk became more lively, mounted to a crescendo.

Ladli watched the entire company wrapt in that special magic which her mother alone could invoke. She was aware of the matrimonial alliance her mother was planning and answered Khusro's courteous queries with equal courtesy.

The banquet was coming to an end. Serving maids came forward with basins, ewers and towels for the guests.

At that moment Laila slipped a small note into Nurjahan's hands. Reading it, she exclaimed in a delighted voice, "You have another grandson, my Lord! Khurram's wife has been safely delivered of her child."

The Emperor called for more wine to celebrate the birth of his grandson; Nurjahan commanded the immediate distribution of alms and largesse in Agra, and Khurram's sisters and cousins besieged him, demanding the traditional gifts from the father.

Ladli stood a little withdrawn from the group of jubilant girls. Another son, another tie, she mused. Another triumph for Arjumand. The gulf between herself and Khurram seemed to widen as the years went by, and her desolation grew as she watched Khurram hurrying through the arched doorway accompanied by her mother and stepfather.

7

"Look at that peacock!" exclaimed Jehangir, pointing with the stem of his jewelled hookah towards the garden.

Thomas Roe, the Inglis Khan, smiled ruefully and glanced at the dancing bird. The peacock had erected its train into a glorious fan to attract the peafowls.

Asaf could barely contain his laughter at the undisguised chagrin on the English envoy's face. He knew that for the past five months Thomas Roe had been endeavouring to obtain firmans bestowing trade privileges from the Emperor, who in his jovial courtly fashion had adroitly avoided all the snares of the foreigner. He turned to Sherrif, who had just returned to court recently from Prince Perveiz's camp in the Deccan.

"Are your camphor plantations flourishing?" Asaf asked.

Sherrif was still slim, amazingly youthful looking and dressed with his usual flamboyant elegance. "Why don't you ask me about the war? Or the state of our Deccan army? What interest have you in trade commodities, Asaf?"

"Don't you know, my dear Sherrif, that next to myself and the Empress, Asaf and his father are the most well-informed people in Hindustan? And the reason he's so interested in your camphor plantations is that I've given him exclusive monopoly of the camphor trade. The Empress has outfitted some ships to carry incense and spices to Mecca, and also pilgrims who are bold enough to venture on a voyage through the pirate-infested Arabian Sea."

Thomas Roe seized the opportunity, and plunged into a bold speech. "Your Majesty, if you would permit us to build our own factories, we would engage to patrol the Arabian Sea and clear it of pirates and Portuguese, who work hand in hand with those Makrani knaves on the west coast to capture your pilgrims and sell them into slavery. We could provide protection for pilgrim ships leaving Mughal ports by sending warships to escort them across the sea."

With a careless wave of his hand, Jehangir said, "You must discuss these matters with my Grand Vezzir or his son Nawab Asaf Khan, the Yamin-ud-Dowlah. Mirza Ghias Beg does not approve of your suggestion... he has often declared that fortified English factories could become a threat to Mughal supremacy along the coastal areas. In affairs of state, the measure which does not have my Grand Vezzir's approval is doomed to failure."

The Inglis Khan, as he was called at the Mughal Court, was an ambitious, restless and brilliant sailor, who had traversed the seven seas and seen many distant lands and strange people. He was more pleasing than handsome with his crisp copper-coloured hair and bright blue eyes, his fine long-limbed form and courtly carriage. He was the only bare-headed man in that assembly, apart from the Emperor. The nobles resented this, for in their eyes it was sacrilege to enter the Mughal palace without a cap or turban on one's head, whereas for the Englishman, it was the courteous custom of his country to appear bare-headed before kings.

He had been recalled to England and he dared not return without a treaty. It was the Empress, he knew, with her implacable resentment towards the English, who was blocking all his moves. And the niggardly gifts sent by King James hadn't helped, either.

Weighing the Emperor's words carefully, Thomas Roe continued in a persuasive tone, "Sire, we have no desire to participate in Mughal politics, or even to own property except for a few factories at important ports. We are not like the Portuguese, who are ruling the entire province of Goa, and are always sending their Jesuits and padres to preach in Mughal territory."

Jehangir spoke with a gleam of amusement in his eyes. "We have nothing against the Jesuits and priests. Indeed, two of my own nephews, Tahmuras and Hoshang, were baptized and instructed in Christianity by the worthy Jesuits."

The nobles nodded their heads in agreement while Sherrif informed the Inglis Khan that Prince Tahmuras was also the emperor's son-in-law by his marriage to Princess Bahar.

Thomas Roe's light blue eyes rested on the Emperor's face for a moment. In this crazy place, one can't take a step without stumbling over his sons and nephews; everybody is related to everyone else; if they are not cousins, then they are in-laws, he thought. He was getting nowhere, and he wondered why the Emperor had summoned him here.

"Have you modified the design of that mosque you're building in the Atka Bazar, Sherrif?" Jehangir asked.

"No, Sire. In Prince Khurram's opinion, if the architects and masons follow my drawings carefully, the finished structure will be most impressive."

"Not if you insist on using purple tiles for the domed roof! What has come over you, Sherrif? You're supposed to be a sensitive artist," laughed Jehangir. "Mind you, I've always admitted that Khurram has a flair for architecture… indeed, whatever energy Khurram can spare from disciplining and equipping his troops he expends in designing palaces and gardens. But purple tiles!"

Before Sherrif could answer, the Emperor's cupbearer entered with water in an exquisitely patterned Chinese bowl. As Jehangir lifted the fragile cup from the tray, a pair of greyhounds came frolicking up to him. The cup slipped from his fingers and shattered into fragments.

Lamenting loudly, the cupbearer bent to clean up the mess. Jehangir looked at Sherrif and said, "The cup was lovely, so the water lost its rest!"

"It saw my love's grief and could not contain its tears!"

answered Sherrif completing the verse.

Thomas Roe wondered if the Grand Mughal was about to command his servant to march forthwith to China to procure a replacement for the broken cup, as had indeed happened not so long ago. But Jehangir merely ordered the cupbearer to summon the artists Mansur Ali and Bishandas with their new portfolios of paintings.

Soon the artists entered, carrying carefully wrapped packages in their arms.

"Bishandas, show the Inglis Khan the miniature he presented us some days ago, and the copy Nawab Sherrif Khan has made of it," commanded Jehangir.

Bishandas unwrapped two identical miniatures painted on ivory, portraits of the divinely lovely English princess, Elizabeth of Bohemia, James I's daughter.

"Can you tell the original from the copy?" asked Jehangir with a mischievous smile playing over his face.

The English envoy studied the miniatures for a long time, frowned and turned them towards the light, but he found them similar in every detail.

"Look carefully. The one in your right hand is the original; you will notice that her eyes are a little round, as though she were astonished at something. Sherrif has given your Princess slightly elongated almond eyes." After a leisurely pull at his hookah, Jehangir continued, "My foster brother Sherrif possesses the rare gift of painting imaginary portraits of people he has never seen, but merely heard of or read about. And the finished portraits are marvellous likenesses of the actual person. Look at this painting of Shah Abbas. A perfect portrait down to the last detail, the Persian Ambassador assures me."

"Indeed!" said Roe, glancing through the folio. "Permit me to keep some of these, Sire, to show to friends at home, for I sail shortly for England."

"That is why we have summoned you here today," observed Jehangir with a charming smile. "We wished to present you with this portfolio of paintings, depicting scenes of Court life, so that you may exhibit them in your own country. In the courtyard outside is a caparisoned elephant, and in the antechamber are gifts of robes, jewelled daggers, and aigrettes of heron plumes for your caps. And this ruby engraved with our name." said Jehangir, drawing off a ring from his finger and presenting it to Roe.

With a courtly bow, Sir Thomas thanked the Emperor, and inquired, "In what way can I serve your Majesty before leaving for Surat?"

"You may use your good offices, worthy Khan, to send us musical boxes, wines of France, muskets of English manufacture, saddles and trappings for our mounts from Spain like the ones you brought before, and a dozen hunting dogs, preferably greyhounds, so that we may establish the breed in Hindustan."

Roe could see that the audience was over now that Jehangir had stated his demands. He was immensely relieved that the Emperor had not demanded expensive gifts like his Grand Vezzir, who had often rejected his offerings with acid comments to the effect that the gifts of the English were inferior to those of the Portuguese and Persians.

After Thomas Roe's departure, Jehangir dismissed his attendants, for he could see Nurjahan's palanquin being carried into the park.

Asaf, Sherrif and Jai Singh of Amber hurried forward to receive her. As Nurjahan returned their greetings, the fragrance of roses which she invariably used, scented the air. The Emperor urged her to sit beside him, and all the others stood respectfully around.

After a little pause, Nurjahan asked her brother, "Has Mother recovered yet?"

"She's improving, but she still tires very easily. And she

keeps asking about you. It's two weeks since you last visited her, my dear Mehrunnisa."

"I always mean to go but with one thing or another, I never seem to have time to leave the palace these days. Oh, well. Mother understands."

"Go by all means, Nurjahan," declared the Emperor. "All things await your pleasure and you must not deny your mother the solace of your visits in what must be a very trying period in her life. In fact you should go to see her as soon as we reach some decision regarding Surat. Jai Singh has just returned from investigating the affairs of Gujarat, and I feel that you should listen to some of his suggestions about the English and their requests."

Maan Singh's young grandson was dressed in a stylish green brocade robe, dark silk pyjamas, and a crimson-striped turban flaunting the fabulous emeralds of Amber. His enormous soulful eyes, sweeping lashes, and delicate mouth, his tall supple figure and air of jaunty self-confidence drew admiring glances wherever he went. His manner was direct; nothing daunted him. He had always been one of Jehangir's favourites and Nurjahan indulged the fifteen-year-old prince because she had always found him amusing and utterly charming. She also knew that Jai Singh of Amber had the ability to see to the heart of problems in spite of his youth. Some said he was more Persian than the Persians, and her father always laughingly called him the Mirza Raja of Amber. For a long while Jai Singh and Nurjahan spoke earnestly about the affairs of Gujarat.

At last Nurjahan declared, "I thought this matter had been settled between you and my father, Sire. The English seek to bind us with a treaty, but we make treaties only with equals like the Shah of Persia. The English would treat any concession as a stepping stone to more concessions. Why should tradesmen need forts? Let them come in their ships and go back in their ships!"

"I hear the Portuguese boarded and plundered two of your vessels trading with Arabia, Gracious One," remarked Jai Singh. "Such incidents would cease once the English were given a free hand in dealing with the Portuguese."

"You are well informed, Prince," said Nurjahan. "But that doesn't mean that we should agree completely to the suggestions of the Inglis Khan. I'm glad he's leaving for his own country soon. What a strange, insistent race the English are! Do the Persians, or the Arabs or even the Chinese demand privileges like these white-skinned men? Others have been trading for centuries with Hindustan, but they are content to come and go without aspiring to establish strongholds on Mughal territory. There's only *one* solution to this problem. We must build our own navy and control the Ocean of Hind."

"My sister is right, Sire. But it will take us years to build and equip ships, and train sailors. In time we shall drive the Portuguese out of Goa. And speaking of the Portuguese, I must mention the Khan-i-Khanan's report. The Governor of Goa has supplied Malik Amber with sixty new cannons and gunners to train his men. Prince Perveiz is finding the siege of Ahmednagar a difficult task."

"It's not the cannons or the muskets or the firangi gunners employed by Malik Amber who are beating back our armies, Asaf. It's those light-armed Maratha horsemen of his who swoop down from their hill fortresses, harass stray columns, destroy our supplies and burn our camps while the troops are forming for battle! They cut adrift our boats on the Narmada and Tapti and since there are no bridges, our lines of communication are jeopardized and we cannot get reinforcements or supplies in time to Prince Perveiz..."

"Is Perveiz surrounded by fools?" demanded Jehangir angrily.

No one answered. After a long pause, Sherrif said, "Well, Sire, I was there observing things for three months. I hate admitting it, but all is confusion in the Mughal camp. Prince Perveiz is too easy going to bend the generals to his will. The Khan-i-Khanan has begun a feud with the young Prince of Marwar, who refuses to obey battle orders, proceeds exactly as he pleases, causing confusion and unnecessary deaths. The generals bicker constantly over their prerogatives and imagined slights. The Mughal troops ravage the countryside, alienating the native populace who might have rendered valuable aid in securing fodder and grain for the camps, besides providing information on the enemy's movements. The soldiers, mostly Rajputs and Afghans, complain of the climate, the country, and the poor rations. Many have deserted, to return to their fields and families."

"Do you know what I think, Nawab? There's something wrong with the Mughal army itself. Too ponderous. Lacks mobility. Needs drastic overhauling. Those elephants are a total disaster in the Deccan, Sire," Jai Singh said.

Asaf made a gesture of annoyance. "You are always full of fancy notions, Prince."

"You've never been a campaigner!" retorted Jai Singh heatedly. "A Mughal army in the field resembles a city on the move. It's ponderous and exposed to attack on flanks and rear, as Sherrif Khan has just pointed out."

Silencing them, Jehangir asked, "What do *you* have to say, Sherrif?"

"Well, Sire, I personally believe that a change in command would bring about a change in our fortunes against Malik Amber."

Jehangir gazed thoughtfully at his life-long friend. He wondered what interest Sherrif could have in suggesting the recall of Perveiz. Did Sherrif believe that he was not aware of the numerous factions at Court, or the hunting for jobs, the intrigues, the exertion of influence, the personal jealousies that distracted his nobles, placing in peril the affairs of the whole Sultanat? He had a special affection for his second son Perveiz, who had never given him an anxious moment in his life, and had always obeyed him without thought of personal profit and reward. Perveiz was the son most akin to himself in temperament, with a love of wine and good living, an inborn courtesy and generosity that endeared him to the people around him.

"No!" declared Jehangir resolutely. "I prefer to leave Perveiz in command at Burhanpur, but I shall recall Mahabat from Kabul and despatch him to the Deccan as my son's second-in-command. Mahabat enjoys immense influence and favour with the Prince, since he was ataliq to Perveiz."

"Very well, my Lord," said Nurjahan, adroitly showing complete lack of interest in the subject. She had become perceptive and subtle after years of marriage to this volatile monarch. Throwing warning glances at her brother and Sherrif, she engaged the Emperor deftly in a discussion about their plans for the winter. Gradually, Jehangir's face brightened and his mood mellowed.

Seizing her opportunity, Nurjahan said with dazzling eloquence, "Have you considered, Sire, that Mahabat and Khurram together would prove invincible against any foe? I think Perveiz needs some well-deserved rest; he has been conducting this campaign for nearly a year now. It was the policy of Akbar Shah, your most venerable father, to replace commanders frequently, so that they might have the opportunity of refreshing themselves with a long sojourn at Court."

Before he realized it, Nurjahan's seduction had worked, and he had agreed to recall Perveiz and send Khurram to the Deccan as commander of the Mughal forces.

"No, no, Sire. Please reconsider. Talk to Khurram, consult the Khan-i-Khanan. Let nothing be done that is repugnant to you," urged Nurjahan. "Here is my father now. Let us find out what he thinks."

As soon as Mirza Ghias Beg entered the pavilion, Jehangir began flinging questions at him. A babble of voices broke out, everyone expressed his own opinion, until Jehangir demanded silence.

At last, choosing his words carefully, Mirza Ghias Beg said, "Prince Perveiz cannot inspire or control his troops, Sire. He is held in esteem, but not in awe. He is too easygoing and kind-hearted to compel obedience from high-ranking Mughal officials and the result is chaos. I am not disparaging his excellent qualities, Sire. Prince Perveiz would make an elegant governor for a peaceful province like Allahabad, Gujarat or Kashmir. Or he could be recalled to Agra and entrusted with the running of the revenue and judicial departments."

Jehangir pondered deeply, and ultimately accepted the Mirza's words, for he knew that Ghias Beg never spoke from malice or prejudice.

Jehangir found Khurram eager to accept the command of the Mughal forces in Khandesh. They sat watching the sunset over the Jamuna from Nurjahan's private terrace. Her ladies had withdrawn after placing bowls of fruit and goblets of wine before the Emperor. Only Ladli sat on a marble bench, her head bent over a piece of embroidery. She could hear her mother and stepfather talking in low tones, and, occasionally, Khurram's resonant voice. Her needle paused in mid-air as she heard him say:

"I'll go, but I have a few requests to make, Sire."

"Let us hear your requests, my son. Perhaps they may be granted." Jehangir spoke fondly; Khurram felt reassured.

"My first request is that the Mughal armies be led by the Crown Prince. It would be more befitting if I followed him as his second-in-command. It will show the world our united might, and victory shall be ours!" declared Khurram.

Jehangir continued to sip his wine thoughtfully. He studied the birds sweeping over the river, and the boats rowing past.

He sat brooding for a while, then he glanced at Nurjahan. She smiled at him, and all his doubts vanished as he caressed her with his eyes.

"What do you suggest?"

Nurjahan's thoughts raced. Khusro, Khurram, Mahabat Khan. The three most dangerous men in Hindustan. Three men she dared not trust. Unlike Sherrif, Mahabat always tried to influence the Emperor, and it was seldom that he agreed with her views. And Khusro would always remain one of the elusive imponderables of her life.

But Khurram was not to be underestimated. Khurram had the urge for power, Khurram had boundless ambition. And of all her stepsons, he alone had consistency. Khurram here at Court, with the Emperor's assured affection, would one day become a formidable opponent. But Khurram waging war in distant Khandesh was another proposition altogether, and Khusro stood very much in his way. She must be careful, thought Nurjahan. The Emperor must believe that the decision was his...

Dusk was falling. Down in the Naubat Khana, they were beating drums and from the women's quarters came the sound of singing. Her fingers brushed his hand as she took her husband's empty goblet and poured wine from the aftaba.

Khurram rose from the cushioned marble seat and sauntered over to Ladli. He glanced at her embroidery and mocked her with a smile.

"You'll ruin those huge eyes, using a needle in this light. "I've forbidden Arjumand to do any embroidery after sunset."

"You won't find me as biddable as my cousin, Prince!" retorted Ladli.

"I have people doing as I like, sooner or later," said Khurram, with a snap of his fingers. Then he strolled back towards the Emperor and Empress.

He overheard Nurjahan saying, "The Prince is right.

Where the eldest son, the undoubted heir of the Mughals, leads, can there be aught but success? My Lord, you must not forget that Khusro has long been out of touch with affairs of state. It's high time he resumed his duties, and proved his ability as general and statesman…"

Jehangir felt a dim foreboding, a sense of impending events which he was helpless to control, but the voice of Nurjahan falling so sweetly on his ears would not allow him to think.

"And your second request, Prince?" asked Nurjahan.

'That the jagir of Surat be transferred to me," he answered boldly, his eyes fixed on his stepmother's face.

A small price to pay, thought Nurjahan. Graciously she answered, gesturing with her hand, "Surat is yours, Prince."

Two weeks later, thc thunder of drums and the awesome sound of war trumpets mingled with the clatter of hoofs and the clink of armour and chai-mail coats as Khusro, Khurram and Mahabat Khan rode out of the great gateway of the Mughal castle.

Nurjahan watched from a latticed window and noticed that Khusro kept glancing over his shoulder at his father standing on the steps of the Diwan-i-Am. Jehangir waved his hand in farewell to his eldest son, stifling an impulse to call out his name, and Ghias Beg sighed, murmuring a prayer. No good would come of this, he felt in his bones.

8

"I do not know where this state of affairs will lead!" cried Ghias Beg, frowning heavily. His marvellous composure had at last given way. Nurjahan looked at her father in bewilderment but the ageing Grand Vezzir kept staring through the open window.

At length, he observed grimly, "No, you will not listen, though I have often warned you that none of us can shape destiny to our dreams. Unfortunately, you have a penchant for interfering with kismet."

"How have I failed, Father? What are these vague accusations?" she asked indignantly. "I have always believed that you at least would applaud and appreciate my efforts to carry the burden of government! I have dealt as best I could with colossal problems without any thought of my own leisure, or comfort, or personal whim."

They were sitting in her father's library. The doors and windows had been opened wide and the curtains rolled up to admit the winter sunshine. Charcoal braziers burned near the divan, and though the Mirza was clad in a quilted satin coat lined with astrakhan, he found the marble-walled room too cold. Shivering a little, he drew his shawl closer round his body and stretched out his hands towards the glowing embers.

His daughter seemed annoyed; her face had lost its gracious expression and her eyes held a defiant spark. She sat stiffly against the cushions, twisting a corner of her veil in the way she would when perturbed.

The Mirza knew that what she said was true. Since the Emperor's recurrent illness and his own retirement after Asmat's death, she had performed the stupendous task of ruling Hindustan with only Asaf to aid her. Despite his sharp intellect, the Emperor was indifferent most of the time to the interests of his empire. The humdrum details of everyday administration bored him; he lacked any obvious warlike inclinations; his energy was expended on collecting fabulous gems, commissioning paintings and laying out Persian gardens.

The secret of Mehrunnisa's ascendancy lay in her ability to shoulder responsibility and assert authority. But absolute power had changed her in some subtle way, and she was no longer amenable to suggestions, realized Ghias Beg sadly.

His daughter Mehrunnisa had been like a fragile flower, bright and innocent. But this woman who sat before him, called Nurjahan, Empress of Hindustan, had grown imperious and ruthless, though towards her own family she still remained loving and generous. He was immeasurably distressed by the change in her and apprehensive of what the future might hold for her, his favourite child.

He must warn her before she forced herself, and half Hindustan too, into the dark abyss of fraternal strife. The Emperor was ailing; all those years of self-indulgence and intemperance had begun taking their toll and no one could say what the future held.

"I'm speaking of Khusro, who died alone and friendless in Burhanpur. A word from you, a mere hint, and the Badshah would have refused to consign the Prince into his stepbrother's care. But that is over, done with. Regrets will not resurrect Khusro from the grave." Ghias Beg raised his hands aloft and sighed. "I have endeavoured to keep the family intact. I have taught my children and grandchildren to live together in amity, for who can destroy the power of a united house? But now you are forcing your kinsmen into rival camps!"

Nurjahan gasped. Whatever she had expected to hear from her father it was certainly not this. A bright flush suffused her face. "Rival camps?" she echoed with disbelief.

'There's still time to reverse your policy, my child," urged Ghias Beg. "Do not interrupt me, please. Do you think us all gullible fools? Do you think I'm unaware of the motives which prompted you to sit silent while Khusro was being slowly poisoned by Khurram in Burhanpur?"

"You surely don't credit every passing rumour against Khurram. Your pious granddaughter Arjumand would never have countenanced such a crime." The Mirza answered with a scornful laugh, "Khurram is not like his father. He makes his own decisions and will never succumb to advice or interference from any woman. Do you know what Mirza Abdur Rahim wrote in reply to my queries about Khusro's death? The truth, he writes, is so frightful that no one can speak about it. This clearly reveals the appalling atmosphere at Burhanpur."

Her father, Nurjahan felt, had grown strangely morbid since her mother's death. She knew that in an age of perfidy and intrigue her father stood like a pillar of integrity at the Mughal Court, and he would refuse to believe that she had not bargained for Khusro's death.

She rose, as if to depart in haughty indignation. Then she remembered the urgent affair that had brought her to her father's house for the first time since her mother's death three months ago.

"Let this matter be, dearest father. And you have just now contradicted yourself! First you accused me of interfering with destiny; now you are upbraiding me for not having intervened on Khusro's behalf. He chose his way. For years I tried to bind him by a matrimonial alliance, but he repeatedly refused to accept Ladli's hand." Shrugging her shoulders, Nurjahan continued, "Inshallah! Ultimately Ladli married Shahryar, the handsomest of my stepsons. He's young, and I have great hopes of him."

She sat down again on a low chair facing her father and

placed her feet on a brocade footstool. Her bright eyes rested with affectionate tolerance on his face.

Ghias Beg realized that his words would not influence his daughter anymore. If only her mother were alive, he thought with aching longing. Perhaps she might have succeeded in instilling some sense into this headstrong woman. The Hindus were right. Our actions bind us, but she refused to believe this. Anyway, he had no desire to wound her. He smiled at her kindly enough, brushing aside his melancholy thoughts. "Let us have some refreshments."

Nurjahan leaned forward to strike the little enamelled silver gong that stood on an ivory inlaid stool before her.

Her father's old retainer Roop Khwass shuffled into the room, barefooted. With a low salaam he asked, "Your commands, Princess?"

She smiled a little as she caught her father's eye. Roop Khwass never bothered to call her Begum or Empress or anything except Princess, exactly the way he and all her father's servants had called her since infancy.

"Bring us some fresh orange juice and sweetmeats," ordered Nurjahan. With another salaam, Roop Khwass withdrew.

Glancing at the enormous uncut ruby Nurjahan wore suspended from a triple strand of Basra pearls, Ghias Beg said, "I see that the Badshah has had his name engraved on Shah Abbas's gem despite my protests. He has ruined that stone."

"On the contrary, he believes that this inscription will enhance its historical value. He would like future generations to know that the largest ruby ever mined in the world once belonged to him. But of what use are gifts and protestations of friendship, when the Shah of Persia denies all knowledge of the siege of Kandahar, and insists on blaming the restless border tribes? The perfidy of the Mirzas of Kandahar is a byword, but Shah Abbas is prevaricating, you admit."

"The Mirzas of Kandahar are undoubtedly the most turbulent and dangerous vassals in Afghanistan," agreed Ghias Beg. "And the Shah of Persia has always wanted to regain Kandahar. You must understand, that part of Afghanistan has long been under Safavid domination."

"That's why I insisted that Mahabat Khan be sent to regain Kandahar while our ambassadors negotiate with the Persians."

"Has the Badshah finally appointed some envoy to the Shah's Court in Iran? I haven't stirred out of the house for days. This weather affects my weary bones; I've never known Agra to be so bitterly cold."

"What a triumph it would be for our family if my brother Asaf could go to the Persian Court as our envoy! Your old enemies in Isfahan would learn that though we were displaced by destiny from our native land, we have become, in the country of our adoption, second only to the Mughal dynasty!"

Though she was smiling, her eyes were wary; she knew it would be difficult to deceive her father, that seasoned statesman.

"Have you spoken to Asaf about this?" he asked, knowing her answer even before she spoke.

"No," murmured Nurjahan, thinking that somehow she must win his support. "I haven't had an opportunity to discuss the matter with him. But if the suggestion came from you, he couldn't turn it down, Father."

For a long time he sat silent. Then he spoke deliberately, hoping she would heed his advice.

"Unless you wish to arouse Asaf's suspicions unnecessarily, drop the matter here and now. Let the Badshah choose from the older nobles one who is personable, eloquent, and discreet, preferably of Persian blood, like Mirza Ibrahim or Mirza Rustam. A time may come when you may have to depend on your brother's friendship and goodwill for your own safety."

"Depend on my brother for my safety!" Nurjahan said

with a scornful laugh. "If his son-in-law Khurram continues to answer the Badshah's firmans insolently, my brother may find himself in a precarious predicament, Father. Instead of assigning sinister motives to me, you had better advise him to dissociate himself from Khurram's faction."

"How wise you have grown!" mocked Ghias Beg gently. "What has brought this change in you, Mehrunnisa? The weight of your crown, or Ladli's wedding to Shahryar? Your schemes, and Asaf's, are of no avail. It is Perveiz who has the support and friendship of Mahabat, Mirza Rustam, the Nawab of Avadh and the powerful amirs of Sindh, Balkh and Badakshan. The chiefs of Sabzawar and Zamindawar are his mother's kinsmen. He has several supporters amongst the Muslim nobility to uphold his claim. That is why I advise you to leave the disposition of empires to destiny."

Nurjahan exclaimed passionately, "You wrong me, Father! My chief concern is for my Lord's health and well-being. I will not allow Khurram to defy the Badshah!"

Before the Mirza could answer, serving maids entered with refreshments. As Nurjahan bit into a coconut ball flavoured with rose petals and cardamoms, aching memories of her mother surfaced. During Asmat's lifetime, her visits to this palace were on festive occasions… the gay, careless laughter of her young nieces, the entertaining gossip of Asaf's wives and those delightful family gatherings round her mother's dastarkhan were all things of the past now…

"I've had no news from Ibrahim for a long while, and I must confess that sometimes I grow anxious," remarked the Mirza, breaking the silence.

"Allah keep him safe in Bengal. Let us be thankful that he was not amongst those who fell with Jahandar, when the Arakani king attacked them near Dacca. Jahandar was a brilliant young prince," sighed Nurjahan, remembering her stepson who had died on his first campaign.

"Most unfortunate. The valiant die young," murmured the Mirza. In the last two years, he had seen death after death. First there was Sherrif, killed at Kangra, then young Jahandar falling on a distant battlefield in Bengal, and Prince Khusro found dead mysteriously at Burhanpur; and finally, the greatest loss of all: the death of his beloved wife, Asmat.

There had been a terrible epidemic of plague in Agra, and Asmat had been one of its many victims. He missed her sorely and often thought of the beautiful young girl he had espoused in Isfahan almost fifty years ago, the gallant young woman who had ridden across Iran with him in their desperate quest for freedom and life. He would never forget that heart-rending moment at Kandahar, when Asmat, his pampered Persian princess, had given birth to their daughter in a trader's tent. Was it a dream or an omen that had convinced her that their girl was destined to become a queen?

Nurjahan dipped her fingers into a Chinese bowl full of warm scented water and wiped them on a silk napkin. It was time for her to return to the castle of Agra.

"You must understand, dearest Father, that my political moves are logical steps which will preserve the Mughal empire. You must not believe that I act whimsically, out of personal hatred or delusion. Oh, well," said Nurjahan rising, and making a low obeisance before her father.

"Allah's peace abide with you," he said.

As he watched the velvet-clad, bejewelled figure of his daughter passing through the garden into the portico where her retinue waited, he became strangely apprehensive. He sighed, his eyes on some drifting leaves blown across the lawn.

Already, his children had embarked on dangerous paths. He was helpless to warn them against the inevitable tragedy he could foresee in the future. The world, he knew, spoke enviously of his children, of the luxurious lives they led, of the eminence of their minds and achievements. What did people know of the disruptive force of ambition at work within his house, of the tangled web round Khusro's death, of the impending clash between Asaf and his daughter?

Children's voices, eager and impetuous, came to his ears, and soon his young grandsons came into the room. In their chatter and laughter Ghias Beg tried to forget his thoughts.

9

When had this distrust between them begun, wondered Nurjahan. Had it begun immediately after their mother's death? Asaf as Grand Vezzir was unyielding and domineering and she could foresee many a struggle for supremacy between them. Or was Khurram, with his evasive, arrogant attitude, responsible for all this trouble between them? Her splendid, ruthless brother was utterly devoted to his son-in-law, she knew. But beneath all their political differences, she still retained for him the softening touch of childhood love. And she couldn't help admiring the courtly way in which Asaf evaded the Emperor's questions.

However, his words didn't deceive her. She knew that Khurram was secretly negotiating with the rulers of Mewar and Marwar, offering them Merta and Nagor in jagir if they would support his cause. She had intercepted incriminating letters from him to Mirza Abdur Rahim and Zaffer, whom he was cajoling with promises of reward to desert her faction. Khurram was even contemplating a matrimonial alliance with a daughter of the Sultan of Golconda, though she felt certain that her violently possessive niece Arjumand would effectively sabotage *that* plan.

Amidst the maze of subterfuge and intrigue that surrounded Khurram at Burhanpur moved Nurjahan's spies, and news of all her stepson's activities reached her ears. She realized that if his arrogance increased any further, he would soon be openly defying the Emperor. And Shahryar with his languid, indolent nature was incapable of anything more fatiguing than hunting, drinking or singing bawdy lyrics to his favourite Kathak dancer Jinnat Jaan.

Jehangir listened to Asaf with a troubled frown. All these

years, he mused, no shadow had marred his affectionate relationship with Khurram, but now all of a sudden they had become involved in endless, intense disagreement. It had begun with vehement protests from Khurram about the transfer of Khusro's jagir of Hissar-Firoz to Shahryar. So many matters could be sorted out, felt Jehangir, if Khurram would attend on him in Agra. But for some reason or the other he refused to move from Burhanpur.

"You are becoming quite tedious, Asaf. These trivial matters can wait till I return from hawking. My grandsons are already assembled in the courtyard below, and I can hear their impatient voices demanding my presence."

Asaf realized that his delays and subtleness were only irritating the Emperor today. Any interference with Jehangir's pleasures always made him short-tempered. With dexterous boldness, he suggested, "All that is required is a firman from you, Sire, granting Sultan Khurram's just requests."

Jehangir brushed his suggestion aside, and said impatiently, "Talk the matter over with the Empress. I can't stay here all day listening to everyone's endless demands."

He moved towards the arched doorway, and Nurjahan said with indignation, "Isn't it odd that Khurram keeps putting off his long overdue visit to Agra?"

Asaf answered with tactful deference, "The Deccan rivers are in spate, my dear sister, and the roads are in a shocking state of disrepair. Though I wish the Prince were here in person to decide this matter…"

"Is he willing to go to Kandahar or not?" interrupted Nurjahan, studying her brother's face.

"We are all aware of your concern over Kandahar," Asaf's smile was mocking. "It's your birthplace, and jagir."

She said with icy hauteur, "Confine your remarks to the matter we are discussing." The Emperor turned to listen to their exchange.

Asaf rejoined with a gleam of amusement in his eyes, "We are also aware that since the Portuguese began dominating the Arabian Sea, our sea traffic with Persia, Arabia and Ethiopia has suffered immeasurably and your revenues have decreased. I have endeavoured to appraise Sultan Khurram of the various implications of the loss of Kandahar. He shall proceed to Kabul once the rains cease, and your worries will be over."

With his thumbs hooked in his cummerbund, Jehangir declared, "Khurram has a genius for military affairs, an unerring tactical sense and the tenacity of purpose required for this campaign. And who knows," he continued enthusiastically, "from Kandahar and Kabul we might be able to launch a two-pronged expedition for the conquest of Samarkand, our ancestral capital."

Like every Mughal since Babur, Jehangir nursed an intense desire to regain the lost principality of Fargana, where their world-renowned ancestor Timur had ruled. Asaf knew that Jehangir had a sentimental regard for his Central Asian heritage; the fabled cities of Mawar-an-nahr and the pastures of the Amu Darya beckoned him enticingly. The Mughals still spoke Chagatai Turkish amongst themselves, though Persian was the official Court language, and Urdu was commonly spoken in Hindustan.

This was dangerous ground, Asaf knew. They had better stick to Khurram and Kandahar. "He has proved his ability to conduct military operations of great magnitude, but before accepting the command of this campaign, Prince Khurram begs that he be granted certain privileges. He wants time to consider…"

"Consider!" cried the Emperor. "Ask for privileges! Doesn't Khurram understand that it's his *duty* to subdue Kandahar, the scene of permanent tension and violence? Persia will always be a source of danger on our Afghan frontier. Is this the time for Khurram to bargain with us?"

At that moment, Jehangir saw his grandson Dawar Buksh hesitating on the threshold. It was difficult for Jehangir to ignore him, so he asked the boy to come in.

"We've been waiting a long time, Grandfather. And the hawks are becoming agitated," protested Dawar Buksh.

He had his grandfather's tawny eyes, an attractive animated face and an intense fascination for all forms of sport. Nurjahan knew that he also took delight in subtle philosophic discussions, and despite her antipathy towards his dead father Khusro, she had always treated Dawar Buksh with affectionate indulgence. She smiled now as he greeted her with charming deference.

"Tell the falconers I shall be down in a moment," said Jehangir.

"The sun will soon be much too bright, Grandfather," pointed out Dawar Buksh.

"These young boys are always impatient," the Emperor remarked, as Dawar Buksh hurried out with jaunty self-assurance. "But this affair must be settled before I go. What are my son's conditions, Asaf?"

"The Prince requests absolute command of the Mughal forces at Kabul. Secondly, he desires the governorship of the Punjab, so that he may raise fresh troops and gather supplies as the need arises. And he begs that the fortress of Ranthambor in Mewar be assigned as a residence to his family while he's engaged in conducting the siege of Kandahar."

An amazed cry broke from Nurjahan's lips. She raised her delicate eyebrows scornfully, "Does Khurram prefer to consign his wife and children to the care of his friend Rana Karan rather than to his most generous and indulgent father?"

For a moment, consternation appeared on Asaf's features. But he soon recovered his composure, and said, "You know that the climate of Agra doesn't agree with his eldest child, Jahanara. That's the only reason why he wants his family at Ranthambor."

Jehangir cut short his explanations with a peremptory gesture. "I won't have it! Prepare a firman ordering Khurram to dispatch all the Mughal forces under his command back to Agra. There are other generals besides Khurram in Hindustan!"

Knowing how useless it would be to argue with the Emperor, Asaf withdrew. Nurjahan could see that her husband was greatly disturbed. She rose, and placing her hand on his arm, cajoled him with soft words to forget the entire affair.

Resting his cheek against her hair, he suggested, "Why don't you come hawking with me? What little time there is in this careworn world for pleasant diversions, Nurjahan!"

She shook her head and gently disengaged herself from his embrace. "I wish I could, for it's a perfect day to be out on a horse, with a hawk on one's wrist. But I've promised to interview the architect Shirazi today, so that the work on my father's tomb may proceed."

"As you please," murmured Jehangir, and kissed her palms.

10

The days slid into weeks, and weeks into months, and still Sultan Khurram remained at Udaipur.

Rana Karan Singh would not permit him to speak of departure. Amidst the diversions offered for his amusement, and the solicitous courtesy of the Rana's people, Khurram's spirits revived.

After his defeat, most of his adherents had deserted him. Branded rebel and traitor because he had refused to command the expedition against Kandahar, hounded from province to province by the Mughal troops, refused aid by Malik Amber and the Sultan of Golconda, Khurram had been forced at last by the plight of his family to seek sanctuary in Mewar.

Realizing the futility of his struggle against his father, Khurram had at last capitulated to Arjumand's pleas, and reluctantly written to Jehangir, begging forgiveness and offering to present himself at Court.

Now he was content to await events in this island retreat, safe amidst the placid waters of Lake Pichola. The Rana's retainers guarded him day and night, and he knew that five thousand Bhils armed with poisoned arrows watched the roads and mountain passes vigilantly.

What irony, mused Khurram, that he, Akbar's grandson, should find sanctuary only in the house of Pratap's grandson. And now after spending so many months in the Rana's capital, he began to perceive the enormity of Pratap's self-sacrifice. Like Amber, Marwar, Rewa and Orchha, Mewar could also have submitted to Akbar Shah. But the Sisodias had elected to fight for independence. For more than half a century the people of Mewar had suffered every woe, pillaged by Mughal, Turk and Afghan.

And yet, the chivalrous Rajput code committed the men of Mewar to his protection, though he was a prince of the hated Mughal dynasty. And the same code, he knew, had estranged him from his mother, who had refused to hear his name pronounced since his revolt three years ago. He had written to her repeatedly, explaining that Begum Nurjahan's scheming actions alone had forced him into armed rebellion, but Queen Jagat Gossain had treated his explanations with silent contempt. It was his mother, that arrogant Rajput princess, who had forbidden her brother Gaj Singh of Marwar to render him aid when he had wandered alone and friendless with Arjumand and his children through the deserts of Rajputana. At last, his friend Karan, learning of his dire distress, had induced him to accept the hospitality of Mewar.

He had offered to send Arjumand back to Agra, of which she spoke with nostalgic longing. Khurram was aware that no matter how he himself might act, Arjumand could always count on her aunt's protection. But Arjumand had refused to leave him. She had always accompanied him wherever he had gone, whether on campaigns or excursions of pleasure. Their love had deepened with the birth of every child, and his respect for her had grown when she had put aside the airs of a pampered princess and tackled the task of caring for her husband and children.

By some mysterious means Asaf managed to correspond with his daughter and son-in-law. From his last letter, dated from Lahore, Khurram had learnt of his father's deteriorating health, of Begum Nurjahan's plans, and the movements of his brother Perveiz. His father-in-law wrote that Mahabat Khan had been recalled from Kabul on his stepmother's express wish. Mahabat's recall might have fearful portents for himself, reflected Khurram.

The Prince paced restlessly in the garden of Jagmandir. He was indifferent to the beauty around him. His face looked drawn and haggard, his mind refused to turn from his unsolved problems.

From the Rana's palace across the lake came the sound of flutes, tambourines, and voices singing ancient Holi songs. Khurram heard oars dipping into water, the scrape of wood against stone, and turned to see a canopied barge pull up alongside the marble embankment of Jagmandir.

Khurram's attendants hastened to welcome the Rana's heir and he watched Jagat striding across the green turf. The shy young lad who had accompanied him to Ajmer all those years ago to attend the Mughal durbar had grown into a tall stalwart man of princely appearance. He was dark like his grandfather Rana Amar, with eloquent black eyes and a high-bridged nose; his saffron turban sat aslant on his head. His white silk fargal was splashed with colours, and for once, Khurram noticed, he wore no arms except a velvet-sheathed dagger in his cummerbund. As they exchanged greetings, Khurram noticed young Jagat Singh's muscular build, and the quick smile that never seemed to be far from his lips.

"Well, nephew!" exclaimed Khurram, his face brightening. "My greetings on this auspicious day. Were the omens good after the Holi burning?"

"Oh, yes," answered Jagat, smiling. "The Brahmins have predicted a year of peace and plenty for Mewar. My father sends greetings; and I have come with the chiefs of Salumbar, Sadri and Badnor to escort you with befitting honour to our palace."

The chiefs stepped forward, greeting Sultan Khurram with courteous deference. After them came the Rana's retainers, to lay at Khurram's feet silver trays full of powdered abhir, gulal, flower petals, saffron, musk, grain and flagons of rose water.

From the palace erected for Begum Arjumand by the Rana emerged the young Mughal princes, Dara, Shuja and Aurangzeb. They were magnificently arrayed in brocades and velvet, with jewelled caps on their heads. Khurram knew that these vestments were the Rana's generous gifts.

They ran up to Prince Jagat, crying eagerly, "Have you come to take us to your palace to see the tamasha, and will the nautch girls really walk a tightrope across the lake from the public ghats to the island temple of Eklingji? Are there crocodiles waiting to devour those who fall into the lake?"

Khurram rebuked his clamouring sons, "Quiet, all of you! We shall leave you behind if you harry the Prince with your nonsense."

At once they ceased tugging at Jagat Singh's clothes and arms, and fell quiet. Dara, a sweet-faced, solemn-eyed boy of eleven turned away to examine the sculptured stone elephants which lined the lawn, throwing jets of water from their raised trunks into a large marble tank. Shuja, with his mother's fair colouring and large hazel eyes, accepted candied sugar and almonds from the stalwart chief of Badnor, popping them into his mouth before anyone could rebuke him. Young Aurangzeb, a restless impudent boy of eight, began chasing a butterfly. The minute he caught it, he tore away its wings, threw them to the ground, and laughed with glee. Called to order, the young Mughals and their father embarked with Prince Jagat for the short trip across the water to the Rana's palace. They were followed by Begum Arjumand and her daughters in a closely-curtained barge.

Khurram watched the island of Jagmandir with its gardens and palaces receding in the distance. He glanced around, appreciating the glow of colour that seemed to surround this lake, these palaces, hills and vales. This was a very original world, he reflected. It was the world of a race who called themselves children of the Sun God; quite different from anything he had ever known before.

Lofty yellowish hills, all crowned with strongholds and crenellated towers, encircled the horizon. To his right, along the banks of the lake, stood temples, ghats and palaces. Huge pipal and banyan trees shaded the dark fringes of Lake Pichola. From the moving boat, Khurram studied the Rana's palace reflected in the placid waters, an unbroken facade of luminous marble. The massive simplicity of white marble against an azure sky struck his keen architect's eye. Along the ghats came an unending procession of women and young girls draped in brilliant hues, carrying earthen pots on their heads, sunlight sparkling on their heavy silver ornaments.

From the courtyard came the sound of bells and conch shells as Khurram's party passed through a multitude of men, showering rose water and flower petals, into a vast colonnaded chamber in which the Rana was waiting with his vassals and kinsmen to welcome his guests.

Rana Karan escorted them into the main courtyard to play Holi. Soon the marble floor was covered with multicoloured powders as the princes and vassals sprinkled each other with abhir and gulal in the customary spirit of revelry. The throbbing sound of tambourines filled the air as the Rana's bards sang lays of Mewar's ancient glory, while several retainers danced in rhythm to the drum beat.

The Rana was here, there and everywhere, meeting delegation after delegation of revellers from the towns and villages, showing equal courtesy to Bhil and Rajput, Brahmin and Baniya, as he accepted their greetings.

Khurram took the wine cup with a gracious smile, declining the sweets and savouries which he knew from experience were always stuffed with bhang on Holi. Sipping the famed asa of Udaipur, the Prince reflected that he had never seen his Rajput hosts in such mad, merry humour. The harvest had been exceptionally good that year and the rayaya was jubilant. He heard rustic farmers who had come from distant villages talk to Rana Karan with amazing familiarity.

His sojourn at Udaipur had taught him many things about

the Rana and his subjects. This was a patriarchal community. These clans, these cavalcades of nobles, these warriors with spears and shields and flowing moustaches, owed unswerving allegiance to this wise King who stood beside him, but they held him in esteem, not awe.

"Do you find our customs strange, Prince?" asked his host, noting his air of abstraction.

"Oh, no!" assured Khurram. "Since the days of Akbar Shah, every major Hindu festival has been celebrated at the Mughal Court."

The noble refined face of Rana Karan lost its anxious look. Yet he wondered: what did this prince, born to the magnificent splendour of the Grand Mughal's Court, think of Mewar's comparatively meagre hospitality?

With endearing friendliness Khurram clasped the Rana's shoulder. "I've envied you two things today, my friend," he said smiling.

"What is there in my humble domain to excite your envy, Prince?" Karan Singh asked, bewildered. "Name them and they are yours!"

"Oh, no!" laughed Khurram. "I couldn't carry away your gifts even if I so desired."

Several people drew closer to overhear their exchange. "Above everything else," continued Khurram, aware of the listening men, "I envy you the loyalty of your vassals and warriors, your Bhils and your rayaya. I'm beginning to understand at last why your ancestors had the courage to defy every invader, from Allaudin Khilji to my own grandfather, Akbar Shah. Had I such men to follow my standard, I would establish my supremacy from the snowbound Himalayas to the ocean-swept shores of the deep south, from Samarkand to the walls of China!" Sipping his wine, he mused, "I wonder why the rulers of ancient Chittor did not venture forth on conquest themselves?"

The Rana smiled with ancient wisdom. "We are content amidst the hills and vales of the Aravallis, where our race has flourished for a thousand years. All we desire is liberty to live according to our ancient Hindu code, molesting none, conquering none, absorbed in pursuits of justice and piety, for they alone can lead to ultimate release, and only then can man's eternal soul be freed from the cycle of birth and death."

"I see," murmured Khurram. He did not add that he found this metaphysical ideal amazing in a warrior king whose ancestors has known nothing but bloodshed and strife.

"Amongst us," continued the Rana, with a distant expression in his eyes, "there is an ancient custom. When we have seen our son's sons grow from infancy to youth, we relinquish the reins of government to our offspring, and retire from public life to spend our old age in silent contemplation of the Infinite."

Khurram suppressed a mocking laugh. Amongst us Mughals, he wanted to say, there is an ancient custom which forces sons into open rebellion against ageing fathers who jealously cling to their prerogative of power. Perhaps the ways of the Hindus were wisest, after all. Without plots, intrigues, or fraternal strife, power passed from father to son.

He broke off his reflections when he heard the Rana ask, "Tell us, Prince, what else have you found to admire in Mewar?"

"Your marble palaces, reflected in the placid water of Pichola, girt by bastioned walls, enclosing lush gardens. We Mughals have not used marble so effectively, but perhaps someday, Inshallah, I may remedy this fault!"

Rana Karan smiled with a gleam of humour in his eyes. He knew what Khurram desired: a crown and an empire; and he knew the Prince would be worthy of both. Khurram would need courageous, steadfast men to aid him; that, of course, would have to be discussed later between them at the appropriate time. He knew all about the endless intrigues, bickerings and frustrations that had finally driven Khurram into open revolt. He was wholly devoted to Khurram's interests. But as long as his father Jehangir lived, he would offer hospitality to Khurram, and nothing more, since he had sworn the oath of fealty to Jehangir. Only when that ailing monarch died would he support Khurram openly against Perveiz or Begum Nurjahan. The Rana brushed aside these thoughts, remembering that on festive occasions one should be free from care.

This was the most joyous, riotous day of the year, dedicated to laughter and playful pranks. Already, half his vassals were drunk on the fiery asa his attendants kept pouring. It was time to escort his guests to the feast prepared in the banquet hall.

Before he could signal Jagat Singh to retrieve Khurram's sons from a rowdy group of young chieftains, he observed a Bhil pushing his way through a knot of men gathered under the portico.

The Bhil slipped through the crowds to Prince Jagat and with a brief greeting handed him a feathered arrow. Round the shaft was wrapped a piece of parchment secured by a string.

Swiftly the Mewar prince undid the note and read it with an anxious frown. He cast a troubled look towards his father.

Khurram too had noticed the Bhil, clad in a scanty loincloth, with a colourful scarf round his head, through which two peacock feathers were stuck jauntily.

A troubled silence fell upon that festive gathering. The singing and dancing ceased at a signal from the Rana.

"What intelligence does the note convey?" demanded Khurram, apprehensively.

The Rana's good humour vanished as he read the message. "Mahabat Khan has crossed the frontiers of Mewar at the head of six thousand Rajput horsemen," he observed with concern. "And strangely enough, my Bhils report, they are riding under a flag of truce."

All eyes turned on Khurram as they watched his reaction. Somewhere a sword flashed, and a proud voice cried, "Let Mahabat Khan beware lest he taste our steel! We want no Mughal minions breaking our borders!"

At once a great shout went up and some ran to snatch up their weapons; others tightened their cummerbunds. The lord of Salumber moved forward, his moustache bristling; the Rathor chief of Badnor swore a furious oath. They understood too well what Mahabat's coming meant.

"Wait!" commanded the Rana. "It's for Sultan Khurram to decide whether Mahabat Khan is to be received in audience or not. Remember he comes under a flag of truce, which must be honoured."

For a long while Rana Karan spoke earnestly to Khurram, urging the importance of making a friend of Mahabat in his own future interest.

After a thoughtful pause, Khurram said, "It's a chance, and I'll take it! Let Mahabat come in peace." Already his brain was seething with schemes. If only he could bind Mahabat to his cause!

The Rana's sons and vassals attended Mahabat's reception armed to the hilt. They came arrayed for battle, resolved at the least hint of danger or discourtesy to their guest, to fall upon Mahabat and his men.

Deliberately, knowing the inflammable temperament of his hosts, Mahabat Khan entered the Rana's audience chamber arrayed in stylish robes, without a single weapon about his person. His attendants too were unarmed.

Besides Mahabat walked Ibrahim Khan Fatehjung, brother of Begum Nurjahan and Arjumand's uncle. As soon as he saw him, Khurram suspected that his stepmother had planned something he had not foreseen.

In the great pillared hall were displayed the sacred symbols and insignia of kingship brought from Chittor. All the doors thronged with warriors, bristling with spears and sabres, their dark eyes watchful in their bronzed faces.

At the end of the carpeted hall Rana Karan Singh sat enthroned under the crimson brocade umbrella of his ancestors. Behind him stood attendants whisking yaktails over his head, and the chanting of Mewar's minstrels and bards filled the hall. On the Rana's right sat Sultan Khurram with his young sons and Prince Jagat was seated on the Rana's left.

Mahabat's proud carriage proclaimed the soldier. Though his hair showed streaks of grey beneath his Afghan turban, no sign of fatigue marred his face. In twenty days, he had travelled from Kabul to Agra and then on to Mewar. All this came to Khurram's mind as he watched this formidable warrior approach.

Most of Mahabat's life had been spent in trying to subdue rebellions and conquer provinces, and Khurram had a healthy regard for his prowess. With his lofty stature and exceedingly long arms, Mahabat was reckoned to be one of the finest swordsmen of the time. He was also an outstanding military tactician and engineer, and Khurram knew Mahabat could use his brains as well as his weapons.

Only after greeting the Rana did Mahabat turn towards Khurram with a salaam, indicating that the Mughal Prince enjoyed no status save that of a guest in Mewar. A muscle quivered at the corner of Khurram's mouth as he waited to hear him speak.

The Rana asked, "What brings the valiant Mahabat Khan and Mirza Ibrahim to Mewar?"

Fixing his eyes boldly on Karan Singh, Mahabat replied, "I have come with a message for your guest, Ranaji. I have not come to discuss terms, but to demand unconditional surrender from the Prince. This rebellion has gone on long enough. The Prince must wait on the Emperor at Agra, and submit himself as a penitent for having listened to evil counsel that strove to sow discord between them. Badshah Jehangir, my ever-indulgent master, is prepared to overlook the youthful transgressions of his son Sultan Khurram, and is willing to restore him to favour. But the prince must throw himself on his benevolent father's mercy."

The Rana received this speech with an expressionless face. But he pondered deeply the words, knowing that Khurram's answer would seal the fate of his kingdom. If the gods so pleased, the shadow of war would pass away from Mewar. But if they were angry, and the goddess of war desired more sacrifices, then he must prepare for another prolonged struggle against the Mughal might. He understood all the implications of Mahabat Khan's unspoken threats. And he remembered that Chittor had been sacked for refusing to violate its ancient laws of sanctuary at Akbar's command. But neither would he ever revoke the sacred bond of friendship that bound him to Khurram.

Before answering Mahabat, he rose, and removing his turban from his head, held it out to Khurram. With a great shout, his vassals and kinsmen also rose, and the hall was filled with wondering voices. Ibrahim and Mahabat watched the Rana and Khurram exchange turbans. With this deeply symbolic gesture, Karan Singh had made his meaning abundantly clear to them all.

Mahabat knew that the Rana would never request Khurram to depart from his kingdom; Khurram knew that his friend had pledged himself to his protection afresh. The chiefs of Mewar knew they were bound by their ruler's action.

"State your terms, Mahabat Khan," said Khurram directly once the tumult had subsided and the nobles had resumed their seats.

"The Badshah commands the surrender of your fortresses in Rohtas and Asir, and the immediate attendance at Court of your sons, Prince Dara and Prince Aurangzeb, to be educated under the personal supervision of their grandfather. Their granduncle Ibrahim Khan Fatehjung has been appointed ataliq. In his magnanimous generosity, the Badshah has decreed that you are to receive your former allowances again, and the governorship of Balochpur."

Khurram glanced reproachfully at Ibrahim. "Was it proper for you to become involved in this affair, Mirza?"

"My niece will be thankful, before this affair is over, for my involvement, Prince," stated Ibrahim with a cool smile.

From the latticed queens' gallery came a smothered moan. Khurram guessed that Arjumand had cried involuntarily at the prospect of parting from her sons. He could plainly see his stepmother's hand in this. Arjumand would find this intolerable. But submit he must, lest he imperil his hosts. He tried to reassure himself: whatever be her faults, Begum Nurjahan was neither inhuman nor callous, and towards children he had always found her curiously indulgent, even to Khusro's son, Dawar Buksh. And Khurram felt that their granduncle's presence was meant to reassure Arjumand of her children's safety on the long road to Agra.

After alternately threatening and beseeching him for three years, she had at last sent Mahabat to subdue him. Someday, Khurram resolved, he would annihilate his stepmother.

The entire assembly waited for Khurram's answer. Would it be peace or war?

After a long pause, Khurram said in a calm, deliberate voice, "I bow to the Badshah's decree."

11

By the banks of the Jhelum sprawled the Mughal encampment, its lamps and campfires visible for miles around in the fast-falling dusk.

After passing the winter at Lahore, Jehangir and Nurjahan were travelling to Kabul with a vast retinue. A host of porters and attendants were moving about the camp, while soldiers armed with spears and sabres stood motionless before each tent. From the Emperor's pavilion came sounds of music and laughter. The Begums and Princesses rested in their tents after leisurely warm baths to dispel the fatigue of travel.

Queen Jagat Gossain sat before a miniature sandalwood temple, performing her evening devotions and chanting hymns to the tinkling of bells and lighting of ritual lamps. Sitting crosslegged on the carpeted floor, Dara watched his grandmother. Between Dara and the Rajput queen was a deep bond, something more than the usual affectionate relationship between grandsons and indulgent grandmothers.

How different it was to travel in state like this, thought Dara, remembering the midnight rides and uncomfortable camps he had known for years, when the shadow of Imperial displeasure lay on his father's life, and they were hunted from place to place.

He tried to control his wandering mind and fixed his eyes on the votive lamps his grandmother had lit before her deity. The cadence of the Sanskrit hymns she chanted absorbed him; the aroma of incense induced a mysterious emotion in his boyish heart. He yearned to fathom the meaning of these rites, these ancient words.

But the sounds of hammering, cutting and sawing from outside were terribly discordant.

As darkness fell, Asaf made a last round of the camp to see that all was well. By his side walked Jai Singh, ruler of Amber, who had been placed in charge of the camp equipment, after Asaf's brother Ibrahim had gone to Agra to govern the Mughal capital during Jehangir's absence.

Asaf recalled the latest story he had heard doing the rounds of the zenanas. The Amber Prince had recently married the haughty, lovely, young daughter of Bundi's chief, and she had continued to wear her voluminous, unsophisticated native garb, at which the women of Amber had scoffed. Jai Singh had once teasingly picked up a pair of scissors and offered to cut his bride's jacket more fashionably. Whereupon the Princess of Bundi had seized his sword and slashed his cummerbund to ribbons. Asaf had heard that in her rage she had laid an interdict on the daughters of her clan: henceforth, no Hara girl was to marry into the house of Amber.

But Asaf dared not risk young Jai Singh's wrath by alluding to the incident even in fun. There was dark work afoot in Mahabat's camp, and he would need the Amber Raja's support if the feud between himself and Mahabat blazed into open conflict. Something had nagged at the back of Asaf's mind ever since Mahabat had been made supreme commander of the Mughal troops by the Emperor.

"What an exhausting day!" exclaimed Jai Singh. "I was closeted for hours with the Badshah and then the Empress wanted…"

"Are you boasting or complaining?" interpolated Asaf.

"Both, Nawab, both!" laughed the Amber Raja.

"I hear Mahabat is holding a celebration in his pavilion tonight," ventured Asaf. "Are you also invited or are you dining with the Badshah?"

Jai Singh laughed, his perfect white teeth gleaming as they passed under lighted flambeaux set before the elephant stalls. "Ram Ram! What are you saying, Nawab? Mahabat suspects me of deep designs, he doesn't want me at his feasts."

"Don't you think Mahabat has grown strange lately? His arrogance hasn't decreased in spite of all that trouble he had about the Kangra treasure, and the scandal of his son-in-law's imprisonment. And yet your Rajputs continue to serve him," observed Asaf scathingly.

Shrugging his shoulders, Jai Singh countered, "Why not? He's liberal and just to his men; they honour him for his valour. Anyway, you know that most of his retainers belong to his mother's clan. And I'm convinced that imprisoning his son-in-law and confiscating the dowry Mahabat gave his daughter was most ill-advised."

Before Asaf could answer, sounds of scuffle and a child's high laughter came to their ears from the elephant stalls. They glimpsed a boy running under the leg of the elephants, while helpless attendants remonstrated and groaned.

"Is that you, Aurangzeb?" asked Asaf sharply, catching sight of the young boy's flushed face.

"Look, Grandfather, no one can catch me!" he crowed triumphantly.

"Come out at once, and cease your foolish tricks, Aurangzeb!" said Asaf with sharp authority.

"Ha ha!" came the mocking reply. "Try catching me first!" The elephants, Asaf could see, were snorting and shifting restlessly with all this clamour after a hard day's march.

Asaf said, "If you don't obey me, Aurangzeb, I shall ask the Empress to send you back in disgrace to Agra. There you will be placed in charge of your uncle Ibrahim, who will take away your horses, weapons and toys and force you to study ceaselessly. Do you want that? Or do you want to see Kabul and the tomb of your great ancestor Babur Shah, besides meeting countless Afghan Begs and visiting the stud farm where Turani horses are bred?"

Covered with straw and dust, Aurangzeb emerged from

under the belly of Jehangir's elephant Alam Goman. Snapping his fingers, he said, "You and your empty threats! My grandaunt is always kind to me; she says I amuse her and make her laugh. She won't send me back to Agra."

"You won't find her laughing if I report your scandalous behaviour to her," retorted Asaf. "If one of those elephants had sunk to its knees while you were frolicking under it, you would have been squashed into halwa! Where's your brother Dara? You would do well to follow his example instead of indulging in these senseless escapades."

"Huh!" snorted Aurangzeb. "Do you want me to sit amidst a lot Kafir women, listening to them chant hymns to their idols? That's what my brother was doing when I escaped from the Queen's pavilion." He ran off, grinning impertinently.

How two brothers could be so different was something Asaf could never figure out. Just as he couldn't comprehend how a prince brought up in the liberal Mughal tradition could be so rude and scathing about his own grandmother's religion.

Asaf upbraided the attendants, saying, "You are unfit to have charge of princes, fools! Do you realize that if anything happens to his grandson, the Badshah will have all of you flayed alive? Go attend to your duties."

"These Mughals!" exclaimed Jai Singh. "There's no curbing them. What use, Mirza, to harangue his attendants, when this princeling is so unbiddable? I was offered his ataliqship, but after observing his antics at Agra, I made my excuses to the Empress. My innumerable military duties would not permit me, I said, to do full justice to the prince's education and training,"

"Isn't it incredible," continued Jai Singh, gazing up at the starry sky. "The Mughals love wandering like nomads across their kingdom. They build magnificent cities and beautiful palaces, but spend all their time living in tents, travelling from city to city and province to province. Now I'm always eager to return to Amber, where my ancestors have lived for countless years."

"That's different," said Asaf, pausing beneath a tamarind tree. "You forget, my Lord, that the Mughals are descended from Chagatai Turks and Yakka Mongols who were wanderers in Central Asia for centuries before they learnt to build cities from us Persians..."

At that moment, they saw Dawar Buksh emerging from the stable enclosure, mounted on a white mare. Asaf realized with a jolt that the two young men riding behind him were Mahabat's nephews, Yaqub and Sulaiman. "Are you planning to go for a ride at this hour, Prince?" demanded Asaf.

Dawar Buksh reined his horse, and answered with a smile, "I had promised to attend Mahabat Khan's banquet, my Lord Vezzir."

Asaf frowned. "Aren't you forbidden to go anywhere unless you are attended by Raja Ram Das Kachwaha, or your grandfather Mirza Aziz?"

Before the Prince could answer, Yaqub exclaimed, "Raja Ram Das is indisposed, Nawab, but we are competent enough to escort the Prince."

"No doubt," said Jai Singh. "But no one is permitted to violate the Badshah's instructions."

Dawar Buksh's deceptively mild smile vanished. He stared belligerently at his cousin, and a wilful obstinate expression came into his eyes. Almost since the moment of his birth, reflected the Prince, he had lived under restraint at his grandfather's Court while the Kachwahas of Amber had done nothing to make his position less intolerable. And Asaf, he reflected bitterly, would continue to treat him like a child even if the Emperor were to name him heir-apparent tomorrow.

"This is intolerable! Must I always submit to interference? Must hordes of people always surround me?"

Asaf realized with a shock that this boy had grown to

resemble his grandfather too much. That wilful set of the mouth and those features were remarkably similar to Jehangir's. Dawar Buksh had the same slender frame and carried himself with the same instinctive poise; even his temper flared with the same suddenness.

He had watched the growing intimacy between the Emperor and his grandson, and only last month the jagirs of Khusro had been transferred to Dawar Buksh despite Nurjahan's protests. Without hesitation Asaf concluded that Mahabat was planning to involve the young prince in some intrigue. But he had no intention of allowing Mahabat to influence Dawar Buksh.

"You may do as you please after obtaining the Badshah's consent," stated Asaf inexorably, while the horses chafed and pawed the ground.

The Prince muttered something inarticulate and rode back to the stables. Mahabat's nephews departed after a heated argument with the Grand Vezzir.

And Jai Singh and Asaf also parted company, each escorted by lamp then bearers to his own tent.

A pale moon rose high in the cloud strewn sky and the gurgling sound of swift-flowing water filled the pavilion as Nurjahan sang softly to her grandchild. The little girl smiled blissfully, her eyelids dropped and she sank into slumber.

Holding the sleeping princess tenderly, Nurjahan recalled with amazement her own indifference to this girl at her birth. She had longed for a grandson, and after two miscarriages, Ladli had produced this tiny daughter. She had resented Arzani, until the day Jehangir had come with gifts for his newborn granddaughter. He had glanced indifferently enough at the child held up to him when all at once his eyes had gleamed. He had laughed and caught her hand, saying, "By Allah! She's your very image, Nurjahan!"

From that moment had begun her utter devotion to this child, and she permitted no one else to interfere with Arzani's upbringing. She placed the child in her cradle, whispered some advice to Ladli and at last hurried to her own pavilion.

There she found her husband standing under an awning, gazing at the moonlit waters of the Jhelum. From the woods beyond came the occasional cry of jackals and night birds.

A twinkle lurked in Jehangir's eyes as he turned to greet his wife. "Must I wait, while you pamper your little princess?"

"Are you jealous, Lord?" she mocked him with a smile.

"Always!" he answered, watching her by the light of the lamps set on onyx stands along her sumptuous tapestried tent.

"I have yet to see you fatigued after a journey, Nurjahan. Didn't the heat and dust bother you?"

"Oh, no!" she answered, walking over to a table and mixing his medicine, As he drank the draught, she continued, "You know I enjoy travelling from place to place. It's you who ought to rest and refresh yourself instead of giving audience to all those people."

With a gesture, she invited him to a couch upon which she proceeded to arrange an enamelled chess board with superbly carved jade and amber pieces. Laila brought the hookah, which the Emperor invariably smoked while playing chess.

Jehangir reclined against the cushions and became immersed in the game. Behind an ivory screen sat the Begum's musicians, softly strumming stringed instruments.

"Someone inadvertently mentioned buzkashi to Arzani, and I had great difficulty in assuring the child that no one uses live goats for the game!" said Nurjahan.

The Emperor laughed. "I shall take her to watch one of those wild buzkashi contests. Of course, the Afghans are no match for the tribesmen of the Amu Darya, where the game originated in all probability."

Nurjahan glanced up from the chessboard. She knew what

was coming next. The Mughals had still not broken free from their Central Asian heritage, and the reconquest of Samarkand was one of Jehangir's favourite schemes.

Jehangir moved his horse into a position which threatened her Vezzir, and continued, "A sovereign should always be engaged upon conquests, otherwise his neighbours will rise up in arms against him. After the subjugation of Kandahar, we must keep these turbulent Pathans engaged in Uzbekistan."

"Your dominions are in too disturbed a condition for you to leave them," Nurjahan pointed out. "Or do you plan to entrust the campaign to Khurram?"

"Do you think I would entrust him with an army of conquest? I was thinking of Dawar Buksh. It's high time he proved himself on a battlefield. Let him prove his mettle by reconquering Samarkand."

Nurjahan knew that the reconciliation between the Emperor and Khurram was embittered by resentment and apprehension for the future. But Dawar Buksh was fast becoming his grandfather's pampered darling. He was a boy of marked potential and imagination, but she often felt that despite his youthful candidness, his true self dwelt alone behind an impenetrable wall. Dawar Buksh would never allow others to manipulate him, she felt.

Anyway, there were things of more immediate importance for her to worry about.

"Can anyone build a future by avenging the past, Sire? We must forget the north and concentrate on the south. Anyway, Dawar Buksh is far too young to head this hazardous venture." She knew that a strong streak of sentiment ran deep in her husband. He enjoyed having his grandchildren around him, and spoiled them with his generosity. Her words would make him reconsider his plans for Dawar Buksh.

"The Amir of Jalalabad come to see me this evening. He swears that his revenues have fallen because all his peasants have harvested the wheat and absconded with the price of their crops," Jehangir informed her.

"I agree, Sire. But he's a loyal fool. Despite misdirected leniency and his revenue problems, he should be left undisturbed. We must remember that he's held in great veneration by his people, and could easily become another troublemaker," said Nurjahan earnestly.

Jehangir moved a pawn forward, and glanced speculatively at his consort. "Perveiz always liked the Afghans. Shall we summon him from Allahabad, Begum, and allow him to handle all these troublesome vassals?"

Nurjahan frowned thoughtfully. "I don't think you should, Sire. If disturbances were to break out in Hindustan while we are in Kabul, then who would control the situation? Unless, of course, you send Mahabat Khan as governor of Allahabad and Bihar, instead of Perveiz."

"Certainly!" said Jehangir. "You have a solution for everything, Nurjahan!" They proceeded with the game.

"Checkmate!" cried Jehangir triumphantly. "Your king is captive in his fort."

Jehangir gave a patient hearing to the tribal chiefs who had come to wait on him. He rewarded some, reprimanded others, ordered his officials to look into their complaints, and decided long-pending matters of justice on the spot.

Afterwards, he gave audience to the innumerable people collected in his audience pavilion. He gave the village headmen grants for constructing roads, wells and sarais. From the children he accepted fruit and flowers with gracious courtesy, and gave them largesse. He sent the rayaya away with good wishes and promises of meeting them again on his return from Kabul.

"Is everything ready for our departure?" asked Jehangir.

Salaaming low, Mirza Rustam answered that they only awaited his command before striking camp.

As Jehangir stepped out of his tent, he saw a vast body of horsemen riding down the avenue towards him. For a moment he thought that his son Perveiz had come to join him from Allahabad. Then he saw Mahabat's familiar figure emerging from the throng. No one was permitted to ride up to his pavilion, except his sons and grandsons, and they too always dismounted at a safe distance, lest the dust annoy him.

"What is the meaning of this effrontery?" demanded Jehangir with icy hauteur as Mahabat approached him.

Mahabat's chainmail coat clinked as he threw himself at the Emperor's feet. "I have come to seek your protection, Sire!"

All the nobles and attendants stood amazed. Wild surmises and fears ran through their minds, as they watched the dramatic scene being enacted before them.

"Who threatens you? Speak!" commanded Jehangir. "Will your feuds never cease?"

Clutching the Emperor's hand, Mahabat cried, "Asaf Khan sent his minions to accuse me this morning of fraud! Must I submit to these insults, Sire?"

"You have lost all sense of proportion, Mahabat! I've overlooked every complaint against you, despite repeated reports of your high-handed practices. Once we reach Kabul, you and Asaf must confront each other in my presence, but I'll tolerate no disturbance on the march. My Grand Vezzir is empowered to demand accounts from any mansabadars. Let me warn you, Mahabat, that if you strive to force a quarrel with Asaf, I will banish you from Court!"

From the corner of his eye, Mahabat watched his Rajputs surround Prince Dawar Buksh. The Mughal forces had long since crossed over to the other bank under Asaf's command, he knew. And by now his men would be guarding all the fords and would effectively block their return.

Mahabat rose with an inscrutable expression on his face.

"It were best if you returned to Lahore under my escort, Sire. The journey to Kabul would prove much too fatiguing for you."

When Mahabat's soldiers drew their swords, the stupefying realization came to Jehangir that he was a prisoner in his own camp.

12

Mahabat had reckoned without Begum Nurjahan's courage and obstinacy.

She had no intention of weeping and relapsing into resignation like the other Begums. By the time her brother had finished speaking, her quick mind was already planning her husband's rescue. "Shall Mahabat Khan's treachery go unpunished? Is the Badshah to be harried by this rebellious vassal? Let the drums and trumpets sound for war!" she commanded the nobles who had assembled round her.

From her elephant she looked down at Asaf, who seemed unmoved by her words. In a clear, resounding voice, she cried, "Do you understand? Let the Mughal troops prepare for war!"

"Yes, I understand," retorted Asaf in a scornful voice. "I understand that you've lost your judgement. Do you imagine that you can win a pitched battle against the combined forces of Mahabat and the other nobles who had a hand in this plot?"

"Ya Allah!" she cried passionately, with blazing eyes. "If only my brother Ibrahim were here! He wouldn't need my urging to send him into battle."

Infuriated, yet held in restraint by the numerous persons listening to their exchange, Asaf Khan said reasonably, "Only some carefully contrived stratagem will succeed where open war is bound to fail, Mehrunnisa. You know that most of our troops were dispatched to Attock three days ago. It would be utterly useless to cross the river with our small remaining force to give battle to Mahabat Khan."

Most of the nobles concurred with him, and Asaf declared that he would escort all the Mughal Begums and Princes to Attock, where the loyal Mughal garrison would defend them.

Her brother's arguments and Ladli's entreaties could not shake Nurjahan's resolve. Quelling them with a scornful glance, she declared imperiously, "Faint-hearted cowards may seek shelter along with the Grand Vezzir at Attock! But I have pledged myself to the Badshah's deliverance."

Jai Singh found her scornful words intolerable. Urging his mount forward, he cried, "Shall the Empress call us cowards? By the gods of my ancestors, no!"

A shout went up, swords were raised, and horses clattered up to Nurjahan's elephant. Steel rasped, pennants were thrust aloft. She looked down, threw the veil back from her face, and counted her supporters. Jai Singh of Amber, with his five hundred Kachwaha horsemen, Jujhar Singh Bundela and his six hundred Rajputs, Fidai Khan the chief of Jalalabad, her nephew, the incomparable archer Bankey Khan, and some Afghan and Persian cheftains whom she had befriended from time to time.

"Our swords shall speak for us!" they shouted.

Ladli knew that there was no reasoning with her mother in this humour. Turning to Dil Aram, who held her daughter Arzani, she said, "Order the mahavat to convey us to my mother's garden on the Jhelum where the Badshah usually halts after crossing the river."

"Dear child, wouldn't it be safer to proceed under your uncle's protection to Attock?" said Dil Aram.

"Do as I command you," cried Ladli sharply. She had no intention of abandoning her mother like her uncle Asaf.

Nurjahan's elephant was already halfway across the ford. She had pulled aside the curtains, indifferent at such a moment of crisis to dictates of custom or of modesty.

Turning to Laila, who sat praying silently behind her, Nurjahan commanded, "Hand me my bow and quiver. Mahabat will pay for daring to hold the Badshah captive!"

At a command from Jai Singh, war drums sounded and

fifes blared out. The place was rent with the sound of Mughal trumpets shrilling over the din of mounts and men. The ford was choked with elephants and horses. Some soldiers stumbled and fell, many were trampled underfoot, others got swept away by the swift current, and only a few were able to cross the stream.

By this time Mahabat Khan's retainers, reinforced by the troops belonging to Perveiz's other adherents, had taken up strategic positions along the river.

As Begum Nurjahan led her forces towards them, battle cries resounded and a fearful clamour broke out amongst the soldiers. Volleys of spears flew everywhere, arrows twanged through the air.

From her elephant, Nurjahan saw Mahabat seated on a fiery charger, his armour shining as he brandished his sword. A fierce rage to kill possessed her and she took a flighted arrow from her gold mesh quiver.

Mahabat heard the whizz of a shaft through the air, and an arrow pierced his chainmail tunic. Only his specially designed armour prevented Begum Nurjahan's unerring shot from wounding him. Seated unveiled on her elephant, rallying the Mughal forces with impassioned cries, she looked formidable with her flying tresses and furious face. He could see a woman sitting behind her, praying with uplifted hands.

What folly had permitted Asaf to allow this truly wild behaviour? He tried to find Asaf in that melee of furiously charging horses and trumpeting elephants. But though he recognized many of his antagonists, he realized that Asaf was missing.

Shields clanked as Jai Singh's clansmen clashed with Mahabat's retainers. The Amber Raja galloped at the head of his squadron and thrust a spear through Yaqub. But he couldn't combat the remorseless pressure of Mahabat's troops. However hard Jai Singh fought, he could not cut his way through the corps of guards who protected Mahabat.

The Afghan chief Fidai Khan, a warrior of formidable repute, dealt death to any soldier or cavalier who dared to cross his path. He wielded his mighty double-edged sword with amazing speed for one no longer young.

Mahabat directed an assault against the ahadis and mansabdars who protected the Empress. She watched the loyal Rajputs surrounding her elephant cut down one by one.

Groans of dying men and the shrill high whinny of terrified horses filled the air. Cannon balls and arrows were falling thick and fast round Nurjahan's howdah; her elephant was wounded and bleeding in many places. One of Mahabat's men took deliberate aim at Nurjahan's mahavat. As the arrow hit him, the mahavat toppled to the ground with an agonized scream.

Now it was Nurjahan who tried to guide the mahavat-less elephant through the enemy lines, all the time seeking Mahabat, the cause of this conflict.

"Let us depart from this field of battle, and leave fighting to men," begged Laila. "It's most unseemly for you to expose yourself to the gaze of all these vulgar soldiers!"

As Nurjahan turned to admonish her, an arrow came flying through the air and pierced her right arm. She reeled at the impact and a sharp cry of pain broke from her. Laila caught the Empress in her arms and felt a tremor pass through her body, as Nurjahan sank swooning with shock. Their elephant wheeled back screaming towards the river bank.

When they saw the Empress leave the battle, the Afghans stopped fighting and broke ranks in panic. Detachment after detachment of ahadis wheeled away and raced towards the river.

Mahabat's horsemen thundered up the river bank, and cursed when they saw the Begum's elephant escaping. Soon the only remaining sound was the clatter of hoofs.

Ladli stood trembling with apprehension in the terraced garden. Her eyes followed the furiously raging battle, and she saw flashes of steel and clouds of dust everywhere. All at once she spotted her mother's elephant stumbling up through the waters below the garden. Her mother's ladies set up a dreadful moaning all around her, but with desperate self-possession, Ladli dispatched Dil Aram to bring news of her mother.

When the women bore the Empress into the garden, a profound silence descended, and everyone gazed with stunned disbelief at her blood-stained form.

Ladli commanded sharply, "Cease your gaping and convey her into the pavilion!"

Nurjahan recovered consciousness much later to find herself in a pavilion bright with perfumed lamps with Ladli bending over her, soothing her brow and tenderly whispering, "Allah has saved you and restored you to us!"

Nurjahan opened her eyes with an effort and said distinctly, "I must go to join the Badshah in Mahabat Khan's camp."

Next morning, Mahabat awoke in a savage mood. This affair had ended in a very different fashion from what he had planned. All he had intended was the Emperor's capture; and only his unshaken belief in Perveiz's cause had forced him into a pitched battle against the Empress. He was determined to hold the Emperor and Prince Dawar Buksh captive until Jehangir signed firmans bestowing the tide, insignia, and jagirs of Crown Prince on Perveiz.

While he strode up and down outside his tent, he heard one of the guards cry, "A palanquin approaches, Master!"

He guessed at once that it was Begum Nurjahan. "Escort the Empress with befitting courtesy to the Badshah's tent!" he ordered.

Jehangir's attendants had retired after helping him with his morning toilet, and he was absorbed in prayer when the sound of marching feet disturbed him. He heard the tent flap fall and the smell of herbs and roses filled the air. "Nurjahan!" Then he saw the bloodstained bandage on her arm.

With a mighty oath, he seized her. His grip was agony, but she choked back her cry. "Who has dared to hurt you? Where are all the mansabdars and ahadis, my numerous queens and concubines? Have they all forsaken me except you?"

In an utterly weary tone, she answered, "They have all gone to Attock with my brother Asaf. Except Ladli."

She sank down on his bed and began to weep softly. He sat down beside her, and kissed her tenderly.

They talked for a long time. "Trust Asaf," he said, consoling her. "Strategems, not swords, will set us free. Don't cry, Nurjahan. Yesterday you proved yourself a valiant queen and I'm sure that somehow, we shall make Mahabat rue his folly!"

"Mahabat is chasing a phantom, I know. But can we trust my brother Asaf?" she wondered aloud.

Jehangir had behaved from the very first day of his capture as if nothing untoward had happened. And so three months passed. Nurjahan waited and watched for a chance to escape.

In Kabul, she saw the breach between Hindus and Muslims widening of. Complaints about the arrogant behaviour of Mahabat's Rajputs began pouring in and when they fought a battle with the ahadis over the right to graze their horses on Crown land, Nurjahan knew that Mahabat's supporters were dwindling.

One afternoon, after an exceptionally unsavoury incident, involving his men, Mahabat came to assure the Emperor that he would publicly disgrace those who had acted against his command.

Jehangir silenced him with a gesture. "Do exactly as you please, Mahabat. I have placed the weight of the empire on your shoulders. The finger of old age has fallen on me and I believe that retirement must be my greatest solace. I now derive pleasure only from peaceful contemplation; the treachery and inconsistency of this world are as clear to me as daylight."

Mahabat withdrew, cursing himself for letting month after month slip by without forcing the Emperor to sign the firmans he had prepared, bestowing the succession upon Perveiz. While he was crossing a courtyard leading to the outer apartments of the Kabul Fort, Begum Nurjahan's chief eunuch accosted him.

"Your pardon, worthy Khan. The Empress desires to pay a visit to the mausoleum of Babur Shah to offer prayers for the Badshah's health. She bids you order your guards not to hinder her departure or return, nor should they annoy her by riding too close to her palanquin and raising dust. She will be accompanied, by her daughter and some waiting women."

"The Empress shall have no cause to complain of my men's behaviour," said Mahabat sharply.

From the window of his apartment, Mahabat saw seven palanquins escorted by fifty of his most trusted men pass along the winding paved path to Babur Shah's tomb. He remembered visiting it for the first time when he was a young boy, flushed with pride at being included in Sultan Salim's entourage. How many years ago had that been?

He sighed and turned away from the window and tried to concentrate on the news reports sent by his agents from all parts of Hindustan. He searched in vain for any message from Prince Perveiz amongst the pile of petitions and reports. Instead he found disturbing reports from his spies at Allahabad about the Prince's deteriorating health.

Meanwhile Jai Singh of Amber set forth unimpeded as usual on his evening ride to Babur Shah's tomb. Mahabat had not bothered to curb his movements, for he knew that as long as Dawar Buksh was captive, the Kachwahas would be powerless to act against him.

In the garden behind Babur Shah's tomb waited three

swift camels, which could travel a distance of more than one hundred miles in a single night.

As twilight fell, Nurjahan watched the palki bearers starting back towards the fort. When the cavalcade of horsemen and palanquins disappeared up the road, she led her group across the park which surrounded the tomb.

When he saw the camels, Jehangir protested, "It's years since I rode a camel, Nurjahan!"

She replied with a low laugh, "And I've never ridden one! Neither has Ladli. Jai Singh and I decided that camels would be safer and swifter than horses. When Mahabat Khan discovers our flight, he will send out parties to search for horsemen. But in our Afghan robes, who will guess that we are not a nomad family moving from Kabul to the land of the Yusufzahis?"

"Let's hurry, Grandfather!" urged Dawar Buksh. "Once they realize that we are not in the fort, they will block all the roads leading from Kabul to the Khyber Pass. If we can reach Jalalabad by nightfall, we shall be safe, for the amir of Jalalabad is loyal to you."

Admiration rekindled in Jai Singh's heart as he assisted the Empress to mount the kneeling camel. She laughed softly and the voluminous folds of her dark silk burkha swirled around her legs. She held out her arms for Arzani, tried to soothe her nervous fears and murmured that she would enjoy the bumpy ride.

When Jehangir and Ladli were settled on their camels, Jai Singh and Dawar Buksh mounted behind them. The men muffled their faces in the folds of their turbans, Nurjahan and her daughter veiled their faces, and very cautiously the little kafila moved down the narrow mountain path leading to the valley below.

Nurjahan restrained an impulse to urge her camel into wild flight. She hugged her grandchild and took a deep breath, exulting in their regained freedom.

13

As the Emperor's health deteriorated, the succession question become acute not only at Court, but throughout Hindustan. There was an air of expectancy at Agra, intrigues grew more involved, and the political situation was so precariously balanced that Nurjahan was compelled to recall her brother from Lahore.

Through the long winter months Jehangir watched the factions trying to outmanoeuvre one another. The humiliation of his imprisonment at Kabul, the death of his second son Perveiz; the revolt of his old friend Mahabat; his Grand Vezzir Asaf's desertion on the banks of the Jhelum; and Khurram's recalcitrant attitude had all combined to break his spirit, and he did nothing to interfere.

After their successful escape from Kabul, events had moved swiftly. News came of Mahabat's flight through Sindh and Gujarat to Khurram, back in Burhanpur. Everyone realized that this could prove a formidable alliance, but Nurjahan was resolute and self-possessed. As long as his sons were held hostage, Khurram dared not stir from the Deccan, she knew.

She summoned her supporters to Agra, and kept a stream of messengers galloping between the capital and the provinces. She held innumerable sessions with the Raja of Amber and her brother Ibrahim. She forced her son-in-law to accept command of the forces deputed to pursue and capture Mahabat. Her brother-in-law Qasim was recalled from Khandesh and made Governor of the Mughal castle.

She still missed her sessions with that wily sage Mirza Abdur Rahim, who had succumbed to old age and his many war injuries, dying at last at seventy.

Though she was reluctant to admit even to herself that the

Emperor's illness was serious, now more than ever did she need her astute brother Asaf. There was trouble and tumult all over Hindustan, she knew. The Persians were invading Baluchistan and Khorasan, the Afghans were treacherous and the Uzbeks hostile. Rajputana was seething with feuding families and warring clans. The Portuguese were up to their old mischief along the coastal cities of Bengal and Gujarat. And as a result of repeated drought and famine in Bihar and Avadh, there was an alarming decline in the empire's revenues, and an upsurge of dacoity and robbery on all the eastern highways.

She wondered if she ought to relent and suggest Khurram's recall. After all, he was the only general capable of driving back the invading Persians.

But months passed by, and her husband remained averse even to the mention of Khurram's name. Nurjahan realized at last that Jehangir would never be able to forgive his once-beloved son. After Khusro's death, he had angrily brushed aside all suggestions of foul play, and told her that these same baseless accusations had been whispered against him when his brothers Murad and Daniyal had died in rapid succession. But when they told him of Perveiz's sudden death, he had demanded the cause. And when no one answered, he had groaned with grief and cried out that something was being hidden from him. After that, he had collapsed completely and the most skilful physicians in the country had been unable to cure him.

Amidst endless administrative problems and ceaseless audiences and receptions, Nurjahan was gnawed by worry over his health. She performed penances, commissioned mosques and serais all over the country, distributed alms, visited the shrines of all the saints in the vicinity of Agra and sent valuable gifts to Sheikh Salim Chisti's tomb. By the end of March she had decided to take her husband to recuperate in Kashmir. In that peaceful valley she would nurse him back to health, she told herself with fierce determination.

Asaf stood with the other courtiers on the steps of the mosque built at Srinagar by his sister Nurjahan in thanksgiving for the Emperor's recovery. Around the Shahi Mosque was gathered a salaaming, cheering multitude. Children jostled and crowded around the marble steps, and from every balcony and window women watched the Emperor.

He heard Zaffar, the Governor of Kashmir, saying emotionally as he helped the Emperor mount his horse, "Sire, it is the ardent prayer of every loyal soul that you may live long to reign over us!"

Jehangir glanced significantly at his assembled vassals. "Life and death are in Allah's hands, but I hope you will continue to serve my successor with equal fervour, Zaffar."

That evening, Asaf invited his old friends Zaffar, Mirza Rustam and the young Raja of Amber to an intimate feast.

Jai Singh found the food delicious and the dancing girls enticing. He sipped the iced wine and murmured compliments to his host, trying to overhear the whispered conversation between Mirza Rustam and Zaffar Khan, one of Begum Nurjahan's staunchest supporters. But the tinkling of anklets and the music drowned their voices and he was unable to catch a single word.

The dance came to an end and Asaf motioned the musicians and nautch girls away. The men were left alone amidst the cushions and flower garlands in the chamber.

After a leisurely pull at the hookah, Asaf turned to Zaffar. "Do you remember what the Badshah said to you this morning, Nawab?"

"Perhaps you could remind me?" Zaffar said.

'This morning the Badshah spoke of his heir. But who is going to succeed him?"

Putting aside all pretence, Zaffar sat up against the cushions and observed soberly, "That is the question I've been pondering for months." Heaving a deep sigh, he continued,

"Why won't he name his heir and put an end to all speculation and intrigue?"

Although Asaf smiled, his voice was grave. "You haven't answered my question, Zaffar."

"The position is one of acute interest to every person, Asaf," interpolated Mirza Rustam. "I've often wondered why the Badshah was so reluctant to bestow the jagirs and insignia of Crown Prince on my son-in-law, Perveiz. He and Begum Nurjahan suffered months of humiliating confinement when a single word could have set them free."

"Let us concern ourselves with the future, Mirza," said Asaf in a compelling voice. The choice of successor might bring disaster to the entire realm, and to each one of us." After a significant pause he added, "Or it may bring a period of unprecedented glory for Hindustan and for us all."

Jai Singh threw Mirza Rustam a speculative glance. A faint smile hovered about his mouth as he said, "Does the Grand Vezzir talk of succession according to the laws of primogeniture or succession according to the rule of seniority?"

"What does the Amber Raja advocate?" parried Asaf, with a glint in his hazel eyes.

"When my grandfather died, I inherited the gadi of Amber as a matter of right, for I was the eldest son of his dead heir. And my kinsmen and vassals uphold my rule," said the Raja with marked emphasis.

There was a moment's silence. Asaf studied Jai Singh intently, then bent his head to sniff the garland of jasmines round his wrist.

"We shall see," he murmured with an inscrutable smile.

In Kashmir, Nurjahan tried to beguile the Emperor with daily diversions. That spring morning, she had invited the entire Mughal family to her new garden on the south bank of the Jhelum beyond the Wular lake.

Standing with her husband under the black marble pavilion, whose windows were made entirely of perforated mother-of-pearl, Nurjahan surveyed the enchanting scene. The mountain peaks were white with snow, and the forests and valleys below them were daubs of indigo and emerald. The canals and fountains appeared to be molten rivers of gold, reflecting the brilliant sunlight.

Around the pavilion lay a large park enclosed by huge chinar, deodar and poplar trees, against which were outlined stiff dark cypresses and Nurjahan's numerous rose bushes and great masses of spring flowers bloomed around the fountains.

To Jehangir, his wife seemed as much a part of this landscape as the lake, which was almost the colour of her eyes. Her pearl-encrusted costume of pale apricot satin seemed to reflect the tints of the flowering fruit trees which they had planted together in the year Arzani, their grandchild, was born. This is the perfect setting for her beauty, he thought, smiling at her.

On a sudden impulse, he asked, "Shall I bestow the province of Kashmir on you and your heirs in perpetuity?"

For a moment she stood gazing at him and the fears which lay dormant in her mind rose up to torment her again. With deliberate effort, she forced herself to think instead of the years that lay ahead, years she had planned so carefully in her own mind. She brushed aside her fears.

"The granting of permanent jagirs is contrary to the Mughal concept of imperial solidarity," countered Nurjahan.

The Emperor glanced at the other Begums and observed with a gleam of amusement in his eyes, "There speaks Ghias Beg's daughter!"

Nurjahan's laughter pealed out and taking her husband's arm, she led him down the shallow marble steps towards a group of his grandchildren talking animatedly besides a fountain.

"Where is Dawar Buksh?" asked Jehangir, smiling affectionately at the eager faces upraised to welcome him.

"Oh, he must have gone with his attendants to watch the boat race I've arranged today. The winner will receive a bag of sapphires from you, Sire, and I believe more than sixty noblemen are contesting for the prize," Nurjahan informed him.

"And the rowers? Won't they get anything, Grandmother?" asked Dara, fixing his large solemn eyes on her face.

"A hundred gold mohurs each!" announced Jehangir in his impulsively benevolent manner. "Let us proceed towards the lake, Begum, for everyone must be eager for the race to begin."

Nurjahan beckoned to Queen Jagat Gossain, and together they all walked towards the embankment through a maze of paved paths enclosed by flowering vines spread over marble arches.

"I wonder if any of you have ever heard the legend connected with the discovery of Kashmir's sapphire mines," said the Emperor.

"No," Nurjahan smiled. "Do tell us."

"Yes, please," chimed in Dara. "You tell such interesting stories, Grandfather."

"Very well," agreed Jehangir. "Years ago, on a day like this, my father went hunting for mountain bears in Kishtwar. By nightfall, he had outdistanced all his amirs and attendants and also lost himself amongst the unfamiliar mountains. Unable to find his camp, he sought shelter in a cave from which came a bright light. And what do you think he found inside the cave? Not a fire, as he had expected, but a strange, awesome sight. At the end of the deep cavern he saw a colossal heap of blazing gems over which sat a Hindu Yogi in an attitude of profound meditation, with serpents coiled round his neck and arms! Undaunted, my father approached the holy man. The story goes that the Yogi recognized the Shahenshah and offered him the pile of precious stones around him. But he imposed one condition. No Mughal was ever to use them for personal adornment, they were to be distributed on suitable occasions amongst the people. Ever since, that cave has been giving us an inexhaustible supply of very fine sapphires, and my father and I have scrupulously refrained from using them or bestowing them upon anyone in our family."

"A diverting tale," said Nurjahan, as they came to the terrace jutting out into the river. A marble throne and benches stood under gold-embroidered velvet canopies.

"Whatever became of the Yogi, Grandfather?" questioned Dara with an eager look.

"No one knows," smiled Jehangir. "Do you believe this fantastic legend?"

"There are many things in this world which can only be described as miraculous, Sire," said Queen Jagat Gossain reprovingly.

"My brother is always ready to credit any nonsense he may hear or read!" scoffed Aurangzeb. "But I know your story is nothing but rubbish, Grandfather."

Immediately his grandmother Jagat Gossain spoke sharply about his manners and commanded him to apologize.

"What are you studying these days, Dara?" asked Jehangir, hastily changing the subject and inviting his grandsons to sit beside him on the cushioned throne.

"Valmiki's Ramayana in the original Sanskrit!" answered Dara with evident pride.

"A great epic, from which we may all learn much," said Jehangir, and reclined against the cushions.

"A stupid, disgusting tale!" declared Aurangzeb, his dark eyes insolent.

"You must not mock the sacred books of which you know

nothing," admonished Nurjahan, aware of the Rajput Queen's growing anger.

"Oh, I've been forced to hear that silly story often enough!" retorted Aurangzeb, with swift impudence. "Just shows what these Kafirs will worship."

"Evidently you found nothing admirable in the story!" snapped his grandmother.

"Oh, yes!" declared Aurangzeb. He was aware that everyone was listening to him. "There's only one sensible person in the entire book, whom I admire wholeheartedly. Queen Kekayi, who induced her Lord to banish his heir so her own son could become king." Jehangir laughed uproariously.

"I haven't heard such diverting opinions since Aziz Koka died!" declared Jehangir. "He should have lived to become Aurangzeb's ataliq. And I swear he would have met his match in my grandson!"

Aurangzeb flashed him an impudent grin while Dara scowled and Khurram's mother sat rigid, but forbore to scold more. She knew that Aurangzeb had developed an incredible antipathy towards the Hindus ever since the day he had been wrenched away from his adoring mother, blaming the Rana of Mewar for their continuing separation rather than the feud between his father and grandfather. Hopefully he would outgrow his prejudice soon and accept the reality of his own Hindu blood.

"Look!" cried Nurjahan, pointing down the river towards a narrow wooden bridge. "The musketeers are lifting their guns, the race is about to begin."

A loud volley of shots followed by the resounding boom of kettledrums was the signal for the boatmen to dip their oars into the water. The gay flower-decked boats skimmed swiftly over the foaming water, while crowds of onlookers cheered lustily and exchanged bets all along the banks. A shrill babble of sound arose, and the boatmen hurled insults at each other.

Jehangir was caught up in the excitement of the race. As the boats approached nearer he could see the turbanned figures straining and swinging rhythmically at their oars. In the forefront were the ornate shikaras of Abu Saiyeed, Shahanawaz Khan and Jai Singh. But soon the Emperor noticed an unadorned boat with upturned stern and bow drawing ahead of all the other boats. It was managed with great skill by rowers muffled in cloaks and scarfs.

"Can you recognize the owner of that boat, Nurjahan?" asked Jehangir.

"Perhaps it belongs to the townspeople, who wish to indulge in the pastimes of our Court! They seem to be well ahead of everyone else," laughed Nurjahan. "The nobles will be vexed if the prize intended for them is won by common folk."

The spectators broke into cheers as the unidentified boat's prow touched the stone embankment. Eunuchs came forward to escort their leader up the stone steps to the Emperor while other harem attendants held up lace screens to guard the royal ladies from vulgar eyes.

A youth approached the Emperor with dignified steps and salaamed low. Only his eyes and the bridge of his nose were visible between the folds of cloth wound round his face and head. Everyone gazed curiously at him, but he accepted the brocade pouch held out by Jehangir wordlessly.

"That was a remarkable exhibition of skill and strength," said Jehangir graciously. "But are we to be left guessing your name, young man?"

With a laugh he unwound the scarf, disclosing a fair boyish face. The Mughal Begums gasped.

"Dawar Buksh!" exclaimed Jehagir. "What mad folly is this?"

The Prince apologized for his trick and laughed. "Fooled you all, didn't I! But you see, Grandfather, I had to disguise myself only because last week, when I won the archery contest some people scoffed and said I had received the prize only because I'm a Mughal, and not because of superior marksmanship! I was determined to show everyone that there are several things I can do on my own."

Dawa Buksh opened the pouch and poured the stones into his palm, where they sparkled and glittered in the sunlight. "These sapphires will make excellent studs, Grandfather! They are superbly matched in size and colour."

But all the humour had gone out of Jehangir's face. "These stones are forbidden to us Mughals, my child. Give them to Asaf's son, Abu Sayeed, who finished second, and I shall permit you to choose anything you may fancy from my own jewellery, which is peerless."

"But I've *won* these gems, Grandfather!" declared Dawar Buksh. "It wouldn't really be the same if I exchanged them. I'm not a bit superstitious, so I'll keep them."

He was gone before anyone could stop him. Nurjahan began talking gaily to Jehangir. She was determined not to let an old legend spoil this day, which had begun so well.

Suddenly, she heard shouts and then a long despairing cry coming from the water. With horrified eyes she saw Dawar Buksh's boat swirling madly in one of those treacherous whirlpools which abounded in this mountain stream, and had often proved disastrous to unwary boatmen.

All the young princes moaned loudly and everyone watched Dawar Buksh paddling furiously to no avail.

Jehangir's face turned ashen as he watched his grandson's boatmen trying to escape the churning waters.

The Rajput Queen cried with desperate urgency, "Do something, Nurjahan. We can't sit here watching Khusro's son drown!"

"To the rescue!" Nurjahan commanded her young nephew Abu Sayeed, who was gaping below in his boat.

Asaf's son gave a sharp command, and the boat rushed across the water. One of the boatmen stood up and twirled a rope in the air. After several attempts, he succeeded in throwing it across to the other boat. Dawar Buksh leaned dangerously forward and caught the trailing end without falling into the foaming, swirling water below.

"Keep cool, all of you!" he ordered, as Abu Sayeed's barge prepared to drag them to safety.

"Hare Krishna!" breathed the Rajput Queen.

"Allah be praised!" Nurjahan said, while Jehangir's eyes blazed relief.

After a while, the drenched and dishevelled Prince sprang down from the boat and walked up the embankment.

"It's those accursed stones," declared Jehangir. "Cast them away, Dawar Buksh, before some other misfortune befalls you."

All the Begums added their objections and entreated the Prince to obey his grandfather.

But their arguments left him unmoved. "Every evil in Hindustan can be traced to superstitions and a slavish belief in legends, omens and senseless customs! It has yet to be proved that mere stones have altered human destiny." And pointing to the Emperor's turban, Dawar Buksh continued with a laugh, "Why don't you cast off the Kohinoor, Grandfather? Isn't there a legend connected with that diamond, of the rise and fall of empires, fraternal strife and woe?"

"These princes!" said Jagat Gossain angrily. "They mock what they cannot perceive, and set themselves up as authorities on matters beyond their understanding..."

Nurjahan intervened swiftly. "Dawar Buksh, your opinions are your own, but your life is more precious to the Badshah, and to us all, than a thousand Kohinoors. All stones are said to influence us, and there are things in this world beyond logic and human comprehension. If my nephew had not gone so quickly to your rescue, that icy Jhelum water would by now be swirling over your head!"

"It would have been a swift, painless death!" said Dawar Buksh with a careless shrug.

14

Jehangir felt the gentle warmth of the afternoon sun on his face as he stood before his pavilion, chatting affably with his grandsons.

At a slight distance stood Asaf, Mirza Rustam and Jai Singh of Amber, with several other nobles, all listening in silent amusement to the vehement opinions expressed by the young princes to their indulgent grandsire.

A cold breeze laden with forest smells ruffled their stiff, elaborately pleated silk robes and teased the plumes on their turbanned heads. Autumn was over, and the first winter chill could be felt by everyone, except the Emperor, it seemed. He lingered on in Kashmir even though November had begun.

Jehangir was in a strange humour. The longing to be on a horse again pushed everything else from his mind. He desired nothing more at that moment than to ride through the hidden forest trails, splashing through swift mountain streams as he gave chase to his chosen prey.

"It's a perfect day to be out hunting, Asaf," said Jehangir, turning to smile brightly at his Grand Vezzir.

Asaf realized, as perhaps very few others did, how much the Emperor chafed at the restrictions placed on him by his solicitous physicians. The prolonged sojourn in Kashmir had helped him recoup, reflected Asaf, and through marvellous good fortune, at fifty-eight, Jehangir still retained his splendid carriage and the beauty of his tawny eyes. He looked imposing and vital in his sumptuous robes, until one noticed the tremor in his hands and the lines around his mouth.

"A hunt is the last thing you ought to indulge in, Sire. I beg you not to jeopardise your health afresh merely for a few hours' pleasant diversion," protested Asaf.

"I haven't been on horseback even once since we left Srinagar! I find it extremely tedious to be carried about in a palanquin like an invalid. You seem to forget, my friend, that my father Akbar Shah indulged in every form of sport and pastime till he was well past sixty. And I'm only fifty-eight!"

He brushed aside the protests of Jai Singh and Mirza Rustam. He had no intention of shooting down any deer kept in an enclosure beyond the camp for the sport of the royal ladies, as Rustam kept suggesting.

"An absurd idea, Mirza!" snapped Jehangir with darkening brow. He would prove to these whining amirs that he could hold his own with any of them, even with young men like Dawar Buksh – that his prolonged illness had not lessened one whit his superb horsemanship or the accuracy of his aim.

Hearing his imperious command ring out, Asaf fell silent. He knew from long experience that no one could persuade Jehangir to change his mind in one of his reckless moods. With swift efficiency, he arranged everything for the hunt, and commanded the huntsmen to be sparing of their master's strength.

The gleeful cries of the young princes could be heard above the ensuing commotion. They were more than willing to break the monotony of slow travel by indulging in an impromptu hunt.

Jehangir remembered the thrill of past hunts as he mounted his pure-bred Iraqi horse slowly and heavily with the aid of his amirs. Gathering the reins with trembling fingers, he threw back his head and laughed to see the anxious disapproving look on his Grand Vezzir's face.

"Let us forget all cares, Asaf, and devote ourselves to the enjoyment of these last precious days, for the world is not to be had a second time!" declared Jehangir, and spurred his horse to a gallop.

In his wake rode a splendid cavalcade with baying hounds

and growling leopards. They were swiftly lost from Asaf's view within the dense woods.

With a thunder of hoofs and a clatter of arms they rode down the forest path into a narrow valley, startling quails and partridges out of the yellowing thickets. Bucks and does, some with spotted fawns behind them, went leaping and bounding into a fringe of trees. The hunters chased them with loud cries and showers of arrows.

While wheeling his horse away from a shallow dry ditch, Dawar Buksh glanced upward, and was thrilled to see a mountain bear clambering up a steep cliff.

"A bear, Sire!" called the Prince, controlling his snorting dappled mount, and pointing excitedly.

"Where?" asked Jehangir, peering keenly as he reined in his horse. Then he spotted the beast. Its fur glistened in the sunlight against the cliff wall. With a triumphant laugh, he cried, "Better sport than deer, by the Prophet!"

"Which way, Sire?" called the Amber Raja, clattering up to the Emperor.

"Up the mountain, close by the ruins of that old Buddhist shrine, till we come up behind him," flung Jehangir over his shoulder with scarcely concealed impatience. Then he ordered his musket bearer to follow close.

Alarmed, Jai Singh cautioned in an agitated voice, "That mountain is rent by ravines and treacherous chasms, my Lord." Jehangir answered disdainfully, "I know these mountains better than you imagine. I've been hunting at Bhimber since long before your birth!" He raced off with his musket bearer, Shamsher, hard on his heels.

The sun in his eyes, the wind on his face, the movement of his mount beneath him, the sound of hooves and the scent of the forest intoxicated Jehangir. He heard a shout from Dawar Buksh, an exultant cry from Dara, and saw his grandsons racing neck to neck. He laughed to see a snowcock rise suddenly from a mass of boulders, flash across the path, and disappear into the dense forest.

The bird startled Shamsher's mare and set it plunging and rearing wildly. And before the musket bearer could control it, the horse bolted off through an opening in the trees.

Jehangir urged his mount forward again, and rode uphill over boulder-strewn ground through which a small stream trickled. He could see the bear silhouetted against the sky. It stood on its hind legs with ears cocked in alarm. He called for his gun, but no one answered him. Moments later, a hideous scream rent the air as Shamsher and his mount went plunging over an unseen precipice.

"The chasm, Sire! Beware the chasm!" shouted Jai Singh, suddenly aware of the crevice which yawned straight ahead.

With a superhuman effort, the Amber Raja swerved his mount away from the sheer cliff, and in another instant leaned forward to wrench the Emperor's reins.

The shrill high whinny of his frightened mount and Jai Singh's despairing shout were the last sounds Jehangir heard as he fell.

After the midday meal, Nurjahan dismissed her attendants, and sat down to embroider the pale cream shawl she had begun a few weeks ago in Kashmir. It was intended as a gift for the Emperor, and she had created an original design of flowing arabesques worked all over in crimson and green silk. Embroidery had always soothed her mind, but today her mind was in tumult. Jewels flashed on her tapering fingers as she bit her underlip, and set tiny intricate stitches in the incredibly soft, warm fabric.

She appeared unruffled and Ladli could hardly guess that her mother had spent a most uncomfortable night.

Nurjahan kept thinking of the horrible dream she had had last night. The lamps and candles in her chamber were suddenly extinguished by an icy blast in her dream, and she had woken up trembling and in tears. And in the morning Dil Aram had only increased her anxiety by urging her to persuade the Emperor to proceed immediately to Lahore.

Her old nurse's vague, sinister allusions had enraged Nurjahan, and she had sharply warned Dil Aram to hold her tongue. But experience had shown over the years that Dil Aram never spoke in vain. What new calamity, wondered Nurjahan, was coming now?

She thought with misgiving of the vital decisions the Emperor had been putting off for months, and realized that ultimately she herself would have to decide everything, issue orders, dictate firmans. Sultanat affairs would not wait upon her husband's whim, and she admitted reluctantly to herself that it was time to entrust Dawar Buksh with the powers and privileges of Crown Prince. That would lessen her own burden, serve as an effective counter-measure to Khurram's soaring ambition and silence the speculating amirs and rayaya.

Though well-disposed towards her stepgrandson, Nurjahan had been unable to decide to what extent he might prove strong or credulous under her brother's adroit handling. She had watched with misgiving as the amirs, led by Asaf, had begun making overtures of friendship to young Dawar Buksh. Already, he was surrounded by sycophants and rapacious relatives who could use him for their own ends. And when she had warned Dawar Buksh a few days ago to keep aloof from matters which his youthful mind could not comprehend, he had heard her out with perfect courtesy, and yet continued to remain on the friendliest terms with his grandfather's Grand Vezzir.

A child's sudden laughter broke upon her reverie, making her pause in her work and look through the rolled-up curtain towards a group of girls playing on the carpeted clearing outside. They were dancing round and round, their tiny veils floating and bangles clinking as they clapped hands and chanted some silly children's rhyme.

Nurjahan smiled indulgently as she watched Arzani, flushed with sunshine and wind. She was amazed afresh at the child's incredible resemblance to herself. A plan which had been forming for a long time crystallized in her mind.

"We shall arrange a betrothal between Arzani and Dawar Buksh, when we return to Lahore," she confided to her daughter.

Ladli sat stunned. "Oh, no, Mother! No, no! Anything but that. Arzani is only a helpless, innocent child. I will not allow her to become a pawn in this ruthless game of power."

Casting a stern look at Ladli, the Empress said, "These things are beyond your comprehension; don't tell me what you will allow or not allow! I alone will plan my grandchild's future. It is for me to decide whom she will wed. She shall be the fragile chain with which Dawar Buksh is bound to my will."

Ladli knew that her mother had always wanted the future consort's crown for herself, but Khusro had frustrated her dearest desire, and now she was determined to secure it for her only grandchild. But these dynastic marriages, Ladli knew only too well, could turn out disastrously. No one had guessed what a burden her mother placed upon her spirit when she had forced her to marry Shahryar, that prince who was born under a malevolent star. Through the years of their marriage, she had watched him lose every vestige of dignity, power, pride and finally even his good looks. Two months ago, her husband had contracted some mysterious disease which had baffled the most learned hakims in the country. It had rendered him completely hairless and revolting to behold. Her mother's scheming had bound her irrevocably to Prince Shahryar, but she would infinitely prefer to leave her own daughter's future to the disposition of fate.

"Inshallah! Whatever is written in the stars for Arzani will be," sighed Ladli, clasping her hands together.

Nurjahan snipped off a strand of silk with a pair of gold scissors. "You may read out those letters and petitions, Ladli, while I endeavour to complete this last little bit. I would like to have the shawl ready before the Badshah returns from his hunt. And I can always rely on your discretion not to divulge information to anyone."

Ladli nodded assent, rearranged her sequinned veil and glanced through the documents which lay piled on her mother's inlaid ivory travelling desk. Her heartbeat quickened, for her mother was watching, and she dared not snatch a letter in a hand she knew well. Instead, she picked up a paper at random and began to read.

An exclamation of disgust burst from the Empress as she listened to a report about some disturbance which had broken out between a detachment of Afghan troops quartered at Benaras and certain Brahmin pundits.

"Of all woes besetting this country, intolerance is the worst!" she declared. "The Afghans are insolent, perhaps it was a mistake to send them to a Hindu sanctuary; but those sanctimonious Brahmins could provoke anyone!" She would have to deal firmly with this matter before religious riots broke out in other parts of the realm.

"Shall I continue?" asked Ladli.

"Yes, let us get through the whole lot if we can," said the Empress. She continued embroidering as Ladli read out petitions and reports.

Her good humour returned when she heard that her brother Ibrahim had successfully concluded the subjugation of Berar and now was pledging himself to the siege of Kandahar.

"Kandahar!" Ladli's lips faltered over that fatal word. Everything had begun with Kandahar; that word seemed to herald every single disaster in her life... her grandfather Mirza

Ghias Beg's death, Khurram's disgrace, the rift between her mother and her uncle Asaf, Mahabat Khan's treachery...

If only Khurram were reconciled to his father, mused Ladli. Her stepfather could hardly be expected to conduct a strenuous campaign. But Khurram could do it. Khurram was the most formidable general in Hindustan. If Khurram recaptured Kandahar, life would become endurable. Her mother would be forced to welcome the conquering prince, and she might live once more in the shadow of his smile.

That was what Ladli now wanted more than anything on earth, but for years she had resisted the temptation to persuade her mother to recall her stepbrother. She was certain that he must have wearied by now of the inaction and disgrace forced upon him by the Emperor's frigid attitude. Perveiz had been dead a long while, the cause would never be known. She felt that the time had come for her mother to work on her stepfather's feelings.

Impulsively, Ladli set down her uncle Ibrahim's letter, and clasped her mother's hand. A torrent of words fell from her lips. "Mother, I've never asked you for anything, though your generosity has never made that necessary. I implore you, entreat the Badshah to relent in his attitude towards my brother! Prince Khurram's presence at Court could not fail to..."

Nurjahan sat upright against the bolsters. The needle pricked her finger, but she ignored the pain. She studied Ladli's face with rising disbelief. Then she spoke with icy hauteur, "I would advise you not to concern yourself unduly with your brother's affairs."

Undaunted, Ladli looked straight into her mother's eyes, and continued, "He has certainly done wrong, but he has learnt his lesson by now! His letters to the Badshah are redolent with humility and loyalty. How long is this estrangement to continue?"

A sudden thunder of drums and blare of fifes almost drowned her last words.

"I'm so glad the Badshah has returned early today. He will not accept it, but these long rides exhaust him beyond belief."

Nurjahan folded her embroidery and put it away carefully in a small velvet bag and called for her ladies. She hadn't been able to complete it after all, she thought regretfully, and now she must prepare to receive the Emperor.

While her women were helping her put the finishing touches to her toilet, she saw Laila enter her pavilion agitatedly. Laila tried to speak, but her breath caught on a sob, and she began to sob hysterically.

The women ceased their appointed tasks while Ladli tried to gather some meaning from Laila's disjointed words. She understood at last that her uncle Asaf was without, demanding immediate audience.

Hurriedly rising from her toilet table, Nurjahan flung on her veil and thrust her feet into the slippers held out for her. As she hastened to meet her brother, she knocked against a cage of parakeets, who immediately set up a fearful clamour. She passed out of the tent, wondering what urgent matter could have induced Asaf to seek audience at such an odd hour.

Asaf was waiting for her in the shadowy audience pavilion, surrounded by a tremulous group of frightened women.

Nurjahan's heart misgave her as soon as she saw the expression on her brother's face. Her lips formed a question, but she could not put into words her inmost fear.

"The Badshah?" she managed at last in a hoarse whisper, her eyes entreating him for reassurance.

In that moment, Asaf forgot that the woman standing before him was the imperious Mughal Empress Nurjahan who with a single word or gesture could set all Hindustan ablaze. He saw only his light-hearted sister Mehrunnisa, whose laughter would be stilled by his words. He thought of the vital, fascinating young girl who had captivated Akbar's heir that summer in Kashmir. That had been many, many years ago, and they had all come a long way since then.

For the first time, he saw fear in her eyes. Slowly, reluctantly, Asaf repeated Jai Singh's tale, that the physicians feared internal haemorrhage. When the full import of his words sank in, the colour drained from her face. Asaf heard her whisper in sick anguish, "Allah aid him!"

A hush fell on the assembled amirs and attendants when Begum Nurjahan entered the Emperor's tent.

Jehangir lay absolutely still on his canopied bed, beside which stood his young grandsons. Sombre men placed blazing charcoal braziers around the pavilion. A tremor shook Nurjahan's body, and an involuntary cry escaped her lips. Terror seized her for the first time, and she realized how emaciated, how exhausted he looked. His eyes were rimmed with dark circles, his immaculate hands were crossed over his breast, a lock of white hair lay on his damp brow.

In his altered face she saw death. And all unbidden, Sheikh Salim Chisti's half-forgotten prediction made to Akbar Shah long before her own birth came to her mind. Murad and Daniyal had died in their camps: was the Emperor also destined to a similar fate? Perhaps, she thought frantically, if she could somehow persuade him to finish the journey to Lahore, his life might yet be saved...

She pleaded with him mutely, and read the answer in his eyes. He would not be moved.

Jehangir studied the faces surrounding him. He saw the stark terror in his grandson Dawar Buksh's eyes, the anxious expression on his Grand Vezzir Asaf's face, the supplicating gestures of men who had served him through the long years of his reign. And the Amber Raja's unflinching stare urging him.

With a determined effort, Jehangir forced the reluctant

words from his lips... words they were all waiting to hear. "The sword and diadem of empire are yours after I go, Dawar Buksh."

A long-drawn out sigh seemed to fill the pavilion as the Prince extended eager, trembling fingers towards the symbols of temporal power. Nurjahan watched him silently as he clutched the jewelled hilt. But before he could gird the sword round his waist the scabbard slipped off, and the sword fell from Dawar Buksh's hand to the ground with a resounding clatter.

From the startled assembly broke cries of "Ill-omen!" In a flash, Aurangzeb leaned over and retrieving the sword, restored it to its scabbard.

She saw her quick-witted brother intervene and pass the imperial sword back to Khusro's son. Nurjahan could have sworn that there was a mocking gleam in Jehangir's eyes.

With a slight gesture, the Emperor banished everyone else from his presence. When the rows of mournful faces had receded, he whispered in a feeble tone. "They will busy themselves, planning their old deceits and fresh loyalties."

His voice sounded inmeasurably tired and feeble. She had to bend low to hear his words. "You will not forsake Dawar Buksh, I know... but remember, do not allow Dara and Aurangzeb out of custody if you wish to hold Khurram in thrall... And when it is all over, bury me in your garden outside Lahore."

At that, she struggled not to break down. Memories of their life together flooded her mind. She pressed her lips to his brow, and wondered at the extraordinary serenity of his eyes.

With a great effort, Jehangir stretched out his hand and stroked her hair, smiling faintly. "Have no fears for me. I have no fear of death."

For a long while he held her close, and breathed the familiar fragrance of her body. He remembered all that she had been to him through the years, the troubles and triumphs she had shared with him, her infectious gaiety and her boundless courage at all times. With a tired sigh, he drifted into uneasy sleep, while Nurjahan kept her lonely vigil at his side.

The hours passed, and she tried to pray silently while he lay still. Suddenly his breathing changed and flecks of foam and blood came to his lips.

An involuntary shudder seized her, and she clutched Jehangir's arm as the wind wailed outside. The braziers gushed smoke, the candles fluttered, and the lamps swayed in the piercing blasts, throwing grotesque shadows across the pavilion.

Outside, his vassals were gathering together in small groups throughout the camp. Already a swift horseman galloped southward to Khurram's stronghold with Asaf's signet. The Raja of Amber had set his retainers around Dawar Buksh's pavilion. Mirza Rustam came with the Sayyids of Barah to mount guard before their dying monarch's tent. Queen Jagat Gossain had taken her grandsons into protective custody.

The wind howled menacingly around the tent and the dying charcoal braziers could not warm Nurjahan. She rose from her chair, and picked up the astrakhan-lined riding cloak, in which the scent of his body still lingered. She wrapt it around her slender frame and it fell in warm folds to her ankles.

Nurjahan choked back a sob and felt her knees grow weak. Suddenly, she sank down on the carpet beside his bed, and buried her face in the velvet folds of his quilt.

It would be daylight soon, the sun would rise, she would have respite from fear. Some miracle would revive him, she told herself fiercely.

Jehangir dreamt that he stood in a bright garden full of fragrant flowers. Near the fountain stood a beauteous young girl, holding two white pigeons against her breast. As he walked towards her, she mocked him with her laughter and set the birds free.

He could hear the sound of fluttering wings. Jehangir opened his eyes, and saw a woman bending over him. It was the woman from his dream. But she was not laughing now.

"Mehrunnisa!" he said, trying to raise himself. Then a misty veil hid her from his eyes and he fell back against the pillows.

As the sun rose over the distant mountains, the agonizing realization came to her all at once that for her, all light, all splendour, was gone with his life.

Her years of loneliness had begun...

Epilogue

After Jehangir's death, his eldest grandson Dawar Buksh was proclaimed Emperor with the support of the Dowager Empress Nurjahan, the Grand Vezzir Asaf Khan and the powerful Amber Raja, Jai Singh. Despite his ill health and unpopularity, Prince Shahryar declared himself king at Lahore.

The moment Prince Khurram received his father-in-law Asaf's signet ring, revealing the death of Badshah Jehangir, he hastened forth from Burhanpur to claim the Mughal empire. Supported by his friend Rana Karan Singh of Mewar, his cousin the Raja of Marwar and the best general in the empire, Mahabat Khan, he lost no time in capturing the Mughal castle and treasure in Agra and ascending the throne as Emperor Shah Jahan on 24th January 1628. The Khutba was read in Shah Jahan's name, coins struck and every male Mughal including his full brother Shahryar, Dawar Buksh and the two sons of Prince Perveiz were put to death at the new Emperor's command.

Begum Nurjahan was spared because of her close kinship to Asaf and the new Empress, Arjumand (Mumtaz Mahal). And also because Nurjahan had no male heir. She was given a pension of sixteen lakh rupees for her private expenses and allowed to live at Lahore with her daughter Ladli and granddaughter Arzani. Nurjahan had the wisdom to spend the seventeen years of her widowhood in retirement, completely detached from the Mughal Court, engaged only in building her husband's tomb at Shahdara, works of charity, composing poetry and prayerful contemplation as she reread all the books she had shared with Jehangir. On her death in 1645, she was buried with quiet dignity besides the grave of her beloved husband.

Shah Jahan was a ruthless but remarkable ruler. Reknowned as a great soldier and architect, he built the great Red Fort of Delhi and the Taj Mahal as a tomb for his favourite wife, Mumtaz Mahal, mother of all his fourteen children.

Aurangzeb became Emperor in 1658 after imprisoning his ailing father Shah Jahan and killing his brothers Dara, Shuja and Murad. While Akbar and Jehangir had fostered Hindu-Muslim unity, Aurangzeb's orthodoxy alienated most Hindus, specially the Rajputs who had helped conquer and administer the Mughal empire. Over-expansion in the Deccan, Assam and Afghanistan made the empire unwieldy. Rebellions and religious uprisings by the Rajputs, Jats, Sikhs and Marathas destroyed the peace of Aurangzeb's last years. His death at ninety left the empire without a strong ruler. Wars of succession between his sons and wars of independence by his governors led to the decline and fall of the Mughal empire in the next fifty years.

Nurjahan's worst fears came true. The power vacuum thus created was filled by the British East India Company, trading under the charter granted to Thomas Roe, against her advice, by Emperor Jehangir. Mastery over the sea routes made Britain a vast maritime empire that included India right up to 1947.